They Were All Dead.

And soon he'd be dead, too. He held out no hope of divine deliverance, harbored no illusions of the cavalry (police) riding up to his rescue at the last minute. Violent, painful death awaited him, probably at some point within the next few minutes. It was a strange and horrible thing, the idea of the remainder of your life being down to a handful of torturous minutes. Thinking about it elicited another helpless whimper. He didn't want to die. Quite the contrary. He wanted to be around for many decades to come, even if that meant living with the guilt of being responsible for the deaths of his friends all that time. Yes, even then.

All he had to do was get to that axe.

Somehow haul his battered body upright.

And then be ready for the bastards when they came for him.

So he drew in a deep breath and began to crawl toward the axe....

BRYAN SMITH

Queen of Blood

LEISURE BOOKS NEW YORK CITY

This one is for my brother Jeff, a fellow pulp fiction junkie. Long live femme fatales, rumpled but tough private eyes, and old paperbacks with yellowing pages.

A LEISURE BOOK®

April 2008

Published by

Dorchester Publishing Co., Inc.
200 Madison Avenue
New York, NY 10016

ISBN 10: 0-8439-6061-2
ISBN 13: 978-0-8439-6061-7

The name "Leisure Books" and the stylized "L" with design are trademarks of Dorchester Publishing Co., Inc.

Printed in the United States of America.

10 9 8 7 6 5 4 3 2

Visit us on the web at www.dorchesterpub.com.

ACKNOWLEDGMENTS

As always, thanks and love to my wife, Rachael. Thanks also go out to the rest of my family, including my brothers Jeff and Eric and their families, Cherie Smith (No. 1 mom of the millenium), Oscar and Dorothy May (grandparents extraordinaire), Jay and Helene Wise (in-laws of the highest caliber). My friends Keith Ashley and Shannon Turbeville. Kent Gowran, David T. Wilbanks, Mark Hickerson, Tod Clark, Bill Lindblad, all the cool people at the Black Circle Saloon and Brian Keene's Message Board of Madness—you guys rock hardcore. Of course, I owe a large debt to all the people who bought *House of Blood* and demanded a sequel. And last but definitely not least, thanks to Don D'Auria for making it happen in the first place.

Queen of
Blood

Headline from the May 1 edition of the Chattanooga Herald:

"HOUSE OF BLOOD" CONTINUES TO MYSTIFY

CHATTANOOGA, TN—Nearly a year has passed since the revelation that an old mansion high in the east Tennessee mountains for years doubled as a house of horrors and a prison for luckless travelers. In that time, remarkably few survivors of the so-called "House of Blood" have been willing to speak to the press.

The known facts are few. Authorities have been as unforthcoming with details as the survivors. The cloak of silence has fueled wild Internet speculation, including persistent rumors of a strange, perhaps supernatural element to the mystery. Many have claimed the house was ruled over by a centuries-old entity, a vampire, perhaps, or an alien creature masquerading as a human man, a man known only as "The Master." And while it may be safe to dismiss these notions as obvious hoaxes and flights of fancy, the truth is they will continue to flourish so long as the public is kept in the dark about what really happened.

A month ago, this reporter set out to learn that truth, only to be foiled at every turn by a seemingly impenetrable wall of lies, misdirections, and general obfuscation. Each of the top law officers in the county refused to talk to the *Herald* for this story, citing the "sensitive nature of the ongoing investigation." Authorities at the state and federal level also refused comment.

Repeated attempts to contact the handful of survivors who spoke with the media in the immediate aftermath of the "liberation" (as they called it) invariably met with the same stony silence. Dream Weaver, 31, is perhaps the best-known survivor. The stunning blonde was a media darling in those first weeks, but she has become as reclusive and elusive as Howard Hughes was in the latter stages of his life. She appeared on magazine covers and was featured extensively in television interviews. Late night talk hosts famously made fun of her colorful name. She eventually married Chad Robbins, 31, another survivor of the House of Blood.

Neither Ms. Weaver nor Mr. Robbins could be reached for this story. One source reports that Weaver and Robbins have separated, though the *Herald* has been unable to confirm this prior to going to press.

We also attempted to contact the man known as "Lazarus," who functioned as a sort of guru to those imprisoned in the cavernous region beneath the infamous house, a place known simply as "Below." He has been described as "charasmatic" and "almost godlike." He appears in only a minimal amount of news footage from that time, and even then only in fleeting glimpses, behaving, some say, like a man deliberately avoiding the spotlight. The blurry images of "Lazarus" have been analyzed and picked apart by legions of amateur online sleuths. One investigator claims to have identified him as a Virginia businessman missing since the early 1990s. Others insist the man is one of a handful of long-believed-to-be-dead rock stars, with the majority of theories centering around Jim Morrison and Elvis Presley. Though these theories are clearly absurd, they will continue to proliferate in the continued absence of any real answers. No one the *Herald* has talked to has seen or heard from "Lazarus" since shortly after the revolt at the House of Blood.

Most of the Master's accomplices died in that revolt. However, two have remained missing and unaccounted for, Giselle Burkhardt and a woman identified only as "Ms. Wickman." Though both women are regarded as highly dangerous (both have been on the FBI's 10 Most Wanted List for several months), the *Herald* has learned that authorities are particularly keen to find Ms. Wickman, whose role at the House of Blood has been likened to that of an SS commandant at a concentration camp. . . .

PART I:
BLOOD RISING

CHAPTER ONE

Five months later

Blood was everywhere.

Sticky gore was on his face and in his hair, hot little rivulets of it trickling down from the gash behind his ear and the larger wound at the crown of his skull. The salty tang of it stung his mouth. Dean wiped more blood from his eyes with a shaking hand and saw bright red splotches on the dirty hardwood floor of the old farmhouse. He lifted his head and saw yet more blood on the nearest wall, huge crimson smears. It looked as if a crazed housepainter had splashed several cans of dark red paint all over the fucking place. Here, in the foyer, all over the goddamned floor. On the front door. And over there, the staircase bannister, it was covered with a slick film of red.

. . . blood everywhere . . .

His blood. Some of it. More blood entered his mouth. Check that. A *lot* of it. Lisa's blood. A fuck of a lot of Lisa's blood. John's blood. And don't forget Debbie. Some of the biggest splashes had erupted from the stump of the poor dimwit's neck when the crazy woman with the axe lopped her head off.

The air was pungent with the combined stenches of spilt blood and recent, violent death, with underlying aromas of piss and shit, the ripest of the latter emanating from the seat of his own soiled britches.

So much blood.

So much motherfucking blood.

Here.

There.

Blood . . . everywhere.

Then, the absurd capper to it all, the guitar riff from AC/DC's "If You Want Blood, You've Got It" began to echo in his head. He closed his eyes again and gritted his teeth, trying to will the old song away—but it just kept playing on an endless loop, that maddening, relentless riff and the dead singer's voice on the chorus.

Over and over and over. Holy hell, how incredibly fucked up was *that?*

His eyes fluttered open again. Drank in the carnage again.

He heard voices. Muffled. He strained his ears and realized the sound was coming from outside. Then came an abrupt burst of mad laughter. The sound made him shake with fear and anger. How could anyone do the things these people had done and laugh about it?

But the answer was obvious. These weren't just people. They were monsters.

And any moment now they'd be back inside, back to finish the night's grisly work. Because he was the only one still alive. He sniffled, the hard reality hitting him again. His friends were all dead. And they had died horribly. After hours of torture and unspeakable violations.

Suffering beyond quantifying.

The memory of the awful things he'd seen taunted him, a dark promise of the shape of his own near future. For some reason he couldn't fathom, they'd saved him for last. He had been beaten. Tortured. Mutilated. Two fingers were gone from his left hand, the stumps a charred mass of blackened flesh where they'd cauterized the wounds with an acetylene torch. But they'd spared him the worst of it, measuring the pain and trauma, keeping him alive and forcing him to watch helplessly as his girlfriend was flayed alive.

He sniffled again, wiped more tears from his eyes.

Something glinted in the periphery of his vision. He turned his head slowly to the left, wincing as fresh jolts of agony sizzled through his body. His breath caught in his throat at the sight of the axe propped against a side of a broken down old sofa in the living room. Lantern light flickered in the room. The old house had no electricty. The old Sutton place had been abandoned for decades. Once in a while kids from town would come here to party and fuck, but even that was a rare occurrence these days. The creaky, termite-infested farmhouse was just too creepy and gross a place to take girls. But tonight had been different, of course. What better night to visit the old Sutton place than Halloween, right?

It hadn't taken much to convince the girls to come out here. The mood of the evening was just right. A clear night sky with a bright moon hanging overhead. A cool fall breeze rolling in. That and a few Corona Lights did the trick. How promising the evening had seemed at the outset. A creepy, fun Halloween with his best friend and their girls. There'd be more beers to drink. Some weed to smoke. Thighs and breasts to grope in the quiet rural darkness. Ghost stories to tell as the evening lengthened toward dawn. Just like last year at the lake.

Only not like last year, as it turned out. Not even a little bit.

He should have known something was wrong upon reaching the end of the old house's long dirt driveway.

For one thing, another car was already there, a gleaming black Bentley parked alongside the long front porch. The old car was no abandoned relic. Its windows were tinted. A silver hood ornament sparkled in the brilliant moonlight, as did the chrome hubcaps. The vehicle was immaculate in every way, and its sleek lines made it look vaguely predatory. The beautiful antique looked as out of place parked outside the old Sutton place as a supermodel in a room full of crack whores.

An argument ensued. They had come so close to turning around and leaving.

My fault, Dean thought, bitterness consuming him as he stared at the blood-smeared blade of the axe. *I had to have it my way. Had to show them all what a big man I am. How fearless . . .*

He'd argued more forcefully than anyone, bordering on belligerence. In the end the others gave in. They always did. They did it to shut him up, not because they'd been swayed by the strength of his arguments. If only they'd stood up to him for once. If only . . .

No.

He couldn't let himself off that easy. Not now. And never again. They were all dead and it was all his fault.

And soon he'd be dead, too. He held out no hope of divine deliverance, harbored no illusion of the cavalry (police) riding up to his rescue at the last minute. Violent, painful death awaited him, and probably at some point within the next few minutes. It was a strange and horrible thing, the idea of the remainder of your life being down to a handful of torturous minutes. Thinking about it elicited another helpless whimper. He didn't want to die. Quite the contrary. He wanted to be around for many decades to come, even if that meant living with the guilt of being responsible for the deaths of his friends all that time. Yes, even then.

All he had to do was get to that axe.

Somehow haul his battered body upright.

And then be ready for the bastards when they came for him.

So he drew in a deep breath and began to crawl toward the axe. *I can do this*, he thought. *I have to do this*.

His hands trembled as the fingernails of his right hand dug into the rotting hardwood floor. He bit down hard on his lower lip and suppressed another whimper. He willed his hand to be still and pulled himself forward another few inches. Then he extended his left hand and gained another few inches. That was harder. The mangled flesh there throbbed horribly. He bit down harder on his lip to stifle a scream. Teeth penetrated flesh and drew blood. The scream stayed inside him, a fire burning in his chest, aching to explode. He extended his right hand again. Then the ruined left hand. He repeated the process several more times, progressing with great deliberation but seemingly infinite slowness. It was maddening. The sheer frustration almost caused him to give up. Then he heard more muffled laughter and anger engulfed him again.

Ignoring the pain as best he could, Dean began to move faster, wriggling forward on bloodied elbows and slightly upraised knees. He began to make serious progress, passing through the archway separating the foyer from the living room. He focused on the bloody axe with a single-mindedness that allowed no awareness of anything else.

He began to grin as he neared the blade. Just a few feet away, now. And then he was there, an electric burst of triumph sparking within him as his right hand closed around the axe handle. He had it, his coveted weapon. Now he just had to tap one last reservoir of strength, somehow get to his feet and prepare to make his last stand. And he would do it. By God, he would. He hadn't come this far to punk out now.

He drew in another deep breath, steeling himself.

His grip tightened around the axe handle.

Then something flashed through his field of vision, a dark blur. He was aware of pressure on his wrist before his eyes could process the image of a woman's high-heeled black shoe pinning his hand to the floor. Then the image crystalized, searing itself into his mind with blazing intensity. The polished black shoe was as elegant as the woman's finely turned ankle. Black was her whole motif. Black shoes, black stockings, and black dress—a fitting wardrobe reflecting the darkness dwelling within the one the others referred to alternately as "Mistress" and "Ms. Wickman."

She applied more pressure to Dean's wrist, eliciting another sob.

Her laughter was soft and mocking. "Such a naughty boy. I suppose you imagined you might use this on me." She wrenched the axe from Dean's grip and tossed it across the room. It struck the far wall and clattered to the floor. "I hope you realize it was intentionally left where you might see it upon regaining consciousness."

Dean wanted to scream, but he didn't have the strength for it. His spirits dipped to their lowest ebb yet. There had never really been any chance for revenge. The hope he'd felt moments ago had only been an illusion. This whole exercise nothing but another sadistic mindfuck. A game.

Anger flickered within him again. He wrapped the remaining three fingers of his left hand around her ankle and attempted to twist her foot off his wrist. He burned inside with the need to topple her, get on top of her, rip her flesh with his fingers and tear her leering eyes out. But he failed to budge her even one millimeter, her leg as unyielding as an iron girder.

Her strength was unnatural. She was a slender woman, about forty, average weight and height. Not unattractive. High cheekbones, but a gaunt, almost ghostly pallor. Her long dark hair was pulled back in a bun, lending her features a slightly pinched, severe sexuality. A shade of lipstick so dark red it was almost black painted the thin lines of her lips, which were curled now in a disdainful sneer. So she was spooky looking, yes, but at first glance she had not appeared to be some kind of evil superwoman. Not someone capable of lifting a teenage girl above her head and throwing her clear across a room. But he'd seen it with his own eyes, Debbie flying through the air, then striking the wall and bouncing off it like a rubber ball.

It defied logic. It was crazy. Impossible.

But . . .

"You've underestimated me again, haven't you, Dean?" She knelt down, pried his fingers from her ankle. "I'm going to hurt you again, child."

An anguished, keening wail issued from Dean's pulped lips. "Noooooo. Please . . . please don't. I'll do anything . . ."

Ms. Wickman snapped his index finger.

Dean screamed. His body convulsed as the pain arced through him, his feet beating a jittery rhythm on the hardwood floor. Through the pain, he was only dimly aware of the front door creaking open. Then there were voices. Those young people. Her followers. They were coming inside, no doubt drawn by the scream.

Ms. Wickman snapped the middle finger of his left hand. The scream this time filled the dust-laden living room like an explosion. He tried to get up. Pure pain instinct was driving him. But Ms. Wickman planted a knee between his shoulder blades and that was that.

She was too strong. Stronger than any human woman should be.

"One finger left, one stubby little thumb," she said, leaning close, her voice an insinuating, malicious purr. "I do enjoy your begging, Dean. Would you like me to spare this one?"

Dean thought about the way this sort of thing usually went in the movies. Your typical cinema hero, facing yet another round of torture, would spit in his tormentor's face and say, "Fuck you." Or some witty alternative.

What Dean said was, "Please don't do it. I'll do anything. I swear."

A brief pause.

"Thank you, Dean."

She snapped his thumb.

Dean's next scream mingled with the laughter of Ms. Wickman's apprentices. Some of the laughter died off as their Mistress gathered his broken fingers in her hand and . . . squeezed.

Then squeezed harder. And harder still.

Tidal waves of pain slammed through Dean. His body bucked. The long, continuous scream that ripped out of him felt as though it might tear his body apart. Dean blacked out for a moment, only to be reawakened almost instantly by the agony blazing in every nerve ending in his body. At some point, Ms. Wickman relinquished her grip on his broken fingers, stood up, and moved away from him.

He heard her talking to her followers. There were four of them, ranging in age from mid-teens to early twenties. The oldest, a thin but tall boy of about twenty or twenty-one, hauled Dean off the floor and deposited him on the old sofa. The sofa reeked of mildew and rot, and it creaked beneath his weight.

Then Ms. Wickman loomed over him again. A long, thin cigarette was pinched between two fingers of her right hand. She took a draw on the cigarette, then blew a thin stream of smoke at the sagging ceiling.

She met Dean's gaze and smiled. "Do you smoke, Dean?"

Dean coughed. "No."

That strange, wicked smile again. Insinuating. Malicious to the core. "Well, you're about to start."

Dean felt terror again, sure, but now another feeling rose to the surface, a weariness he felt from the depths of his soul. "I don't care anymore. Please kill me now. Get it over with."

The woman's eyes widened in mock surprise. "Oh, Dean, honey, I'm afraid there's been a misunderstanding between you and me."

Dean drew in another sharp breath as she sat next to him on the sofa and draped an arm around his shoulders. He trembled beneath her touch, tried to cringe away from her, but of course was unable to move.

She leaned into him, her breath hot on his ear as she spoke. "I think we've gotten off on the wrong foot here, Dean. You see, we're not going to kill you."

Dean's gaze swept over the mad woman's followers, cataloguing a variety of minor injuries and mutilations. A missing finger here, a livid scar there . . . and the tall, thin boy was missing an ear.

Dean shook his head as more tears filled his eyes. "No. No, no, no. You can't make me. I won't . . . won't be like . . . them."

A dark-haired girl in a raggedy black dress and black Doc Martens laughed. "Where have I heard that before?"

More deranged laughter.

Ms. Wickman leaned closer still, her lips moving softly against his ear as she said, "You'll be whatever I want you to be. You belong to me now."

Then she put out her cigarette on the back of his mangled hand.

Dean screamed yet again.

And watched aghast as smoke rose from the seared pucker of flesh.

CHAPTER TWO

Two years later

Dream Weaver was a drink or two shy of being truly drunk. She had every intention of addressing that deficiency within the next few minutes. But first things first. She needed to get her game face on before wading back into the action. So she extracted a tube of lipstick from her Prada knockoff purse, uncapped it, and leaned over the sink as she applied a fresh coat to her full lips. She capped the tube and dropped it in her purse, dabbed away the excess with a square of toilet paper, then teased out her hair a bit with her fingers.

The image looking back at her from the bar bathroom's tiny, cracked mirror looked less and less like a stranger with each passing day. This was a good thing. She wanted to obliterate every trace of the woman she'd been. Erase her. Replace her with something completely different. Whether or not that "something different" was something others would consider admirable was of no consequence.

Her flowing blonde tresses were gone, replaced by a choppy, dyed-black cut that made her look like a punk Bettie Page. Her formerly perpetual tan was also a thing of the past. The extremely tight and skimpy black top she wore accentuated her womanly assets and displayed a lot of very pale flesh. It looked as though the sun's rays hadn't touched her in years, which wasn't too far from the truth. Ultrashort denim cutoffs hugged her still shapely ass. She turned to admire herself from a side angle, peering over her shoulder to get a glimpse of the new black rose tattoo on her lower back.

She looked good. Hot. She was a beautiful woman. None of the potential cosmetic changes available to her—short of a splash of boiling acid to the face—could change that essential aspect of her existence. But she was cool with that. It was the one thing about herself she had no desire to change. She was a much shallower human being these days, a thing she had no problem admitting to herself. Gone was the ditzy girl who fretted so about the feelings of others and worked to avoid using her looks to unfair advantage. In her place was a cool, cold-hearted bitch who knew damn well she was prettier than just about everyone else— and didn't hesitate to make full use of the fact.

Someone pounded on the bathroom door, rattling the cheap hook-and-eye lock. "You about done in there? Other people have to piss too, you know."

"Wait your fucking turn, cunt!" Dream snarled, her face twisting in a sneer.

Dream slipped the strap of her purse over her shoulder and stared at her reflection some more. The only flaw in the otherwise perfect reflected visage was the tell-tale hint of red in her eyes. She dug a Visine bottle out of her purse, squeezed a few drops into each eye, and blinked away excess moisture until she could see clearly again.

The bathroom door rattled in its frame again.

Dream smiled. And waited. The redness was already fading from her eyes.

She waited another beat longer, until the door rattled yet again. Then she went to the door, popped the lock out of the hook, and opened the door. The girl waiting to use the bathroom was a scrawny thing, almost waifish. Flat-chested and curveless. She wore thick glasses and her short hair was dark with streaks of blonde.

Dream smirked. "There she is . . . Miss America."

The girl rolled her eyes and tried to push past her into the bathroom. Dream stepped aside, allowing her entry. Then she shut the door and locked it again.

The girl's face twisted in a scowl. "What are you doing? Are you a dyke or something? I don't swing that way."

Dream adjusted the purse strap on her shoulder and stepped forward. "I don't care."

She slammed the girl against the wall and punched her hard in the stomach. The girl's eyes went wide with shock and pain. Her legs gave out, but Dream held her up and punched her again. Then one more time.

She stepped away and the girl dropped to her knees. A sheen of sweat broke out over her face and she lunged toward the toilet, flipping the lid open an instant before her stomach voided its contents. When she was done heaving, she looked at Dream, her lower lip trembling as she said, "Why . . . why . . ."

She lifted her glasses and swiped at a sudden flood of tears, unable to comprehend the outburst of violence.

"Because I'm a bad person." Dream knelt next to the trembling girl, lifted her chin with a finger. "And you don't fuck with bad people."

The girl twisted away from Dream and cried some more.

Dream stood up. "Get yourself together. When you're done here, pay your bill and leave. Don't say a word about this to anyone, ever."

Dream watched her a moment longer, then turned and left the bathroom.

The Villager Pub was a tiny place, with a short bar just inside the front entrance. There were two tables opposite the bar, a jukebox (silent now), and an old Galaga tabletop video game. Between the bar and the bathrooms was an open area for dart players. Dream waited for a pause in the in-progress dart games, smiled her thanks to the waiting players, and made her way to the bar. She felt the gazes of the male dart players on her every step of the way. The lust they felt as they drank in her long, long legs and abundant curves was a palpable thing. It made her feel good.

And powerful.

She took a seat at the end of the bar, a good place for watching the dart games. The players were all college-age boys. A look through their wallets would reveal more than one fake ID. Maybe tonight the mark would be one of them. These young guys, bursting with hormones and fueled by too many beers, would be easy. She would lure one of them to a motel room. Dope his drink. Maybe even fuck him before he lost consciousness. Then rob him blind and light out of town before sunrise. It was the way she lived now. Town to town. Mark after mark. Sometimes, when she'd dosed them just right, they were delirious enough to share credit card PIN numbers. There was an art to timing everything just right. She was getting better at it all the time.

One of the players elbowed his buddy—a square-jawed, bushy-haired frat type—and nodded in her direction. Frat Boy saw her looking at him and grinned.

Dream smiled and lit a cigarette.

The barmaid—a thin woman of about forty with long, dishwater hair—approached her and said, "What'll you have?"

"Shiner Bock."

The barmaid removed a frosty pint glass from a cooler behind the bar and began to fill it from the tap.

Dream licked her lips as she watched the amber liquid fill the frost-rimmed glass. She loved the taste of the stuff, but more than that she craved the fuzziness of mind it would bring, that added buffer between her present life and the painful memories of her past. The barmaid placed a napkin in front of Dream and set the nearly overflowing mug on it. Dream waited for the head to settle before taking a first sip of the deliciously cold, cold brew.

The skinny girl emerged from the bathroom and wobbled through the game area, oblivious to the men with their darts. She bumped into one, eliciting a startled yelp.

Frat Boy sneered. "Watch where you're going, bitch."

One of his friends snickered and said, "Yeah, skank."

The girl didn't say anything. Dream watched her from the corner of her eye as she continued toward the bar. She experienced a flash of sense-memory, a vivid moment in which she again felt the girl's soft flesh yield beneath her hard fist.

The girl gave her a wide berth, continuing down to the far end of the bar, where she paused long enough to dig into her purse and extract several rumpled bills. She tossed these on the bar and left in a hurry, the bell over the door jangling behind her. An untouched pint of Bud Light gleamed in the light of the neon Miller sign mounted behind the bar.

The barmaid frowned. "Well, shit, girl didn't even drink her beer."

A middle-aged man in a cowboy hat rose from his seat at one of the tables. "Hell, I'll drink that, darlin'."

The barmaid shrugged. "What the hell, it's paid for. Today's your lucky day."

Cowboy Hat gripped the mug's handle with a beefy hand and winked at Dream. Dream kept her expression blank and returned her attention to the young boys playing darts. Frat Boy caught her eye again and grinned. Dream flashed another smile, hoping to encourage the kid to make a move. He'd better get the hint soon, because she had a feeling Cowboy Hat would lumber over any moment and hit on her. But Frat Boy's attention was again on the dartboard. He was squinting, a dart pinched between thumb and forefinger held at about shoulder level.

It was then she heard the slightly labored breath behind her and knew the time had come to shoot down another dirty old man. The bar stool to her left creaked as a weight settled onto it. Dream set her mug down with a sigh. She looked longingly at Frat Boy a moment longer, but he was still too focused on his damnable game. Vowing to make him pay for that later, she swiveled around on her stool to tell Cowboy Hat off . . .

But the smackdown went undelivered, the words dying on the tip of her tongue as a paralyzing numbness swept rapidly through her body.

There was someone on the bar stool next to her, but it wasn't Cowboy Hat.

The apparition smiled hideously through rotting lips. "Hello, Dream."

A ghost. A fucking ghost. Or a hallucination. That was more likely, she supposed, but how could anyone tell the difference?

It was Alicia Jackson, her one-time best friend in the world. Alicia had been dead for more than three and a half years. She didn't look like an old-time movie ghost, though. She wasn't flickering or floating in mid-air. She looked as solid and three-dimensional as the bar stool under Dream's ass. She was a walking corpse, her flesh bloated and rotting. The back of her head was a pulped, sticky mess—the exit wound from the self-inflicted gunshot wound that had ended her life. She wore a slinky little black dress, which meant a lot of visible putrescent flesh. The tortures she'd endured prior to her suicide were much in evidence, including the uncountable razor-blade cuts the demonic Ms. Wickman had inflicted on her. Each wound weeped blood.

Alicia's gruesome smile widened, exposing rows of teeth that protruded alarmingly from her blackened, shrunken gums. Maggots trickled from one corner of her mouth. "It's been a while, girl." She laughed and more maggots tumbled from her mouth. "Oh, I know what you're thinking—I'm not real. But you're wrong. I'm not a ghost. Not exactly. And I'm sure as shit no hallucination."

Dream opened her mouth to say something, managed a single, incoherent syllable before falling silent again. Her mouth hung open in astonishment. She simply couldn't speak. What could she say to this . . . thing? The idea of holding a conversation with it was absurd.

Alicia chuckled. "You're still not believing it."

Dream nodded, a very slight downward tilt of her head. She didn't want anyone in the bar to see her interacting with this thing that looked like her old friend. She knew they'd only see a thirtysomething chick in slut gear conversing with an empty bar stool. An aging barfly with severe mental problems would be the likely perception.

She picked up her beer mug and drank deeply from it again. She looked at the television mounted on the wall behind the bar. *The Simpsons* was on, and she pretended to pay attention to Homer's shenanigans.

Alicia scooted closer and slapped a cold, clammy hand down on Dream's upper left thigh. Dream sucked in a deep breath. The hand on her leg felt rough and leathery. She glanced down, noted the contrast between Alicia's rot-brown hand and her own pale, unblemished flesh, and began to feel light-headed.

Alicia leaned closer still and Dream felt the dead woman's bony knee press against her. "There, girl. Do I *feel* like a motherfucking hallucination?"

Dream trembled. She gripped the handle of her beer mug tighter. Her eyes flicked toward the bar's front door. She could go. Just slide off the stool and hit the ground running. Bang through the door and leg it across the street to the lot where her old Honda Accord was parked. Then drive. Get the hell out of this stinking, gray, miserable New England town, find some other place to prowl for a while.

Alicia's dead hand gave her thigh a squeeze. "Don't matter where you go, baby. I'll be there. It's like I said, I'm not exactly a ghost."

Dream looked at the bar and kept her voice as low as possible. "Then what are you?"

"I'm something you created."

Dream frowned. "Bullshit."

"Oh, it's true, all right." Alicia laughed again, and Dream saw a single maggot strike the mahogany bartop and begin to squiggle across the polished wood. "You and I both know you left that fucking house of horrors a changed woman. And I don't mean just changed in the head. You got yourself some of the same supernatural mojo that Master asshole had. You always had it in you, but he woke it up. You can *do* things normal people can't. You're stronger. Smarter. And you can change the shape and substance of the world around you, just by thinking hard enough about it."

Dream shook her head. "No."

"Yes." Alicia's fingers began to stroke Dream's inner thigh. "You know it's true. And it scares the shit out of you. So you've done everything you can to hold that power back, to suppress it. But the pressure's building up inside you. Some of that psychic energy is spilling out. And me . . . well, I'm one of the consequences of that. Some of that energy mingled with the bit of my essence you've carried with you all these years. And that got all mixed in with your guilt. It was inevitable I would manifest." Another soft, dry laugh. "And that I would look this fucking awful, I guess. Seriously, I ought to bitchslap you for this Night of the Living Dead Black Bitch look you've stuck me with."

Dream was still shaking her head, but it was just automatic, desperate denial. Another part of her—a part the booze was meant to numb—acknowledged the truth of Alicia's words. But truth changed nothing. She would work harder to suppress it. Drink more. Drug more. Whatever it took. "I have to get out of here."

The barmaid looked up from the glass she'd been polishing. "Whatever. Go talk to yourself somewhere else. But you owe me three bucks for that beer."

Dream fumbled with her purse, digging for bills. "Okay. Sorry."

Alicia continued to stroke her thigh. "I'll tell you a secret, Dream, something I never seriously considered telling you when I was alive. I always wanted to get it on with you. You were the only chick I ever felt that way about. I was always too scared to tell you, of course. Didn't want to risk ruining our friendship."

Dream's hands were shaking as she at last managed to extract her wallet from the purse and undo its snap. She withdrew three dollar bills, considered withdrawing a fourth for a tip, but decided against it when she got a look at the barmaid's face, which was a mask of pity and disdain.

"Remember what I said. You made me. I'm not a ghost." Alicia's fingers ceased their stroking motion and squeezed. Hard. "I'm also not exactly the woman you remember. But I'm close, Dream, I'm real fucking close. And I am always with you." She squeezed even harder, really bearing down. "And I was with you in the bathroom when you put the hurt on that geek. That was some fucked-up shit, baby. Nothing like the sweetheart I remember. Shit, you should change your name to

Nightmare, would suit you better these days." She ran the coarse end of her gray tongue over her bloated lips. "Personally, I think it's an improvement. You don't get anywhere in this world without kicking some ass."

Dream threw the three single bills on the bar and slid off the stool. Some instinct caused her gaze to flick toward the young dart players, and she felt something stab her heart as she saw the way they were looking at her. Frat Boy's finger made a circle in the air around his ear, the international loony symbol.

She hurried out of the bar and stood outside on the sidewalk, watching the traffic on the two-lane street whiz by. She heard music wafting from another bar on the same side of the street, "People Are Strange," that old Doors chestnut. Hearing it now, in these circumstances, raised gooseflesh on her arms and the back of her neck. A creeping sense of paranoia threatened to overcome her. She sensed that something important—something on the order of a seismic shift in her life—was on the cusp of occurring. The feeling scared the shit out of her.

She glanced to her right and saw Alicia standing there. The dead woman's eyes were stained a milky white, but they remained oddly expressive, conveying a hint of amusement.

"Look, Dream, here comes a bus. I think if I were you, I'd consider stepping in front of it."

Dream looked to her left, where a block away a traffic light was turning yellow. In another few moments, the traffic would slow to a halt and she would be able to cross to the parking lot on the opposite side. She knew she should just focus on getting out of here and ignore Alicia.

But curiosity forced her to ask the question: "Why?"

Alicia smiled. She wiped another trickle of maggots from her lips and flicked them away. "Nasty things. There's trouble coming, baby. You're strong. Powerful, even. But this may more trouble than you can handle."

Dream squeezed her eyes shut. Enough. This was clearly just some especially malevolent corner of her shattered psyche fucking with her. Alicia was a hallucination, and the things she was saying were issuing from somewhere inside her, not from the mouth of some maggot-spewing ghoul. She hoped the realization would make the dead woman's voice halt in mid-sentence . . .

. . . but Alicia kept talking. "You thought it was all over when you left that evil place up in the mountains. But it ain't, girl, not by a long fucking shot. The evil is still out there. It's been dormant for a while, but it's just been restoring itself, getting strong again. That woman, the one who killed me, she's gonna come looking for you soon."

Those last words sent a deep, resonant chill through Dream. "No . . ."

Alicia didn't respond this time. Dream opened her eyes and looked to her right. The apparition was gone. She breathed a sigh of relief, but the chill invoked by the dead woman's words remained.

She shivered and began to thread her way through the stalled traffic. She unslung her purse and looked for her keys as she entered the parking lot. She cursed, not finding them at first, but then her forefinger snagged the key ring. Before she could get the keys out, though, she heard a vaguely familiar voice say, "That's her."

Dream tensed. She'd reached the far end of the lot. It was darker here, removed as it was from the main thoroughfare and the lights of the bars. She heard movement to her right and her head snapped in that direction. She gasped. The girl from the bathroom was standing there, an ugly smirk on her face. Two boys were with her. Dream's heart pounded. They stood between her and the Accord. Which meant she only had one option available—to turn and make a desperate dash back toward the street. But just as she started to turn, she sensed more movement behind her.

Something hard and metallic struck the base of her skull and she crumpled to the asphalt. Her vision wavered for a moment, went black, and when things came back into focus another girl, this one taller and somewhat prettier, was standing directly over her. There were others, now, a total of five arrayed around her. One held a tire iron that was wet with her blood.

The girl standing over her smiled.

Then she spit in Dream's face, the gob of saliva hitting her between the eyes.

Dream tried to stand, but a booted foot smashed into her side, causing her to curl into a fetal ball. Then she felt rough hands on her, dragging her upright.

And the girl said, "Get her in the van."

Dream struggled as they dragged her toward the open back of an old van. She opened her mouth to scream, but someone hit her again.

The world went black.

CHAPTER THREE

The smell of cooking meat wafted in from the kitchen. A faint undertone of Indian spices accompanied the aroma. The muffled sound of a television also emanated from that direction, as did the occasional clank of pots and pans being moved around.

Chad Robbins closed out his e-mail and browser screens and flipped the laptop shut. Allyson poked her head around a corner of the hallway arch and smiled broadly at him. "Dinner's almost ready, baby. Put the silly Internet away and come help me get the table ready."

Chad looked at her and smiled. Her long blonde hair was in pigtails, but wild strands of it hung over her sparkling eyes and over her ears. She was a pretty girl, with a sweet, almost angelic face. The pigtails and her relative youth—she was twenty-four—endowed her with an almost Lolita-like quality. She could pass for a girl in her late teens. But she was slighter than Dream, smaller and less curvaceous.

And this was a problem, that way he was always comparing the two of them. It wasn't fair to Allyson. Especially given his still-vivid memories of the emotional abuse he'd suffered during his time with Dream. Allyson was special in so many of her own ways, and her presence in his life had done much to prevent a slide into the kind of despair and guilt that had crippled his ex-wife.

Chad rose from the recliner and followed her into the kitchen. The table was already covered with a crisp white tablecloth. Set upon it were two lit candles in silver holders and a tasteful arrangement of fresh flowers. Chad opened a cupboard above the counter and withdrew two plates, which he set at opposite ends of the table. From a drawer he selected the appropriate silverware and set these next to the plates. Allyson selected glasses from another cupboard while Chad set about opening a bottle of wine.

The cork came out with the usual mild pop, the rich wine aroma immediately mingling with the scent of the spices in a pleasant way. Chad poured a modest measure of the red wine into each of their glasses. He then pulled his seat out and sat down, taking a sip of the wine as he watched Allyson transfer the food from the little island in the middle of the kitchen to the table. He experienced a mildly salacious tingle as he observed her moving through her domestic-goddess-in-training paces. He especially liked it when she would turn and flash him a look at her exquisitely toned calves. The dress she wore had a somewhat prim aspect to it, with no plunging neckline to reveal cleavage. However, the conservative effect was offset by a high hemline that fell just inches shy of miniskirt territory. The big pink apron she wore over the dress inexplicably heightened the erotic charge Chad derived from watching her, so much so that he was almost disappointed when she removed it and hung it from a peg on the pantry door.

She flashed him a dazzling smile as she settled into her own seat at the table. "Let's eat, shall we?"

Chad needed no further prompting. He dug into the spiced lamb with enthusiasm, letting out a moan of almost sexual satisfaction as the tender meat penetrated his taste buds. Similar moans accompanied each of the next several bites.

He paused long enough to take a deep breath and say, "Allyson, dear, you have outdone yourself."

Allyson received the compliment in what had become her usual way, by smiling sweetly and saying, "Thank you, sweetie. When we're done eating, you can thank me again by fucking the daylights out of me."

The eye contact between them in that moment was electric. Chad sucked in a hissing breath through clenched teeth. Talking dirty at the dinner table was one of Allyson's kinks. No dinner ever elapsed without some amount of what she called "naughty talk."

Chad returned her smile and said, "I'd like that."

Allyson licked her lips after another delicate sip from her wine glass. "Of course you would. But I think I'll sit on your face for a while first." She laughed softly as she dipped a spoon in her curry. "After all, you'll want to show your appreciation for all my hard work, won't you?"

Dinner continued in that manner for a time. Moments of relative silence during which they enjoyed the food, followed by increasingly ribald verbal exchanges. Chad's body was vibrating with need by the time he finished his meal. His fork clattered on the plate and their eyes locked across the table again.

Allyson smiled. "We're going to the bedroom. Fuck cleaning up. It can wait."

Chad nodded his enthusiastic agreement. "Yes."

He hurried around the table and pulled Allyson into his arms, her body slamming against his as she hooked her arms and a leg around him. Their mouths met. Their tongues danced. They gasped and moaned. Chad's erection thrust against the fabric of his trousers. Allyson squealed as she felt it and writhed against the hardness, making Chad shudder and reach for the hem of her dress, snatching it up over her ass.

"Hell with the bedroom," Chad managed between gasps. "I want you now. Right here."

A sound like a growl emerged from Allyson's throat and a corner of her mouth curled in a carnal snarl. "Yes. Yes. Do it."

Chad spun her around, grabbing a handful of her dress and pushing the flimsy bit of fabric up over her ass as she braced herself against the table.

She looked back at him over her shoulder, biting her lip as she said, "Hurry. Hurry."

Chad was reaching for his zipper when they heard the heavy double knock.

THUMP-THUMP.

Someone was at the front door, pounding the wood with the base of a fist rather than using the brass knocker.

"God-DAMMIT!" Allyson slapped an open palm against the table top and stood up straight. "Who the fuck could that be?" She glanced over her shoulder at Chad again. "Please tell me you're not expecting anyone. You would've told me, right?"

Chad frowned. "Who would I be expecting?"

The question was rhetorical. Allyson was the only person he'd allowed to get close to him since moving to the Atlanta suburb of Buckhead. He had no friends. The friends he'd had in his former life in Tennessee were either dead, estranged, or missing. And he'd made no new friends here. He was a financial analyst for Aerodyne in Atlanta, where he met a lot of people, but he'd intentionally maintained an air of aloofness with his fellow employees. And he met all gestures of potential friendship with a wall of coldness. With Allyson as the one welcome exception, of course.

THUMP-THUMP came the double-knock again.

Chad groaned. "Christ. You know it can't be anyone I know."

Allyson sniffed. "Well, I don't have any friends here either, remember?"

It was true. Allyson had moved to Atlanta only a week prior to Chad's relocation there. They had met by chance at a coffeehouse, the chemistry between them instant and undeniable. And since then they'd been too involved with each other to bother meeting new people or getting entangled in the local social strata in any way.

THUMP-THUMP-THUMP!

"Fuck!" Chad moved past her, anger boiling inside him again as the knocking intensified. "Okay, time to get rid of this asshole."

"Be careful." Allyson hurried after him, the slap of her bare feet on the kitchen tile becoming a whisper as tile gave way to living room carpet. "For God's sake, Chad, don't just open the door. It could be anyone. Remember that home invasion last week."

Chad's hand paused on the doorknob. She was right. He'd read the newspaper stories. A wife and daughter had been raped. The wife's husband was tortured until he'd given up the combination to the safe in his office. No one was killed and everyone had said how lucky that was for the victims. Except that Chad knew that was bullshit. Those poor people would carry the mental scars of that night with them the rest of their days.

It had happened in this neighborhood. And the perpetrators had not been caught. They were still out there.

Somewhere.

THUMP-THUMP.

And this stupid fucking door didn't have a peephole. *Fuck.* His hand still on the doorknob, Chad looked at Allyson. "Maybe you should get a phone, be ready to speed-dial 911."

Allyson nodded and hurried out of the room. She came running back a moment later, a slim, silver cell phone clutched in one slightly trembling hand. Chad flashed her a reassuring smile and shifted his attention back to the door as the most insistent knock yet rattled the thick slab of wood in its frame.

Chad cleared his throat and made his voice loud, projecting it the way a stage actor would: "You can stop knocking, asshole! Who are you and what the hell do you want?"

The knocking stopped. Chad held his breath and sensed Allyson doing the same. Then he heard a very dim, muffled sigh. A tired sound. A weary sound.

Chad frowned. There was something faintly familiar about it.

Something—

Chad's hand closed around the doorknob and yanked the door open. Allyson let out a gasp of surprise, but Chad barely heard it.

He gaped at the figure standing on the darkened front porch for nearly a full minute before managing to say, "Oh . . . shit . . ." Then he broke into a broad grin. "I can't believe what I'm seeing." He stepped back and waved a hand toward the interior of the house. "Come on in, man."

The dark figure stepped forward into the light. The wryest of smiles touched the very edges of his mouth. He looked better than the last time Chad had seen him, years ago. Leaner and less haggard. The bushy mane of gray-flecked brown hair had been shorn to a longish shag. He looked especially great for a man in his early sixties.

Chad shut the door as the man stepped into the house. "Christ, Jim, I can't believe how good you look. Last time I saw you—"

The man Chad had once known as Lazarus shrugged.

"Being an unrepentant sinner is a well-documented course to a healthier life."

Chad's grin remained in place as he turned to introduce his friend to Allyson. "Hey, honey, this is the man I've told you about—" His grin faltered as he registered her sullen expression. "Honey—?"

"I don't care who the fuck this is." Sullen, nothing. She was fuming. "We were in the middle of a nice, quiet dinner. I can't believe you're inviting this person in, regardless of who the fuck he is."

"Honey, I'm sorry, but—"

"Whatever." Allyson brushed past him and yanked the door open again. Her face was a tight mask of controlled fury as she turned toward him. "You boys catch up. Jerk each other off. Whatever, I don't fucking care. I'm going for a walk."

She stepped outside and slammed the door behind her.

Chad gaped in disbelief at the door for a long moment. He'd never seen Allyson so angry about anything. He understood her frustration about the interruption. He still felt some of that, too, a rippling undercurrent of unspent sexual energy. But storming off like this—well, it seemed a bit out of proportion.

Jim cleared his throat. "Sorry to cause you trouble, friend. But there are things we need to talk about."

Chad turned and looked at his friend, a ghost of the faded grin returning to his face. "Okay, but I think I need a drink now."

Chad led the way to the living room and the liquor cabinet.

Allyson waited until she was two blocks from the house before flipping open her cell phone and punching in the number she'd memorized so many months ago. She held it to her ear and listened as it rang and rang.

She cursed as she counted a tenth ring and considered hanging up. But she couldn't do that. The time had come and she couldn't afford to turn back now. She made herself wait some more and her patience paid off as the phone was at last answered on the twentieth ring.

A tired male voice said, "Yes?"

Allyson snapped at the man: "What the fuck took so long?"

A pause. Then: "Who is this?"

"This is Allyson fucking Vanover. You recognize that name, don't you?" Her voice was shrill, rendered almost brittle from the combination of fear and anger coursing through her. There was another strong emotion at work, as well, one she couldn't afford to think about, not if she meant to see this through. "After all, you're the reason I'm in fucking Atlanta, remember?"

The man sighed. "Of course. I do remember. I told you—"

"You told me to call this number only if I had news. This is the first time I've called, but trust me, the news is big."

The man's attitude changed immediately. His voice resonated with eagerness as he said, "Do you mean—"

"Yes." Allyson paused. She allowed a final pang of regret to pierce her deeply. Then she made herself say, "The man you've been looking for, the one you told me to keep an eye out for . . . he's here."

"Excellent. Are you still at the same location?"

Allyson hesitated only a moment, regret stilling her tongue a second longer than necessary. But she knew it was too late for second thoughts. The wheels had been set in motion. Regardless of what she said from this moment forward, there was nothing she could do stop it.

"Yes. It's the fourth house on the left on Jacobsen Avenue. 505 Jacobsen Avenue." Her hand was shaking. She forced it still. "There's a late-model silver Porsche parked on the road in front of the house. Your people won't be able to miss it."

"Good. You've done very well, Allyson." Soft laughter issued from the other end, wherever that was. Allyson had Googled the number, but there was no record for it, nor any other indication of its origin. Which was kind of spooky, but it figured. "And as previously agreed, you'll be handsomely rewarded."

"I better be." She forced a toughness into her voice she didn't feel. "That money better hit my account by the end of business tomorrow."

More soft laughter. "Oh, it shall. All one hundred thousand. And remind me, that would be your secret account, correct? The one Mr. Robbins doesn't know about?"

Allyson closed her eyes. "Yes. That one."

"The money will be there by the appointed deadline, rest assured. You'll want to be well out of town by then."

"You can count on that."

"Good." A sigh. "We can consider our business closed, then. You will never speak of this to anyone, of course."

Allyson's eyes fluttered open. Two kids were playing with a glow-in-the-dark Frisbee two houses down. Somewhere a dog was barking. Through a window of the house to her immediate right she could see the warm glow of a television. She imagined a family gathered around the box, enjoying their evening's familiar and comforting entertainment. Though part of her was loathe to admit it, she had come to appreciate that a life in the suburbs could be a good, perhaps even blissful one.

She snapped the phone shut without another word and turned back toward home.

CHAPTER FOUR

Ms. Wickman smiled at the boy on the floor. His name was Terry. His dead sister's name had been Sherry. Such unimaginative parents. No wonder, then, that the siblings had crumbled so predictably through the course of the evening's long and bloody festivities. Refugees from the shallow end of the gene pool, these children. Not that it mattered. Ms. Wickman had a slight preference for more intelligent victims, but in the end she was an equal opportunity sadist.

This Terry had a blandly handsome face, though its handsomeness was offset somewhat by a pudginess she found distasteful. He stared up at her with wide, pleading eyes. Snot dribbled from his nostrils. A large red welt on his left cheek further marred his bland good looks. His bleeding lower lip trembled uncontrollably.

"Please d-don't hurt me . . . again." A whimper issued through his sputtering lips. "I d-did it. Did what you t-told me."

Ms. Wickman's smile broadened. "Yes, you did." She clapped her hands in a slow, mocking way. "And congratulations on the murder of your sister." She leaned over him, her long, brown hair falling over her shoulders. "I did so admire the gusto with which you committed the act. Such savagery. Why, one would think there'd been more to it than the cowardly exchange of your life for hers."

She looked at the boy kneeling at Terry's head, a broad, gleaming knife clutched in his three-fingered left hand. "Dean, did it seem to you that Terry enjoyed killing his darling sister?"

Dean looked at her through hollow, sunken eyes. Long strands of greasy hair hung over those eyes. "Yes, m'am." He laid the edge of the knife against Terry's trembling throat and drew forth a trickle of blood, making the doomed boy squeal. "Matter of fact . . . I think he was getting off on it."

Ms. Wickman nodded. "You know, I believe you may be right. You see, Terry, one of the things that most interests me is exposing the barbarian that exists in all of us. Human beings are taught to live behind a mask of civility, to govern their lives by an arbitrarily imposed set of concepts of right and wrong. You lived all eighteen years of your miserable life with that mask wedged firmly in place, but tonight we stripped it away. Tonight we saw the ugly, craven beast that's always lurked in the depths of your now thoroughly tainted heart."

Anger flashed in Terry's eyes. "Fuck you. Fuck you and fuck all of your evil little helpers. Are you going to lecture me all damn night, or are you going to fucking kill me?"

"Boys, hold Terry very still, please. Dean, make certain he is unable to move his head."

Terry's abrupt surge of anger died, terror again twisting his features. "No. I'll do anything. I'll kill anyone. Whatever you want."

"So sorry, dear. I'm afraid I find you too boring to join the ranks of my Apprentices." Ms. Wickman's voice conveyed boredom, with an undertone of mock regret, a parody of an interviewer turning down a job applicant. "So now, yes, you die."

Then she positioned herself so that she was standing directly over Terry's head. "Now, no peeking up my dress, you naughty boy."

Terry sniffled. "You're . . . crazy."

"Perhaps. But I'm not the one about to die helpless and broken."

Two Apprentices worked to keep Terry's legs pinned to the floor. Two more of the black-clad boys kept his arms still. Dean kept the big blade pressed to his throat, while his other hand was wound in the boy's sweat-soaked hair.

Ms. Wickman lifted her right foot and placed the sole of the black stiletto against the boy's forehead. The point of the long, narrow heel hovered just above his dancing eyeball. Normally she wore a more modest heel, but she'd worn the stilettos tonight with this very purpose in mind. She watched the jittery dance of his eyes a moment longer, savoring his terror, enjoying his helplessness.

One of the apprentices snickered and said, "Oh, look, he's pissing his pants."

Ms. Wickman directed a last bit of mocking laughter at her victim. "Pathetic. You're clearly too worthless to continue existing in this world, Terry. Convey my regards when you meet your sister in hell."

She eased the point of her heel down and it touched his eyeball. Terry squealed and jerked against the grip of his captors. But it was no use. The Apprentices managed to keep the boy still as she continued to press down. She watched in almost breathless fascination as the point of the heel dimpled the surface of the eyeball, causing the tissue to well up around it. Then she increased the pressue still more and there was an audible, liquidy pop as the point of the heel pierced the eyeball. Terry screamed yet again and jerked harder against his captors, almost dislodging the boy pinning down his left arm.

But it was too late to matter now.

Ms. Wickman bit her lower lip and thrust the heel downward, angling it so that it pushed through the eye and into his brain. Blood jetted from the socket and the boy convulsed violently for a moment before going still. The curved back end of her shoe conformed against the curvature of the dead boy's eye socket in a way she found aesthetically pleasing. She wished someone had a camera to take a picture of it. Ah, well. She admired the darkly delicious juxtaposition of shoe and eye socket a moment longer before extracting her heel, which emerged slick with blood and tissue.

A breath of shuddery, sensual satisfaction issued through her lips. She straightened her dress and brushed back her hair. "Dispose of this trash, children. I'll be retiring to my quarters for the evening."

She exited the living room without another word and continued through the gleaming foyer to the ornate staircase that led to the many floors above. She had learned many useful things from the Master, among them the ability to manipulate aspects of the physical world. The necessary magical energy was derived from appeasement of the death gods, entities that derived power from suffering and death, which she happily supplied in generous portions on a daily basis.

This house was outwardly decrepit. When glimpsed from the bottom of the long, dusty driveway, the abandoned farmhouse looked as it always had to generations of locals—like an uninhabited, decaying thing, a rotting collection of ancient timber and drywall that through some miracle managed to remain upright.

But any wanderer unlucky enough to step through the front door would instantly know they had entered a strange place far removed from the natural world. On the other side of that creaking front door was the interior of a huge mansion, a place far too large to be contained by the ancient farmhouse. And yet, once inside, there was no denying the apparent reality of it.

And once inside, Ms. Wickman reflected with a stiff smile, no could ever hope to escape.

She had learned from the Master's mistakes. Her new kingdom was formidable in its own right, but it was not so large and out of control that she was unable to maintain a firm ruling hand. The slaves she had were not allowed to talk to each other, lest they have their tongues removed and fed to them. The silence rule drastically reduced the possibility of a revolt.

Everything was so very close to perfect now. The lone remaining large task was the ongoing effort to hunt down the surviving House of Blood revolutionaries. But the hunt was going well and she knew she'd have them all soon, kneeling before her and begging for mercy.

She entered a long corridor lit by candles flickering in wall sconces. Each side of the corridor was lined with doors that opened to bedrooms that doubled as torture chambers. Ms. Wickman glanced through one open doorway and saw a thin blonde girl in skintight black leather.

"Hello, Gwendolyn. Enjoying your work tonight?"

The girl flashed a smile as she flicked a bullwhip at a middle-aged man strapped to a four-poster bed. "Loving it. As always, Mistress."

Ms. Wickman watched the whip slice away a strip of blubbery flesh and flashed a smile of her own. She then left Gwendolyn to her work and continued to the end of the corridor where a set of double doors marked the entrance to her chambers. The doors opened at her approach, sweeping backward as if triggered by an electronic sensor. They closed again as she moved into the room. The room was huge and well-appointed, a living area fit for a queen. A massive four-poster bed with a velvet canopy was set against one wall at the far end of the room. A library and bar dominated another corner of the room.

She paused at what appeared to merely be a smooth expanse of unadorned wall. Her fingers brushed the wall's surface and the outline of a doorway formed. A tap of her forefinger caused the door to open. The door, a huge stone slab, made a gritty sound as its bottom end slid over the stone floor of the hidden chamber. Through this door was a deep, sticky darkness, a blackness so impenetrable and compelling that many who glimpsed it feared it would swallow them forever. A fear not far from the truth.

Ms. Wickman stepped without hesitation into that clingy darkness. The stone door slowly closed behind her and the blackness enveloped her. She felt for a moment like a wandering soul suspended in some void between worlds. But the feeling was fleeting, because this was her realm. Her darkness. She commanded the spirits and the elements in this place. She was the only thing to be afraid of here, and knowing that aroused her, caused her nipples to stiffen against the fabric of her elegant dress.

The sound of a muffled whimper penetrated the silence.

Ms. Wickman snapped her fingers and the wicks of several candles sparked and grew thin columns of flame.

Another, louder whimper, just this side of a moan.

Ms. Wickman's nostrils flared. She ached to touch herself. Instead she placed her hands on her hips and approached the cage that hung suspended from the ceiling by a stout chain. The dark-haired girl whined and scooted to the back of the cage. The motion caused the cage to spin slightly, and the twisting chain links made a grinding sound.

Ms. Wickman stopped a few feet from the cage. She

threw her head back and laughed with sudden, shocking heartiness. Just as abruptly, the laughter died. She stepped closer and pressed her face between two cage bars.

"Hello, dear." Her voice was a breathy whisper, barely audible. "How are you settling into your new home, hmm?"

The girl said nothing.

Ms. Wickman turned the cage. The chain links groaned and the girl attempted to scoot away again, but Ms. Wickman caught one of her slender arms just above the charred stump of her left wrist. A loud moan emerged from the cage. Ms. Wickman gave the girl a savage yank and she crashed against the cage bars. The girl's other stump flailed uselessly. Her hands were both gone, of course, removed to make the rendering of dark magics next to impossible.

Ms. Wickman pulled the girl closer and said, "I'd tell you struggling is useless, which is true enough, but I do so enjoy reveling in your terror, Giselle."

The girl abruptly stopped struggling.

She sagged against the cage bars and shuddered as the room grew colder.

CHAPTER FIVE

Something shifted in the darkness. Dream was dimly aware of a subtle rolling motion. The sensation reminded her of early morning fishing trips with her father when she was a little girl, the way those slowly rippling lake waves would make the boat gently sway in the murky green water. The memory was fleeting, the vivid colors bleaching from the vision before it blew apart like a puff of fog. There was a pang of loss, but then that too was gone, lost in the shifting black tides of unconsciousness.

Shifting . . .

Dream felt it again, the slow, almost imperceptible roll of her body, only this time the sensation was clearer, more of the real world than the comfortably numb land of sleep. She wasn't awake yet, but some part of her knew consciousness was approaching and wasn't happy about it. This dark place was better than what awaited her on the other side of the wall of sleep.

Then she became aware of another sensation, even sweeter, a hand moving slowly over her naked body. Her breath quickened and she moved closer to consciousness. The hand slid up her inner thigh, moved very lightly over her tingling pussy, then roamed over her flat stomach and up between her breasts. When the hand cupped a breast, Dream moaned and arched her back, offering a swollen nipple to her still invisible lover.

She was almost awake now. Her eyes fluttered once before closing again, allowing her a glimpse of a formless shadow. Her lover's mouth closed over the proffered nipple, making her moan again as the person's tongue swirled around the stiffened flesh. It felt good. So good. An animalistic grunt came from the region of her breasts as the mouth shifted to her other breast and showed it the same hungry, aching attention.

Dream was awake now, but she kept her eyes closed, reveling in the delicious sensations rippling through her body. The mattress below her rolled again. A waterbed, she finally realized. Which meant she was likely in some cheap hotel. Which further meant the person suckling at her breasts was some sleazy guy she'd picked up somewhere. Not that his identity mattered. In the end he'd be just another faceless mark, the latest in a succession of men she wouldn't have to care about the next day.

Dream decided to keep her eyes closed while the mytery man did these delightful things to her body. She was enjoying too much the notion that he could be anyone. He could even be . . .

The image that came to her then arrived with such sudden and shocking vividness that it made her gasp. A part of her mind rebelled. *No.* The man she was remembering was a monster. He'd done awful, horrific things. And he'd been responsible for the deaths of her friends. But the Dream who'd cared about such things was the part of her psyche she'd worked so hard to suppress. That Dream was dead. The person she'd become accepted darkness, welcomed corruption.

So instead of pushing the vision away, she allowed it

to further crystallize in her mind. She imagined the Master on top of her, his naked body gleaming in the flickering candlelight the way it had the one night she'd spent with him. The sex she'd shared with him that evening had been astonishing, better by far than anything she'd experienced before or since. Her body twisted on the bed, delighting at the feel of his rough, masculine hands kneading her soft, yielding flesh. The fingers teasing her sex abruptly pushed inside her, curled and flexed, triggering a first jolt of orgasm and eliciting a shuddering cry of ecstacy. She lifted her ass off the bed and thrust her pelvis at the still-flexing fingers.

She ached to be penetrated by something else and said so. "Take me . . ." A gasp. Another flex inside her. "Do it. Please . . ."

Then the mouth came away from her breast and a voice said, "Afraid I can't do that, baby."

Dream's eyes flew open and she gaped at the sight of Alicia Jackson's smiling face. "I don't have the necessary equipment, so sorry." Alicia's tongue darted out and flicked at Dream's still engorged nipple. "But this I can do all night long if you like . . ."

Dream's face twisted in disgust as a maggot tumbled out of Alicia's mouth onto her breast. "Get away from me!" Her body jerked away from Alicia's touch, sinking deeper into the yielding mattress. The tiny maggot clung to her skin and Dream instinctively tried to brush it away, but her arms wouldn't move. They were stretched at sharp angles behind her. She glanced back and saw that she was tied to the bed. She jerked her hands against the restraints, but the lengths of new-looking rope abraded her flesh and refused to yield.

Fully awake now, she began to take in more details of her surroundings. She saw a ceiling fan above her. Tufts of dust along the edges of the unmoving blades. A book-case filled with haphazardly stacked old paperbacks. An old television with a rabbit ears antenna atop an old dresser. Piles of dirty laundry on the floor. Chintzy cheap curtains drawn across the room's two windows. A creased and much-folded poster of Robert Smith on the closed bedroom door. And a faint piss smell she associated with cats. Then she felt the sticky wetness beneath her and realized she'd pissed the bed while she was unconscious.

Gross.

"Where am I?"

Alicia's hand slipped out of Dream's vagina. The dead woman smiled and licked moisture off her bloated fingers. "Mmm . . . you're not in Kansas anymore, baby."

Dream's mouth curled in disgust. "You're not Alicia."

The dead woman rolled her milky eyes. "How tiresome. We've been over this. I——"

"I know you're real," Dream cut her off. There was fire in her voice now. "But you're not my dead friend. She'd never do anything so vile to me."

"You didn't think it was so vile a minute ago."

Dream's face reddened. "A minute ago I thought you were——" She faltered, her mouth hanging open a moment before she lamely finished, "——someone else."

"Oh, I know what you thought, baby." The dead woman shifted position on the bed, stretching a leg across Dream's midsection. Then she sat up, straddling her. She was still wearing the slinky little black dress; it rode up high on her thighs now, exposing mottled flesh that had once been smooth and toned. "You figured I was some dude you picked up at a bar, but what you were really thinking about was——"

"Shut up!" Dream vainly tugged at her bindings again. "And get off me, you fucking disgusting . . . thing."

"I will not." She cupped Dream's breasts in her swollen hands and tweaked the nipples with her thumbs. Her nails were abnormally long and yellowed; seeing them graze her flesh made Dream's stomach twist. "You're in no position to demand anything. And let me be clear about this one more time. I am Alicia Katherine Jackson. And though you didn't mean to, you brought me back, restored me to this undead state of existence. And let me tell you, I'm not feeling all that charitable toward my old best gal pal these days. It's not a lot of fun being a half-decayed walking corpse."

Dream still couldn't accept it. Buying into what the grotesque apparition was trying to sell her would mean she was some kind of monster. "No. You're not her. You're lying. You're some thing masquerading as her to cause me misery."

"Nonsense. You think I'm some random ghoul playing head games with you? What kind of sense does that make? No, I'm what I say I am and you're just going to have to deal with that." Alicia picked at a weeping razor wound with a yellowed nail. "These hurt, by the way. Thanks so much for making me corporeal, Dream. Thanks for making me feel things. Everything hurts, Dream. Everything feels like it wants to come apart, but the magic you filled me up with won't let that happen. So, from the bottom of my dead-but-beating heart, thank you so very fucking much. Cunt."

Dream's vision blurred. She sniffled and blinked back the tears. "I'm sorry." Her voice was small, soft, the sound of a beaten, broken thing. "I never meant to hurt you."

Alicia's smile faded. "I wonder how many times you've said that in your life. You know, I never thought I'd say it, but I'm beginning to think Chad-boy was right about you all those years ago. You love drama. You wallow in self-pity. And at the end of the day, all you've ever really done is hurt people."

"Stop it." Dream's eyes misted over again. "Please . . ."

There was a sudden sound of voices from the other

side of the closed door. Alicia sighed and climbed off the bed, moving to a spot near the bookcase. "The fuckers who nabbed you earlier are back. Guess I'll just sit back and watch the show. Hopefully they'll at least leave me some sloppy seconds."

The door flew open and several young people swarmed into the room. Dream counted seven altogether, including the girl she'd assaulted in the bathroom of the Villager Pub. There were two other girls and four boys. They all appeared to be in their late teens or early twenties. One boy was carrying a huge Igloo cooler. He flipped the top open and pulled out a can of Pabst Blue Ribbon. A few of the others grabbed beers, too. A girl wearing a black gypsy dress had hair bleached a platinum shade of blonde with inch-long black roots. Black fishnets with several rips exposing pale flesh encased her slender legs. She fired up a clove cigarette and sat down on the edge of the bed.

"Hello, sleeping beauty."

Dream didn't say anything. Though the girl was smiling, the expression didn't reach her eyes, which were hard and flat. A barely contained rage pulsed just beneath that smiling surface. Dream's eyes again filled with tears. She would probably die in this room. And despite the hell her life had become, she didn't want that to happen.

The girl blew rancid clove smoke in Dream's face. "I hear you beat up my sister tonight." She indicated the girl Dream remembered from the Villager Pub with a nod. "She says you beat the living shit out of her for no good reason at all. Now, you're not getting out of here no matter what. I guess you know that, so you might as well be straight with me. Is my sister telling the truth?"

Dream met the girl's merciless gaze and swallowed hard. Though she was still terrified of what was about to happen, a part of her was already resigned to it. So the girl was right, there was no point in telling anything but the truth.

"Yeah. I did it."

The girl nodded. "Good." She blew more foul smoke at Dream's face. "It's good that you admitted it, I mean. It'll make this easier for both of us. We'll know what we're doing is justified. And you'll know you're getting what you deserve."

"What are you going to do?"

"We're going to kill you."

The bluntness of the statement elicited a helpless, sudden sob from Dream. For a long moment the only sound in the room was her rising anguish. Then the girl put her cigarette out on Dream's thigh, making her scream and jerk away from the source of the pain.

The girl waited until Dream's screams died away to a low, blubbering moan. "We're going to kill you," she said again, "and we're going to take our time doing it. You may wonder why we didn't gag you. We're kind of out in the country here, which means you can scream your fucking lungs out and no one will ever hear you."

One of the boys, a lanky, long-haired kid with acne, had been slouching in a corner, his arms wrapped over his knees, a can of Pabst dangling from one hand. He abruptly came out of the crouch and moved into the center of the room, beer sloshing out of the beer can. "Am I the only one who thinks this is kind of fucked?" There was agitation in his voice, real anger and in-credulity, but the words were slightly slurred. A little much liquid courage, Dream figured.

He turned in a slow circle, eyeing each of his friends in turn. "Come on, you assholes. You know this is wrong. You can't kill a person over something like this."

No one said anything for a while. Several of the kids

shifted uneasily. They studied the floor or briefly glanced at each other before turning their gazes to the ceiling or an inexplicably interesting patch of blank wall.

Then the girl sitting next to Dream said, "Am I going to have to worry about you, Michael?"

Michael was staring at another boy in the room, one to whom he bore a strong resemblance. They were siblings or very close cousins. Michael's brother or cousin stared hard at the floor. His hands were shaking. Dream did a quick scan of the faces arrayed around her and saw evidence of fear in all of them, including the girl she'd so stupidly vented some of her free-floating rage on in the pub bathroom. The one exception was that girl's sister, who was eerily calm.

The girl rose from the bed and approached Michael. "I asked you a question. I'd like an answer. *Now.* Am I going to have to worry about you?"

Michael gave up trying to engage his relative's attention and faced the girl. "Or what, Marcy?" There was real venom in his voice now, a harshness only slightly blunted by the boozy slur of his words. "Are you afraid I'll turn narc?" He gulped Pabst. "And what if I do, huh? What then? Are you going to kill me, too?"

Marcy said nothing at first. She pried the Pabst can from Michael's shaking hand. She drank what was left and tossed the empty can into the open cooler. Then she put a hand on Michael's shoulder and said, "No more beer for you tonight. It's making you crazy and you need to calm down."

The kid was trembling all over. Something about Marcy being so close terrified him. He wanted to flinch away from her touch but didn't quite dare. And he did seem perceptibly less bold without a beer in his hand.

His voice was very soft as he said, "We can't do this. It's wrong."

Marcy slapped him, the sound shockingly loud in the otherwise silent room.

Alicia barked laughter and said, "Damn."

No one reacted. The kids couldn't see or hear the dead woman. Dream glanced at her. Alicia winked and blew a kiss. Dream forced herself not to react and made a mental note not to respond to anything else Alicia might say. She sensed a delicate balance in the room, her fate perhaps hinging on whether this kid had the fortitude to continue making his stand. Her case wouldn't be helped any should she start talking to invisible people.

Marcy cupped the boy's chin in her hand and leaned close. "We're gonna do this. Nobody does what this bitch did and gets away with it, not when it comes to my family, motherfucker." The boy was shaking more than ever and Dream despaired, sensing the fight was already lost. "And about your question, Michael? Let's just say you don't want me thinking for even one second that you might narc." She released his chin and stepped back. "Can I trust you? And please tell the truth, because I'll know if you're lying."

Michael sighed and nodded. "Yes."

"And it's not like she'll be the first person we've killed." This was Michael's brother or cousin finally speaking up. "Nobody talks about it, but we all know that bum we jumped in Overton Park last summer didn't survive."

Dream's heart lurched at the revelation. Again, no one said anything for a time. The general anxiety level skyrocketed. There was a lot more nervous shuffling of feet. A lot of fidgeting. Marcy's sister looked very pale, as if she might throw up at any moment.

A ghost of a smile brushed the edges of Marcy's mouth before vanishing. "That's very true," she said, breaking the silence. "Thank you for reminding us, Kevin. Now back to business."

She returned to the bed and appraised Dream candidly, her gaze moving slowly over the length of her splayed, nude body. Then she looked Dream in the eye and said, "You really are gorgeous, you know that?"

Dream didn't bother responding.

But Alicia moved to the other side of the bed and appraised her in much the same way. "Girl's a gothed-out skank, but she speaks the fucking truth." She smiled broadly and blood leaked from cracks at the corners of her mouth. "Hey, maybe if they really kill you, you can come back like me. Wouldn't that be a kick? Little Miss Hot Stuff all rotting and stinky?" She cackled. "Well, I'd get some satisfaction out of it anyway."

Again, Dream ignored the dead woman's commentary.

"Somebody bring me a belt."

Michael's cousin reacted instantly to Marcy's command, crossing the room within the space of a heartbeat and yanking open a closet door. He rummaged around in the closet's dark interior for a moment, then emerged with the requested item.

Marcy accepted the belt from him, winding one end twice around her right hand while letting the end with the brass buckle dangle. "Seriously, you really are the most beautiful thing I've ever seen in person. You could be a model or a movie star." There was plain, honest admiration in her voice as she said these things, but then her tone darkened. "But beautiful people like you always look down on people like us. That's if you think of us at all. Or if forced to think of us, you see us as, like, insects, or rodents, something less than human."

Dream struggled to keep a quaver out of her voice as she said, "Th-that's not true. I never—"

"SHUT UP!"

Marcy's arm snapped out like a striking cobra and the belt whipped across Dream's belly, the buckle gouging her flesh. Dream cried out and the belt snapped across her body again. Then again. A thin trickle of blood ran down her side from where the buckle had nicked her.

Dream's chest heaved and tears rolled down her face. "Please . . . please . . ."

"I told you to shut up." Marcy's voice was surprisingly calm again, belying the act of violence. "You should do as I say."

Dream stifled the whimper that wanted to come, reminding herself that her pleas were less than useless, serving only to further stir the ire of her tormentor.

Marcy resumed her speech as if nothing had happened: "Beautiful, privileged people think nothing of bullying people like Ellen, my sweet little sister. Poor Ellen's been pushed around by people like you all her life." She paused and sat down again at the edge of the bed. "One time a couple of cheerleaders followed her into a bathroom. This was sophomore year of high school, I believe." She glanced at her sister for confirmation. Ellen wouldn't meet her gaze, but she nodded. "Do you know what those fucking nose-in-the-air bitches did to her?"

Dream shook her head. "No."

"I'll tell you." Marcy leaned over Dream so that their faces were separated by mere inches. The hate pulsing out of the girl's hard, dark eyes made Dream shiver. "They pulled her into a stall and pushed her face down into a shit-clogged toilet. They held her there while she struggled and shit and toilet water filled her mouth."

Dream sniffed. "I'm sorry."

Marcy grunted. "Yeah, you should be, because it might as well have been you who did that. I hold all your kind responsible. You wonder why I'm so angry? Maybe now you're beginning to have a clue. When you attacked Ellen tonight, you were making her relive that all over again."

Dream's breath hitched in her throat and tears rolled in a steady stream from her eyes. "I'm . . . so sorry . . . I wish—"

"Shut up."

Dream again fell silent.

Marcy unwound the belt from her hand and slipped the thin length of black leather behind Dream's neck. Dream tensed, her heart pounding as Marcy fed the end of the belt through the brass buckle and pulled it taut around her throat. She wound the end around her hand again and stared into Dream's suddenly bulging eyes. "I wanted to go after those fucking cheerleaders so bad when I heard what they'd done, but I didn't have the nerve back then. But not this time. This time someone's going to pay."

She stood up and pulled on the end of the belt. Dream sputtered, her face turning a bright shade of red as the loop tightened around her neck. She was dimly aware of someone else in the room saying "Oh God" over and over.

Then Marcy relaxed her grip on the belt and Dream was abruptly able to breathe again. She drew in huge gulps of air and listened to her heart slam against her chest wall.

Marcy was smiling now. "You didn't think I'd kill you so quickly, did you? That would've been almost like mercy. This is just the beginning, cunt. A warm-up. You've got a long night of pain ahead of you and I'm going to enjoy every sweet fucking second of it."

A black rage stole into Dream's heart then, obliterating the terror completely, sweeping away any lingering trace of guilt she felt over what she'd done to Marcy's sister. Her mouth curled in a sneer of disgust and fury. Dark, malicious energy swirled inside of her, dormant power awakened and focused by the overwhelming strength of her anger. There was no room in her heart now for anything other than hate and a blind need to inflict pain on everyone around her.

Everyone else felt the change, too.

The other girl in the room, a somewhat plump thing with hair dyed a bright shade of auburn, shivered and said, "Did it just get really fucking cold in here?"

Someone else said, "Yeah. Jesus, what's going on?"

Marcy looked into Dream's eyes and flinched. She let go of the belt and began to rise from the bed. Then she froze, suddenly unable to retreat any further.

Dream snarled, hissed like a snake. She flailed at her bindings, rocking the bed violently and causing a lamp to topple off the nightstand. The auburn-haired girl screamed and ran for the closed door. Dream loosed a tremendous cry that filled the room like the concussion from a bomb blast. The auburn-haired girl's body slammed against the door, then spun around and fell to the floor. When she tried to stand, blood was leaking from every orifice, spilling in trickles from her ears, mouth and nostrils. A bright redness stained the whites of her eyes and she wobbled as she tried to take a blind step toward the bed. Then she collapsed, hitting the floor with a resounding thump that elicited more screams and cries of shock from her friends.

The screaming went on for a while.

The girl on the floor was absolutely still. Dead. Dream knew she'd somehow killed her. She hadn't done it intentionally, but she'd done it nonetheless, some instinct causing her to strike at the girl with the power she'd tapped.

Her voice emerged as a growl. "No one gets out alive." And she meant to do it. Kill them all. Make them suffer on an epic level. Wallow in their pain.

She focused on Marcy now, drawing in some of that thrumming energy, preparing to unleash a lethal blast of it straight into the bitch's pounding heart. She felt a tingle of arousal. She hadn't felt so deliciously debauched since that long ago night in the Master's bed. Each of her senses was heightened to an unnatural degree. She could hear each thudding beat of Marcy's heart. The girl tried to jerk away from her again, but remained held in place by invisible puppet strings.

She whimpered. "Please . . ."

Dream smiled. "I'm going to kill you."

Marcy winced at the sound of her own words thrown back at her.

Dream focused energy in a tight, pulsing ball, drawing it in like a ball stretched backward in the elastic band of a slingshot.

Then, as abruptly as it had come over her, the power blinked out. It was just gone, as if someone had thrown a switch. There was a moment of frozen shock, an abrupt and dramatic shift of atmosphere. Dream sagged into the sloshing waterbed mattress, so tired now, her body depleted of energy. She could fall asleep right now, even surrounded by these enemies. Her eyes fluttered, almost closed. And Marcy stumbled backward, tripped over the dead girl, and tumbled to the floor.

She was back on her feet in an instant. Her eyes were wild and darting, moving from the dead body to the stunned faces of her friends, then to Dream. She was breathing hard, like someone who'd just finished a marathon. Then she was screaming and gesturing wildly at her friends.

"EVERYBODY OUT!" She yanked her sister out of the chair and shoved her stumbling toward the door. "GET OUT! GET THE FUCK OUT OF HERE! NOW, GOD-DAMMIT!"

Michael was the first to snap out of it. He yanked the door open and Ellen staggered through it. The others followed in rapid fashion. Marcy was the last out the door. She turned and paused with the door half-shut.

"I don't know what just happened here—" She was working hard to project an approximation of the malicious calm she'd evinced before. "—but I'm not fucking through with you. Somehow I'll make you pay."

Then she was gone, the door slamming shut behind her.

Dream felt only a mild apprehension at the girl's threat. Her eyes fluttered again. She mused in a vague way over the awesome power she'd so briefly channeled, wondering where it came from, and whether she could summon it again if needed.

Alicia was standing over her again, but her image was blurred, hazy.

Dream was almost asleep now.

But she remained aware long enough to hear her dead friend speak. "That was pretty impressive, Dream. Those kids are scared shitless, what with you makin' like Linda Blair in the motherfuckin' *Exorcist*. But this ain't over." Alicia gave her head an emphatic shake. "Uh-uh, not by a long shot. But listen, you remember what I told you before about trouble comin', don't you? I wasn't talking about these kids, honey."

Dream's eyes closed. "Whatever."

Alicia leaned close. Her rancid corpse breath hot on Dream's ear. "Trouble's out there, Dream. Lurking, waiting for you to show yourself. And let me tell you something—if you somehow walk out of here alive, somewhere down the line you'll wind up wishing these punks *had* killed you."

Dream sighed.

She could think about Alicia's warnings later. Maybe. Her breathing evened out.

At long last, the world went away again.

CHAPTER SIX

The sound of the television emanating from the bedroom abruptly silenced. Allyson looked at her reflection in the bathroom mirror and listened to the muffled sound of Chad yawning. He was tired. Not surprising, given how long a day it had been, and given how many glasses of whiskey he'd downed over several hours of conversation with the man he called Jim.

Allyson had returned to the house less than fifteen minutes after storming off, making sure to stay out just long enough to allow Chad to believe she'd only been blowing off some steam. She had to stay in character. So she'd come home just soon enough, smiling and apologizing to their uninvited "guest," but not making too big a deal about it. The men retired to the den while she cleaned up in the kitchen. And while she cleaned, she worked at not thinking about the hard, dangerous men who would soon be here. Whether they were coming to kill or merely apprehend, she did not know. And didn't want to know.

Or so she told herself, over and over.

It wasn't supposed to matter. Chad was just a mark, and his friend was just a person some other people wanted to get their hands on. She'd done everything asked of her, working her way into Chad's life, earning his trust, making him love her. Being there when the moment her employers said would arrive finally did. She knew she should continue to be cold and emotionless about it, just wait until the opportunity arose to slip away in the middle of the night, but . . .

The damnedest thing.

She liked Chad. There was no use denying it. The line between playacting and reality had become blurred at some indistinct point. The moments before placing that phone call earlier had been like walking up to the very edge of a high cliff and deciding whether to jump. She had taken that leap after only a minor hesitation, believing her second thoughts would evaporate with the deed done.

But those thoughts were still swirling around in her head, taunting her with images and fantasies of possible futures that could no longer be. They were all the more maddening for the obvious impossibility of taking it all back.

What's done is done, she thought, silently addressing her reflection. *Just leave it be and when you board that flight tomorrow morning start working on forgetting there ever was a Chad Robbins.*

Right.

She had a feeling that was going to fall into the category of things easier said than done.

And as if she didn't have enough to fret about, there was the matter of this mystery man. Chad clearly liked and respected the man a great deal, which added yet another layer of regret to her betrayal. There was something so naggingly familiar about the man. So she'd decided to eavesdrop on their conversation, kicking off her shoes and padding on her bare feet to a spot in the hallway just outside the den.

They had talked of small things at first. But the tone

of the conversation abruptly shifted when Jim at last told Chad why he had come to see him after all this time. Allyson's eyes widened and her heart skipped a beat as he talked of danger on the horizon. Some survivors of the House of Blood had gone missing and another had been found brutally murdered. He urged Chad to "go underground."

Allyson had been able to bear no more of it, retreating from her eavesdropping position and heading in a hurry to the spare bedroom. There she retrieved from the closet the bag she'd packed months ago. It was a big black canvas bag stuffed full of clothes very unlike the fashionable wardrobe she'd adopted for her big role as Chad's love interest. Tucked away in a zippered side pouch was the $10,000 cash advance she'd been given for the job. Her getaway money. Another pouch contained an array of flawlessly produced false credentials and ID, including a passport, a Tennessee driver's license, a birth certificate, and a card identifying her as a consultant for something called Franklin Security Solutions. All bore the name Jennifer Campbell.

Chad likely would invite his friend to spend the night, and she could too easily imagine the man stumbling upon the stuffed traveling bag. A man like that would operate at a base-level of paranoia every day. He would open the bag, see the fake ID and documents, and . . . so she stashed the bag at the back of her own closet in the bedroom she shared with Chad.

Well. It was taken care of now. No one had any reason to suspect she was working with the bad guys. She turned away from her reflection and returned to the bedroom. She went to the bed, watched Chad's sleeping form. He was snoring lightly. She prayed for him to turn over and see her in the expensive Victoria's Secret lingerie they'd picked out together from a catalog. It would arouse him. It always did. A good, energetic fucking might be just the thing to get him talking again. She pictured herself in his embrace, their bodies naked and covered with a sheen of sweat in the afterglow of love. The intimacy of the moment leading him to confide in her again, sharing his fears and telling her of the danger Jim claimed they were facing. And it would then be so easy to fuel the fires of that fear, manipulating him with her own show of terror.

They would run.

Rouse Jim, grab a few necessities, and get the hell out of Dodge.

Chad shifted position on the bed, rolling from his side onto his back. Allyson held her breath for a hopeful, tense moment.

He didn't wake.

Damn.

Allyson pulled on a tiny silk robe and slipped out of the bedroom. As she moved down the hallway toward the living room, she paused at the doorway to the guest bedroom. The door was partly open, but the interior was dark. She could just vaguely make out the sleeping form of Mr. Jim, Lazarus, or whatever his name really was. She heard an intake of breath and thought for a moment that he might be awake. Awake and watching her watch him. Her heart raced at the thought. Without waiting to verify whether the man was awake or asleep, she hurried past the darkened doorway.

She retrieved Chad's laptop from his office and carried it into the living room. She settled into the plush sectional sofa and propped the little computer on her lap. She opened it and tapped the power button. The computer came out of hibernation mode to present her with a screen that offered the option of signing on to her desktop or Chad's. She moved the cursor to Chad's name and clicked on it. The desktop icons quickly loaded and she signed on to Chad's AOL account. She opened his mailbox and scrolled through the list of e-mails, looking for anything that might be from someone looking to tip him to Allyson's true role here. She couldn't imagine who might be in a position to do that, but paranoia drove her to periodically check his messages on the off-chance anything that needed intercepting did show up.

Seeing nothing out of the ordinary, she clicked over to his saved mail folder and opened the two-year-old e-mail from Dream Weaver. She read through it again, even though she knew the words by heart. And she felt again the familiar stab of ridiculous jealousy. Ridiculous because the woman seemed to be gone from Chad's life forever. And doubly ridiculous given the true nature of her own relationship with Chad.

But the feeling was there nonetheless.

The note read:

Chad,

Yes, I know it's been a while since you've heard from me. Yes, I know you're worried. I can tell because there's about a gazillion e-mails jamming my inbox. I don't even need to read them. The subject headers tell me all I need to know.

Sorry if that sounds cold. Sorry if I sound like a bitch. But you need to let go and move on with your life. Stop pining for me, because I'm telling you right now, once and for all, I am never coming back.

I don't say these things to hurt you. I honestly don't. It hurts me to say them this way. I'm trying to be forceful and firm—yes, bitchy—because I need you to accept the way things are. What we had is

*broken and cannot be fixed. I'm broken. I love you
with all my heart, more than I could ever love anyone else, but our lives are on very different paths.*

Paths, Chad, that will never cross again.

*This is the last time you will ever hear from me.
Please don't reply to this message. I'm cancelling
this account and it will just bounce back to you.*

*Have a nice life, Chad. Please find someone nice
and forget about me.*

Goodbye,

Dream

Allyson closed the e-mail and clicked out of Chad's AOL
account.
Dream Weaver. As usual, Allyson's blood boiled at the
thought of that gorgeous woman and her ridiculous
name. *That fucking cunt.* Dream had put Chad through
so much drama and strife. He always swore he was over
her. But why, then, would he continue to save a two-
year-old e-mail?
Cunt. Fucking cunt.
She'd been asked to keep an eye out for her, too. She
wished the bitch *had* been the one to show up tonight.
She would've called hell down on her without a second
thought. But she'd been told from the beginning that
Lazarus, as they still called him, was far more likely to
one day grace Chad's door. And . . .
Allyson frowned.
Wait a minute . . .
Chad's name for the elusive Lazarus was Jim. It didn't
require a lot of thought to conclude that Jim was far

more likely the man's real name. Allyson clicked over to Google Web search and entered the following:

"Lazarus Jim House of Blood"

She clicked on the first search result, a two-year-old *Chattanooga Herald* story that recounted everything then known about what had happened at that remote mountain house. One paragraph stood out immediately. It told of the wild Internet speculation about the true identities of the men known as the Master and Lazarus. One theory in particular made Allyson gasp. She'd heard it before, of course, but had forgotten about it or dismissed it as obvious nonsense.

Now, however, she wasn't so sure.

She clicked back over to the image search tool and with trembling fingers typed in the name of a dead rock star. The images of this man were plentiful. She scrolled through them before clicking on a thumbnail image of the man at his most grizzled-looking. His face was bloated from alcohol overindulgence. His hair was a big brown mane and he had a thick, bushy beard. The hair was shorter now and the beard was gone, but the penetrating eyes and high cheekbones were the same.

"Fuck—"

Jim. Lazarus. That voice . . . no wonder it'd seemed so naggingly familiar.

Allyson clicked out of the browser window and closed the laptop. She sat there in a state of numb astonishment for several more minutes.

Then a noise from outside the house—a metallic thunk—snapped her out of it. She set the laptop on the coffee table and surged to her feet, her heart thumping in her chest as she moved hurriedly through the living room and into the foyer. Adjacent to the foyer was a small sitting room lined with bookcases. She slipped

into this room and moved to a big window that over-
looked the front lawn. She moved the curtain back
slightly and peered outside.

A big, dark-colored van was parked on the other side
of the street. As she watched, two men clad entirely in
black moved away from the van and crossed the street.
Light from the streetlamps glinted off something shiny
in the lead man's hand. A pistol. Allyson's breath caught
in her throat. She made her shaking hand come away
from the curtain. Without thinking about what she was
doing, she raced out of the sitting room and headed
back through the living room at full speed. Then
through the kitchen to the door that led to the garage.
She yanked the door open and reached for the light
switch. Her hand froze on the switch.

No, she thought. *Can't let them see light.*

She hurried down the three steps to the garage floor,
making her way around in the darkness by memory
and feel. Her bare right foot landed on something sharp
and she let out a squeal of pain. But she made herself
keep going. The men in black and their guns would
have reached the house by now. She didn't have much
time. Her heart felt like it might explode out of her chest
at any moment.

Then she reached the back of the garage and her
hands moved over the dim shapes of tools hanging from
a neatly arranged set of pegs. She dislodged a hammer
that landed on the cement floor with a loud clatter. A
fresh jolt of terror flashed through her at the sound. But
it was nothing she could do anything about. The men in
black had heard it or they hadn't. Her eyes at last discerned the shape of the axe on one of the highest pegs.
She seized its handle and yanked it off the peg.

She was back in the kitchen when she heard a soft tin-
kle of breaking glass. The sound was shockingly close
and she realized the men had scaled the fence to make

a rear entry. A glint of something shiny at the far end of the kitchen seized her attention. A big hand was reaching through a shattered pane toward the handle of one of the doors that opened to the patio and backyard.

Allyson moved to the wall and edged toward the door, blood from the wound to her foot making a slick trail on the kitchen tiles. As she neared the door, she adjusted her grip on the axe handle and raised it over her head. She held her breath and tried to make herself be calm.

Why are you doing this!? a panicked part of her mind railed at her. *You only had to let it happen and collect your fucking money! You're fucking crazy to be doing this!*

Allyson knew that. And she had no answer for the question. All she knew was it was too late to do anything but what she was doing right now.

She was committed.

The man's hand grasped the handle, found the lock, and turned it.

The door popped open.

One man moved through the opening. He was dressed all in black and his face was smudged with black makeup. A pistol was gripped tight in his hand. Another man attired in exactly the same fashion followed him into the kitchen.

Neither man sensed her presence until it was too late.

Allyson stepped forward and brought the axe down, the finely honed blade chopping through the second man's wrist with ease. Blood jetted from the stump. Hand and gun struck the floor. The man screamed as the first man into the house whirled around. He gaped in astonishment at his comrade's mutilated arm. Then he saw Allyson and began to raise his own gun.

But the blade of the axe flashed and cleaved through his neck before he could aim the gun at her. He reflexively squeezed off a shot that blew another pane of glass out of the rear door. Blood pumped out of his severed jugular vein in great gouts and he dropped dead to the floor. The other man reeled about the kitchen, then reached for his severed hand and gun with his good hand.

Allyson brought the blade down yet again, planting it between his shoulder blades and making him cry out again. But it was a weak, dying sound. She yanked the axe out. Blood bubbled from the wound and the man cried out again. He mewled and crawled a few feet away from her, his right arm spewing blood in an arcing fountain as it flopped about uselessly.

Then there were more voices. Shouts and the sound of approaching footsteps.

The kitchen abruptly flooded with light.

Someone gasped.

Allyson blinked at the stark sight of all that bright red blood sprayed all over the kitchen. She looked at the dying man. A pale length of ragged bone protruded from his bleeding wrist. The man looked up at her with drowsy, condemning eyes.

Allyson dropped the axe.

Then she stumbled.

Fell.

Landed in someone's outstretched arms.

Fade to black.

CHAPTER SEVEN

Giselle awoke to the sensation of something crawling up her leg. Something about the feel of it triggered an instant feeling of revulsion. It was fuzzy and many-legged, a large spider probably. She swatted at it and missed, the charred stump at the end of her right wrist brushing uselessly over the still-moving creature. Her mind still fuzzy from sleep, it took her a moment to remember that she no longer had a hand to swat with. But apparently her nerve endings still hadn't accepted this awful reality and continued to taunt her with this damnable phantom limb sensation.

The fuzzy spider continued its progress up her inner thigh. Its insinuating presence on her bare flesh felt like the light touch of a would-be rapist stroking the sleeping form of an intended victim. The concept of violation galvanized Giselle. There was no telling what the thing on her leg really was. Perhaps it outwardly resembled a spider—though she couldn't verify that in the absolute blackness of her suspended prison—but it could very well be something else entirely, a deadly magical construct conjured by Ms. Wickman. She thought about the deliberate way it seemed to be moving toward her vagina and imagined it entering her, saw it expanding and transforming itself inside her, becoming something hideous and bloated.

And as she thought these things, the big spider's body did seem to swell slightly. Giselle's breath caught in her throat as she realized her suspicions were true. Though conjured by the evil woman's magic, the creature was all too real. She suspected Ms. Wickman had designed the thing to adjust its shape and appearance according to its victim's worst imaginings. And the slight swelling while it was still outside of her was a powerful indicator of the scope of its shape-shifting abilities. Once it was inside her and able to directly tap into her mind and feed on her worst fears . . .

Giselle focused every bit of will still available to her and worked to suppress the phantom limb sensation. The effort seemed to yield results. A dim tingle remained, but now she felt the low throb at the end her scarred stump. She concentrated harder still and jabbed at the creature with the stump. The stump skidded past the creature on the first attempt, just brushing its fuzzy legs. The thing was mere inches from her pubic thatch and was still moving. Panic rose in her throat like an exhalation of poison gas. She sat up straight and jabbed downward. The suspended cage swung slightly on its chain, but she made direct contact this time. Her stump pinned its body against her leg. She felt it trying to escape from the pressure, exerting more strength than so tiny a thing should possess. Giselle gritted her teeth and pushed down with all her strength. Instinct and revulsion made her want to knock the thing off her body, but she knew she had to kill it while she had the chance.

The creature swelled beneath her stump, its legs growing longer and thicker. Giselle leaned forward, applying upper body leverage. Then there was a squeal as the thing's body burst and a thick, gooey substance exploded against her flesh. Its legs twitched another time and stopped moving. Giselle gagged and flicked the tattered body away. Coated in goo, the thing's body clung to the cage for a moment, then fell between two of the steel bars and landed with a sickening plop on the stone floor.

Giselle's chest was heaving. Sudden tears erupted from her eyes and spilled in hot trails down her cheeks. She pawed at the mass of goo coating the center of her body, wiping as much of it away with her stumps as she could. The phantom limb sensation returned and she made a mess of the job, spread the goo over a wider area of her body. She managed to gather a fair amount of the vile stuff on her stumps and flick it away, but without hands it was impossible to clean herself thoroughly.

The room abruptly grew colder and her tears turned to frost on her cheeks. The atmosphere in the room was clearly being artificially manipulated. Yet another spell constructed by Ms. Wickman, likely designed to start working should Giselle somehow manage to thwart the shape-shifter. Knowing the cold was a product of magic did nothing to alleviate the spell's effects. The temperature plunged several more degrees and Giselle moved into a corner of the cage, drew her legs up to her torso, and wrapped what was left of her arms around them. Her body shivered uncontrollably in the deepening cold, making the cage sway again on its chain.

And though they shamed her and added to her discomfort, her tears continued to flow, etching icy paths down her cheeks. She was so frustrated and afraid, more afraid than she'd been in years. More than that, she felt powerless. She still couldn't accept that this had happened to her. A few years earlier she'd been at the height of her powers, the Master's mountain kingdom destroyed through her efforts and years of patient planning.

In the aftermath of that triumph, she used her deep

knowledge of magic to build a comfortable place for herself in the world. She returned to the home of her youth, Boston, where she was able to manipulate wealthy, powerful people in her special way, reaching into their minds and convincing them that it was their own idea to hand over large sums of money to the beautiful and tantalizing young girl. Money to buy a mansion in an exclusive neighborhood. She led an easy, comfortable existence in that big house, her every need and desire attended to by a large staff of well-paid and loyal servants.

Giselle's teeth chattered as she recalled with dim bitterness the betrayal of one of these ostensibly trustworthy employees. It was to have been a lovely evening out at the opera. One of the world's leading tenors was performing, and she'd managed to procure choice seats and backstage access. Her regular driver, the impeccably mannered and attired Mr. Thorne, pulled up to the mansion that evening in a limo. She recalled how he'd smiled and bowed slightly to her as she came down the mansion's steps in her expensive evening gown, a fake fur shawl wrapped about her bare, slim shoulders. She'd felt not the slightest twinge of alarm as Mr. Thorne opened one of the limo's rear doors, allowing her a glimpse of the legs of an elegant woman and two men wearing tuxedos.

These would be her companions for the evening. Her neighbor Angelica Anderson and her husband Henry, and her own date, Robert McDowell, a financier who'd been one of the many contributors to her still-growing fortune. As she approached the open door, she gathered up the hem of her gown and dipped her head in preparation for sliding into the car.

Then she froze, her eyes going wide and her heart stopping for an instant as she saw that the woman inside the limo was not Angelica Anderson. She was Ms. Wickman, flashing a mad grin as she laughed at

Giselle's shocked expression. The men with her were two wild-eyed boys barely into their early twenties. Giselle tried to back away, but then she felt Mr. Thorne's firm hand at the small of her back.

His voice was fierce and hot against her ear, full of venom and so unlike anything she'd ever heard from the proper British man, "You're not going anywhere, cunt."

Then he shoved her inside and the hands of her enemies were upon her. She was too stunned to fight back instantly—as she should have—and by the time it occurred to her to strike at them with her magic it was too late, her powers blunted by the elaborate web of counterspells spun by Ms. Wickman. And when one of the men produced the machete from an inner pocket of his tux, Giselle knew that the battle was lost.

She cringed at the memory of the heavy blade punching through her wrist, the awful grind of steel on bone, then the blade passing into the upholstery beneath. And her hand coming away from her wrist, the explosion of blood across black seat leather. She screamed and thrashed, to no avail. And through it all remained the wild and desperate belief that one or more of her many servants would come running to her rescue.

It didn't happen.

Her assailants were able to go about their grisly work unimpeded and unhurried.

Ms. Wickman raised the blade again.

And one of the men holding her down thrust his crotch against her ass as steel chopped through flesh again.

She'd been sure she would bleed to death there in the back of the limo, but then Ms. Wickman calmly accepted something passed to her from outside the car by Mr. Thorne. There was a glint of light on some metal object. Then she discerned the cylindrical shape of the object and knew at once they weren't here to kill her after all. They wanted her to suffer, though. There was a whoosh and the acetylene torch grew a bright blue and red tongue of flame. Another hoarse exhalation of purest terror tore out of her as the flame was lowered to her violated flesh. And yet another, shriller scream as the flame made contact and burned brighter, cooking her flesh as the limo's interior filled with the aromas of smoke and burning meat.

The flame burned and burned and it seemed like the torture would go on forever. Then there was a click and the whooshing sound stopped. Giselle saw her hands, one on the seat next to Ms. Wickman, the other on the shiny black floormat. A glimpse of protruding bone made her stomach knot. Her blood was everywhere. Splattered across the upholstery and all over the tinted windows. A zigzag pattern of coagulating gore across the front of Ms. Wickman's black dress. Everywhere.

Instinct caused her to aim a strike of lethal dark energy at the grinning madwoman, but the anticipated blast fizzled and the energy dispersed. Giselle had forgotten about Ms. Wickman's web of blocking spells. And the removal of her hands had eliminated her most powerful method of focusing and unleashing magical energy.

Ms. Wickman laughed. "Your power is gone and you are mine now, you pathetic whore."

And Giselle had choked back the tears long enough to say, "Damn you."

Ms. Wickman's eyes gleamed with amusement. "Oh, that's right. The former mute can speak now. Bonus." Her smile vanished then. She seized a handful of Giselle's long black hair, twisting it and eliciting a yelp. "Righteous hypocrite. What do you deserve? How many people did you torture and kill while in the Master's employ, hmm? Including your own brother, as I recall."

Giselle didn't reply because the answer to Ms. Wickman's question was obvious. And because the pain was coming back, overwhelming the temporary numbness of shock. Instead she'd said, "Just kill me. Be done with it."

Ms. Wickman threw her head back and laughed again, long and heartily, until she was almost crying. "Oh, you of all people should know better than that, Giselle. We're taking you to a special place, dear. You'll be there for a very, very long time and your suffering will go on forever."

And so she was brought to this place, many hundreds of miles from Boston.

Despair overwhelmed her as it became clear Ms. Wickman had truly mastered the most advanced forms of dark magic, working to appease the death gods, drawing immense power from them through daily blood sacrifices. The scent of blood—fresh and flowing—was strong in the air.

Giselle knew she would ultimately be offered as a sacrifice to the death gods. Her sadist's soul would be particularly prized by them. She would die.

Unless . . .

Yes. There was one avenue yet left to her. It was a slim hope at best. And any possibility of success would hinge on a price perhaps too heavy to bear, even given the grim reality she was facing already. She hesitated, contemplating what manner of unspeakable atrocity might be asked of her in exchange for the help she needed. Time moved forward. She felt the minutes unspooling like the ticking of the Doomsday Clock. Death was coming for her soon. She could almost hear the Reaper's footsteps on the stone floor. She saw him in her mind, raising a gnarled hand to point an icy finger at her.

Then the vision of the Deathbringer dissolved and

was replaced by an image of Ms. Wickman's mad grin as the cleaver separated Giselle's hands from her body. A low sound like the warning growl of a wounded animal rumbled out of her throat.

She brought her right forearm to her mouth. The taste of her own flesh on her tongue made her pause for a moment, anticipation of pain momentarily freezing her resolve. Then she sank her teeth into her arm, driving them deep, shredding flesh and filling her mouth with salty blood. She drank the blood, drawing it down into her stomach as she continued to slurp more of it from the wound. Then she pitched forward and pressed her face against the cold metal bars of the cage floor. She opened her mouth and expelled blood, allowing it to coat the metal. The pain was bad, but she ignored it and initiated the blood ritual by repeating the phrases she'd memorized years earlier. Rhythmic phrases from an alien tongue. A chant. A summoning spell.

Ms. Wickman had removed her ability to wield magic as a weapon, but she had not deprived Giselle of her knowledge. She had one ally among the death gods. A rogue who had aided her efforts to overthrow the Master. He would help her again. If only she could reach him . . .

She placed the tip of her tongue against the cold metal and tasted her own blood again. Then she focused what psychic engergy she could and sent a message into the wall of darkness and the ether beyond.

Azaroth, I beseech you.

Another taste of blood, metallic and tart.

I offer you my blood. My pain. Please come to my aid. I will do anything.

Nothing.

Despair again began to encroach on her thoughts, threatening the necessary focus and spiritual purity of the ritual. She tasted her blood yet again, used the feeble power it contained to focus her wavering will one last time.

And the message went out again: *Azaroth, I implore you . . .*

Then she felt it, the death god's presence manifesting at first as a warmth that allowed her temporary respite from the freezing atmosphere of the torture chamber. She drew in a deep breath and exhaled slowly, forcing herself to relax. And as she relaxed, a bright, warm light displaced the darkness of her prison, enveloping her in an ethereal radiance that felt like a loving embrace.

Something dark swirled in the midst of all that brightness, a cloud of energy that became luminescent and began to mold itself into a humanoid shape. The entity was forging a human appearance, one that exactly replicated the form Giselle remembered from her prior experience with this being.

When the process was complete, Azaroth smiled at her with his human mask.

Ah, Giselle. I see you have need of my assistance again.

Tears misted Giselle's vision. The spark of hope became a flame.

I do. My enemies have taken me. They have maimed me. And I fear what they've done to me is only the beginning. They will not rest until they have done the same to all those who rose up against the Master.

Azaroth's expression changed subtly. His eyes continued to glow with that lovely radiance, but the set of his features shifted to something approximating a frown. *You speak of the woman who served the Master and her new set of followers.*

Giselle gathered her courage. Here was where things might get tricky. *Yes. She chopped my hands off to blunt my magic and imprisoned me in a dark place. I'll do anything you ask of me if you can help me.*

Azaroth's features shifted again, displaying a fluid grace that made the god look like something from an animated motion picture. He was smiling again, but there was a hint of something very dark behind the expression.

What you ask will require a sacrifice.

Giselle nodded. *Of course. Anything.*

Azaroth was silent a moment, his not-quite-real-looking brows knitting in apparent concentration. Then his expression became solemn. *I can restore you, Giselle. Make your body whole again so that you may combat your enemy on equal footing. But to justify this I will need you to do something that will wound your soul very deeply.*

Giselle suspected what was coming. She held her breath and nodded tensely.

There is a man who is special to you.

Giselle thought, *Oh, Eddie . . .*

Azaroth paused for a beat, hearing her thought. *Yes, the very one. I will grant you temporary restoration and temporal transport to his current location. You will be there just long enough to kill him.*

And though her heart was pierced to the core by the thought of murdering the one person left in the world for whom she felt genuine affection, Giselle knew there was no other choice. She alone possessed even a slim chance of defeating Ms. Wickman. A part of her hated Azaroth for forcing her to make this difficult choice, but the feeling was muted by the knowledge that this was merely the nature of the death gods, this exchange of blood and breath for aid.

And once this has been done . . . I will be whole again?

The death god's expression darkened slightly. *As I*

have said. You know I keep my bargains. Do what is asked of you and you will be more than whole again. The cast of his features shifted again, projecting a shimmering glow as he smiled. *You will be stronger than before. More powerful. You will be a fearsome adversary for the one who took you, her equal in every way.*

Giselle thought again of Ms. Wickman's many vile transgressions against her. The memories stoked her anger anew.

I am ready to do what you ask.

The god laughed, a sound that echoed like rolling thunder in this place between worlds. *I believe that you are. And now . . . go from here.*

His words seemed to shift the fabric of reality around her, lifting her and moving her at astonishing speed through a place of swirling shadows and strange colors. The journey passed in utter silence, but ended with an audible pop that signaled the end of a temporal displacement.

She blinked against a flash of light. The real, human world reconstructed itself around her in the space of that blink. Then she was standing in the empty kitchen of a woman's apartment. She based this supposition on the general cleanliness and the array of frilly touches and knick-knacks. The sound of a television tuned to a talk show emanated from another room. Giselle felt a strange tingle and lifted her arms to look at her freshly restored hands. She flexed her fingers, marveling for a moment at the ease of movement and the smooth, unblemished flesh connecting her wrists to her hands.

Azaroth had been true to his word. And now it was left to Giselle to fulfill her end of the bargain. She heard voices from that other room, one male and one female. One achingly familiar and one not.

Giselle opened a likely-looking drawer and found a

carving knife with a broad, flat blade. A gleaming and very, very sharp blade.

With a final sigh of regret, she walked out of the kitchen toward the source of the voices—trying all the while to block out the underlying hints of contentment and happiness she sensed there.

CHAPTER EIGHT

The ground in the woods was still wet from the recent rains. The topsoil yielded easily to shovel blades. The going got rougher approximately a foot down, but between the two of them they were able to dig a grave of acceptable size in just over an hour.

Marcy tossed her shovel aside and climbed out of the hole. "That's enough."

Michael palmed sweat from his forehead and wiped his hand on his dirty jeans. More swollen droplets of sweat gathered at the ends of his eyebrows. "You won't get any argument from me." He threw his own shovel aside and followed Marcy out of the hole. He was breathing heavily, unused to such heavy physical exertion. "That's, what? Maybe four feet deep?"

"It's enough." Marcy screwed the top off a water bottle and drank deeply from it. She'd changed into jeans and a Bella Morte T-shirt for the job and they were soaked from her exertions. But she felt good. It was a strange thing. A woman she intended to kill was tied to her bed back at the house. The dead body of one of her friends was in the same room. Her other friends were freaking out. She should be beside herself with panic.

But she wasn't. She was as calm as a monk in the midst of prayers.

Michael straightened and brushed more sweat from his forehead with the back of an arm. He was shirtless. Sweat glistened on his pale torso, the diffused early morning sunlight making him look like a ghost caught in its slanting rays. Marcy watched him and felt a stir of libido. He was slim and reasonably good-looking, at least compared to the rest of them. And he was smarter than the others. Too smart, maybe. Unlike the rest of them, he didn't just accept her every pronouncement as gospel. But maybe she could bring him more firmly under her thumb if she fucked him.

He looked at her and frowned, seeing the glint in her eyes. He shifted his eyes away from her, studied some vague point in the middle distance. Marcy supposed he'd mistaken her expression for something other than ardor. Which was understandable. He was very afraid of her. They all were at this point.

Marcy moved closer to him and laid a hand on his shoulder. "Is there something you want to say to me, Michael? Something that worries you . . ."

Michael jerked at her touch. She could feel the tension thrumming through his body. "I just think this is a rotten idea."

She squeezed his shoulder and moved another step closer. "You shouldn't worry. Everything will be okay, I promise."

He was shaking now. "No. I really don't understand why we're doing this. We should've called 911 last night. Or maybe just taken Sonia to the ER ourselves."

Marcy didn't reply to this right away. She was too enthralled by the live-wire trembling of the boy's body, which seemed to grow more pronounced by the moment. She moved her hand from his shoulder to the small of his back. Michael drew in a sharp, involuntary breath. Marcy leaned against him and slipped her other arm around his back. A small sound that might have been a whimper emerged from his mouth.

Marcy smiled. "Are you a virgin, Michael?"

The sound he produced this time was louder, somewhere between a moan and a whimper. "I'm . . . that's . . . what's that got to do with anything?"

He abruptly broke out of her embrace and stalked away to a point several feet away from her. He pointed a shaking finger at her. "We can't do this. It's wrong. Sonia deserves better than being buried in the fucking woods. We need to let someone know what happened to her. We don't even have to tell the truth, Marcy. We'll get rid of that bitch you had us grab first, dump her in this hole, and everyone will figure Sonia had some kind of hemorrhage."

He lowered the accusing finger, but his eyes remained bright and glowering.

Marcy put a hand to her face, rubbed at her tired eyes with thumb and forefinger. A dull ache had flared behind her forehead. Her own rage was building, rising up within her like a black storm cloud. She fought to keep a grip on her emotions. Nothing good could come of a fight with Michael. Things were too precarious as they stood. On an objective level, she knew the course of action she'd chosen wasn't a smart or rational one, but instinct had driven her down this path. This was the way she wanted things to be. The way she *needed* them to be. It felt like the first step down the road to her ultimate destiny (though she had no clue what that might be).

So fuck it.

Michael would not ruin this for her. No one would.

She lowered her hand and saw Michael still glaring at her. Her own expression hardened, the corners of her mouth curling slightly in a humorless smile.

Michael's brow furrowed. His eyes reflected fear.

Good.

She darted toward him, closing the distance between them before he could even consider retreat. She drove a fist into the softest part of his stomach, making him splutter and double over. She crashed the same fist against the side of his head and he pitched backward onto his ass, landing at the side of the open, empty grave. He instinctively sought to brace himself, but one of his grasping hands reached into the hole and offset his balance. He tumbled into the hole and landed with a thump at the bottom. Marcy picked up one of the shovels and moved to the edge of the hole. She turned the shovel around, holding it like a baseball bat while she waited for the boy to climb back out. She heard him sit up and groan. She tightened her grip on the handle.

Michael exhaled heavily and groaned again. "Jesus, Marcy . . . that was pretty fucking uncalled for. I'm only trying to make you see some goddamned sense."

Marcy made her voice soft and placating. "I know. And I'm sorry. I got carried away. Now come up here so we can talk things out. Maybe you're right about everything. Maybe I'm being overemotional and crazy about things."

Michael grunted. "Ya think. Jesus, but I'm glad to hear you talking sense for a change. Okay, I'm coming up now."

She heard him shifting position; then he got to his feet with a groan of effort. He blinked and frowned at the sight of Marcy holding the shovel. He remained perplexed as she lifted her arms and brought the shovel blade around. It was as if he simply couldn't fathom the idea of Marcy doing this to him. Only at the last possible instant did it occur to him to lunge away from the arc of the blade. He almost made it, but the tip of the shovel blade clipped the side of his face and sent him spinning back down into the hole.

Marcy jumped in after him, planting a foot at either side of his prone form. Michael groaned and looked up at her through a mist of tears. He still couldn't believe what was happening to him. The dumb bastard. Marcy adjusted her grip on the shovel handle, taking it by the base and holding it in front of her like a jackhammer. Michael squealed and tried to back away, but there was nowhere to go. The back of his head connected with moist earth and he stopped moving. His mouth opened to issue a last plea for mercy.

Then Marcy squatted and drove the shovel blade into his throat. A fountain of blood erupted around the dirty blade, and Marcy watched the gory cascade with a mixture of revulsion and fascination. Michael bucked beneath her and flailed at the shovel handle. He had to know he was doomed by now, but he was fighting her with everything he had. She leaned forward and used upper body leverage to drive the blade deeper into his throat. The grind of steel on bone made her stomach lurch, but she kept bearing down and finally Michael died.

She swallowed hard and let go of the shovel handle. Her heart was racing and her breathing was shallow. She stared at Michael's very still face and tried to make herself feel something other than numbness. The strange positive buzz of before seemed to have at least temporarily deserted her. She stared into the boy's unseeing eyes and tried to discern some hint of the human being he'd been, but whatever he'd possessed that had made him uniquely Michael was gone forever.

And she'd caused that. She was a killer. She thought about the bum in Overton Park the previous summer, recalling vividly the way he'd dropped and not moved after the second blow to his head with the heavy wine bottle. They'd taken his booze and pitiful handful of pocket change. Marcy remembered the way the dark blood had oozed from the gash at the back of his head to stain the grass beneath him. She was almost positive he hadn't been breathing when they'd left him. There'd never been any verification of the homeless man's death. But Marcy's gut told her she'd become a murderer for the first time that summer evening.

This was different in so many meaningful ways. The old wino had been little more than a walking casualty anyway, a ruined shell of a man no one could possibly care about, as evidenced by the silence of the local media on the matter. It was as if he'd never existed at all. But she'd known Michael since childhood. Had watched him grow up and struggle to fit in before gravitating to her little clique of outcasts. She knew his likes and dislikes. His favorite bands and books. She knew each member of his family by name. In a way killing Michael was sort of like killing family.

She touched his face, stroked his cooling cheek. "I'm sorry this happened, Michael. If only you'd been quiet and fallen in line like the rest of them . . ." As she said the words, the vague sense of purpose—of destiny— she'd felt earlier reasserted itself. "I did what I had to do, damn you. Wherever you are now, I hope you know that. But I'm sorry anyway, okay?"

The dead boy said nothing.

Marcy got to her feet and hauled herself out of the hole.

Then she noticed for the first time that the front of her clothes was splattered with sticky, coagulating blood. There was more gore on her hands and arms. Shit, it was everywhere. She'd have a hell of a time explaining all that blood to everyone back at the house. Then there was the matter of Michael's absence. It wouldn't be terribly difficult to put two and two together.

Dammit!

Marcy flicked blood from her hands and shook her head in disgust. This was what she got for acting rashly and not thinking things through. But the burst of self-directed anger soon dissipated. She'd done this thing and there was no way she could take it back. She could only move forward and maybe devise a way out of this mess on the fly.

She spied the pile of freshly turned earth next to the grave and had an idea. She grabbed a shovel and dug into the pile, working feverishly to return the earth to the hole. She stopped when she reached the concealed layer of topsoil at the bottom, the damp earth that was nearly like mud. She knelt next to the diminished pile and scooped up handfuls of the dark soil. And she smeared the damp dirt across the front of her shirt. The mud blended nicely with the blood, effectively obscuring the gore without cleansing it, which would have to be good enough for now. She smeared more handfuls of mud over the front of her jeans. Using the remaining water from her bottle, she was able to remove most of the dried blood that clung to her forearms.

She would look more of a mess than she should, she supposed. As for Michael, she would tell the others he'd gone for a walk. The fiction should buy her some time, maybe enough to clean up and concoct a better story.

Satisfied that she'd done all she could do to cover up what had happened, she turned away from the half-filled grave and began the short trek out of the woods. She soon emerged through a line of trees and entered the large field behind her house. The field was overgrown with weeds and was dotted here and there with ancient, discarded farm equipment. Marcy trudged through the weeds toward the house, which sat on a hill a quarter mile away.

She and her sister had inherited the property a year

ago, after their parents were killed when their Subaru stalled on some train tracks. They were drunk and messed up on some other stuff. As usual. With the radio blasting, maybe. And so they probably never heard the blaring horn of the locomotive that eventually plowed into them, crushing them like bugs in a can. Marcy initially had a vague notion about reviving the property as a farming enterprise. But she'd soon recognized the idea as foolhardy. She wasn't up to all the work it would require anyway.

Most people would love to have a place of their own that was paid for, but Marcy mostly found it to be a pain in the ass. She was bad at remembering to pay things on time. And there was so much to remember. Property taxes, water bills, power bills, and miscellaneous upkeep expenses out the goddamned wazoo. She'd already squandered much of the money her parents had left behind, of which there'd not been very much, and there was no new money coming in. The prospect of having to get a job filled her with dread and made her want to bolt. She wondered if the crazy things that had happened since the summer—the murder of the bum, the abduction of the woman, and Michael's slaying—were symptoms of some kind of self-destructive downward spiral. Then she thought about that some more and laughed. The laughter was manic, verging on hysterical.

She reached the rear door of the house and—as silently as possible—let herself into the empty kitchen. She heard muffled but obviously agitated voices. The sound seemed to be coming from the living room. Moving as stealthily as possible, she crossed the kitchen and entered the hallway that led to her bedroom. She paused at the archway that led to the living room. The voices suddenly stilled. Not that it mattered. She'd heard enough to know they were talking about her. And not in a positive way.

She glanced in and smiled weakly at their apprehensive faces. "We're about done. Michael's gone for a walk, but he should be back shortly. I'm gonna get cleaned up and then we can talk everything out, okay?"

Ellen was sitting away from the others. She was on the floor in a corner of the room, her knees pulled up to her chest. Her eyes were full of tears when she looked at her sister. Then she frowned, noticing the mud on Marcy's clothes. "Are you . . . okay?"

Marcy made her smile go brighter and nodded. "Yes. Absolutely. Cheer up, little girl. Everything's going to be just fine."

The smile fell off her face as she turned away from them and continued down the hallway. Her room was at the very end of the hallway. The door was still closed. No one—not even Marcy—had managed to work up the nerve to venture into the room again. And no wonder. The woman bound to her bed possessed some level of telekinetic or supernatural ability. Marcy experienced a chill as she recalled the way the woman had reached into her mind and temporarily shut down her motor control. She wasn't too thrilled with the idea of being in the strange woman's presence again. But there was just no way around it—she needed something in the room.

As she neared the door, she detected a stench emanating from the other side. The source, of course, was Sonia's corpse, which remained exactly where it had fallen several hours earlier. Marcy paused at the door, her hand hovering shakily over the doorknob. She put her ear against the thin wood and listened for any indication that the woman was awake. She heard nothing at first, but then detected the low sound of very shallow breathing. Not giving herself a chance to think about it any further, Marcy gripped the doorknob and turned it, rushed into the room and closed the door behind her.

Her gaze went immediately to the woman tied to her bed. She was lying very still. Her head was turned to one side, a sheaf of jet-black hair falling across her face like a veil. Her chest rose and fell very slightly, and the softest of snores confirmed that she was asleep.

Marcy hurried to the dresser to the left of the bed. She knelt and opened the bottom drawer, brushing aside some puttering-around-the-house raggedy clothes to find the L-shaped lunk of metal concealed at the bottom. The 9mm Glock felt good in her hands, the molded plastic grip seeming to adhere to her flesh like a living thing. She stood up and looked at the sleeping woman. It would be so easy to kill her now and remove one big fucking problem once and for all.

But the others would hear the shot and freak. Maybe run.

She swallowed hard.

Just do it.

"Right."

She went to the door and opened it smoothly, stepping back into the hallway with as much stealth as she could muster. She was midway to the living room archway when Michael's cousin stepped into the hallway, saw her holding the gun, and opened his mouth wide.

Marcy raised the gun and squeezed the trigger.

The bullet hit his chest dead center. Redness like a rose petal stained the front of his shirt as his body was propelled backward. Marcy blanked all thought from her mind then. She hurried into the living room and saw that the other boys were on their feet. Two of them were standing near the sofa and screaming at her. The other one, an Asian kid named Kim, was edging toward the front door. Marcy swung the Glock in Kim's direction and squeezed off two shots. One whizzed by him and punched through drywall. The second drilled a hole through the back of his head. Then she swung the gun back toward the remaining two boys, who were backing away from her now, their faces shiny with tears as they begged for their lives. Marcy squeezed the Glock's trigger two more times and both boys fell dead to the floor.

Marcy's ears rang from the boom of the gunshots. The air in the room was thick with the pungent stench of cordite. A long moment later she realized someone was screaming. Her eyes found Ellen, still huddled in the corner, her eyes wide and frightened. Next Marcy heard her hammering heart and a moment later the hard reality of what she'd just done crashed in on her. She'd killed all her friends. *Oh, God.* What little remained of her sanity was hanging by a thread. This thing she'd done made no sense on any obvious level. And yet there remained that sense of selfish righteousness, that she was doing only what destiny required, no matter how crazy it seemed.

She lowered the gun and went to her sister, knelt next to her and smoothed back her hair with a trembling hand. "I meant what I said, baby sister. Everything's going to be okay. You'll see. This . . . it had to be done. This was a . . . a cleansing. And maybe the beginning of something new for you and me."

Ellen sniffled. "You . . . you're not going to . . . kill me?"

Marcy felt something give inside her. She dropped the gun and drew Ellen into her arms as her own eyes filled with tears. "No, no, no, Ellen, don't you ever think that. I could never hurt you. You're my baby girl, my only family, and I love you more than anything."

Ellen sagged against her sister and wailed like a baby for a time. Marcy held her and patted her back, allowing her as long as she needed. Her own tears dried up faster than she expected as her mind turned back to practicalities. They had no close neighbors, so she wasn't worried about anyone reporting gunfire. Regardless, they

were going to have to leave this place. At some point rel-
atives of the dead would report their loved ones missing
and sooner or later the law would come sniffing
around. And there was no conceivable way to cover up
this much carnage or explain away a bunch of missing
friends known to spend most of their free time in her
company.

Marcy gently eased out of her sister's embrace and
picked up the Glock. "We're going to be leaving, Ellen.
Going on the road." Seeing that her sister wanted to
protest, Marcy put some steel in her voice as she said,
"We're going and that's that. It's too late for regrets or
second thoughts. We have to go on the run, get some
place far away from here. Maybe Florida, way down in
the Keys. Wouldn't that be nice? If we get out of here
within the next couple of hours, we might have as
much as a day's head start before the cops start looking
for us."

Ellen chewed on her lower lip and frowned. "But . . . I
didn't do any of this. Can't I just stay?"

Marcy's expression went slack. She stared coldly at
her sister for a long moment. Then she put the Glock
against Ellen's temple and said, "You're going with me. I
love you, Ellen, but I can't leave anyone behind. Do you
understand that?"

Ellen was shaking again. "You promised you wouldn't
hurt me."

"Look around you, Ellen," Marcy snapped. She eased
her finger off the trigger, but kept the Glock's barrel
pressed to Ellen's head. "I really don't want to hurt you. I
do love you. But I'm not feeling very stable right now and
you don't want to upset me. Do you understand that?"

Ellen nodded. "Yes. I'm sorry. I'll go with you."

"Just remember, sister, you put all this in motion
when you came running to me with your sob story
about the bitch attacking you in the bar."

Ellen started crying again, her thin shoulders heaving beneath her black blouse.

Marcy lowered the Glock and stood up. "I'm sorry, Ellen, but that's just the way it is. I need you to see that we're in this together from the beginning to the very end. Do you see that?"

Ellen continued crying, but she managed a weak nod. "I do."

"Good." Marcy didn't doubt Ellen's sincerity. She was too scared to lie. "I'm going to take care of some loose ends and clean up. You'll hear one more shot. You know what that will be."

Ellen nodded again. "Yeah."

"And while I'm busy, you'll need to pack a bag for the road. Make sure to bring as many clothes changes as you can. And any hair care products you have. We'll be wanting to cut and dye our hair wherever we stop to-night."

"Okay."

Marcy held out her free hand and Ellen slipped her own hand into it, allowing her older sister to haul her to her feet. "Come on."

They walked hand-in-hand out of the living room and into the hallway. Marcy saw Ellen flinch at the sight of the first boy she'd shot. He apparently hadn't died in-stantly. There was a trail of blood along the hallway car-pet to the place where he'd ultimately expired, just a few feet shy of the kitchen archway. Marcy turned her sister away from the sight and led her in the opposite direction. She relinquished Ellen's hand when they ar-rived at her bedroom. Ellen slipped into the room and began rummaging through her closet. Marcy watched her a moment longer. She was pretty sure she wouldn't have shot Ellen. As sure as she could be given the way this insane day had developed. She did, however, feel a tremendous relief as she watched the younger girl make preparations for departure. An acquiescent Ellen would make the whole process so much smoother.

She turned away from Ellen's door and continued down to her own bedroom. The door was standing open, as she'd left it. The black-haired woman was still asleep. Marcy drew in a steadying breath and entered the room. She was going to get this over with now. Put the gun to the cunt's head and pull the trigger. But as she strode into the room she was immediately aware of something not right. The door swung shut behind her and Marcy spun about, raising the gun and applying pressure to the trigger. But her finger froze before squeezing off a shot.

Her mind reeled at the sight of the intruder, a shapely black woman in a slinky black dress. The woman was alive and smiling, but she looked like a walking corpse. Maggots wriggled from the corners of that hideous smile, falling onto the black dress and the bare tops of her bloated breasts.

Marcy took a step backward. *"Holyjumpingjesusfuckingshit!"*

The black woman laughed and more maggots tumbled out. "Yeah. About sums it up, I guess."

Marcy's hands were shaking. "Stay away from me!"

The black woman chuckled and took a step toward her. "I'm not afraid of you, Marcy."

Marcy squeezed the Glock's trigger. The gun boomed and the bullet punched a hole in the door behind the woman. The black woman didn't flinch. She never stopped smiling. "I'm not afraid of you, Marcy," she repeated. "And the reason for that, in case you haven't already figured it out, is that I'm already dead."

Marcy was shaking her head and moving backward again. The backs of her legs met the foot of the bed and she stopped. "No. That's not possible."

"Oh, it's possible, all right, thanks to that bitch tied to your bed."

Marcy frowned. "What the fuck are you talking about?"

The black woman pried the gun from Marcy's suddenly numb hands and tossed it on the bed. "I was her best friend back when I was alive. But then I died. Which should've been the end for me, but she conjured me back to . . . undeath, I guess you'd call it."

Marcy was shaking. She turned her head away from the dead woman's rancid breath. "This is insane. It can't be happening."

The black woman slapped her. "But it is. It's real as a motherfuck. Hell, I'm getting more real by the goddamn minute. You didn't see me last night, but I was here all the time."

Marcy couldn't deal with this. It felt like the very fabric of the world was unraveling. Soon she would go spiraling away into some unfathomable void. Which would kind of be okay at this point.

The black woman grinned again. "And speaking of insane, that was some wild display of batshit crazy you just put on, girl."

Marcy felt bile rise in her throat. "I shouldn't have done it. Any of it. Something's really wrong with me."

"Don't you second-guess yourself, baby." The black woman wrapped her arms around Marcy and pushed her rotting flesh against her. "You did what you had to do, and you know it. Hell, it's the main reason I've decided not to kill you."

Marcy shivered in the dead woman's sickeningly intimate embrace. "What do you mean?"

The black woman laughed softly. "We're all going on a very long trip together. Just us girls on the road. Won't that be fun?"

"Where are we going?"

"To a bad place, Marcy. A very bad place." She smiled in a way that might have been intended to reassure, but the effect was offset by the sight of more wriggling maggots. "But along the way we're going to have big fun and see many wondrous things. You have my word on that."

Marcy frowned. So much for an escape to a tropical paradise. She felt a vague instinct to fight against this, but she recognized the idea as futile and it quickly withered. And anyway, maybe this was the true unescapable destiny she'd sensed was waiting for her beyond this place. "So when are we leaving?"

The black woman's smile widened. "Oh, soon. Now give me a kiss."

Marcy sucked in a breath. Then the dead woman was kissing her.

Maggots fell into her mouth and slid down her throat.

Marcy closed her eyes and prayed for an end to the nightmare.

CHAPTER NINE

The old Ford pickup slowed as it passed a green high-way sign announcing the last rest station for fifty miles. When its turn signal began blinking, Chad flicked on the Lexus's blinker and glanced at Allyson. She looked disheveled and tired. They'd talked very little during their three hours on the road, with Allyson sitting very still the entire time and staring straight ahead at the un-furling highway.

He supposed he couldn't blame her for not wanting to talk. She was a young woman from the suburbs used to a life of relative peace and quiet. Chad, however, had some experience with sudden, shocking violence, mostly from his time in the place called Below, the cavernous under-ground prison beneath the House of Blood. Even now, three years later, nightmares of that time still occasionally jolted him out of sleep.

And now Allyson, who had swept into his life like some divine angel of mercy, had likely been condemned to years—and perhaps a lifetime—of similar nightly tor-tures. The thought of it made him grip the steering wheel harder as his anger began to build again.

He hadn't known the dead men in his kitchen; Jim seemed sure they were emissaries of the long-missing

Ms. Wickman. And Chad had believed him. Which was why they were on the road now, bound for some vague destination Jim had assured them would be a safe haven. Citing "security concerns," he refused to specify the precise location of the place, asking that they instead follow him to wherever it was they were going. It wasn't that Jim didn't trust Chad and Allyson with the information. Rather, he refused to allow even the remote possibility of the location being extracted from them via torture should more of Ms. Wickman's agents intercept them en route to the place. Which was paranoid as hell, but Chad didn't blame the man.

The old Ford slowed some more and eased off the highway onto the curved white lane that led to the rest station. The parking lot was about half full. People were milling about around the vending machines and talking to each other on the long sidewalk. Other people were having lunches at the nearby picnic tables. A dog ran across the sloping lawn to the left of the rest station, chasing a yellow Frisbee that arced across the sky. Chad felt the knot of tension in his gut ease a bit. After the long, silent hours on the road, it felt good to be among people again. Normal people doing normal things.

He followed Jim's brown-and-tan truck to the end of the lot. Then he shut off the Lexus and twisted in his seat to look at Allyson. She still had that stunned animal look, her eyes dull and staring at nothing at all.

He put a hand on her shoulder and said, "Honey? Let's get out and stretch for a bit, okay?"

Her head swiveled toward the sound of his voice. The corners of her mouth dimpled, a smile so soft and weary that it made Chad's heart ache for her. "Sure."

She unbuckled her seat belt and reached for the door handle, stepping out of the car before Chad could reply. She threw the door shut and moved rapidly to the sidewalk, where she paused to stretch her arms and neck. Chad remained behind the wheel a moment longer and watched her, enjoying the simple, supple grace of her lithe body. She caught him looking at her and smiled. Chad smiled back as she reached into her handbag, retrieved a pair of black sunglasses, and slid them on. She waved at Chad and headed for the rest station's main building.

Chad watched her go, the slight sway of her hips beneath the thin fabric of her dress making his heart race just a little faster. She slipped into a small throng of people standing beneath the building's pavilion and disappeared from sight.

Then he got out of the car and threw the door shut. Jim was leaning against the side of the old Ford, one booted foot raised and braced against a rust-flecked door. He was wearing dark sunglasses and smoking a cigarette. He turned his head slightly and blew a stream of smoke up at the clear sky. "Nice day." He tapped the cigarette and ash fluttered to the faded asphalt. "When I was young, days like this would inspire me to write poetry." He smiled. "Or chase girls."

Chad raised an eyebrow. "Yeah?"

Jim chuckled. "Oh, yeah. That or get drunk. Or all three at once."

Chad grinned and shook his head. "Sounds a little tricky. You know, there are still times when I can't get over the fact that I know you. Did you ever see that movie made about you, the one where that pretty-boy actor played you?"

Jim smiled. "Yeah. Wasn't bad . . . for such a load of shit."

"Yeah, well, I was a kid when that came out. I saw it a bunch of times. There was a scene in there—"

"You should believe only ten percent of any given scene in that film. There's some truth, sometimes just a grain of it, but much of it embellished and manipulated for dramatic effect." Jim flicked away the cigarette butt and reached again for his Winstons. "I don't mind, of course. It's what filmmakers do with works based on the lives of real people. The same thing happens in real life. People tell stories intended to convey a particular image or idea about themselves. From what we might call white lies, basically harmless fictions, to wholesale, malicious untruths meant to dupe the victims of con artists and other criminals."

A frown stole across Chad's face as he listened to Jim's seemingly incongruous oratory about truth and lies. "Um . . . what's this got to do with the movie?"

Jim took a drag on his fresh cigarette and said, "Can I ask you a question?"

Chad hesitated. He had a feeling he knew what was coming, but he didn't want to hear it. It was something insane, a thing he'd attempted to relegate to the darkest, remotest recesses of his mind. But it had remained just beneath the surface, a niggling nag of a notion that kept trying to capture his attention. He wanted more than anything to keep pretending it wasn't there, and he certainly did not want the idea verbalized. But an image that made the ground beneath him feel slippery intruded on his thoughts—Allyson shoving an overstuffed black travel bag he'd never previously seen to the back of the Lexus's trunk, then quickly covering it with two more hastily packed bags.

He sighed. "Ask me."

Jim removed his sunglasses and nailed Chad with his piercing dark eyes. "How well do you really know Allyson?"

Chad felt dizzy. He put a hand to his head and said, "I have to sit down."

Jim nodded in the direction of the picnic tables. "Over there. We'll get out of the sun and talk this out."

He flicked away the cigarette and set off toward the tables.

Chad numbly followed.

Allyson brushed past a pair of doddering elderly ladies and banged open the restroom door. It was a long room with a line of gleaming silver stalls against one wall. Nearly all the stall doors stood open, indicating disuse. Two of the nearest were closed. A woman in her thirties leaned over the basin, checking her makeup in the long mirror. Allyson kept her head down and strode quickly to the very last stall, stepped inside, and shut the door behind her. She sat on the toilet seat, fished her cell phone from the depths of her pocketbook and thumbed the red power button.

She'd turned it off at some point after killing the intruders, fearing a call she wouldn't be able to explain to Chad and the annoyingly suspicious old rock star. A displayed message informing her she had received seventeen missed calls and had three voice mail messages. She was not surprised to find each call was from the same number. Allyson's heart pounded as she pressed the button to dial her mailbox. She drew in a calming breath and raised the phone to her ear. The first message was a brief burst of shrill panic. "What the fuck is going on out there? Call me back."

The caller's voice was more relaxed during the second message. But the content of his message sent a bone-scraping chill winding through her: "Ms. Vanover, we know you have betrayed us. This is not a very smart thing you have done. Those who betray us are always made to pay the highest price. Rest assured, I mean to hunt you down and exact vengeance personally. I have a lovely picture of you right here, by the way. It appears to be a still from a pornographic movie. Your hair was different then, but the image is unmistakably that of Allyson Vanover. Or as you were known then, Sinthia Fox."

Allyson felt the earth shift beneath her. She closed her eyes and gripped the phone tighter as the man's calm voice continued. "I'm going to show this picture and others like it to your boyfriend just before I go to work on your delectable body with a knife. I wonder what he'll be thinking as he watches you suffer and die. Will he be crying out for blood and revenge when I shove the knife up your cunt? Or will he still be too stunned by the images of double penetration and girl-on-girl pussy-licking to care?"

The message ended and Allyson sat there shaking for a time before working up the nerve to hear the last message. She didn't want to hear the man's insinuating tone again, but she knew she had to hear what he had to say. So she pressed a button and heard the following: "I imagine you are very frightened now. Afraid not only of what's coming for you, but hoping against hope that Chad doesn't begin to piece some things together. But he will, Allyson, and you know it. He's a smart man. Even now he is thinking hard about many puzzling things, and in time he will ferret out the truth about you. And when that happens, you will be tossed out like the trash you are."

There was a silence then, the recording continuing as he paused long enough to allow her time to think about what he was saying, the obvious truth of it. She worked hard to imagine an alternative possibility, but every time she tried to see a happy future with Chad the forced images glimmered with a plastic sitcom phoniness for a fragile moment before dissolving.

Then the man drew in an audible breath and slowly exhaled. "Not a pretty picture. But you know what, Allyson? I'm feeling generous today. I'm going to offer you a way out of this mess."

Allyson tensed and closed her eyes again.

"Call this number when you arrive at your destination. Tell us where you are, then slip away when no one's watching. If you do this, your death sentence will be rescinded. You will not be getting the hundred thousand dollars originally promised you, but you've probably already figured that out. You'll get to keep the ten grand we fronted you . . . if there's any left, that is. Which I doubt, if you've still got that nasty porn star coke habit. So that's the deal, bitch. Take it or die. Remember . . . before sundown."

The message ended and Allyson pressed a button to delete it. She did not dismiss out of hand the offer she'd been given. It was a simple way out of a very complicated situation. One phone call. She could do that and haul ass out of Jim's "safe haven," whatever or wherever the hell that was. She still had every penny of the ten-thousand-dollar advance. She'd shed her coke habit prior to coming to Georgia and had successfully resisted every temptation to dip into the fund. Ten thousand dollars wasn't as comfortable a stake as the one hundred thousand dollars upon which she'd based her original plans, but it would be more than enough to start a new life somewhere else.

Allyson flipped the cell phone open and punched in a number. She held the phone to her ear and listened as it rang. The man answered on the second ring. "Hello, Allyson. Have you accepted my offer?"

Allyson allowed a moment to pass before responding. She was still thinking. Still unsure. She didn't know what she would say until the words came out of her mouth. "You'll never find us, you son of a bitch," she said, voice emerging without even a slight quaver. "And there's not a threat in the world you can make that scares me. I've told Chad everything and he's forgiven me. And even if you do figure out where we're going, I'll kill anyone you send after us, just like I killed those men last night."

There was a long pause from the other end. Then the man grunted and said, "Next time you won't have the advantage of knowing my men are coming. One night when you're sleeping they'll slip into your room and take you. And then they'll bring you to me. And then—"

A soft laugh.

And then the line went dead.

The phone slipped out of Allyson's hand and landed with a clatter on the floor. She stared at her shaking hand, willing it to be still again. The man's final, implied threat had rattled her more than she would've expected given everything else she'd been through. The voice of cowardice rose within her again, imploring her to pick up the phone and call the man back to tell him she'd reconsidered.

Allyson did pick up the phone. Then she stood up and smashed the delicate device against the concrete wall. The casing cracked, but that wasn't good enough for Allyson. She wanted to destroy the thing completely, to vent her fear, frustration, and rage on this symbolic link between herself and the bad people she'd so foolishly aligned herself with all those months ago. So much had changed since those early days in Georgia. She no longer felt dead inside. The world was wide open and alive with possibilities she'd never imagined for herself. And she'd be damned if she'd allow that snide cocksucker and his threats to taint that. So she flipped the phone open. The hinge connecting the two halves of the device let go with a snap as she smashed it against the wall two more times. Then she separated the two halves with a savage twist and stood there breathing heavily for a moment.

Then she stepped out of the stall and strode to the

end of the bathroom, where she dropped the pieces of the ruined cell phone in a waste bin. She moved to the basin and examined her reflection in the mirror. Her cheeks were slightly flushed, but otherwise she looked okay. Definitely nothing like a woman who'd just been forced to make a potential life-and-death decision. She slipped the strap of her purse over her shoulder, slid her sunglasses back on, and exited the bathroom.

Remembering what she'd said about getting a soda, she paused at one of the vending machines and fed change through a coin slot. A can of Coke thunked into the slot. As she bent to retrieve the frosty cold can, she glanced in the direction of Chad's car and dimly perceived a shape behind the wheel. Jim was leaning against his pickup and smoking a cigarette.

The old man made her nervous. She was certain he suspected her of something. It was in the way he looked at her and the subtly doubting tone of his voice when he questioned her. In the aftermath of her confrontation with the intruders, he'd asked her a series of questions that made her uncomfortable. He wanted to know why she'd been up at that late hour. Wanted to know every tiny detail of how things went down. She explained everything in minute detail. It helped that much of it wasn't made up. She'd been restless and had come into the kitchen for a late night snack, she'd told them, and that was fiction. The rest was stone cold truth.

More or less.

So it was aggravating that Jim clearly wasn't buying it. This despite understanding why he was suspicious of her. She was an unknown quantity as far as he was concerned. He was a hard guy to figure out, not much at all like the wild rock-and-roll madman portrayed in movies and books. He was calmer, quiet, and coldly analytical. He'd hauled the dead men away in the bed of his pickup and disposed of them somewhere. It was chilling how unfazed he'd been by that.

Once the cleanup chores had been completed, Jim made the offer of sanctuary at his "place in the mountains." He made the offer explicitly to Chad, pointedly leaving her out. But Chad would only go if Allyson accompanied him. Jim acquiesced without argument, but his demeanor told the real story—he'd didn't trust her.

Allyson straightened and took a large gulp from the can. The cold soda felt good going down. Slightly invigorated, she set off toward Chad's Lexus. She smiled at Jim as she passed him and he nodded, his eyes unreadable behind his dark sunglasses. Then she opened the Lexus's passenger door and slipped inside.

"Thanks for stopping. I feel so much better after getting—"

Then she saw the thing propped on the dash and her voice died in her throat. It was an ID card with her picture on it. At the top in cobalt blue block letters were the words FRANKLIN SECURITY CONSULTANTS. Beneath her picture in small black type was the name Jennifer Campbell, and beneath that the title Senior Solutions Specialist.

The back door on her side opened and someone slid into the seat behind her. The door thunked shut and Allyson detected a faint scent of tobacco. *Jim.* No one said anything at first. Allyson's face reddened as sweat appeared on her forehead. The air in the car felt close and hot. The slick Coke can began to slide from her fingers. She set it in the cup holder with a shaking hand and tried to think of something—anything—to say.

Chad cleared his throat and said, "Is there anything you want to tell us, Allyson? Or should I call you Jennifer?"

His tone thrummed with equal measures of anger and hurt. Hearing that hurt snapped her out of the state of speechless panic. The partial admission that followed came before she could take even a moment to consider it. "I'm an ex-porn star and drug addict. Allyson Vanover is my real name. I'm from Los Angeles originally, but I ran away from my life there because it was out of control. I did twenty-four pornos in just under two years, and the ten thousand dollars is what I had left from that when I met you. I used to do so much coke my nose bled all the time and I wouldn't sleep for days. I had to get away from that or I was going to die. Jennifer Campbell is the alias I came up with in case I needed a new identity to really start over."

The words had come out in a rush, tripping over the tip of her tongue like pebbles tumbling wildly down a waterfall. As with her previous explanations in the aftermath of last night's carnage, her story now was comprised of interweaving strands of truth and fiction. And, again, much of it was truth. But she had no faith at all they would buy the whole package this time. She suspected the combination of Jim's paranoia and Chad's hurt feelings would conspire to put her out on the street. The thought filled her with a black despair. She'd done many bad things, but she was doing her damnedest to make up for them. The unfairness of it burned, coming so soon after taking her stand against the bad guys.

Chad blinked slowly, his face registering shock. "Um . . . porno?"

Allyson's nod was emphatic. Her eyes were shining, imploring him to believe her. "I swear to God." She glanced at the rearview mirror, met Jim's stoic gaze, and looked again at Chad. "I don't know what you guys are thinking or what you suspect, but I swear it's fucking wrong." A quaver entered her voice and tears began to roll from the corners of her eyes. "I'm not a bad person. I love you, Chad, and I didn't tell you the truth about my past because I knew you wouldn't want anything to do with someone so . . . trashy."

The tears gave way to sobs, a display of genuine emotion devoid of even the smallest hint of fakery. She had known all along the real Allyson Vanover was not the kind of person who could ever hope to move in the same circles as a Chad Robbins, much less ever hope to marry a man of his quality. And now that this part of the charade was over, she felt like crawling into a hole and never coming out.

Jim shifted in the backseat and spoke up: "I don't suppose you have proof to offer of the veracity of this tale?"

Allyson's eyes went wide and she said, "Chad! Your laptop, please get it."

Chad's brow furrowed and he stared at her in a searching way for a moment. Allyson expected to see judgment in his eyes, but it didn't seem to be there. Or maybe he was merely holding everything in for a big explosion to come. But then he sighed and got out of the car. He popped the trunk with the electronic key fob, and Allyson glanced again at Jim as she listened to the rustling sound of baggage being moved around. His sunglasses were off now and he was staring hard at her.

She made herself hold his as gaze as she said, "I'm telling the truth."

Jim's nod was barely perceptible. "I'm sure you are." Then he smiled, an expression untouched by humor. "But I don't think you're telling all of the truth."

Allyson looked away from those cold eyes. "I'm not lying. You'll see."

Jim didn't reply.

Chad returned to the car, sliding back behind the wheel and moving his seat back before flipping open the laptop. The computer came out of hibernation mode, its screen a bright glare in the sunlight. Chad tapped some keys and said, "Lucky us, there's a wireless network in range. We're connected." He glanced at Allyson. "What are we looking for?"

Allyson swallowed hard before replying. She didn't want Chad to see the things she was about to show him. But she knew she'd been left with no choice. "Do a Google image search on Sinthia Fox. That's S-i-n-t-h-i-a Fox."

Her fingernails etched grooves in her palms as Chad tapped the keys. The search immediately produced pages of results. And though the glare of the sun obscured the shameful images somewhat, she was able to see enough to know she'd delivered her promised proof. Her hair had been a darker shade of blonde then, the sandy shade that was her natural color, and the makeup she'd worn for the movies and photo shoots had been starkly whorish and slutty. But it was her. Chad stared at the thumbnail pictures without saying anything for long moments before clicking on one that showed her fellating a dildo. He winced at the enlarged image and flipped the laptop shut. Then he looked up and stared straight ahead, eyes focusing on nothing at all.

"I'm sorry, Chad." Allyson's voice sounded small, defeated. "I understand if you kick me out now."

Chad finally looked at her again. She saw pain in his expression. The withering aspect of judgment she expected was still missing. "I'm not kicking you out." His voice was softer now, entirely devoid of the rage and implied accusations of before. "I wish you'd told me the truth before. It would've saved us all some grief. But I understand why you didn't. It'll take me a while to come to terms with this, but I want you to know that I care about you, too." He indicated the closed laptop with a nod. "I know how hard it must have been for you to show me those . . . things."

He reached out to her, stroked her cheek with the

back of a hand, and Allyson melted inside. She grabbed his hand and held on for dear life. "I'm so sorry. Chad, I'm so sorry."

Jim said, "I take it you're satisfied, Chad?"

Allyson blinked her tears away and watched Chad as he hesitated for only a moment before nodding. "Yeah, Jim. I'm satisfied."

"Fair enough."

Jim opened the rear door and swung his legs out. He paused before getting the rest of the way out. "I trust you, friend, and if you choose to place your trust in this woman, I'll abide by that. But we're going to a place I can't afford to compromise. We'll stop ahead of arriving there and blindfold young Allyson. She'll ride the rest of the way in with me. That condition is non-negotiable. Understood?"

Allyson answered before Chad had a chance to open his mouth. "Understood. I'll do whatever you say."

Jim nodded. "Good."

He departed without another word, throwing the door shut and returning to his pickup. Allyson settled back into her seat and felt her eyes flutter shut. There was so much else she wanted to say to Chad about her old life in California, so much she needed to explain, but she didn't have the energy now.

Darkness took her as the Lexus followed the old Ford back to the highway.

CHAPTER TEN

Giselle Burkhardt opened her eyes in darkness. She was back. She felt the cold steel of the cage beneath her bottom. Giselle sat upright and grasped the bars of her prison. Then she pulled them apart as easily as a child deconstructing a clumsily assembled Lego building, the steel yielding with stunning ease to her strength. She climbed out of the cage and dropped to the floor. Instinct guided her to the room's only point of egress, a place where the texture of reality was thinner and more susceptible to the manipulation of magic. She splayed her hands on the cool stone wall and focused her will.

It was easy.

A door formed in the wall. It swung open before her and she stepped into a large room that was a precise replica of the Master's old chambers. The door closed behind her, its outline vanishing instantly. An odd sense of peace settled within her as she surveyed the uncannily familiar surroundings. Giselle had emerged from her dank and freezing prison a changed woman. It was as if she'd shed an old skin with her passage back through Azaroth's portal. The missing parts of her body had been restored, obviously, but there was an inner change as well.

The murder of Eddie and his woman seemed to have

erased the last traces of her conscience. She was no longer a redeemed sinner. There was fresh blood on her hands. Innocent blood. She'd taken it willingly, even eagerly. So she was no longer afraid to shrink from the core truth about herself. She was a murderer. A sadist. And by killing Eddie she'd unleashed the tamed beast she'd kept hidden in the darkest part of her soul for so long.

She thought of Eddie and tried to feel some trace of her former feelings for him, but those feelings now seemed as dead as he was.

She had done it fast, sprinting across the apartment's living room floor toward the oblivious couple seated on the sofa. They were watching a movie and laughing. Their arms were around each other, the woman's head on Eddie's shoulder. Giselle gripped a handful of Eddie's hair and yanked his head back. Eddie gagged as his eyes rolled up to look at her. His woman screamed. There was a moment of recognition in Eddie's terrified expression. His eyes may have expressed pain over the betrayal. The knife slashed across his throat, blood leaping from the gash as Eddie's woman disengaged herself from the dying man and tumbled to the floor. She got to her feet and ran for the door. Giselle hurried after her, moving with the speed and grace of a wolf. Unnatural, unhuman speed. She gripped the screaming woman by the shoulder, spun her around, and slammed her against the door. Then she drove the knife through yielding flesh, plunging it in just below the sternum. The woman screamed and thrashed some more, but Giselle held her in place with a strong hand to the throat. She held the knife in place a moment, coldly holding her agonized gaze, then yanked it out and thrust it in again to the hilt. The woman died and Giselle returned to Eddie and drank blood from his still-bubbling wound, knowing the obscenity would further honor Azaroth and the other death gods.

Killing the woman hadn't been strictly necessary. But it had seemed the right thing to do. So she had killed the woman, a primal, reptilian part of her enjoying the act of senseless murder. She had a feeling Azaroth and the other death gods would appreciate the additional blood offering. And even in the midst of those savage moments she'd known that something within her had changed forever.

Now, standing here in Ms. Wickman's lovingly re-created version of the Master's chambers, Giselle under-stood that other things had also changed, including her immediate plans for the future. The things she wanted now were no longer the things she'd coveted prior to summoning Azaroth.

A full-length oval mirror on a swivel-stand caught her attention. She walked over to it and appraised her reflec-tion. She was as flawless as ever, her flesh porcelain-white, body slender and shapely. Her face was delicately beautiful, almost angelic, with exquisitely fine lines and angles that belied her capacity for savagery. Her long hair was jet-black and straight, a shimmering raven mane that starkly contrasted her pale flesh.

Giselle smiled. She looked good.

Better than ever, in fact.

She turned from the mirror and moved past the large four-poster bed to the French doors at the end of the room. One of the doors was standing open. Giselle moved through it and stood on a long balcony. She moved to the edge of the balcony, braced her hands on the metal rail and looked down. The vista that unfurled below took her breath away. The balcony was high in the air, maybe as much as a half mile above the ground. The landscape beneath was a pockmarked, blasted place. The red terrain made her think of pictures she'd seen of the surface of Mars. She spied a big bonfire in the distance and a thick haze of black smoke rising toward the horizon. Teams of men in black hoods worked together to haul huge stones of varying chiseled shapes in the direction of the bonfire. Other men with machine guns and whips prodded them onward.

These activities were likely connected to Ms. Wickman's own efforts to appease—and draw power from—the death gods. The thought made Giselle smile. Ms. Wickman was powerful and ruthless, but she did not have Azaroth on her side.

Giselle turned away from the tableau of horrors and returned to the bedroom. This time she went directly to the bed and spread herself across the plush and luxuriant feather mattress. She let out a low groan of satisfaction and rolled across the mattress a time or two, reveling in the decadent cradle of comfort. Then she repositioned herself, propping her head on the plump pillows and staring up at the heavy velvet canopy.

She heard a cough and turned her head to see a bare-chested man with a studded leather collar around his throat. The man was lean and sinewy, the exposed flesh of his torso a map of scars and abrasions. He stared at Giselle with eyes that were wide with fear and confusion.

Giselle eyed him coldly. "Stop your gawking, boy, and go fetch your Mistress."

The man flinched as if slapped, then turned and hurried across the room. He tripped and tumbled to the floor, smacking his head against a marble pedestal. A sculpted bust of someone Giselle failed to recognize rolled off the pedestal and split in half as it struck the floor. The man scrambled to his feet and resumed his flight from the room.

Giselle closed her eyes and allowed her mind to drift. It was amazing how at peace she felt now. Life was so much easier minus the tiresome complications of moral concerns. The apparent obliteration of her conscience did not alarm her. One risked these things when making deals with gods, especially of the darker variety. She fell into a sleep state, entering a dream in which she sat on a high throne made of gold. An audience of slaves knelt in rows below her, chanting, their arms extended in praise of their queen.

Then the creak of a door opening roused her from the dream state, and her eyes fluttered open. She turned her head and saw Ms. Wickman and a coterie of followers enter the room. Ms. Wickman, as always, was elegantly attired, wearing a simple black dress with a hemline just above her knees. She wore black stockings and black heels. A single strand of glittering white pearls encircled her throat. The last time Giselle had seen Ms. Wickman she'd worn her long brown hair down, but now her hair was gathered in a bun at the back of her head, the way she'd always worn it during her time as the Master's top servant and de facto second-in-command.

Two of Ms. Wickman's entourage were muscular men clad in black, militaristic uniforms, complete with gleaming black jackboots and crisp black caps. These men flanked her. Both were armed, one with a machine gun, the other bearing a sidearm in a holster. Giselle felt a faint flicker of amusement. In so many ways Ms. Wickman had exactly resurrected aspects of the Master's former regime. Behind the guards was an assortment of Apprentices and servants, among them the bare-chested slave Giselle had sent to fetch Ms. Wickman.

Giselle stifled a giggle as Ms. Wickman paused next to the pedestal and stared at the shattered bust. There was a subtle atmospheric change in the room, a gathering of energy sensed by all present. No one said a word, but some of the Apprentices were smirking, sensing what was coming. Even Giselle felt a surge of excitement as she felt Ms. Wickman's always considerable anger build and build.

Ms. Wickman at last lifted her gaze from the shattered bust and looked in Giselle's direction. She smiled. "I'll deal with you in a moment, dear, but I need to address a housekeeping issue first."

She turned and brushed past the armed guards, her head down like a bull's as she strode purposefully toward the cowering, bare-chested slave. He shook his head, whimpered, and held his hands out in a beseeching way. He backed away, but Ms. Wickman moved fast. In a moment she had the man's head locked in her strong hands. Then there was a sickening snap and the slave fell dead to the floor.

One of the Apprentices, a young girl with pale skin and golden blonde hair, applauded. "Bravo."

Ms. Wickman smoothed her dress and smiled at the girl. "Thank you, Gwendolyn. Could you get rid of this . . . mess for me?"

Gwendolyn smiled. "Of course." She unfurled a whip and snapped it at two nearby slaves, barking strident instructions at them as the whip peeled away strips of their flesh. The slaves worked together to hurriedly haul the dead slave from Ms. Wickman's quarters. Gwendolyn and two other Apprentices followed them out.

Ms. Wickman made eye contact with Giselle now, holding it as she circled the bed and came to a stop on the side nearest the French doors. Giselle shifted position slightly, rolling to her left a bit to better observe her adversary.

"I'm impressed by what you've accomplished, Giselle." Ms. Wickman's tone was even and devoid of any hint of emotion. Amazing. The woman's self-control was remarkable. "Clearly you possess magical capabilities far beyond what I suspected. In retrospect, I should've had you killed immediately."

The guard with the sidearm moved toward the bed. "Should I execute this woman, Mistress?"

Then Ms. Wickman smiled again and said, "No, Captain. This . . . girl . . . presents no threat. Stand back, please."

The guard nodded and retreated to his former position.

Ms. Wickman said, "You puzzle me, Giselle."

Giselle arched an eyebrow. "Oh?"

"Oh, yes. I suppose I should have you killed now, as the Captain suggests, but my curiosity has been aroused." She licked her lips and allowed her gaze to slowly travel the length of Giselle's naked body before again settling on her face. "I would like to know some things. For instance, with your level of ability, you could easily have escaped this place already. Instead you summoned me. Why?"

Giselle smiled. "Because I do not wish to escape."

Now it was Ms. Wickman's turn to raise an eyebrow. "Oh? That's surprising, given the nasty things that have been done to you here."

Giselle raised one of her restored hands, bending it at the wrist for better display. "Nothing that was permanent, as you can see." She lowered her hand and smiled again. "You'll want to know about that, of course. A god assisted me. Do you have any direct experience with the death gods, Ms. Wickman?"

Ms. Wickman's gaze hardened. "I do not." Her terse manner indicated this was an admission she was furious to have to make in front of her followers. "But I know a death god would not assist you without a suitable offering . . ."

"A sacrifice, you mean." Giselle moved a hand over the empty patch of bedsheet next to her, enjoying the feel of the smooth silk beneath her restored flesh. "Yes, a death god granted me temporal transport to a location far from here. There I made the required sacrifice by killing one of the men instrumental in the Master's demise."

Ms. Wickman grunted. "How very fitting."

"The Master should never have died," Giselle said, the sincerity in her voice surprising even her. "I've changed. And I've seen the error of my ways. I want to serve here with you, Mistress, to honor and exalt you. I want to kill for you. Torture for you. Anything you desire . . ."

Ms. Wickman continued to regard her coolly for several long moments, her expression giving away nothing as she mulled over Giselle's words. Then she said, "Is there anything else you want, Giselle?"

Giselle patted the smoothed-down silk sheet and said, "I would like for you to lie here with me for a while."

Something subtle sparked in Ms. Wickman's dark eyes. Giselle felt a deep satisfaction at having prompted it. Without moving her eyes from Giselle's face, Ms. Wickman barked out a single command: "Leave us!"

The others in the room reacted as if slapped. They scurried almost as one out of the room, even the guards, responding to the undeniable imperative in their Mistress's tone. The big door slammed shut, the sound echoing in the large room for a moment.

They were alone. At last.

Ms. Wickman held Giselle's gaze a short moment longer. Then she turned her back on Giselle, dipped her head, and said, "Unzip me."

Giselle got to her knees and moved to the edge of the bed. She took the tiny zipper tab at the collar of Ms. Wickman's dress and began to slowly draw it down, unveiling a wedge of flesh nearly as pale as Giselle's own. Then a surprise, a hint of color as she pulled the zipper further down. Then further still, Giselle's breath catching in her throat as she slid the zipper all the way down to Ms. Wickman's waist.

"Oh, my . . . that's . . . beautiful."

She gripped the flaps of the dress and pulled them

farther apart to better admire the illustration. Ms. Wickman had a large and intricate tattoo of a dragon etched into the flesh of her back. Its scales, nostrils, teeth, talons, and glaring eyes were all stunningly rendered. Giselle touched a forefinger to the back of Ms. Wickman's neck. Her flesh was cool and marblelike, but warmed nicely to her touch. She drew the tip of her finger down the length of her spine, moving through the dragon's mouth before stopping at the small of her back. Then she splayed her fingers and moved her hand slowly over the bared flesh. Ms. Wickman made a soft sound and reached behind her to undo the bun at the back of her head. She shook her hair loose and turned around.

Giselle's excitement level rose yet again. They were no more than a foot apart. Ms. Wickman placed a hand between her breasts and shoved her backward. Giselle fell into the plush mattress and watched as Ms. Wickman pulled the dress off and tossed it to the floor. Then she stepped out of her heels and climbed onto the bed, moving toward Giselle on her hands and knees, stalking her like an alley cat about to pounce on its prey. Giselle squirmed backward, toward the headboard, then stopped as her head met the pillows. Ms. Wickman reached Giselle and climbed atop her, one leg to either side of her waist, hands braced on the pillows above Giselle's shoulders. She lowered herself slightly and her erect nipples brushed Giselle's soft breasts. Giselle placed her hands on Ms. Wickman's waist and urged her even closer. Their faces were only inches apart now. An electric sensuality tingled within her as she looked into Ms. Wickman's wide, hungry eyes.

Ms. Wickman let out a heavy breath that was almost a moan. "I suppose I shouldn't be surprised by this. You have always been such a resourceful little whore."

Giselle caressed Ms. Wickman's back before allowing her hands to settle on the woman's upraised ass. "And you have always been a consummately evil cunt. We were made for each other."

Ms. Wickman's eyes flared again, and this time the carnal need was unmistakable. She abruptly lowered her mouth and kissed Giselle with a hunger Giselle met with equal enthusiasm. They squirmed against each other, hands grasping and probing, wet tongues thrusting between cries of pleasure. After several minutes of this, Ms. Wickman moved lower, her mouth drawing in each of Giselle's engorged nipples in turn. Giselle moaned and squirmed, running her hands through Ms. Wickman's long, unfettered hair. Then Ms. Wickman moved lower still, Giselle spreading her legs as the other woman's tongue found her clit and began flicking at it energetically. Giselle thrashed on the bed as waves of intense pleasure crashed through her. She grabbed the iron bars of the headboard behind her, arched her back, and let out a piercing scream. And after Giselle had been made to scream and pant several more times, Ms. Wickman eased away from her throbbing pussy and laid down next to her.

Giselle let out a feral grunt and rolled on top of the woman. "Your turn."

Ms. Wickman made a growling sound and scooted toward the headboard, better positioning herself for Giselle's attentions. Giselle kissed Ms. Wickman lightly on the mouth before sliding down and taking a nipple into her mouth. And now it was Ms. Wickman's turn to moan, writhe, and pant. After a little of this, Giselle moved south, her tongue tracing a wet trail down Ms. Wickman's flat belly. She laid a hand flat on Ms. Wickman's stomach.

"I made you want me, you know."

Ms. Wickman moaned again and said, "Mmm?"

Her eyes were closed and her mouth open, her lips

curled back to bare her teeth. She writhed slowly and clutched at the bedsheet with both hands. She arched her back and lifted her pelvis, her thighs and stomach muscles quivering with the force of her need. For Giselle, that need was a lovely thing to behold. It was gratifying to see the cold and merciless Ms. Wickman reduced to this helpless animal level. She was a prisoner of overpowering desire—just as Giselle had planned.

Giselle moved her hand in a slow, circular motion over Ms. Wickman's stomach, drifting to a stop at a spot just below her prisoner's sternum. She brought her fingers together, forming a wedge of flesh that pushed against Ms. Wickman's soft abdomen. "You've forgotten some things about me, cunt, beginning with how adept I was at sex magic when I served under the Master. Haven't you wondered why you were so quick to dismiss all your lackeys and leap into bed with me?"

Ms. Wickman's eyes fluttered open and her gaze floated lazily toward Giselle's intent face. She wasn't quite alarmed yet—the erotic charge sizzling through her body was still too powerful—but Giselle's words stirred a part of her mind that had been sleeping. "What is this?" She grunted and lifted her pelvis again. "Please . . ."

Giselle sneered. "Pathetic. You want me to penetrate you? Okay."

She leaned forward and thrust her hand forward with all her considerable strength, the wedge of fingers splitting Ms. Wickman's flesh as easily as if she'd shoved them into jelly. Ms. Wickman's eyes opened wide and her mouth stretched to issue a scream, but Giselle slapped a hand over the opening and muffled the sound. Her other hand delved further into Ms. Wickman's body, pushing aside organs and digging through layers of muscle to reach for her heart. Ms. Wickman thrashed in agony. She scratched and flailed at Giselle's

face. But Giselle held on with ease. She was stronger
than Ms. Wickman now. She pressed her face against Ms.
Wickman's, staring into her bugged-out eyes as her
questing fingers found the throbbing mass of muscle.
She held that gaze a moment longer, savoring the mass
murderer's agony and terror. Then her hand closed
around the heart, gave it a savage twist, and yanked it
from her body, her dripping red hand emerging from the
hole beneath the woman's sternum with a moist plop.

Ms. Wickman went still at once. She was dead.

Ding-dong, Giselle thought, and giggled.

And without her heart, this particular wicked witch
would never rise again. Again, Giselle felt satisfaction,
but there was no righteousness attached to the feeling.
She had not done this thing to avenge the thousands of
deaths Ms. Wickman had been responsible for over the
decades. Her role now was that of usurper. The dead
woman's kingdom would belong to her now.

She brought Ms. Wickman's dripping heart to her
mouth and tore a chunk out of it. She chewed it slowly,
enjoying the tough, raw taste of meat and muscle. A
groan of satisfaction escaped her lips as the morsel slid
down her gullet. Then she tore another chunk out and
devoured it more quickly. Followed by another chunk,
and then another, until it was gone, until she'd symbol-
ically eaten the woman's essence and her magic. This
Giselle did to preserve the work Ms. Wickman had
done with this place. Otherwise this magically constructed edifice and the fiery realm beyond would turn
hazy and wink out of existence. Giselle licked her lips
and sighed with the satisfaction one derives from a fine
meal.

Now that the deed was done, she allowed herself to
marvel over how easily it had been accomplished. If
anything, Azaroth had understated how amplified her

abilities would become with the sacrifice of Eddie King. The power coursing through her was such that she felt like something so much more than a mere sorceress. In the past, even the simplest magic had required some rudimentary form of spellcasting. Now, however, she was able to wield magic merely by focusing her will, thinking about what she wanted to happen, and directing the core of magical energy within her to make it happen. That Ms. Wickman had succumbed to sex magic spoke volumes about the staggering intensity of that energy. Giselle had long been able to manipulate normal people by amplifying the automatic sexual response to certain scents given off by her body, but other practitioners such as the Master and Ms. Wickman had been immune to this brand of magic. No longer. She felt capable of absolutely anything—and of everything all at once.

What she felt like, actually, was a goddess.

She decided to experiment. She flexed her will and heard the large doors at the far end of the quarters creak open. She thought of the people who had accompanied Ms. Wickman into the room earlier and focused on one of them. A few moments later, one of the black-clad guards came staggering into the room, his legs propelling him forward jerkily as if he were a puppet on a string. He pawed at his holstered sidearm, but his hand twisted painfully away from the weapon with a sound of grinding bones. His eyes popped and jittered with the helpless terror of one not in control of his own body. Then he saw the limp form of his dead Mistress and let out a squeal of fear.

The man Ms. Wickman had referred to as "Captain" came to a swaying halt at the foot of the bed as Giselle relinquished much of her physical control over him (though she kept his hand twisted away from the pistol).

Giselle licked blood from her fingers and smiled at the terrifed man. "Tell me your name."

In a trembling voice the man said, "I-I am . . . C-Captain Girard of the B-Black Brigade. The military wing of the M-Mistress's . . . organization."

"I see." Giselle tongued the last of Ms. Wickman's blood from her fingers, then wiped them clean on the bedsheet. She climbed off the bed and approached the trembling captain. "As you can see, you no longer serve Ms. Wickman. I am Mistress of this place now, and you will answer only to me from now on. Is this clear?"

Captain Girard appeared to be too stunned by the inexplicable coup d'etat to immediately supply the only acceptable answer. He kept glancing at Ms. Wickman's body, perhaps expecting her to rise from the dead and reassert her authority. Which, given the condition of her body, was just stupid. Impatient, Giselle snatched the 9mm pistol from his holster and shot him in the face. By the time his corpse struck the floor more black-clad armed men had stormed into the room. Giselle usurped control of their minds in a millisecond. They stood there, terror shining in their eyes, mouths hanging open in shock, their fingers frozen over the trigger guards of their useless weapons.

Giselle stepped over the fallen Captain and advanced to within six feet of the nearest trembling man. "Ms. Wickman is dead. I rule this place now. Captain Girard is dead because he could not accept that. He was a stupid man." She eyed each of the men in turn before saying, "Are the rest of you as stupid?"

A chorus of muttered denials brought a very slight smile to her face.

"Good. Then know this. I do not wish to kill any more of you. Nor do I wish to upset the essential order of things around here." She clasped her hands behind her back and strode slowly back and forth in front of them like a marine drill sergeant addressing a rank of fresh boot camp inductees. "This is a change of command, nothing more. Your Black Brigade will remain intact. If anything, you will have more power than before."

Giselle allowed a moment for that to sink in. A new, hungry gleam stole into the eyes of several of the men. Giselle supposed the message was getting through. These men had been something of an elite force before, but now they would be backed by power far greater than that wielded by their deceased Mistress.

Giselle said, "I need to speak with your top officer privately. The rest of you go about your business at once."

All but one of the men hurried out of the room. The big door slammed shut yet again. The Black Brigade officer who remained with her was a tall, thin man with cold blue eyes and close-cropped steel-gray hair. He glanced briefly at the bodies of Ms. Wickman and Captain Girard. Giselle watched him closely, but his eyes registered nothing at all. He was over any shock he'd felt at this turn of events.

Giselle moved closer to him, almost to within touching distance. "And what is your name?"

The man's face remained expressionless as he said, "Lieutenant Schreck, Mistress."

Giselle suppressed the smile that wanted to come. *Mistress.*

"The Black Brigade is yours to command now, Schreck. Anyone above you will be demoted or eliminated." Giselle smiled. "Whichever you deem necessary."

A corner of his mouth twitched, the first indication of any emotion lurking behind the man's mask of cool indifference. "I understand."

Giselle moved away from him and sat at the foot of the bed. She crossed her legs and set the pistol next to one of Ms. Wickman's unmoving feet. "Please bring me up to speed, Schreck. Brief me on the things I most need to know about this place."

Lieutenant Schreck cleared his throat and began a concise recitation of a number of basic facts. Some of what she learned then increased her contempt for Ms. Wickman. Her handling of the slaves, for instance, bespoke a pathetic lack of confidence in her ability to forestall an uprising like the one that had brought down the Master. This would not continue under the new regime. More pleasing was what she learned about the ongoing efforts to rein in the survivors of the Master's former domain. She wanted to see those people again.

The briefing finished, Giselle allowed herself a silent moment of contemplation. She looked at Ms. Wickman's corpse and felt a tingle, a ghost of the powerful erotic charge that had flowed through her own body during their brief but electric coupling. That tingle intensified and Giselle became keenly aware of an awakened taste that had not yet been sated.

"Tell me, Lieutenant. You are no doubt familiar with all the Apprentices in service here. Of the females, whom would you say is the most beautiful?"

Schreck's answer was immediate. "That would be Ursula, Mistress."

"Have someone fetch her for me. But first . . ." Giselle turned her head to look at the open French door and the red sky beyond. "Have this cunt's body taken to that barren place and burned. I would like to watch this happen from my balcony."

"As you wish, Mistress."

She dismissed him then and he departed the room at once. Giselle again arose from the bed and ventured back out to the balcony. She observed the diminutive forms of the hooded, toiling slaves and thought of what Schreck had told her about the edifice they were constructing.

An actual pyramid, she thought, wonderment again filling her as she imagined it.

She smiled again.

She couldn't imagine a more appropriate place for the sacrifices to come.

PART II:
THE CRIMSON HIGHWAY

CHAPTER ELEVEN

One month later

The strange little girl in the yellow rain slicker was looking at her again. Laughing at her again. The girl made her
nervous. She had a weird glint in her eyes. And there was
something about the set of her features and the angle at
which she was holding her head that made her expression look like a grown-up leer. A hint of lasciviousness
one shouldn't see in the eyes of one so young. Though
Dream couldn't hear the sound of the girl's laughter over
the wind and the rushing water below, she was certain it
possessed a mocking tone.

She wasn't positive the little girl was really there. Another apparition, maybe. She was glad of the dozen or
so yards that separated them. If she moved any closer,
Dream would bolt back across the bridge to the parking
lot where they'd left Marcy's van. The girl put a cupped
hand to her mouth to cover a giggle.

Dream shifted her attention back to the natural wonder in the distance. The stiff breeze stirred her hair and
the fine mist of rain made her flesh glisten as she
leaned over the railing of the Rainbow Bridge and
watched the distant churning foam of the water at the

bottom of American Falls, the U.S. half of the famed Niagara Falls. The sky was overcast and the temperature
had dropped into the thirties, with the stiffening wind
adding an extra bite to the chill. It was late afternoon
drifting toward evening, and the already bruised sky
was growing darker by the moment. The nasty conditions had thinned the usual tourist crowds to nearly
nothing. Dream had an eerie sense of standing alone at
the very edge of the world as all of existence teetered
on the brink of some unfathomable apocalypse.

Dream shivered as the swirling wind abruptly redi-
rected and gusted across her wet face. She tucked her
hands under her arms and wished for better protection
against the elements than the light jacket she was wearing. She leaned further over the railing and looked at the
rushing stream of water directly beneath the Rainbow
Bridge. An image leapt unbidden to her mind then, one
that stirred horror within her, but was not without a certain morbid appeal. She imagined herself climbing over
the slick railing and leaping spread-eagled into the
drink, her arms outstretched as she soared for one glorious moment before plunging into the cold, cold water
and the darkness beyond.

"It's tempting, isn't it?"

Dream flinched at the sound of Marcy's voice. The
fragile—but achingly vivid—illusion of perfect alone-
ness was wrecked again. On the other hand, there was
a measure of comfort to be derived from the proximity
of an undeniably flesh-and-blood human being. Dream
considered asking Marcy whether she could see the girl
in the yellow rain slicker, but decided against it when
she realized she wasn't certain which would unsettle
her more, a yes or no answer.

Marcy took up a position a few feet to her left and
leaned over the railing. The wind blew her bottle-
blonde hair wildly about her face, but she seemed

oblivious to the conditions. She glanced down before looking at Dream again. "I kind of wish I had the guts to do it. Just climb over and . . . jump." Her tone turned wistful as her gaze was drawn back to the water. "It would solve a lot of problems."

Dream sighed and finally acknowledged her presence. "So do it. I won't stop you, I promise."

Marcy grunted. "If you hate me so much, why don't you just kill me? Make my brain explode like you did to my friend. Or have your freaky zombie friend rip my head off or something."

Anger stirred within Dream as she listened to Marcy rant. The girl had been nearly as silent as her meek little sister during their first days on the road, but in the last week she'd grown increasingly bold with her verbal jabs. Dream knew she was testing her, probing to see just how far she could push. She was treading a very thin line. The pressure building within Dream was immense. It wouldn't take much to trigger an explosion. And she had a feeling her next explosion might wipe out anyone within range.

Dream shivered again and looked at Marcy. "That thing isn't my friend. Not really."

Marcy smirked. "That's not what she says. She says—"

"I know what she says." Dream turned away from the railing and leaned close to Marcy. She caught a glimpse of Alicia over Marcy's shoulder. The black woman was standing at a spot some twenty yards to the left, her gaze trained on the waterfall. "And maybe she even believes it. But she's not Alicia. She's not even Alicia's ghost. There may be some little strand of Alicia's essence inside her, something some part of my subconscious always carries with me. If anything, she's some kind of fucked-up clone or copy. There's a lot of what I remember about Alicia in that . . . thing, but it's all distorted." She frowned. "I don't know how to put it exactly."

Marcy's brow furrowed. "Like a garbled data transmission, then? Static or interference causing some information to be left out and other bits of it scrambled all to hell."

Dream shrugged. "Something like that, I guess."

Marcy nodded. "Yeah. The supernatural gumbo inside you created a shell based on your last memories of Alicia, then downloaded a faulty blueprint of her psyche to her regenerated brain." She laughed and shook her head. "It's all very late night Z-movie. Not sure I believe it, but I guess it makes at least as much sense as the idea of a genuine walking corpse."

Dream didn't respond to that. She looked over Marcy's shoulder again at Alicia. The slinky cocktail dress had been traded in for jeans, a long-sleeved thermal shirt, and a light jacket similar to the one worn by Dream. She looked almost normal now. And it wasn't just because of the clothes. The wounds and corpse bloat were still there, if you looked close enough, but these things were fading, the open, weeping razor incisions closing and becoming scars. Every day she looked a little better, and Dream suspected she would soon be fully restored. Her improvement was disconcerting, although it wasn't as unsettling as the realization that other people could see the dead woman now. It reduced the likelihood that she was hallucinating or losing her mind, a scenario that bothered her far less than the idea of having actually conjured Alicia into being through some unconscious use of raw magic. A vision of the girl in the yellow rain slicker formed in her mind then, and Dream was again made to consider the possibility that if she could perform the feat of creation once, then she could surely do it again.

She thought about that. She assumed the dead woman was feeding off the power lurking within Dream, drawing some of that energy out to make herself more real. That they were tethered together in some way was

clear, but Dream had no way of knowing the depth of
that connection. But she wondered just how much Alicia
still needed her now that she had form and substance in
the physical world. She had a feeling the creature
would've ceased to exist had those idiot kids killed her
outright that night instead of abducting her, either blinking out immediately or continuing in a fuzzy state of
semi-existence for a brief time before fading away.

But now . . .

Now she was here to stay. Dream could take a swan
dive off the Rainbow Bridge and Alicia would remain
up here behind the railing. She would watch the water
take Dream and sweep her away. Then she would leave
this place, taking Marcy and Ellen with her as she resumed her meandering search for Ms. Wickman.

Which, of course, was crazy. The thing that resembled her dead friend might not actually be Alicia Jackson, but she certainly bore her grudges as tenaciously
as the real thing. She meant to see Ms. Wickman dead,
preferably at the business end of a straight razor. Dream
was not bothered by the idea of being made to partici-
pate in the murder of that woman. She deserved death
and worse. What did bother her was the obvious impos-
siblity of making this happen. There was a whole wide
world into which Ms. Wickman could have disappeared. They could never hope to find her.

Except that . . .

Well.

Except that Alicia believed Ms. Wickman had already
established a new kingdom similar to the one formerly
ruled over by the Master. She also believed Ms. Wickman
had scores of operatives scouring the country for Dream
even now. She wouldn't say why she believed this, but
the strength of her conviction was clear. Alicia hoped to
somehow draw the attention of these agents, induce
them to capture them and transport them back to this

supposed new kingdom. Which would eliminate the necessity for all this endless, aimless hunting. Dream figured it was the only remotely plausible way Alicia might get what she wanted. And even the remote possibility of again gazing into the awful Ms. Wickman's cold, dead eyes chilled her to the bone.

Marcy noted Dream's continued scrutiny of Alicia and smiled. "Hey, at least the maggots are gone."

Dream laughed. "Yeah. There's that."

"So it's not all bad."

"Right. Now it's only 99.98 percent bad."

Dream watched the dark form of a bird swoop through her field of vision before disappearing into the gathering darkness on the horizon. The rain grew harder, falling in silver-white sheets across the sky. The temperature seemed to have fallen another five degrees in just the last twenty minutes. Though it had been her idea to come to this place, she was beginning to regret it. It was one of a number of places she'd always wanted to visit, and when she'd realized they were wandering close to this area, she'd insisted on a slight course change to bring them here. Niagara Falls was as beautiful as she'd always imagined, and the sight of all that rushing water inspired the expected sense of awe. And that overwhelming beauty was enhanced now with the advent of twilight. The spotlights behind the falls had been switched on, adding a lovely soft green tint to the pouring water. The problem was that it was too beautiful a thing to share with her current company. She should be seeing this in the company of a lover, here or on one of the closer observation platforms, holding hands and leaning against each other, enjoying a classic romantic moment.

The train of thought plunged her into a sudden depression. For the first time in a while she thought of Chad and the life she'd left behind. Scenes and aural snippets from their screaming arguments came back to her then. Arguments that nearly always centered around the same thing—her deepening booze and pill dependence. Chad railed endlessly against this "self-medication," insisting that she needed professional help to deal with her guilt over the deaths of her friends. This was followed by Dream's usual litany of bitter recriminations, unfairly blaming him for everything that was wrong with her. Even then she'd known how unfair she was being, but she hadn't cared. She would not be denied her only real solace, the numbing effects of her chosen poisons. Things came to a head the time Dream whizzed an empty bottle past Chad's head, barely missing him before it exploded on the living room wall. And then she'd hit him. And that'd been the end of it. She moved out the next day and never returned.

Tears stung Dream's eyes and she was glad for the obscuring effects of the rain. A flicker of movement to her right drew her out of the painful reverie. She glanced in that direction and saw the girl in the yellow rain slicker again. Only now she was closer than before, the distance between them nearly halved. The rain slicker flapped in the wind and the hood blew back a bit, revealing long wet strands of blonde hair. The girl's eyes were a brilliant shade of blue that sparkled even in the gloom. She was a pretty young thing, one might even say adorable but for that insidious grin and that strange, mocking laughter Dream realized she could actually hear now.

Dream cast her gaze about for any sign of the child's parents, but there was no one nearby who obviously fit the bill. A few other people were present, but they were mostly dark, indistinct forms in the distance. And surely no parent of any worth would allow a child so young to wander from sight on a place like Rainbow Bridge. She didn't want to believe the girl was another apparition or magical construct, but the sense that she was wouldn't go away. The idea that the power she possessed was so far beyond her control terrified Dream.

But there was another thing to consider. From which submerged corner of Dream's psyche had she emerged? There was nothing instantly familiar about the girl. Except for the blonde hair, she didn't much resemble Dream as a young girl. Nor did she much look like any of the childhood friends she could recall. Then something occurred to Dream, a flash of insight so stark and compelling she couldn't help but believe it. Perhaps, on a subconscious level, the girl was Dream's idea of how her own daughter might look. She was a woman, and perhaps on some primal level lurked a need unfulfilled, a biological imperative that combined with what Marcy called the "supernatural gumbo" inside her to produce this leering manifestation.

Her eyes still locked on Dream, the girl laughed harder, her little body rocking with the force of her mirth.

Dream shivered and moved back a step.

The girl was closer by half again, maybe ten feet away now, and Dream had not seen her move. It was almost as if the physical distance between them was shrinking of its own accord, the fabric of existence retracting or disappearing to draw them closer. Which was an insane, impossible thing, but Dream had seen and experienced enough not to discount a thing merely because it shouldn't be possible.

She moved back another step and said, "Stay away." She bumped against Marcy and her voice rose in pitch as tears flowed freely down her face. "Stay the fuck away! Leave me alone!"

Marcy shuffled away with a startled grunt and said, "Who are you talking to, Dream?"

The little girl was five feet away and looking straight at her now. She raised a hand and pointed a slender forefinger at her. The pale digit looked ghostly in the gloom. Like something only half-formed or incomplete. This impression, combined with Marcy's question, formed the impetus for what happened next.

Dream ceased her retreat. The terror was still rising inside her, an inferno that threatened to scorch what precious little remained of her sanity. But there was another emotion now, as well. Anger. Raw, burning hatred. Hatred for a part of herself she couldn't control. A thing she feared might consume her.

She loosed a cry of rage and dashed forward. The girl's hand fell to her side and her evil little grin gave way to a look of shocked surprise. Dream seized her by the shoulders and began to lift her up. A scream of terror ripped from the girl's lungs, but Dream ignored it, knowing only she could hear the sound. She would not be swayed from doing what had to be done, would not allow this awful thing to feed from her and grow stronger, become a part of the real world. The girl's body was quaking as Dream lifted her higher and moved toward the railing. She sobbed and pleaded, but Dream blanked it out and focused only on the task at hand, moving the light little body out over the railing.

Marcy was yelling at her: "Dream, what the hell are you doing? Have you lost your fucking mind!?"

Other people were yelling, too. Shouts and exhortations, desperate words that failed to penetrate the roaring in her ears. She also failed to hear the sound of several pairs of feet pounding across concrete toward her, but she did feel the grappling hands of the would-be rescuers a moment later, felt them pulling at her arms, tugging at her hair and clothes, desperately digging for any hold at all to pull her back from the brink. But Dream was resolute and would not be moved. The dormant core of power within her switched on and filled her entire body with a strength several times

greater than that of all the people assailing her combined. Though she didn't think it consciously, there was
an underlying sense that these people were attempting
to pull her back from an apparent suicide leap.

She leaned even further over the railing, effortlessly
shrugging loose all those grasping hands as she lowered the girl and prepared to drop her. The girl abruptly
stopped thrashing and looked up at Dream with wide,
pleading eyes. Then her mouth was moving. Dream
couldn't hear. what the apparition was saying, as the
roaring in her ears continued to obliterate all external
sounds.

This was it. All Dream had to do was relax her hold
on the girl and let her slip away, and this one little
phase of the ongoing nightmare that was her life would
be over. But Dream hesitated. She stared at those thin,
chapped lips as they moved. Saw the girl's crooked
white teeth and the pink wedge of tongue behind them.

The roaring in her ears ceased.

The rush of the water below returned. Then she
heard the screams and the words of the people grabbing at her, words too frantic and intercut to make any
sense. Dream focused on the motion of the girl's lips
and was at last able to hear her voice, its soft timbre
somehow rising above the cacophony of sound from
the bridge. The girl's actual words were channeled in
another direction as something alien pushed these
words through her vocal cords: *"The Master awaits you
in hell, slut."*

She let go of the girl and jerked backward. The bodies of all the people behind her prevented a full retreat
and she watched the little body drop and tumble, the
rain slicker flapping up and briefly lifting her arms like
a tiny sail. Then she hit the water and sliced through its
surface like a scalpel cutting flesh. In the next moment
she disappeared from view and the people behind her

went running toward the other side of the bridge. Staggering, Dream turned around and watched their retreating backs as a frown began to work its way across her stunned features.

Someone grabbed her by the arm and she shrieked. Something inside her reflexively lashed out and she was aware of a sensation like fire blazing through her body, its sizzle banishing the cold as a wave of heat pulsed outward from her center.

Marcy screamed and jerked her hand away, shaking it like a person who has touched a scalding surface. "Dream, that was fucked up. We have to get out of here before the mob comes back for you."

Too late for that.

Several people were still leaning over the railing on the opposite side of the bridge. One woman was slumped against the concrete barrier and wailing like a grief-stricken mourner at a funeral. The impression formed like a cold fist around her heart and the heat pulse abruptly fizzled out.

Dream swallowed a lump in her throat and thought, *Oh, no . . .*

Three men were striding rapidly back across the bridge toward her. The man in the lead was thirtyish, tall and muscular with a thick mop of curly brown hair and a beard. His eyes were dark with a bottomless rage. Every aspect of his bearing unmistakably conveyed murderous intent. The rigid set of his features. The huge, curled fists that looked capable of slamming holes through layers of steel.

Dream shook her head.

Oh no. Ohnoohnoohno . . .

The girl had been real.

And this man was her father.

Dream's eyes filled with tears as she took an unconscious step backward. Her back met the railing. She briefly considered letting herself fall backward into the water. It was what she deserved. Christ, how could she have been so wrong? She'd known her long-tenuous hold on reality had been slipping for some time, but she'd never imagined such tragic consequences. She'd murdered a child, sacrificed her on the altar of her crumbling sanity.

Yes, she deserved to die. She even felt ready to meet that fate at last.

Then the man was closing in on her, eyes blazing and teeth bared as he raised one of those big fists high in the air. Then something inside Dream flexed and the man froze. A surge of energy so strong it was nearly visible pushed outward and slammed into the man's chest like a freight train, lifting him off his feet and blasting him back across the bridge. Dream saw his eyes go wide with shock before the surge carried him away. And then he was gone, flying over the railing on the opposite side and hanging suspended in midair for a moment before dropping to the water below.

Marcy let out a breath and said, "Holy shit. Holyholy-holy fucking shit!"

The men who'd followed the father across the bridge were lying flat on their backs, blown off their feet by the energy surge. They looked up at Dream with twin expressions of horror and began to scoot backward, scrambling to put as much distance between themselves and the monster as possible. That's what they saw when they looked at her. A monster. Not a woman. Not a human being. But an incomprehensible abomination. A *thing*. And they were right.

The people on the other side of the bridge were looking at her and cringing, crouching down against the concrete barrier as they huddled together and awaited the monster's wrath. A few of them were armed men of some authority in uniforms. But they were as helpless and terrified as the wailing woman Dream assumed was the dead girl's mother. Dream stared at them for a long moment and felt the awakened energy burning inside her, aching to be utilized again. And it would be so easy. She could flatten them all and walk away from this place unscathed.

A weak, frightened voice next to her: "Dream . . . seriously . . . we have to leave."

A peculiar smile contorted the corners of her mouth as Dream turned to look at Marcy. "I'm a monster, Marcy."

Marcy put a hand to her mouth as her eyes filled with tears. "Dream. I—"

"Shhh." Dream touched the girl's shoulder and felt her body go still. She was every bit as terrifed of her as the strangers huddled on the other side of the bridge. And who could blame her? "Don't say anything. It's funny. A minute ago I felt so much guilt, but this thing inside me burns that away when it's working." She lowered her voice a bit and leaned closer to Marcy. "I could kill all those people over there just by thinking about it. Part of me really wants to. I shouldn't do that, should I?"

Marcy's face twisted with a mixture of sudden grief and black humor. She laughed once, a small, empty sound. "Look who you're asking. I'm a monster, too."

Dream smiled. She released Marcy's arm and touched her face. "Yes. Yes, I suppose you are. And I'll tell you something, Marcy. I don't think I hate you anymore." She looked past Marcy at Alicia, who remained in the same spot she'd been throughout the episode. The dead woman watched them in a remotely curious way, a small smile playing at the edges of her mouth. Dream met and held Alicia's gaze for a moment, then looked Marcy in the eye again. "I'm going to leave you now, but I'll see you again."

Marcy frowned. "Where are you going?"

"Into the water."

Marcy's expression abruptly sobered. "But—"

"Don't worry about me. I'll be okay." She gently stroked Marcy's face and the girl covered the hand with one of her own. "You've seen how strong I am. The river will take me away, but it won't kill me. It's the only way out of this for you. Too many eyes will be on me. You and Alicia go back to the van and your sister. Get away from here. I'll find you again. I promise."

She moved away from Marcy and threw one leg over the rail. She looked at the black water below and tried to decide whether she believed everything she'd just said. Then the energy swelled within her again and a shroud of warmth enveloped her.

She smiled again and said, "Go, Marcy. Now."

Marcy stared numbly at her before nodding and beginning a retreat. "Okay . . . and, Dream?"

"Yeah?"

Marcy's expression was somber as she said, "I don't think I hate you anymore, either."

Then she turned away and began a hurried retreat back down the bridge toward the parking lot. A moment later Alicia turned to follow without so much as a backward glance. Dream watched their backs until they dwindled to barely perceptible specks in the darkness.

Until they were gone.

Dream shot one more look at the people huddled at the other side of the bridge. One of the armed men was fumbling for his sidearm. Dream reached out with her power and made his hand freeze. She was getting better at controlling this thing by the moment. The knowledge was at once terrifying and exhilarating.

Dream swung her other leg over the railing.

Then she stood up and leaped, her arms spread before her as she'd envisioned earlier. She hung suspended in the air, flying for a single, incandescently glorious moment.

Next came the slap of the water against her body, harder than she expected.

Then the world was blackness and a cold deeper than anything she'd ever imagined as the water carried her away.

CHAPTER TWELVE

The axe handle felt good in his hands. The muscles in his arms ached from the strain of his physical exertions, but it was a good ache. Chad was a man used to cool, air-conditioned offices and the soft comforts of a home in the suburbs. Physical labor in the so-called great outdoors had occurred only on rare occasions over the course of his thirty-four years on the planet. His thrice-weekly workouts had been confined to hip gyms filled with other trendy and pretty young professionals. Trim and toned bluebloods clad in fashionable workout outfits, iPods affixed to their bronzed biceps as they power-walked on treadmills that hummed with quiet efficiency. And always there had been the relaxing sauna afterward, not strictly necessary but an enjoyable reward for forty-five minutes worth of light maintenance working out.

Chad swung the axe and watched with satisfaction as the blade chopped the log cleanly in half down the middle. He added the halves to the steadily growing cord of firewood before propping another log atop the big stump he was using for a chopping block. The screen door screeched open and flapped shut behind him. He turned and saw Allyson emerge from the rear of the building Jack Paradise referred to as the "mess hall." She came bearing two brown bottles of beer, one of which Chad accepted with a grateful nod. They were enjoying an unseasonably warm patch of fall weather here in the mountain country of east Tennessee, and the dripping bottle of beer looked like the nectar of the gods as the glass reflected the shining afternoon sun.

He gulped Budweiser and looked at Allyson. Clad in cutoff denim shorts and a dirty white blouse tied off at her sleek midriff, she bore little resemblance to the trendy suburbanite she'd been a month ago. Chad felt a stir of lust as he looked at her long and slender legs. Then, as was nearly always the case lately, he thought of the sheer number of people—men *and* women—who had been between those legs during Allyson's time in the adult film industry and his ardor waned. They'd had sex exactly once during their month at the compound, a brief and awkward coupling that easily ranked among the most unsatisfying encounters of Chad's life. They hadn't talked about it much, but it was obvious Chad had developed a mental block in the aftermath of Allyson's tawdry revelations.

She noticed his scrutiny of her body and smiled. "Got something on your mind, Chad?"

Chad frowned and looked away. A huge red ant crawled across the dry ground at his feet. "Not really."

Allyson moved closer, sidling up against him to whisper in his ear: "Is there anything you ever wanted to do to a woman but didn't have the guts to ask?" Her breath was hot against his ear. Her soft lips brushed the lobe and sent a pleasant tingle through his body. "Anything you want, you can have. *Anything*."

The tip of her tongue flicked lightly against his ear, and Chad's cock twitched as she moved a soft palm over his bare, sweat-covered torso. These physical ministrations were exquisitely pleasurable. The heat of her body and the feel of her silken flesh against his made his heart pound. Allyson was so very skilled at making a man feel good. Too good, maybe.

Chad pushed away from her and said, "Maybe later," the words emerging as a halfhearted mumble. "Got work to do."

He set the bottle down and raised the axe again. Allyson watched him in silence as he split several more logs. Then she departed without a word. Chad kept working as he listened to the sound of her retreating footsteps, not stopping until he heard the screen door flap shut again. When he was sure she was gone, Chad slammed the axe blade into the old stump and picked up the beer bottle. He retrieved his flannel shirt, pulled it on, and left it hanging unbuttoned. Then he walked away from the mess hall and moved across the sloping, green grounds of the compound toward the little cluster of cabins where most of the inhabitants of "Camp Whiskey" had their quarters.

Men attired in green camos patrolled the wooded perimeter of the compound, some out in the open, others lurking behind the line of tall trees. They carried machine guns and had walkie-talkies clipped to their belts. These were serious, stern-faced men. Many of them were former U.S. military. Recruited and commanded by Jack Paradise, they were the compound's main line of defense against the enemy Jim seemed so certain would come for them one day.

He approached the door of the nearest and largest cabin and the armed—and heavily armored—guard stationed there stepped aside to allow him entry, acknowledging his exalted status at Camp Whiskey with a single, terse nod.

Chad remained a hero to the other survivors of Below. They all remembered well the instrumental role he'd played in the House of Blood revolt. Which was fine. But the deference with which they treated him made him uncomfortable.

This was the only place he ever felt truly at ease anymore.

So Chad knocked on the wooden door once and loudly announced himself. Then he opened the door and stepped inside. It was dark inside, the windows covered with a heavy dark canvas material. The only illumination was courtesy of the glow from a red bulb in a wrought iron floor lamp and a handful of flickering candles. Little wisps of smoke were visible around the heads of the people seated at the table in the center of the room. Chad smelled cannabis, tobacco, and bourbon. Soft sitar music emanated from the tinny speakers of a small boombox propped atop a crate containing rifles.

Jim acknowledged his arrival with a lazy wave. "Chad. Join us."

Chad nodded and approached the table, pulling out a wicker chair opposite Jim. "I see you're deep into the day's meditations." He settled into the creaky chair and set his beer bottle on the dusty wooden table. "Uncovering any new universal truths today?"

Jim's eyes were hidden behind dark sunglasses, but a lazy smile slowly formed at the corners of his mouth. "What we're doing, Chad, is engaging in the ancient ritual known as getting fucked up beyond all recognition. You should join us."

Jack Paradise lifted a glass containing two fingers of brown liquid and chuckled before taking a drink. "Jim's getting fucked up. Me, I always indulge at a slow maintenance level." He stared at the glass cupped between his large hands. His eyes had a haunted look. "After all, the shit could hit the fan at any time."

Jack was seated next to Jim on the opposite side of the table. Directly opposite Jack was Wanda Lewis, formerly known as "Wicked Wanda" during her time Below. Wanda's dark hair was drawn back in a ponytail. She wore form-fitting dark clothes. A thin brown cigarette smoldered between two fingers of her right hand. She looked at Chad with a soft, druggy smile and said, "And I wouldn't exactly say I'm fucked up, but I ain't quite sober either." She laughed and leaned back in her chair, bringing her hand to her mouth to puff at the brown cigarette. "Could be me and 'fucked up' will be having a rendezvous sometime in the near future."

Chad noticed a simple plastic bong at the center of the table. It was the sort of thing a frat boy might buy for fifteen bucks at a campus head shop. Next to it was a .45 automatic, a clip for the .45, and an open box of ammunition. As Chad watched, Jim picked up the empty clip and fed bullets into it. He did this slowly and with much deliberation, clearly determined to perform this task with precision despite his high level of inebriation. Then he flipped the safety on and set the gun back on the table.

Jim removed his sunglasses and tucked them in his shirt's front pocket. He leaned across the table and regarded Chad with eyes that were bloodshot but somber. "So what's on your mind, friend?"

Chad picked up the Budweiser bottle and twirled the long neck slowly between his fingers without taking a drink. "Things are still weird between Allyson and me. I don't know what to do about it. And I keep wondering whether bringing her to this place was the right thing to do. Maybe I was wrong about that. A girl like Allyson was made for life in the city. I can sense her getting restless already."

Jim's expression grew more intent even as he reached for the bong. "You need to have a serious talk with that girl, Chad, regardless of whether things are 'weird' between you."

Chad leaned back in his chair and let the Bud bottle hang by his side. "Yeah, I know, okay?" He watched Jim fire up the bong and wondered whether a hit or two of the potent weed might improve his mood.

He was reaching for the bong when Wanda said, "Maybe I should have a talk with her." She shrugged when Chad showed her a puzzled look. "Hey, why not? She might feel more comfortable talking this shit out with a woman."

Jim passed the bong to Chad and said, "I agree. Let Wanda talk to her. Open up some new channels of communication and see what happens."

Chad accepted the bong. He put the lighter to the bowl, covered the carb with a fingertip, and inhaled a lungful of smoke. He held the smoke inside for a full twenty seconds before blowing a white stream at the ceiling. A few moments later he felt some of the tension go out of his body. He did a few more hits and felt even better. At some fuzzy point the sitar music gave way to the Velvet Underground. Chad was aware of laughter, but his sense of the ongoing conversation became garbled and disjointed. He hardly noticed when Wanda stood up from the table and left the cabin.

Allyson's fingers were starting to cramp from all the hours she'd spent chopping vegetables for Camp Whiskey's cooking crew. A big feast was in the works for the evening and all day long the mess hall's kitchen had been a bustle of activity. But now it was late in the afternoon and the other women she'd been working with had knocked off for a final break before the last big pre-dinner push. They hadn't invited her to join them outside, which was typical of the way she'd been shunned from the beginning. Though Chad denied it, she suspected the thinly disguised ill will toward her was a result of Jim's lingering distrust of her.

Allyson's life prior to arriving at Camp Whiskey had not been an easy one, but she was pretty and personable and so had always managed to find a way to fit in wherever she went. This ostracism was something new. Being surrounded by people who would barely talk to her or look at her was worse by far than merely being alone. It hurt her in a fundamental way that she'd never truly experienced before. And, of course, they all knew of her past in the porn industry. Someone—

Jim, she thought, her blood boiling.

—had decided to share this bit of information with his inner circle. And the juicy tidbit had filtered down through the grapevine until everyone knew about it. Chad's apparent unwillingness to stand up for her made it worse. It was almost as frustrating as her several failed attempts at seducing him. He didn't seem at all interested in her physically anymore, and Allyson was beginning to feel it was pointless to keep trying.

Thinking about it caused her to grit her teeth and start chopping the carrots faster. She wielded the gleaming blade in her hand with a swift efficiency. Something about the task made her recall how easily the axe blade had punched through the flesh of the men sent to retrieve Chad and Jim. She imagined the blade in her hand pressed to Jim's throat. Saw his eyes go wide as she eased the sharp wedge of steel into his flesh and drew blood, his pleas for mercy going unanswered as she made him pay dearly for the humiliation she'd suffered. But the fantasy brought no real satisfaction. Her wounded pride aside, she ached to fit in and be accepted. Ached to have Chad like and respect her again.

She didn't realize her eyes had filled with tears until she heard the sound of boot heels on the kitchen floor. She wiped her eyes with the back of a hand and looked up to see Wanda Lewis entering the kitchen from the mess hall. The woman was tall and slender,

and possessed of a striking prettiness that made
Allyson want to touch her. Which was just odd. Allyson
had performed sexual acts with women before, but
never outside the context of porn films. Hetero was her
default orientation and she was happy with it, so it was
a strange thing to feel that little tingle of arousal every
time she saw Wanda's face.

There was a small, enigmatic smile teasing the corners of the woman's mouth as she approached Allyson
and placed a hand on her arm. "Come for a walk with
me, Allyson. I'd like to talk with you about some things."

Allyson looked into the taller woman's luminous
green eyes and felt something melt inside her. Maybe
Wanda had approached her as a peacemaker. Perhaps
she'd even been sent by Jim for that very purpose. The
prospect of being accepted at last by the inner circle
made her heart skip a beat. She felt like crying again,
but she managed to keep the tears at bay. She dared not
get her hopes up too soon.

She let go of the knife and wiped her hands on the
dirty apron tied about her waist. "Okay." She untied the
apron and tossed it over the back of a chair. "I'm about
sick of this women's work bullshit anyway."

Wanda smiled again and moved toward the screen
door at the rear of the kitchen. Allyson followed her outside and noted at once the mixture of disdain and curiosity playing across the faces of her co-workers. Most
of them puffed at cigarettes and pretended not to notice
her, but one man, a soldier who'd moved away from the
nearby woods to talk to the gathered women, looked
her in the eye for a moment. A flicker of some unreadable emotion passed over his face and disappeared.

Allyson hurried to catch up to Wanda, whose long
strides had nearly carried her to the edge of the woods
in the time Allyson had paused to study the soldier's
expression. She stepped through the line of trees and

put an extra spring in her step as she glimpsed Wanda's back in intermittent flashes through the maze of trees. They were moving along a winding, ill-defined path. She moved quickly along lengths of bare ground, then had to take her time negotiating areas covered with thick bramble and blocked by low-hanging branches.

She was nearly out of breath by the time she emerged into a small clearing. Wanda was standing in the center of the clearing with her back turned. She moved closer to the other woman and said, "It's . . . kind of . . . nice out here." She laughed once, a sound rendered brittle by her live-wire nerves. "If you're into the whole back-to-nature thing, I mean. I'm not, really, but I'm trying to get used to it."

Wanda laughed. "I wouldn't worry about that, Allyson."

She turned around and Allyson gasped at the sight of the gun pointed at her chest. Her knees went weak and her stomach did a slow roll. "Wh-what . . . is this?"

Wanda moved closer. "Get on your knees, Allyson."

Allyson knew she should turn and run. A mad dash back into the woods was her only chance of escape. But the sight of that looming gun barrel was so intimidating. The strength drained from her legs and she dropped to her knees. Wanda's smile broadened as she approached Allyson and placed the warm gun barrel against the center of her forehead.

She laughed at the sight of tears spilling down Allyson's cheeks. "Poor little thing. Did you really think I brought you here for some heart-to-heart, girl-to-girl talk?"

Allyson was shaking uncontrollably by now. The steel biting into her flesh felt like the cold finger of God, the Almighty laying His judgment down on her. She'd done a lot of bad things in the past and now the time of reckoning had come.

Wanda pressed the gun harder against Allyson's forehead, making her look up into her leering face. "I've been assigned by my Mistress to act as your executioner. You shouldn't never have fucked us over, bitch."

Allyson's eyes blinked in confusion. "Wh . . . ?"

Wanda's forefinger began to exert pressure on the 9mm's trigger. Allyson knew she was an instant away from dying. She should be praying to God for forgiveness in hopes that He might show her some mercy once she crossed to the other side. But instinct sent her mind scrambling to make sense of what Wanda had said.

It almost seemed as if . . .

BLAM!

Allyson screamed as the shot rang out, the blast echoing in the clearing as Wanda toppled backward and fell hard to the ground. Allyson remained frozen for a moment, unable at first to comprehend that she was still alive and that the person who'd meant to kill her had been struck down. Then she gasped as she heard heavy footsteps moving past her toward the fallen woman.

The soldier she'd glimpsed outside the mess hall knelt next to the woman he'd shot and felt for a pulse. Then he showed Allyson a grim expression and said, "She's dead."

Allyson nodded.

Then the world went fuzzy and she fell into unconsciousness.

CHAPTER THIRTEEN

The view from the balcony pleased her more with each passing day. A small, ramshackle community was rapidly taking shape out there in that alien desert, with numerous primitive huts and a handful of prefab buildings and trailers dotting the landscape. The huts functioned as the new living quarters for the slaves. The prefab buildings and trailers—which were surrounded by a chain-link fence tipped with barbed wire—housed the Black Brigade compound. Plans for the near future included the establishment of a large, open-air marketplace, drinking halls, and places of entertainment, where the live sex and torture shows once enjoyed by the Overlords of Below would be resurrected.

Giselle's intent was to fashion the incipient city into a bustling center of filth and decadence, of tawdry spectacle and ultimate corruption. She imagined the new community several months hence. A fully realized city of the damned. Used-up prostitutes bleeding to death in alleys, razor-wielding psychopaths prowling dark streets, murderers and petty criminals alike strung up from public gallows, children ripped from the arms of their parents and made to watch as mommy and daddy were raped and slaughtered in the streets by Black Brigade soldiers, and all-night fetish/torture sessions in a lounge reserved exclusively for an elite few in the Brigade's power structure.

The vividly imagined atrocities brought a smile to her face.

Beyond the embryonic city, hundreds of slaves clad only in loincloths and sandals continued to work at hauling huge slabs of stone toward the steadily rising structure just visible at the edge of the horizon. The technology and machinery necessary to greatly speed up the construction process was available, but, as with so many other things, Giselle preferred to do the job the old-fashioned way. She liked watching the slaves toil. But there was a purpose to the method beyond the simple joys of casual cruelty. The human misery honored the death gods, who drew sustenance from pain and gave power to those who appeased them. The city taking shape beneath her would also honor the death gods. Giselle would provide the old ones with a veritable feast of suffering and death, a nonstop carnivale of depravity unlike anything they'd seen before, eclipsing anything from Medieval times or modern war. Her forces were working continually to cull thousands of sacrifices from normal human communities, mostly the marginalized people no one in authority cared much about. Poor people. Prostitutes, runaways and drug addicts. This in addition to the handful of societal castaways who managed to find their way here by accident every year. Ms. Wickman had largely contented herself with the random strays who happened into her territory, but Giselle had no interest in conservatism. She was determined to be bold. To do big things, bigger even than the Master had ever envisioned.

She heard a click of heels behind her. A moment later Ursula was standing to her right, leaning over the balcony railing to stare intently at the bustling, busy forms a half mile below. "Wow, Razor City is really coming along."

Giselle glanced at her lover and smiled. "Yes. I enjoy watching it grow."

Ursula was wearing a long, cream-colored backless dress woven from a thin, clingy fabric. It adhered to the pronounced curves of her long, slender body in a way that made Giselle's breath quicken. Her hair was an almost white shade of blonde. It was long and straight and fell in a brilliant spray across the pale expanse of her back. Her flesh was the incandescent white of one who has spent nearly all her life indoors. That and her fine, regal features made her look like an ice queen from a fairy tale. Ursula turned her head to look at Giselle and the spray of hair across her back rippled and shifted, revealing a small birthmark on her left shoulder.

Ursula lifted an eyebrow. "Are you having naughty thoughts, Mistress?"

Giselle moved closer and laid a hand on her lover's back, enjoying the way Ursula shuddered slightly at her touch. "Perhaps." She moved her hand slowly over Ursula's back. "Are you in a mood to tempt me?"

Ursula licked her lips and said, "Always."

Giselle pulled the woman into a sudden embrace and kissed her with vigor. Ursula matched her hunger and grabbed at her hair, pulled her head back to kiss her throat and the hollow between her breasts. Then Giselle grabbed her by the hand and led her back into her quarters and the huge, plush bed they'd shared so many times over the last month. They disrobed quickly and fell upon each other in the bed, rolling over the soft sheets, limbs shifting and intertwining, mouths warm and seeking, hands rubbing and probing. A little later, when they lay sated and still in each other's arms, Giselle said, "I feel like giving you a present."

Ursula squealed with delight and sat up suddenly, bouncing up and down for a moment before exclaiming, "I *love* presents!"

Giselle smiled. "Would you like to play tonight?"

Ursula's eyes opened wide and an eager grin made her pale flesh almost glow. "We haven't played in *days*! Oh! Do I get to do whatever I want to our playmate?"

"Anything your heart desires."

"*Anything?* Seriously? Even . . ."

Giselle laughed. "Even that."

Ursula moved to the side of the bed and lifted a bell off a marble end table. "Should I ring for Mr. Schreck?" She shook the bell by its black handle (though not hard enough to produce a tone) and grinned. "Have him fetch one of the fresher arrivals, perhaps?"

Giselle pulled Ursula close again and stroked the girl's long, shimmering hair. Hair the color of sunshine. "You've wanted a playmate and you'll have one. But I want to properly show my affection for you. No mere slave will do."

Ursula gasped. "You can't mean . . . no, you can't, surely not. Do you mean . . ." She made a sound of exasperation. "Oh, I can't make myself say it."

Giselle clasped hands with Ursula. The younger girl's chest was heaving as she struggled to control a burgeoning euphoria. It was a lovely, delicious thing to see. "Darling, is there any one person you hate more than anything else in the world?"

Ursula's eyes blazed with a degree of intense excitement Giselle normally only glimpsed in the deepest throes of passion. "Gwendolyn."

Giselle smiled. "I thought as much. Which is why I've taken the liberty of planning ahead."

Ursula clapped her hands together and squealed. "Yes!"

Giselle got off the bed and strode quickly to a nearby wardrobe. She opened the wardrobe and withdrew a pink satin bathrobe, which she shrugged into and closed by loosely knotting the white sash at the waist. Then she crooked a finger at Ursula and said, "Follow me."

Ursula hopped off the bed and hurried to catch up with Giselle, who had just come to a stop at a blank patch of wall. "Why are we staring at this wall?" Ursula crossed slim arms beneath her breasts and frowned. "I want *Gwendolyn*."

"This is no ordinary wall, dear."

Ursula's frown deepened. "Stop teasing me and get on with it."

The girl's impatience made Giselle pause a moment longer. She wanted to spoil Ursula. Wanted to pamper her, give her everything she desired. But her behavior at the moment was a shade shy of outright insolence. She considered delaying gratification for Ursula a while longer, even briefly thought of withdrawing the gift altogether.

But Ursula must have sensed her anger because she suddenly smiled and said, "Please."

Most of Giselle's anger melted at the sight of that smile. She decided not to withhold the promised gift. She would discipline Ursula later.

"Very well."

She looked at the wall and focused her will. A dim, door-shaped outline formed in an instant, then quickly became more defined. She directed energy at the door and it began to move inward, revealing a wedge of darkness so black it seemed like a living thing, an unfathomable predator waiting with infinite patience to draw the unsuspecting into its sticky embrace. Giselle had a reflexive shudder of fear at the sight of it, but the sensation passed quickly. That strange dark energy was hers to command at will now. Once the door was fully open, she grasped one of Ursula's hands and was unsurprised to find it cold and trembling.

Ursula let out a shuddery breath. "I don't know if I want to go in there."

Giselle chuckled. "Nonsense."

Then she tightened her grasp on Ursula's hand and led her into that deep darkness. Despite the reassurances, the girl clutched at her as they moved further into the room, a helpless, barely audible whine issuing from the back of her throat. She shrieked when the heavy stone door behind them slammed shut with an echoing boom.

Giselle decided to show a measure of mercy and released a small energy pulse. An array of candles and torches sparked to life, columns of flame driving back the oppressive darkness in places.

Ursula cupped a hand over her eyes and blinked against the sudden glare. Then she glimpsed the small form huddled in a corner of the suspended cage and grinned. She let go of Giselle and moved to a spot almost directly beneath the slowly swinging cage. Her mouth opened wide as she stared in rapt awe at the sight of her imprisoned rival's nude—and only slightly bruised—body.

"So . . . beautiful." Her voice was low and reverent. "I can't believe she's really mine."

Giselle smiled. "Believe it. Nothing's too good for you."

Ursula abruptly came away from the cage and pulled Giselle into a rough embrace. "Thank you so much." She kissed her hard on the mouth, then beamed at her again. "I love you for this."

"You deserve it, Ursula." Giselle smiled. "I would do almost anything for you."

Ursula touched her face. "I know. You spoil me."

Then she stepped out of the embrace and moved back to her previous position under the cage. Giselle felt a small pang at her departure, craved the return of that special warmth. A troubled look crossed her face.

She had become one of the most powerful creatures on earth. *Nothing* should trouble her. She should be able to do as she pleased with impunity, with absolutely no concern for consequences. But she did worry about her deepening feelings for Ursula. In the immediate aftermath of killing Eddie, she'd believed herself to be cleansed of the capacity to feel things like love for other creatures. And in the beginning, she'd been able to believe that all she felt for Ursula was a simple animal lust.

Then a week passed and Ursula was still sharing her bed. A week after that it was apparent a real bond of some sort was forming between them, something beyond the obvious balance-of-power connection between Mistress and slave. And now, a full month after their first night together, they had progressed to a stage that could only be construed as romance. Given the way her heart seemed to swell against her chest wall every time Ursula so much as looked at her with a certain glint in her eyes, no other label for what was transpiring could be appropriate.

Yes, there could be little doubt now.

I'm falling in love with her, Giselle thought. *How stupid*.

Stupid because the very act of falling in love with a person carried with it an implicit vulnerability. It meant the other person in the relationship possessed the ability to hurt you more than any other person possibly could. The potential was there—albeit slight—for someone else to influence the girl against her. She was relatively certain that, despite being firmly under her thumb, every person in her employ was satisfied with their position here. One of the first things she'd done after assuming power was to identify potential troublemakers and purge them from the ranks. But it was just possible that someone who sought to avenge Ms. Wickman's death remained, and Giselle would be a fool to assume such a person would not at least entertain the notion of recruiting Ursula as an assassin. She doubted very much that the girl could be swayed to an enemy's side, given her newly exalted position, but one could not afford to be complacent about such things.

Ursula had retrieved a torch from one of the wall sconces and was raising it toward the unconscious form in the cage. The leading edge of the billowing flame licked at Gwendolyn's body, and Giselle cringed at the memory of the acetylene torch applied to her mutilated flesh in the back of a limo. Gwendolyn awoke with a shriek and jumped away from the searing heat, making the thick metal chain that held the cage suspended above the floor groan as the cage swayed wildly. Ursula laughed and shifted position beneath the cage, raising the flame again. There was a faint sizzle of burning meat as Gwendolyn danced away from the flame and began to plead for mercy. Giselle felt a tiny flicker of sympathy. Not so long ago she'd been in the same position. Desperate, her spirit broken, her dignity gone.

An intense sense of déjà vu made Giselle want to leave the concealed dungeon at once. Ursula danced beneath the swaying cage, raising the torch again and again as she grinned and giggled at Gwendolyn's tears and cries of pain. The delight she took in her adversary's pain made Giselle think about vulnerability again.

The smart thing to do would be to eliminate the potential threat engendered by her feelings for Ursula. Kill her. Or cast her out to the slave city, which might be even worse for her. But even as she considered these ideas Giselle knew she would not harm her lover. There were other, less lethal precautions she could take. They weren't as foolproof as death, granted, but they would be better than nothing.

"Ursula."

"Yes, Mistress?"

Giselle kept her voice even and her face expressionless as she said, "There are some things I must attend to. In the meantime, I'll leave you to play with your toy. I'll leave the door open in case you need to leave, okay?"

Ursula nodded. "Okay." She smiled. "Thank you again. I can't tell you how much this means to me. I . . . love you."

Giselle's heart raced. "I love you, too."

Then she turned away from Urusla and strode out of the dark place. Back in her quarters, she hesitated a moment, considering whether she should simply close the door and seal Ursula inside forever.

But the girl's words came floating back to her: *I . . . love you.*

And Giselle again was unsurprised to find she still lacked the will to implement an obvious solution to her dilemma. She would instead summon Schreck and have some simple restraints affixed to the big bed.

But something else caused her to delay summoning Schreck. It was the other thing that worried her and which she strove not to think about. An inexplicable thing. She approached the full-length oval mirror that stood next to her wardrobe and stared at her reflection for a long moment, her hands clasped tightly just below the sash. The pink bathrobe didn't look good on her. She was meant for darker shades. But that, of course, wasn't the thing that was bothering her.

She sighed. *Oh, just do it!*

She untied the sash with fingers that trembled slightly and pulled the front of the robe open. She stared for a moment at her full breasts and flat stomach, then she turned to her side and allowed the robe to slide down her arms to her elbows.

It was still there.

A month ago her back had been a smooth expanse of pure white. But now much of that flesh was covered with a large and intricate tattoo of a dragon. The same tattoo she'd seen on Ms. Wickman's back. She'd seen it the morning after Ms. Wickman's death, glimpsing it in a mirror after her bath. The sight of it, unexpected as it was, had almost stopped her heart then. And it still scared her. She had no idea what the tattoo's appearance on her flesh might mean. It didn't seem to be affecting her in any obvious way, but, as always, it wasn't the obvious things that worried Giselle.

She abruptly pulled the robe back over her shoulders and tied the sash. There was nothing to be done about it. It was probably a harmless consequence of having devoured the dead woman's magic when she ate her heart.

She turned away from the mirror and summoned Schreck.

Somewhere on the other side of the world, a slim woman wearing a black shirt and black slacks entered a dimly lit room. Her bare feet whispered across carpet as she approached a man who sat cross-legged on the floor. The man's eyes were closed. He was meditating. The woman waited in respectful silence until the man's eyes opened and he acknowledged her presence.

She bowed her head and presented him with an envelope, which he accepted with finely wrinkled fingers as dry as crepe paper. The man flipped the envelope over and saw that it bore the seal of the Order of the Dragon. He winced slightly at the sight of it. The Order normally preferred to conduct its business in more subtle ways. The arrival of this letter could only be a portent of darker, more dangerous times to come. He didn't need to read the letter to know this.

He nonetheless tore the envelope open, unfolded the single crisp sheet of paper it contained, and read the two paragraphs with mounting fury. The intent of the letter was twofold—to serve as a summons and to inform him of the passing of a member of the Order. The old man stood and moved to a table upon which was an ornate sword in a scabbard and a single flickering candle in a silver holder. He fed both letter and envelope to the flame, watched as they turned to black ash and fell to the table's polished surface. Then he removed the sword from the scabbard and held the blade upright before him. He ran the ball of a thumb along the edge of the blade. The sharp edge nicked his flesh and a thin stream of scarlet ran down the blade.

The anger coursing through his body invigorated him, made him feel like a much younger man. He turned away from the table and quickly crossed the room. The other man in the room cringed at his approach, but he could not get out of the way of the doom bearing down on him. This other man was tied to the only chair in the room. The rubber ball in his mouth muffled his screams as he watched the long, flashing blade arc toward him. And then he felt nothing as the blade separated his head from his body.

The old man watched blood erupt from the neck stump and felt nothing. The anger that had possessed him a moment ago had deserted him. Nor did he feel remorse for the life he'd taken, which was only the latest of hundreds. He summoned servants to dispose of the body. The slim woman in black returned and asked if he had any orders for her.

He did.

Beginning with the scheduling of his first trip to North America since World War I.

CHAPTER FOURTEEN

The lighting in the dingy gas station bathroom left something to be desired. The single low-wattage bulb in the exposed ceiling socket flickered and buzzed. Marcy leaned over a sink covered with mildew and studied the dye job Ellen had helped her with in a fleabag motel outside of Newark the night before. The jet-black shade made her vaguely resemble Dream. She didn't have the supermodel face and figure Dream possessed, but she didn't look bad. She could almost pass for Dream's slightly less-blessed younger sister. The important thing was she bore little resemblance to the high school era pictures of herself that had appeared on CNN and the front pages of newspapers across the country.

Now she touched up her eyeshadow and applied a dark red lipstick. She returned the lipstick and eyeshadow to her purse. Then she moved to the bathroom's single toilet, dropped her jeans, and squatted on the cold seat. As she relieved herself, a fat cockroach moved across the blue-and-white floor tiles. The place was a pit, but she'd become inured to unsanitary conditions during her month and a half on the run. You couldn't very well stay at the Hyatt when you were trying to fly under the radar.

Alicia was waiting outside when she exited the bathroom a moment later, shifting her weight from foot to foot. She glared at Marcy as she barged past her. "What were you doing in there? Counting the fucking tiles?"

Then she was gone, the gray metal door slamming shut behind her. Marcy sighed and shook her head as she moved across the parking lot toward the old van. Alicia's progress from freakshow walking corpse to fully functioning living woman still wigged her out. The formerly dead woman hadn't required drink or food for weeks. Then, as she began to "heal," normal human appetites reasserted themselves. At first she'd only nibbled on fries and sipped at fast-food sodas. But now she consumed full, regular meals and guzzled jugs of Red Bull and vodka like a nightclub slut. Very little visible evidence of her original corpselike appearance remained. There was one faint little scar just above her collarbone, but Marcy suspected even that would be gone soon.

Marcy stepped through the van's open side door and slid into the seat next to Dream, who sat slumped against the window on her side. She clutched a bottle of Boone's Farm wine in her hands, holding it tightly against her chest. Her eyes were bloodshot and an odor of alcohol clung to her like a second skin. She smiled weakly as she glimpsed Marcy sitting next to her. "Hey, girl." She offered the bottle. "Have a drink."

Marcy accepted the bottle from Dream's shaking hands and put it to her mouth. She tilted her head back and let the warm wine wash down her throat. Then she passed the bottle back to Dream and wiped her mouth. "Thanks."

Dream sipped from the bottle and leaned her head against the window again. She looked through the window at the gray sky and the cars passing by on the wet street beyond the gas station parking lot. "Where are we now?"

"Back in New York. Near Rochester."

Dream grunted. "We ought to go south."

"That's where you're from, right?"

Dream nodded without shifting her gaze from the dreary view. "Yeah. Good ol' Tennessee. But anywhere in the South would be good. It's so cold and dark and nasty here all the fucking time." Her tone was laced with melancholy. It was how she always sounded these days. "I wanna go where I can feel the warm sun on my skin. And smell flowers . . ."

Marcy watched Dream's eyes flutter closed as her voice drifted. She gently pried the wine bottle from Dream's numb fingers to keep it from falling to the floor. The van's interior already smelled enough like an accident at a liquor store. She put the bottle to her lips again and drank as she watched Dream drowse. She was even more beautiful in repose. In sleep the demons haunting her weren't so apparent, and in these moments Marcy fancied she was seeing Dream as she'd been years ago, back before her life had turned into a perpetual horror show. She looked at her closely now and tried to imagine her with the longer blonde hair she remembered from the old newspaper pictures. It was easy to picture and part of her ached for Dream, for what she'd lost. Yes, she was still pretty now, but she was harder inside than she'd been and that showed in the lines at the corners of her eyes and mouth. The hard living was taking its toll.

"Has she passed out again?"

Marcy watched the gentle rise and fall of Dream's chest. "Yeah." She held the bottle toward the front seat. "You want a hit of this?"

Ellen was ensconced behind the wheel of the van. Early on in their quixotic quest she'd assumed the role of driver. It gave her something to do. And Ellen having a defined role in the scheme of things was good. This little bit of structure helped keep her balanced in the midst of the insanity swirling around her. She'd also changed her hair, letting it grow out some and dropping the mix of blonde and black in favor of a dark shade of auburn. The new look brought out her features and made her more attractive, which had also served to boost her confidence. Marcy liked that. Little sister was a mousy doormat no more.

She'd only relinquished her position as driver once in recent weeks. That being when Alicia had briefly taken over in the aftermath of the Rainbow Bridge incident. Alicia remained behind the wheel as they followed the course of the river, tracking Dream's downstream progress via some internal means Marcy couldn't comprehend. Marcy remembered how she'd fretted over the course of that grim hour, worrying that Dream's confidence in her ability to negotiate the rapids had been unfounded, that she'd drowned out there in those cold depths. But Alicia kept going, staying as close to the water as possible. And then they'd seen her, sopping wet and sitting cross-legged in the grass by the side of the road. Shivering and smiling in a vacant way as she waited for them.

Ellen turned from the steering wheel and stared through the gap between the front seats. "We should get out of here."

Marcy frowned as Ellen took the bottle. "What?"

Ellen sipped some wine. "You heard me. We should toss Dream out while she's unconscious and that freaky bitch is away."

Marcy shot a nervous glance back toward the gas station. No sign of Alicia. And the bathroom door was still shut. She frowned and looked at Ellen again. "Why would we do that?"

Ellen rolled her eyes. "Because something bad will happen if we don't. Duh. We might even get ourselves killed trying to find these people Alicia is after."

Marcy's frown deepened. "So . . . you want to ditch our friends and step out of the line of fire? That's kind of a shitty thing to do. Cowardly, even."

"They're not our friends." Ellen's tone was thick with exasperation. "You seem to have forgotten that somewhere along the way. We had some real friends, but you fucking killed them all. Remember?"

Marcy's expression hardened. "They would have gone to the police. They would have ruined everything." Her hands curled into tight fists. She didn't like talking about this, and Ellen fucking well knew it. "And anyway, I'm really only talking about Dream. I don't care what you think about her. She's my friend. I won't abandon her. I sure as shit won't leave her alone with Alicia."

Ellen scowled. "I can't believe you. How anyone can go from wanting to kill a person to being their best pal is beyond me."

"I'm not asking you to understand it. Just accept it."

"Unfuckingbelievable." Ellen passed the nearly empty wine bottle back to Marcy. "Take this shit. It's awful."

Marcy took the bottle and drank from it again. She wouldn't admit it out loud, but she knew her sister had a point. They were well out of their league. Yes, the impulsive murders she'd committed at the farmhouse constituted a spectacular lapse of sanity. But anyone could snap and go off like that. It happened several times every year. Regular, everyday people who suddenly lose it and shoot up a schoolroom or workplace, with images of the aftermath beamed into your living room courtesy of CNN and Fox News. But these were tragedies rooted in the real world. They were almost mundane, despite the immense horror and grief suffered by the survivors and loved ones. There was nothing the least mundane about Dream Weaver and Alicia Jackson.

She looked at Dream and thought about that night

on Rainbow Bridge. That was when it had all changed for Marcy. In many ways it had been an awful and tragic evening, but for Marcy it had also possessed a kind of strange and dark beauty. She recalled with a shiver the *frisson* of that moment just before Dream had taken her dive into the river, a sudden shock of recognition that had passed between them, an awareness that beneath the hate and their differences they were kindred souls. Marcy couldn't explain it to Ellen in any way that didn't make it sound like she had some kind of dippy girlcrush on Dream. That wasn't the case. Rather, she understood Dream and her compulsions. She'd come to feel more closely bonded to Dream than she ever had to her own flesh-and-blood sister. So, no, she would not abandon Dream. If necessary, she would follow her to the ends of the earth. With or without Ellen.

Dream stirred and lifted her head off the frosty window. She looked at Marcy through bleary eyes and smiled. "Have I told you how good your hair looks like that?"

Marcy blushed. "Yeah. A few times. But thanks again."

Dream took the bottle from her and knocked back a belt. She looked at the bottle and shook it. "We're gonna need more booze soon."

"I saw a liquor store back down that way." Marcy nodded at the road. "We could stock up before heading out to the highway again."

Dream yawned and stretched. "Sounds good."

Ellen sighed. "Wonderful."

Marcy felt her anger come back in a rush. She leaned forward in her seat and thumped the back of the driver's seat. "Something you want to say, Ellen?"

Ellen met her sister's gaze in the tilted rearview mirror. "Yes. You're all drinking too much. It's not a moral fucking judgment or anything. I'm just worried someone will get sloppy and somehow make a cop look at us a little too hard."

Dream drained the rest of the Boone's Farm and flung the empty bottle through the gap between seats. It exploded on the dash, making Ellen shriek and jump in her seat.

Then Dream was laughing. "Sloppy like that, you mean?"

Ellen sat very still for a moment. Marcy's heart pounded as she waited to see how her sister would react to the sudden violence. Then Ellen undid her seat belt and reached for the door handle. "Fuck this, I'm out of here."

The humor drained from Dream's face at once. "Stay."

Ellen's hand froze on the handle. "Please. I can't do this anymore."

"You can and you will." Dream's voice was cold. Devoid of compassion. "I don't want to hurt you, Ellen. So put your seat belt back on. Please."

Marcy let out a relieved breath as Ellen relinquished her hold on the door handle and did as instructed. Though her loyalties had shifted somewhat, she didn't want to see her sister suffer. And Ellen would damn well suffer if she resisted Dream's will.

"That's better." Dream pushed up out of her seat and moved into the gap between the front seats. Marcy couldn't see Ellen now, but she heard the other girl gasp. Then Dream went to her knees between the seats and laid a hand on Ellen's arm. "Listen up. I know you don't like me and I guess I can't blame you for that. But you're gonna have to work at putting all that shit behind you, because we're a family now."

"*Right.*" Ellen's tone dripped sarcasm.

"Yes, a *family*, goddammit." Marcy hadn't heard Dream speak with such conviction in weeks, if ever.

Okay, we were forced together by circumstance. It's a fate thing, you see. And so we're like any other clan—we don't get to choose family. And you don't run out on family. Do you understand what I'm trying to say?"

Marcy blinked tears from her eyes. "I do."

"I know you do, Marcy. I'm proud of you. We're sisters, all of us. I love you like I would a birth sibling." Dream moved further into the gap between seats. "So I want to feel the same commitment from you, Ellen, and know you're in it to the end, too."

Ellen didn't respond at first. Marcy leaned forward and saw that her hands were locked in a death grip on the steering wheel. Then her sister's head dipped forward and touched the hard molded plastic. She sniffled once, her shoulders heaving. Then the floodgates opened and her body quaked with a series of sobs. Dream stroked her back and made sounds of reassurance. Marcy wiped hot moisture from her cheeks. Nothing had ever moved her as strongly as Dream's speech. Never had anyone so plainly expressed love for her. She swiped at her eyes again, then a flicker of something in her peripheral vision made her head snap to the right.

Alicia was there, standing just outside the open side door. Her mouth was twisted in a smirk. "Sheesh, I go away for ten minutes and you fuckers start writin' your own motherfuckin' Lifetime movie."

Marcy turned up a middle finger and extended it.

Alicia's smirk deepened. "Crying fits and obscene gestures." She opened the front passenger door and began to pull herself inside. "Time for the Estrogen Express to hit the road before one of you bitches starts quoting lines from *Thelma and Louise* or some dumb thing."

She paused at the sight of the glass shards sprayed across the front seat area. "I missed some kind of drama, I guess." She looked hard at Dream, her dark eyes flat and unreadable. "Anything I need to be worried about, Dream?"

Dream did not wilt beneath that unforgiving gaze. Her lips curved upward. "Of course not. Just having an old-fashioned heart-to-heart with Ellen. I think we've come to an understanding." Her eyes flicked toward the still-sniffling girl. "Haven't we, Ellen?"

Ellen at last managed to compose herself. She lifted her head off the steering wheel and wiped her face dry with a sleeve. Then she did something that astonished Marcy—she looked Alicia in the eye as steadily as Dream had a moment ago and said, "That's right. I had a weak moment."

Alicia's trademark smirk returned. "Latest in a long, long series, I'd say."

"That's right." Ellen reached for Dream and clasped hands with her. "And Dream called me on it. Think what you want, but I see things differently now. Wherever this road takes us, I want to be there. I want to see what's at the end of it."

Alicia picked glass shards off the passenger seat and tossed them on the parkling lot asphalt. "Whatever, Dorothy." A small piece of glass nicked the ball of her thumb and drew blood. She popped it in her mouth and sucked on it. "Mmm." She withdrew the glistening digit and stared at it. "I don't know exactly what's at the end of our yellow brick road, but I know it's a bad place, a place like the one where I died."

Marcy said, "The House of Blood."

Alicia wiped her thumb on her jeans and climbed into the van. She pulled the door shut and turned in her seat to look at Marcy. "That's right, girl. And I know one more thing. There'll definitely be a wicked witch waiting for us when we get there."

Marcy shoved her hands into the pockets of her

brown hoodie and slumped further down in her seat. "Ms. Wickman."

"Damn straight."

Marcy's brow furrowed. "And you're sure you can kill her."

"Ain't sure about shit. But I'll either kill the bitch or die trying."

Marcy's mouth twisted in a humorless smile. "That'd have to be a real kick in the ass. Dying twice at the hands of the same person."

Alicia scowled. "I don't—"

"Any a you ladies spare some change?"

Marcy jumped at the sound of the gravelly voice and turned to look at the homeless guy standing outside the van. He smelled like a sewer and Marcy was surprised he'd gotten this close undetected. He had limp brown hair tucked under a ratty New Jersey Devils cap. His face was seamed and his nose sat like a swollen red ball in the center of his face. He wore a heavily stained yellow windbreaker over raggedy clothes.

He leaned in through the open door and sniffed. "Smells like wine in here. Good stuff. 'Spose I could get a taste?"

Ellen piped up from the driver's seat. "Fuck off."

"We don't have anything for you, bum." Alicia directed her eerily intense gaze at the old drunk. "I'd advise you to leave before you stir up trouble you can't handle."

The man sneered at her, displaying a mouth missing most of its teeth. "Whaaaaat?" He drew out the syllable and laughed. "You ladies don' wanna tussle wit' the likes a me. Tell ya that much." He leaned further into the van and his rheumy eyes roamed over its interior. "Aw shit, just gimme a bit of pocket change and I'll be on my way."

Marcy shifted in her seat and turned slightly to the

right. The bum's aggressiveness stirred an old memory. That night in Overton Park. The homeless guy. The bottle. The first time she'd taken a life. Her fists clenched at the edges of the seat.

"Say, you bitches look kinda familiar." The bum scratched at a cheek with long nails turned brown with infection. "Yeah." He waved in the general direction of the convenience store. "Over there at the paper boxes, last week I think it was." He looked at Marcy and squinted. "I seen you staring out at me. You the one killed all those kids. Maybe I oughta go to the cops, huh?"

The atmosphere in the van turned frigid. Marcy's heart raced as a paralyzing sense of panic began to set in. This was it, then. The end of the road. But it wasn't right. Their journey wasn't over. Not even close. Anger rose inside her.

The old guy sneered again and said, "Or maybe I'll keep my mouth shut if that one—" He nodded at Dream. "She gives my pecker a good suck and I'll keep quiet. Come on, bitch. Whatcha say?"

Dream surged past Marcy, seized the bum by the front of his black sweatshirt, lifted him off his feet, and pulled him inside the van. He yelped and flailed a little until Dream slammed the top of his head against the closed door on her side. The man went limp and Dream cradled him in her arms like a child. Her eyes pulsed with cold energy as she looked at Marcy. "Close the door."

Marcy swallowed a lump in her throat and nodded, then shut the door.

And then she watched in horrified fascination as Dream closed her hands around the unconscious man's neck and began to twist.

A man in a powder blue 1970s Plymouth set his paper coffee mug in the plastic cup holder he'd purchased at a truck stop the previous night. The cup holder was clipped inside the ash tray and dipped precariously as it accepted the mug's weight. He hated the old jalopy, but the people in charge said it was better for tailing people than something new and flashy. The man disagreed. He thought the old piece of shit stuck out like a sore, infected thumb, but what did he know, he was just a goon with a gun.

A creepy three-fingered kid named Dean sat in the passenger seat. He kept playing with his favorite knife, running the edge of the blade over the fabric of his jeans, up and down his inner thigh, over and over. The kid was a world-class geek, but he was stone psycho and a merciless killer.

"What do you reckon the odds are we just got ol' Ducky killed?"

The corners of the kid's mouth lifted slightly. It had been his idea to send the old bum over to check things out. Ostensibly, the plan had been for "Ducky," as he called himself, to report back to them with his findings, but that looked to be out the window. "He's dead. I can feel it."

The man nodded and removed a pack of smokes from his shirt pocket. He tapped a Winston out and wedged it in a corner of his mouth. "I reckon you're right, boy. So what do you think? Seems pretty certain these are the ones the Mistress wants."

The boy licked his dry lips. "Yeah."

The van's tail lights came on and the van began to glide out toward the street just as the man was applying a lighter flame to his cigarette. "Oh, shit."

He flipped the lighter shut and tossed it onto the dashboard. Then he twisted the key in the ignition and listened to the engine groan. He twisted it again and got a rattle. He looked up and saw the van cross the intersection and pick up speed.

"Fuck!"

The kid was looking at him now. The big knife was pointed vaguely in his direction. "It better start."

The man spoke around the cigarette: "No shit."

He was trying hard not to sound afraid, but inside he was coming apart. He couldn't afford to blow this. Not when they were so close. He knew the kid was just looking for an excuse to gut him and resume the chase on his own. So he sent out a silent prayer and twisted the key again.

The engine sputtered, caught, and roared to life.

He let out a big breath and grinned at the kid. "Have faith, kid. They ain't gettin' away."

He gunned the engine and the car lurched forward.

CHAPTER FIFTEEN

The night was cold, the chill cutting easily through her sweater and the shirt beneath. Allyson scooted closer to the crackling campfire and rubbed her hands together. The warmth from the fire helped, but all in all she'd rather be back inside, huddled beneath a blanket with Chad's naked body spooned against her back. But Camp Whiskey's inhabitants had warmed to her somewhat in the aftermath of her close call in the woods. This was the first time she'd been invited to hang out at one of these little gatherings of what she still thought of as the "inner circle," and she was determined to make the best of the rare social outing. She wanted them to see that she was a good person, a friendly and warm person, and that none of them had anything to fear from her.

Hell, she just wanted to fit in.

Someone on the opposite side of the campfire strummed an acoustic guitar and the low babble of conversation abruptly ceased. The man with the guitar was sitting cross-legged and was wearing a heavy denim-and-wool coat. Jim was stretched out on the ground next to him, but now he sat up and withdrew a harmonica from a pocket of his brown shirt. Firelight glinted on the polished silver surface of the instrument as Jim brought it to

his mouth and began to blow. The guitar player intensified his strumming and the two soon found a bluesy
rhythm that made Allyson bob her head as she listened.
The jam went on for a few minutes. Then Jim lowered the
harmonica and began to sing.

A shiver went up her spine at the sound of his voice.
Chad returned from his trip to the outhouse and sat
next to her, draping an arm around her shoulders. She
snuggled closer and laid her head on his shoulder.

Jim paused in his singing to blow a few more bluesy
notes on the harmonica. Then the old singer surged to
his feet and belted out the song's chorus with a passion
that was exhilarating to see:

"Devil come a'risin'
Devil gonna come
Devil on the highwaaaaaaaaay
Devil on the way"

Jim's whole body was moving. Or at least that's the
way it looked to Allyson from the other side of the
campfire. He was doing a kind of Ray Charles headroll
while the rest of his body rocked to the beat the gui-
tarist was now thumping out on the body of his guitar.
Jim looked like a man possessed as that beat intensified, his facial features twisting and twitching, his hands
held out before him in a kind of supplication. Allyson
watched the performance with mounting awe. There
was an undeniable electricity in the air. And no wonder. The man was a legend for good reason.

The beat slowed but grew heavier, the other guy slapping the guitar's body with the flat of his palms as Jim
resumed singing:

"Devil come a'risin'
Devil gonna come

Devil at the crossroads
Think I might explode"

Jim abruptly raised a clenched fist high in the air and struck a rigid pose. The guitar player ceased his thumping, shifted the guitar in his lap, and began picking out a subdued, haunting melody, a series of wistful notes that felt like a cold breeze rolling across an open plain.

Jim slowly lowered his fist and finished the song in an equally subdued manner:

"Reckon time has come to pay that bill
Devil comin' up that hill
Lord, I always knew this day would come
Time to get . . . gone."

The last word was spoken rather than sung. Jim lowered his head and held his hands clasped before him as the guy with the guitar plucked a few final notes, the last of which seemed to hang suspended in the air for a long, achingly lovely moment. Then it was gone and there was just the sound of the campfire and the ambient noises of the wilderness at night.

Allyson released a breath she hadn't realized she'd been holding.

A young woman to her left said, "That was incredible. What was that?"

Chad craned his head to look past Allyson. "That was 'Pay The Devil,' an old blues standard."

Jim was still standing on the other side of the fire. He put the harmonica away and tapped a cigarette from a pack. "Man's correct. Blind Cat Jones's version from the 1930s is probably the best known." He lit the cigarette and rolled it into a corner of his mouth. "Used to have it on an old 78." He smiled around the cigarette and blew out a puff of smoke. "Long gone now, like most things from my past."

Allyson surprised herself by speaking up. "I've heard that." She met Jim's gaze across the campfire and felt goose bumps form on her flesh as the corners of his mouth lifted in a small smile. "Years ago I saw a PBS documentary about delta blues. Blind Cat's version was beautiful, but yours was just amazing."

Jim exhaled more smoke. "My humble thanks to you, Allyson. And now, if you good people don't mind, I'll be retiring for the evening."

He flipped the cigarette butt into the fire and began to move back in the direction of the cabins. A pair of machine-gun-toting men in camos fell in behind him and trailed him down the slope. Some of the others seated around the fire gathered their things and began to make their exits as well. Allyson stayed where she was, watching Jim and his guards move in and out of shadows as they moved downhill. He disappeared through a door when they reached their destination and the guards moved to flanking positions at each side of the little cabin. She wondered what his inner life must be like. Did he live wholly in the present, or did he spend a lot of time thinking about the lost glories of his past? Did he ever regret the strange path he'd embarked upon in the early part of the 1970s? She hoped to talk to him about these things at some point. She suspected there was much he could teach her about coping with regret.

Allyson and Chad eventually joined the slow-motion exodus, rising to their feet and walking hand-in-hand toward their own cabin.

The bottle of Beam was calling to him again. Jim dropped the cigarettes and harmonica on a table and picked the bottle up by the neck. He looked at the brown liquid inside the bottle. The stuff didn't control him as completely as it had in his youth—he'd be dead for real otherwise—but booze remained a significant factor in his life. He'd reduced his daily intake to a small fraction of what it had once been, both to improve his health and prepare for the struggle he knew was on the horizon. But sweet lady alcohol was always there in the background. He drank at a measured pace throughout the day, careful to never get too intoxicated. At night he would indulge a little more deeply, but even then he remained cognizant of his responsibilities.

He was a leader now. But more than that, a symbol of a past victory for the refugees from Below. They would naturally look to him for inspiration and guidance. It was a role in which he still felt some discomfort. Within him there yet lurked a faint spark of the wild spirit that had driven him to such reckless extremes in the past. That part of him wanted to down the whole bottle of Beam, consequences be damned.

He spun the cap off the bottle and brought the neck to his lips. The booze filled his mouth and he savored the sweet taste for a moment before swallowing. A little shiver of pleasure rippled through him. Then he took another little sip, screwed the cap back on, and returned the bottle to the table.

A faint sound from the other side of the room made him turn around. There was no one there. But he'd heard it, of that he was certain. A woman's voice. He sighed. He occasionally heard voices when he was alone. Sometimes he could even make out words. Once in a great while the voice was distinct enough to recognize. And always it was someone who could not actually be there, at least not in a physical form. These were people from his distant past he knew to be long dead, ghosts he supposed he would carry with him until his final days.

But this was different. He wasn't certain why, but he

felt it on a level that resonated in his bones. A little tingle of fear started at the base of his spine and worked its way up. Instinct drove him to pick up the bottle again. This time when he screwed the cap off, he tossed it on the table and drank deeply from the bottle. The influx of booze settled him and drove back the chill. He carried the bottle by the neck as he paced the width and length of the small room, paranoia driving him to conduct a search, even though there was plainly no place for an intruder to hide.

Except . . .

He dropped to his knees, grunting as the old joints creaked. He lifted the edge of a blanket and peered beneath the small bed. No one was there, of course, with the exception of a few crawly bugs and his personal effects. The tattered old backpack he'd carried on his travels through Europe and Africa in the 70s. Two boxes, a small one and a somewhat larger one filled with some of his favorite books. He sighed and stood again. He moved to the other side of the bed and sat down. He swigged from the bottle one more time before setting it on the floor. Then he reached beneath the bed and withdrew the smaller of the two boxes, an old cigar box with a length of twine tied around it. He untied the loose knot and flipped the lid open.

The box contained an assortment of faded pictures and other mementos of the life he'd left behind so long ago. He'd carried it with him everywhere for decades, even Below, where most of the banished people were stripped of their personal belongings. But though the box was important to him, only in his most melancholy moments did he remove its contents to examine and reflect upon. The last time had been more than a year ago, when he'd first heard rumblings of the threat that was out there.

In the time since then, he'd worked hard to prepare

for the coming confrontation, and the heavily fortified Camp Whiskey was the fruit of those labors. The goal had been to establish a haven impenetrable by any enemy. Thanks to the resources and contacts of Jack Paradise, the community enjoyed the protection of a small but world-class army. The camp should undeniably be the safest place for the survivors of Below. And yet there remained intangibles that might yet make them vulnerable, things they couldn't anticipate.

Things like the treachery of Wanda Lewis, who had once been a significant player in the plot that ended the Master's reign of terror. Jim could not imagine how so strong a woman had been swayed to the other side. He had taken her loyalty for granted and bringing her into the fold had been a priority. But she'd been unusually difficult to locate, even given the slippery nature of many House of Blood survivors. She resurfaced a month before her attempt on Allyson Vanover's life, explaining that she'd been busy eluding a particularly tenacious group of would-be assassins. Which seemed a believable enough cover story. But Jim began to hear reports of some strange behavior on Wanda's part. She was seen talking to herself, appearing to have animated conversations with people who weren't there. Once she was spotted engaging in a paganistic prayer ritual in the woods. There was nothing worthy of condemnation in these behaviors, but they were far enough removed from the Wanda Lewis he'd known to be troubling. And so Jack Paradise had passed along instruction to the soldiers to keep a watchful eye on her. Which had turned out to be a good thing for Allyson Vanover.

He was thankful Allyson was still with them. He had a strong feeling there was more to her story than she was willing to share. The question of why Wanda had attempted to kill her remained unanswered and presented a host of bothersome questions. Allyson's account of things had been too vague to provide any real answers. But his gut told him Allyson was not a threat. She clearly loved Chad, and Jim sensed she was struggling toward an inner change for the better. He could appreciate that.

As he sorted through the stack of mementos—mostly age-yellowed photographs—Jim reflected on the uncountable number of mistakes he'd made in his life. At the top of that list, as ever, was the impetuous decision to "kill" his public persona. He'd felt so overwhelmed then, with the press and their lies, with evading an American court system determined to make him serve hard time for a supposed act of public indecency, and with the pressure to record a new album that could never live up to ludicrously high expectations. And, of course, his judgment had been clouded by the drugs, enough so that faking his death and going underground had seemed a perfectly reasonable way out. He'd like to go back to that time and force his younger self not to go down that road. In the first few years after his "death," he'd occasionally entertained notions of resurfacing. But something always held him back. Then, as the years stretched into decades, he began to realize he would never return to public life. For better or worse, this twilight existence was his lot.

He came to a picture of Pam, his old love, and his eyes misted. The picture showed her seated outside a cafe in Paris, not long before the end of his old life. She was looking away, not wanting to be photographed. She had just learned of the crazy thing he was planning and was unhappy about it. He wanted so much to talk to her again, tell her she'd been right, that he'd made a horrible mistake. But she was dead and beyond reach now. He touched the photo with the tip of a shaking finger and imagined he could feel the softness of her flesh again. The photo slipped from his fingers and tumbled

to the dusty cabin floor. He was reaching to retrieve it
when he caught sight of the photograph that had been
beneath it.

His heart lurched.

And now the entire stack of old photos and mementos slipped from his suddenly numb fingers and fluttered across the floor. The new photo—the one he
knew had never been there before—landed upright
amidst a sea of white. He felt a tightness in his chest as
he looked at it again. The picture showed a nude
woman on a plush bed. Her eyes were glassy and her
face was twisted in a frozen expression of agony. She
had been disemboweled by some means not immediately apparent. Blood was everywhere and a small loop
of intestine was visible. Jim forced himself to look beyond the gore for some hint as to why an interloper had
seen fit to insert the gruesome photograph in the middle of a stack of older pictures he looked at so rarely. At
first no obvious solution presented itself. But then he realized there was something familiar about the dead
woman . . .

His stomach knotted as the realization hit him:
"Ms. Wickman—"

The wicked witch was dead. The proof was at his feet.
This should be cause for celebration. Surely there was
no longer anything to fear now that she was gone. Why,
then, did he not feel like celebrating? But he knew why,
really. It was the inexplicable appearance of the picture.
That and simple instinct. Something very wrong was
happening and he didn't have the first clue what it
might be. An unacceptable state of affairs. The thing to
do now was summon Jack Paradise and begin an investigation.

But first . . .

He was reaching for the bottle of Beam when he felt
a weight settle on the bed behind him. He tensed,

expecting to feel the blade of an assassin slide beneath his rib cage at any moment. It should have been impossible, even for the stealthiest of assassins. The windows were boarded up. The front door, flanked by heavily armed guards, was the only way in or out of the little cabin. Logic dictated this was someone who'd been here all along. He could only assume the intruder had employed some magical means of cloaking their presence.

The intruder was closer now. He could feel her breath on the back of his neck. That the intruder was a woman was a thing he sensed on a primitive level. He knew he should leap to his feet and make a break for the door, but his feet felt nailed to the floor. He was as incapable of movement as a statue—and would remain so until the intruder released him from this paralyzed state.

Anger flared inside him. "Stop fucking around and do it."

Then he felt the cold sting of a large blade laid flat across his throat and closed his eyes. No need to wonder how it would feel. He'd had a would-be assassin's blade in his body before, back during his time Below. He'd survived that attempt on his life, but he sensed this would be different. And less clumsy. This blade would open his carotid and his blood would splash across the spilled evidence of his formerly exalted place in the world.

The intruder leaned against him. A pair of soft lips pressed against his ear. And a voice, wholly unfamiliar, whispered the following: "Don't you want to live?"

Jim swallowed hard. "Why are you toying with me?"

The woman turned the blade, pressed the sharp side to his trembling flesh. "Answer my question." Her free hand slithered like a snake around his midsection and moved to his crotch, where it grasped and squeezed. "Answer . . . Jim. Or I'll cut this off and feed it to you."

"Honest answer . . . I don't know."

The woman slid off the bed to stand before him. Jim's brow knitted in confusion at the sight of the stranger. She was wearing a black *gi*. She was slim and small, maybe two or three inches over five feet. Her features were Asian, though her voice had been smooth and inflectionless.

"Who the hell are you?"

She knelt before him and snatched up the picture of Ms. Wickman's gutted body. "I am of the Order of the Dragon. My name is not important." She waved the picture at him. "I am here to speak to you about this. And to make a proposition."

Jim realized the woman had relinquished her psychic grip on him. He grabbed the Jim Beam bottle and chugged from it. Then he sighed and wiped his mouth with the back of a hand. "Does this proposition involve any sort of threat to my people?"

"It involves the removal of a threat. For my organization, it is a matter of vengeance. This may mean sacrifices. You will have to decide how high a price the removal of this threat is worth."

An ache began behind Jim's eyes as a familiar spiritual pain lanced him. For maybe the millionth time, he wished he'd not chosen to assume a position of leadership. He loathed being the man who had to make life and death decisions for a larger body of people. His father had been such a man. Alas, such regrets were useless at this juncture. The die had been cast for him long, long ago.

He looked at her and spoke evenly: "Speak to me. Tell me your proposition. And then we'll see just how much I feel like living or dying."

CHAPTER SIXTEEN

Giselle awoke to the sound of birdsong. She opened her eyes and saw a large and multicolored creature perched at the foot of the bed. It was a strange synthesis of parrot and vulture, with brightly colored feathers, a long, black beak, and large and very sharp talons. The creature stared at her through glassy black eyes. She found its scrutiny unnerving and wondered for a moment how the thing had gained entry to her quarters.

Then she recalled the previous evening's festivities in a series of flashing images. She and Ursula had consumed large quantities of a very expensive wine imported from France. There had been music, a girl playing a guitar. A large number of Apprentices gathered in her quarters at her invitation. Slaves were brought in and put to use in various ways as entertainment. Clothes were discarded and the party devolved to pure orgy. Giselle had partnered with several different men and women through the course of the evening, exploring every possible sexual combination and position with Apprentices and slaves alike.

It had been, she recalled with a tired smile, the most purely debauched evening of her entire life. There had been interludes during which slaves she'd fucked were then tortured and humiliated. Then things would shift back to party mode, with the consumption of still more wine and numerous more carnal indulgences. As evening progressed toward dawn, the wine flowing through her system caught up to her and things became a blur. She vaguely remembered accosting Ursula, violently removing the young Apprentice perched atop the girl and then dragging her out to the balcony. Here her memories became even blurrier. She recalled some frenzied moments of passion. But she'd been rough with the girl, maybe too rough, and there'd been anger. And then . . .

a sound, the loud crack of her fist across Ursula's jaw . . . the girl's eyes rolling back in her head as her body topples backward, falls against the balcony railing . . .

Giselle's head snapped to her right and let out a sigh of relief as she saw Ursula lying beside her. The girl was unconscious, her mouth hanging slack against the silk pillowcase. Her jaw sported a deep brown bruise and her flesh was gouged in other places where Giselle had struck her. But she otherwise seemed okay. Giselle listened to her racing heart and felt her eyes moisten as she realized how close she'd come to killing her lover.

She wiped the tears away at once. They were a sign of emotion. And emotion equaled weakness. She could not afford to be seen as weak. Also, Ursula was not in the restraints Giselle normally put her in at bedtime. The lapse angered Giselle. She'd left herself vulnerable, another thing she couldn't allow to happen, a thing she'd worked hard to prevent.

Until last night.

She sat up in bed and surveyed the aftermath of the orgy. The physical effort amplified a dull ache in her head. Her mouth felt as dry as parchment. She had a hangover, her first in more years than she could recall. She felt a touch of nausea at the back of her throat, a sensation exacerbated by the pungent scents of piss, semen, and blood. This annoyed her, but not nearly so much as the sight of unconscious bodies lounging everywhere. The crashed-out revelers were all nude or nearly nude, some of them with their limbs still in-twined, having passed out after sex. They were on the floor and in chairs. A young male slave was lying atop a table in the library section of her quarters. A male Apprentice, nude, lay next to him, an arm draped across the slave's waist.

There was a lot of blood. Big splashes on the floor and the furniture. The decapitated head of a female slave sat impaled on the tip of a spear, which was propped against the wall opposite the bed. Giselle couldn't imagine where anyone had gotten a spear. But that minor bit of mystery was forgotten as she noted the dark entrance to the secret torture chamber. Her heart thudded. She couldn't remember opening the door. The unnatural cold from the chamber was seeping into the air in her living quarters. There was something in-sinuating about the chill, a hint of something alive and malignant, and her first instinct was to seal the door at once. But she restrained herself, knowing she would first have to check the chamber for signs of anything amiss.

The missing bits of her memory stirred the self-directed anger again. She had been sloppy. Unforgivably so. The party-cum-orgy had been Ursula's idea. She had become petulant of late, resentful even, chafing under the new restrictions imposed upon her. She especially disliked being restrained in the evening, rebuffing Giselle's initial attempts to soften the loss of her total freedom by turning it into a kind of kinky game. Worst of all, from Giselle's point of view, she'd become more subdued during sex, feigning passion and being quite unsubtle about the fakery.

At first Giselle told herself she didn't care.

But she did.

And the longer the situation went on the less she enjoyed lovemaking with Ursula. She missed that feeling of unquenchable erotic hunger. The sex had become a rote act in recent days, a matter of going through the motions. She ached to feel that fire again. The need bothered her, though. It was weakness. She could have her pick of lovers. Yet she only wanted Ursula. Wanted her *completely* again. And so when Ursula begged for permission to throw the ultimate decadent party—along with an unsubtle hint that she would show her gratitude in the way Giselle most desired—she'd acquiesced, had even allowed herself to believe it might be a good idea to get loose and liven things up. She saw clearly now how wrong she had been. She thought of the Master and the relentlessly merciless way he'd exerted authority. He'd managed to survive that way for centuries before he was finally killed. Giselle had loathed the Master, but she decided she could yet learn some valuable lessons from him.

The strange vulture/parrot hybrid opened its beak and trilled another bit of song at her. It peered at her with simple animal curiosity. Giselle smiled and held out an arm. The gentlest of mental nudges caused the creature to flap its wings and move from the foot of the bed to Giselle's extended forearm. She cooed at the creature and gently stroked the back of its head. It tilted its head again and trilled another lovely burst of birdsong.

Giselle wrapped her fingers around its neck. Its eyes bulged a little and it emitted a little chirp as Giselle cooed reassurance. Then it squawked as she tightened her grip and began to twist. Panic set in and it raised talons to slash at her, but another mental nudge stilled the act of self-defense. And Giselle stared into the creature's bulging eyes as she snapped its neck with excruciating slowness.

There, she thought.

Something relaxed inside her and she studied the dead bird's limp body with grim satisfaction, puzzling over why she felt so good about killing so helpless a creature. An impulse caused her to look at Ursula. She imagined taking Ursula's neck in her hands and doing to her what she'd done to the bird. She licked her lips and felt her nipples stiffen. Then the girl stirred in her sleep, groaning and stretching out her body.

Giselle stared at the tender, exposed flesh of the girl's slender neck. So pale. So lovely. She watched the rise and fall of her breasts and thought of how they felt in her mouth, in her hands. And she sighed, knowing she still could not kill Ursula. The girl would require a still greater level of discipline, that's all.

She got out of the bed and carried the dead bird out to the balcony. The other world's sun bathed her body in heat, dispelling the cold that had seeped into her bones from the open torture chamber. She peered over the railing at the bustle of activity in the rapidly expanding slave community everyone called Razor City. Here was something of which she could be proud. Her vision for the community far exceeded in scope and daring anything the Master had accomplished with Below. There were many more hovels along the perimeter of the community now, with more being erected every day to accomodate the steady influx of new slaves. The large marketplace was open for business. Numerous other buildings were under construction. It was becoming a real city, albeit a primitive one, like something from a twisted version of the Middle Ages. The community's name derived from the high, razor-tipped fences that defined its borders. Giselle loved the sound of it. *Razor City*. It sounded like a place where nightmares would go to live. So apt. The endless suffering of its pitiful denizens would exceed the suffering of any oppressed group in human history, honoring the death gods enough to make her powerful almost beyond reckoning.

She tossed the dead bird over the railing and returned to her quarters. The nude revelers remained unconscious and for a moment Giselle considered killing every one of them, such was her distress at the tainted condition of her quarters. She picked up the spear and pried the dead slave's head from its tip. She tossed the head aside, examined the sharp and blood-coated tip, and imagined plunging it through the hearts of all present. The brutality would afford her a few moments of cold satisfaction, but she decided against it. Several of the sleeping Apprentices were very good at what they did, and capable Apprentices were significantly harder to replace than slaves.

And anyway, she knew she was only delaying the inevitable.

She braced herself with an intake of breath and stepped through the open entrance to the darkened torture chamber. The cold seeped into her bones again. She muttered a spell and the ranks of candles grew flames. Her gaze was drawn immediately to the limp figure splayed across the bottom of the dangling cage. No one else was in the room and there was nothing obviously amiss. She still couldn't recall opening the chamber, but she guessed Ursula had coerced her into doing it somehow.

Giselle moved deeper into the chamber and the figure at the bottom of the cage stirred and turned toward the sound of her approach. Gwendolyn lifted her head and several tangled golden locks fell across her face. She smiled weakly through lips puffy and coated with dried blood.

"Why, it's the great usurper. What a privilege it is to be in your presence, Mistress." She laughed, a ragged sound followed by a deep, hacking cough. "Come to finish me off, have you? Where's your kept girl, then? I'd think she'd want to be here for this."

Gwendolyn's flesh was covered with bruises and livid scars, many of which pulsed with active infections. Patches of abraded skin leaked blood and pus. She was missing an ear, a nipple, and several toes and fingers. There were multiple burn marks on her abdomen and thighs. And her pussy had been sewn partially shut. Giselle had not participated in any of these tortures, but she had been present for most of them, observing in a detached manner as Ursula enjoyed herself. But her lover's endless abuse of the prisoner had become tiresome, having dragged on for weeks beyond the point at which the former Apprentice should've been put out of her misery.

Giselle smiled and moved closer to the cage, adjusting her grip on the spear as she worked to decide on the best possible angle for a kill thrust. "Your tormentor is passed out on my bed. A touch too much wine last night, I'm afraid."

Something flickered in Gwendolyn's eyes as she watched the bloody spear tip move closer. The instinctive fear of one who senses impending death, perhaps. But that impression was belied by the small smile that dimpled the corners of her puffy lips. And she didn't retreat as the spear tip passed through cage bars and touched a spot between her breasts. Giselle's body tensed as her hands tightened on the spear shaft. The girl was making it easy for her, almost offering herself up for sacrifice. Which should not have been surprising. She had suffered immensely. Almost anyone in her position would welcome the release of death.

And yet . . .

That smile.

Giselle frowned. "Something is wrong."

Gwendolyn's smile broadened, displaying bloody gums and cracked and chipped teeth. "You don't know the half of it, Mistress." Another ragged laugh, followed by another whooping cough. She spat blood. Then she spoke in a singsong tone: *"I know something you don't."*

Instinct told her to ignore the doomed girl's vague insinuations. This was likely nothing more than one last mind-fuck, an empty game designed to delay the impending end of her life a few minutes more. She pressed the tip of the spear forward a millimeter or two, piercing pale flesh and drawing forth a trickle of blood that spilled along the girl's protruding rib cage before dripping through cage bars to splash the stone floor below. Gwendolyn winced as the spear tip entered her flesh, but that damnable smile barely faltered.

"I don't think you know anything." Giselle twisted the spear tip, widening the gash between Gwendolyn's breasts. A thicker stream of blood flowed over the tip, fresh gore commingling with dried red flakes. "This is just a last-ditch shot at saving your ass."

Gwendolyn winced again and gritted her teeth as the spear tip continued to twist and delve deeper. "You fucked up when you killed Ms. Wickman."

Giselle arched an eyebrow. "Oh? How so?"

"The tattoo on your back is lovely. It's funny. Usually the only tattoos you can't remember getting involve massive amounts of tequila and a road trip to Tijuana." Gwendolyn smiled again as the spear tip stopped twisting. "Got your attention, did I?"

Giselle's heart pounded. "What do you know about the tattoo?"

"Oh, a lot. I wonder if Ursula told you I was Ms. Wickman's favorite, hmm?" Gwendolyn pushed the spear away and sat up, making the stout chain groan as the cage swayed slightly. She pressed her face between cage bars and leered at Giselle. "She told me things.

Secrets. Tell me, Giselle, what do you know of the Order of the Dragon?"

Giselle swallowed a lump in her throat. She'd heard of the organization. Vague whispers of an ancient and powerful order founded on principles of extreme self-discipline. But that was the extent of her knowledge. The Order, to her mind, was like the Masons or the Illuminati. Formless phantoms lurking in shadowy, unknowable segments of society. They served as fodder for popular fiction and gave conspiracy theory crackpots something to obsess over.

"Are you implying Ms. Wickman was a member of the Order?"

Gwendolyn licked her puffy lips. "I'm not implying it. I'm flat-out saying it. And that tattoo on your back makes you a marked woman." She laughed. "Every Order tattoo is unique in some way. The Order is coming for you, Giselle. One look at your back and they'll know I was telling the truth."

Giselle tightened her grip on the spear shaft again. She was genuinely rattled now, but she didn't want Gwendolyn to see that. "They'll never get to me. They can't. I'm too well-protected."

Gwendolyn smirked. "Do you really believe that, Giselle?"

"Stop addressing me by my first name!" Giselle pressed the spear tip against Gwendolyn's stomach. "I'll not tolerate insolence."

"Fuck you. The true Mistress of this house is gone. You're just a pretender." She flexed her torso, made the spear tip cut into her flesh again. "And I'll call you whatever I want, Giselle. You bitch. You fucking cunt. You'll pay for what you've done."

Giselle's shoulder muscles tensed again. Anger overwhelmed fear. "Time to die, Gwendolyn."

Gwendolyn smiled. "Yes. But one more thing."

Giselle knew she shouldn't listen.

Kill her, she thought.

Poke this fucking thing through her and be done with it.

But again she hesitated. Fear reasserted itself. She imagined black-clad Order assassins coming to her in the middle of the night, could almost feel the killing blade at her throat, and her helpless to prevent it despite all her power. She was possessed by a sudden conviction that only a greater depth of knowledge would keep her alive.

She lowered the spear again. "Tell me."

"You're afraid. Good. I hope you spend the few nights left to you consumed by your fear. And while you're lying awake at night waiting for them to come for you, please think of me. I sent them the photo of Ms. Wickman's body. I tipped them off, Giselle. I'm the reason all your grand schemes are about to collapse." Gwendolyn's smile faded and her voice was laced with a more sober tone. "But I didn't do it alone."

"I don't believe you." Giselle swallowed with difficulty. "What are you saying?"

"There are traitors in your midst, Giselle. Other people burned by your fucking coup d'etat. Here's a question you'll no doubt ponder over those long, sleepless nights—who took the picture I sent to the Order?"

Giselle jabbed at her with the spear. The tip of it plunged into a spot beneath her sternum. Gwendolyn gasped and fell backward, rattling the cage. The heavy chain groaned and twisted. But then the girl was laughing again, a maddening display of mirth that assailed Giselle's ears like a swarm of buzzing locusts.

"Tell me who the traitors are!" Giselle jabbed with the spear again, opening a long gash along the back of a thigh. More blood spattered the stone floor beneath the cage. Another savage jab pierced a buttock. Still more blood sprayed the floor.

Gwendolyn sat up, lurched toward the side of the cage again, and sneered at Giselle. "You'll never know, cunt. Not until it's too late. But I have one more surprise for you. One of them left me a present."

She uncurled a fist and revealed a shiny razor blade.

Giselle's eyes widened. "No."

Gwendolyn laughed one last time and drew the blade across her throat in a flash. Her flesh opened like a zipper and blood fountained from the wound. Then she fell backward and the razor slipped from the remaining fingers of her right hand. Her body jerked once and went still. Giselle stared at the unmoving form in open-mouthed shock for several moments. The turn of events seemed unreal. In a few brief moments, her deepest fears had been revealed as truth. People in her employ were actively working against her. For a moment she found it difficult to breathe. The cloying darkness lurking just beyond the candles seemed to reach for her . . .

Giselle hurried out of the chamber and sealed it. She was shaking as she turned to survey the damage to her quarters one more time. Most of the hungover revelers were still unconscious, but a young male slumped in a recliner yawned and began to rise.

Giselle slammed the spear through his chest. His eyes went wide and he had a fraction of a second to realize what was happening to him. Then the spear tip passed through his back and impaled him briefly on the recliner. A bottomless rage sizzled through her as she yanked the spear out of the dead boy and moved to a sleeping couple entwined on the floor. The spear penetrated their bodies with equal ease, magic fueling her body with strength even as it sent bursts of wild energy darting through the room. More of the sleeping people began to wake up, only to find their bodies on the business end of a spear already coated with blood and lumps of viscera. Some tried to flee, but froze in their tracks, their bodies and minds paralyzed by a single small flex of Giselle's raging magic.

And the slaughter continued until they were all dead.

All of them, that is, with a single exception.

Ursula was sitting up in the bed, a sheet pulled up over her bosom. The pointless modesty might have made Giselle laugh under other circumstances.

She pointed the spear at her lover. "Don't ever betray me." The tip of the spear touched the hollow of Ursula's throat. "Ever. Not fucking ever."

Ursula swallowed carefully and gave a slight nod. "I wouldn't." Tears trickled from the corners of her eyes. "I . . . love you."

And I love you, Giselle thought. *Which probably makes me an idiot.*

She tossed the spear aside and climbed up on the bed. She yanked the sheet out of Ursula's hands and forced the girl onto her back.

"Prove how much you love me."

Ursula just stared at her for a long moment, her eyes still bright with residual fear. Then, at last, that gleam faded and she reached for Giselle.

And here it was, that thing she'd been missing for so long.

The hunger.

The *need*.

It was glorious.

And, for a time, it allowed her to forget the things that troubled her.

CHAPTER SEVENTEEN

"Are we gonna kill this fucker or not?"

Dream didn't reply to Marcy's question right away. She had two fingers wedged between slats of a window blind and was peering through the small opening at the motel parking lot. The place was a moldy dump on the outskirts of Columbus, Ohio. They'd been holed up here for two days, lying low after a robbery gone bad in Cleveland. A cop was dead and surveillance video of the crime had made the national news. Some genius with the FBI had connected the dots, linking the bloody convenience store holdup with a string of other brazen crimes, including the murder of a young girl at Niagara Falls and a mass murder at a New England farmhouse. The common denominator being a group of young women traveling together, three whites and one black. The female gang angle made the story a sexy one and thus a natural for the chattering talking heads on the twenty-four-hour news networks. But the whole thing really blew up when Dream was identified from her appearance in the surveillance tape. Now the reportage was virtually non-stop, and Dream found herself wishing for a major terrorist strike or something, anything to divert the media's attention in another direction.

The parking lot was somewhere just shy of half-full. Most of the cars she could see were old and in shabby condition. A nearby Caddy sported a leopard-print steering-wheel cover. A pair of fuzzy dice dangled from the tilted rearview mirror of a Plymouth Duster. The Starlite Inn did not attract an upwardly mobile class of clientele. But that didn't bother Dream. Among other things, it meant their old Dodge van didn't look out of place.

She turned away from the window and looked at the balding, middle-aged man cuffed to the headboard of the queen-sized bed. Blood leaked from his nose and trickled over the strip of duct tape covering his mouth. He wore rumpled black slacks and a blue polo shirt that was at least a size too small. His bloated belly stretched the fabric of the shirt and made him look pregnant. Marcy was pointing her Glock at his head. Two nights ago a bullet fired from the same gun had ended the life of a Cleveland officer on routine patrol. It was an ugly weapon. A brutal, merciless thing. And the sight of it pointed at another likely victim made Dream's stomach churn.

Despite everything, it was still hard to deal with all this killing.

But it was getting easier. Some. And that was maybe the worst thing of all.

She sighed. "You can't shoot him. Too much noise."

Alicia cackled. "Ooh, this should be good." She sat at a little table at the far side of the room. She aimed a re-mote control at the television and hit the mute button. She turned in her seat to get a better view of the bed. "So what's it gonna be, Dream? Gonna reach inside his brain, make the motherfucker hemorrhage?"

A toilet flushed and Ellen returned from the bath-room. "No, that's boring. Make his head explode, like that dude in *Scanners*."

Marcy laughed. "That would rock."

Ellen's eyes were wide and she was blinking rapidly. She kept licking her lips and wiping her mouth with the back of a hand. Snot dripped from her nose and Dream could see little white specks above her upper lip. Marcy was just as twitchy. The two had spent much of the evening snorting the cuffed man's cocaine off the back of a Gideon Bible. The stuff had turned up during a search of his belongings, several white Baggies hidden in the lining of a scuffed and dented old suitcase. Turned out the guy was some low-level middleman in the drug trade, information he'd coughed up after a pistol-whipping from Marcy.

Dream sat at the edge of the bed and looked the man in the eye. A muffled whimper issued from beneath the frayed edges of the duct tape. She'd given him a thrashing earlier in the evening, back in those first moments following their invasion of his room. He'd opened his door to step out for some reason. And the moment the door was open Dream and her companions swarmed out of the van and bludgeoned their way into the room. He'd been full of bluster at first, hurling threats and a barrage of sexist epithets. So Dream had been rough with him, surprising him with her strength. She remembered the feel of his nose breaking beneath the force of her fist. She'd pulled the punch. Otherwise the man's head would've come right off his shoulders. She was that strong now. And getting stronger all the time, the power inside her growing by leaps and bounds every day. And full of a fury that had nothing to do with the man's apparent misogyny. It was only an extension of the darkness that had taken root in her soul, a sickness of the spirit she could only assuage with violence.

Dream pinched the man's nostrils shut and watched his eyes go wide. He thrashed and managed to dislodge her fingers, sucking in air through the narrow passages.

Dream climbed up on the bed and straddled him. Marcy let out a whoop that made her sound like a drunken sorority girl at a kegger.

Ellen dropped to her knees at the side of the bed. "Do it." Her hands were clasped in a way that was almost prayerful. "Suffocate the pig."

Dream ignored it all as the man continued to buck beneath her. Her body rolled with the motion of his struggles. She thought of the time she'd ridden a mechanical bull in a bar in Florida. That had been fun. So was this, in a deeply twisted way. There was something distinctly sexual about it, in fact. She hadn't been with a man in months. A mad impulse to rip the fat man's pants off and suck his cock to hardness flashed through her. She pictured herself riding the man's dick and felt a dampness between her legs. She could kill him while he was still inside her, rip his throat out with her bare hands.

Then Ellen's breathy whisper: "Hey . . . this is kind of . . . hot."

The words broke the spell. Dream would not sate her needs with this man. He wasn't worthy. And she wasn't quite debased enough to relish the notion of playing the starring role in a live sex act for her friends. Not yet. So she exerted her strength and pinned the man firmly to the bed. He still thrashed with all his might. Useless. Dream felt that darkness rise inside her again, that sickness aching to feed. She raised her fists and brought them crashing down on his face. She felt bones and cartilage splinter and yield beneath her hands. His head whipped side to side, the motion a blur, like a punching bag in a gym. His face was a bloody, pulpy mess by the time she broke off the beating.

But he was still alive.

Still breathing.

A blood-red snot bubble welled from the end of a

crushed nostril and popped. Dream stared at the man's ruined face and felt the same numb disconnect she always experienced in the immediate aftermath of her violent outbursts. The pillow cushioning the man's head was flecked with blood. More dark red droplets dotted the backs of his flabby arms. His hands had gone limp, the metal handcuff bracelets having slid down to a spot directly behind the crown of his skull. Looking at him triggered the same muted repulsion she sometimes felt when watching an especially gruesome horror flick. Then the numbness was gone, completely, and she owned this again, this twisted reality that was sicker by far than any cheap bit of celluloid exploitation.

Now you finish it, she thought. *This guy's an asshole, but he's a human being. End his suffering.*

The strip of duct tape had loosened during the beating. She pressed it down and pinched the man's nostrils shut again. It didn't take long. He regained consciousness for a brief moment. His hands jerked once against the brass headboard slats. Then he went still. His eyes glazed over and he was gone.

Dream's shoulders slumped and her chin dipped toward her chest. And here was the next necessary stage she'd come to expect. This abrupt agony of remorse. The tears came, hot and plentiful, spilling in rivulets down her cheeks to moisten the collar of her T-shirt. No one said anything. They were used to this by now. Her friends. She'd started out hating them all. Not anymore. She belonged with them. They understood her. Accepted her. She'd told Ellen she thought of them as family. And it was true enough. Sort of an all-girl version of the Manson family, yes, but family nonetheless.

She sighed and the tears abruptly stopped. The remorse was gone. And now the dead man beneath her was just a slab of meat. A thing to be dealt with, no more significant than a bag of garbage.

She swiped moisture from her nose. "Let's get this bag of shit out of here."

Alicia leaned across the bed and unlocked the cuffs. She removed them from the dead man's limp wrists and tossed them onto the table. Dream climbed off the bed, slid her arms beneath the big body, and lifted him as easily as she'd lift a small child. There was a distant ache in her knuckles as she turned and carried him toward the bathroom. The slight pain was nothing. A normal person's knuckles would be broken and useless.

Ellen raced ahead of her and threw the bathroom door open. Dream turned sideways and moved through the opening. Ellen followed her in and opened the shower's sliding glass door. Dream dumped the body inside. It landed awkwardly on the gleaming white tile, one leg tucked beneath a fat buttock, the other splayed across the edge of the tub. The strip of duct tape had come off again and his plump lower lip looked like a rancid sausage. Dream closed the glass door and turned away from the ugliness.

Ellen continued to stare at the dead man. "Look at him. Pathetic. He deserved that."

Dream shrugged. "Maybe. Maybe not. I don't really give a shit."

Ellen followed her back out to the main room, skipping across the beige carpet like a child on a playground. Dream shot her a look of mild rebuke, but the girl didn't notice. She was bouncing off the walls. That damn cocaine. And now Marcy was chopping fresh lines on the back of the Gideon Bible. The sisters took turns kneeling over the table, inhaling white lines through a clipped fast-food straw. Ellen did the last line and tossed her head back, loosing a manic shriek of exultation.

Dream frowned. "Too loud."

"You need to loosen up, Dream." Marcy shook the last

bit of white powder from the Baggie and went to work with the razor blade again. "Little Miss Gloomy all the time." She grinned. "Haven't you had enough of feeling on the verge of doom every waking moment? I know I have."

"Yeah!" Ellen leaped into the air and clapped her hands. Then she dashed over to the nightstand next to the bed and started fiddling with the little alarm clock radio. "Let's have a fucking party!"

The radio's tinny speaker emitted a long buzz of static as the red dial indicator moved all the way to the left before at last hitting a surprisingly strong signal that turned out to be a college radio station. A student DJ spoke in a monotone before introducing a Violent Femmes song. Ellen shrieked again as the first herky-jerky notes of "Blister In The Sun" rattled the little speaker. Then she leapt up on the bed and began a manic dance that made her look like a person having an extraordinarily violent seizure. Marcy hopped up on the bed and mimicked her sister's spastic moves. The mattress springs squeaked in loud protest and the headboard slammed against the wall over and over.

Dream shook her head. "You guys weren't even born when that song came out."

The sisters didn't hear her. They sang along loudly, the combined volume of their voices overwhelming the meager capability of the radio-clock speaker. Dream experienced a reflexive bit of annoyance, but it felt half-hearted. The beginnings of a smile tugged at the edges of her mouth. How strange. Circumstances dictated the exercising of caution at every turn. Otherwise they could wind up cornered by half the cops in Ohio, the last moments of their wild spree playing out on television screens across the country, providing vicarious entertainment for millions of disapproving good citizens in safe suburban homes.

But as Dream watched the sisters some of their enthusiasm began to infect her. "Blister In The Sun" ended and a more modern tune she didn't recognize began. The girls evidently recognized it, as they let out identical shrieks and continued to torture the mattress springs.

She moved to the table and sat down. She pulled the Bible close and stared at the little mound of powder.

Alicia chuckled. "Go ahead. Have a toot."

Dream picked up the clipped straw. "I've never done this before."

Alicia braced her elbows on the edge of the table and leaned toward her. "Dream, you just killed a man. That's five motherfuckers you've knocked off since we hit the road. Every John Law in the whole goddamned country is looking for your ass. Most people would be shitting themselves just about now, maybe be ready to swallow a bullet rather than face the music. But not you. Uh-uh." She made a clucking sound and shook her head, grinning broadly. "Because you've got these super freaky powers. On some level you feel invincible. Am I right?"

A corner of Dream's mouth turned up. "Could be."

"Damn straight." Alicia slapped the table and laughed. "Ain't nobody takin' you down and you know it. You're the baddest bitch ever lived, bar none. And you're telling me you're afraid of a little powder." She leaned back in her chair and folded her arms beneath her ample breasts, shaking her head. "Well, shit."

Dream sighed. "Okay. Stop giving me static."

She picked up the razor blade—another thing pilfered from the dead man's belongings—and scraped the powder into a thin white line. Then she wedged the straw into her right nostril, pressed the other nostril shut with a finger, and bent toward the cocaine. She inhaled hard. The stuff hit her nasal passage and she almost sneezed. She didn't care for the physical sensation at all. But she inhaled again and finished off the line.

She dropped the straw and rubbed at her nose. "God-*damn*."

Alicia cackled. "Kinda grabs you by the short and curlies, don't it?"

Ellen shrieked and pointed at Dream. "Ohmigod! Ohmigod!" She grabbed a still-bouncing Marcy by the shoulder and made her look at Dream. "Dream's gone crazy! She's got white-line fever!"

The girl flopped onto her back, making the bed springs squeal again. Then she rolled onto her side and pressed her face into the pillow, kicking her feet and convulsing with hysterical laughter. Marcy hopped off the bed and made a beeline for Dream. There was a wild gleam in her eyes, a hint of something wicked. She slid onto Dream's lap and pushed her tongue between her lips. Dream's initial reaction was shock bordering on revulsion. This wasn't her thing at all. But the cocaine was working on her now. She felt wild and up for anything. So she let Marcy kiss her, even started kissing her back.

Then she heard something.

A click.

She broke the liplock with Marcy and turned her gaze to the hotel room's front door. The brass doorknob moved. The motion was slight, careful. She heard another click and knew someone was breaking in. She pushed Marcy off her lap and got to her feet as the door swung open and two men rushed into the room. One was a middle-aged man in a cheap suit. The other was a wiry, black-clad kid with scraggly hair that hung in his face. The older man had a .38 clutched in a beefy fist. The kid brandished a large and quite lethal-looking knife.

The older one kicked the door shut with the heel of his shoe and leered at them. He dropped a lockpicking tool into a suit pocket. "Party's over, bitches."

Dream opened her mouth to tell the intruders they were messing with the wrong people. But the words never made it past the tip of her tongue. Things started happening. She saw it develop like a slow-motion scene from a cheesy '70s cop movie. But the impression was a false one. It was happening fast. Too fast. She felt a hot surge of panic as Ellen rolled off the bed and made a grab for Marcy's Glock, which was on the nightstand now. The wiry kid flipped the blade in his hand and snapped his arm back. His arm came forward as Ellen brought the gun around. A scream filled the room. Marcy. The knife was a blur as it spun through the air. The blade buried itself in Ellen's side. Her finger jerked on the Glock's trigger, squeezing off a reflexive shot that sent a bullet whizzing by Dream's head. The bullet punched a hole through the television and Ellen dropped to the floor.

Marcy screamed again and rushed to her sister's side. The man in the suit aimed his gun at her back. He was going to kill her. Dream understood this in a flash. Anyone close to the Glock was a threat. She saw his finger begin to exert pressure on the trigger. A thought formed in her head. *Heat.* The gun glowed red. The man's flesh started to sizzle. He yelped and dropped the gun. It hit the floor and the carpet ignited. Dream looked at it and another thought filled her mind. *Ice.* The temperature in the room plummeted and the incipient fire fizzled. Dream felt a mixture of astonishment and exhilaration. She'd never so precisely controlled and directed the power inside her. She felt capable of anything. The feeling was at least partially attributable to the cocaine rush, but a larger factor was this sudden epiphany—the impression that she had at last become the thing she was meant to be from the beginning. Not a human being, but a thing. A supernatural monster of some sort, just as the Master had been. And Alicia's words rang truer now— she did feel invincible.

The man in the suit edged close to the door and reached for the doorknob. Dream focused her will again and the doorknob turned hot in the man's hand. He shrieked and let go. The scraggly-haired boy's fingers were moving toward another concealed weapon, something tucked in the waistband of his pants. The grasping hand was missing two fingers. It was the same hand that had sent the knife on its lethal trajectory toward Ellen. A grin that hinted at madness spread across the boy's face as his fingers slipped beneath the dangling tail of his shirt and emerged with another knife.

The switchblade snapped open.

Dream looked into his eyes and felt his pain. He'd suffered immensely in the past. But any good he might once have harbored had been eradicated through torture and brutalization. This impression formed in less than the space of a second. She knew, then, that the interlopers were no ordinary predators.

Another wail of anguish spiraled out of Marcy's tortured lungs.

Dream rushed the boy and seized him by the wrist. She pried the knife from his fingers with ease. And she thought of Ellen as she slammed the blade into his abdomen. Poor Ellen. The girl she'd once victimized and whom she'd come to regard as a friend. She'd blossomed in the two months they'd spent on the road, becoming stronger and more confident. And now she was crumpled on the floor. Maybe already dead.

The boy's only reaction to the pain was a wince. His grin remained in place as the fingers of his other hand came around to claw at her face, grasping for the soft tissue of her eyes. Dream swatted the hand away and slammed him against the dresser, rattling the mirror mounted on the wall behind it. She yanked the knife out of his stomach and punched it in again. And again. The mirror's reflection showed her a black-haired, wild-eyed woman in the grip of a murderous frenzy. A woman who had embraced madness and had no desire to turn back. Not anymore.

She threw the boy to the ground and straddled him. His eyes turned glassy. But still there was no fear reflected there. He grinned. A soft burble of laughter emerged between pale pink lips.

The man in the suit made another move toward the door, but Alicia intercepted him. The gun he'd discarded was in her hand now. She whipped it across the man's face and blood leaped from his smashed nose. She dragged him further into the room and threw him down at the foot of the bed.

Dream shifted her attention back to the boy. His grin broadened and he even stuck his tongue out at her. Dream forced his mouth open and plunged the knife inside. The pain at last took its toll on the boy. He tried to jerk his head out of her grip, but he failed to budge her at all. Blood bubbled from his mouth, along with a mewling, inarticulate plea. Dream turned his head carefully to one side, allowing the blood to flow out rather than letting him choke on it. Then she pushed the blade into each of his eyes, penetrating just enough to blind him. More mewling. More inarticulate pleas. She worked on him with the knife for a long time, molten rage driving her to mutilate the body of her friend's murderer in the most obscene ways possible.

And finally he was dead.

Dream stood up and looked at her reflection again. Her thrift-store clothes were covered with blood. Blood was everywhere. She turned away from her reflection and saw Marcy sitting on the floor against the side of the bed, her sister's motionless body cradled in her arms. She looked up at Dream, her face shiny with tears.

Marcy's anguish melted some of the hardness that had seized her soul.

"Is she—"

Marcy nodded and sniffed. "Yes."

Dream felt her own anguish rising up, but she clamped it down. A member of her adopted family was dead and there would be real grief to deal with, but for the moment there were more pressing matters at hand. She yanked the man in the suit to his feet and leaned in close, their faces separated by no more than an inch.

"Who sent you?" Her voice was low, her tone even, but the ruthlessness beneath came through clear as a bell. "Was it Ms. Wickman? It was, wasn't it? I saw it in that boy's eyes before I blinded him."

The man swallowed with difficulty. His bloodshot eyes danced in their sockets. His breath reeked of cheap beer and cheaper cigarettes. He licked blood from his lower lip and swallowed again. He sensed her implacable determination and understood there was no room for anything but the truth.

"Not Ms. Wickman. She's gone. Dead." He licked his lips again and shivered. He was afraid of Dream, yes, but he also clearly feared whoever had sent him. "Another has taken her place. Mistress Giselle."

Alicia was on her feet again. "The bitch is dead? For real?"

The man nodded. "Yes. And she's worse than Ms. Wickman. The old broad sent her people after House of Blood survivors. I figured that'd be off with her dead, but no, the new Mistress wants you, too. I don't know why and that's the whole fucking truth."

Dream smiled. "I believe you. What's your name?"

The man coughed. "Harlan Dempsey. People call me Dempsey."

Dream heard sirens rising in the night. A lot of them. Drawing closer by the moment. Then a sound of tires squealing in the parking lot. She let go of the man's shirt and pushed him away. He stumbled over the edge of the bed and flopped down on the mattress. She heard voices in the parking lot. Shouts and commands. Flashing red and blue strobe lights were visible at the edges of the window blinds.

Alicia shot her a worried look. "Dream?"

"It's okay, Alicia. I'll deal with it. And after I've taken care of things, Harlan here will take us to whatever pit of hell this Giselle cunt is holed up in. Isn't that right, Harlan?"

Harlan's gaze flicked from the windows to Dream and back again. He swallowed hard and nodded. "Sure. Yeah. Whatever."

Dream looked at Alicia. "The quest isn't over. Ms. Wickman's dead, but we still have a destiny to meet, okay?"

Alicia nodded slowly. "Yeah. I hear you, Dream. And I'm with you all the way." She glanced at the front door. The level of frantic activity outside was increasing by the moment. "But are you sure you can get us out of this?"

Dream's eyes glittered. "Yes."

Marcy was on her feet now, the Glock in her hand again. "I'll help you."

Dream smiled at her. "Thank you. But that won't be necessary. Just stand back and watch the show."

She went to the front door and grasped the knob, which had cooled again. Then she steeled herself with a deep breath and opened the door.

More shouts.

A voice squawked through a megaphone, issuing commands she ignored. Dream stepped outside and moved fearlessly toward the array of raised handguns and rifles. She smiled and spread her hands wide. Someone yelled at her to get down on the ground. Then there was a pop from behind her. Marcy at the door, firing the Glock and ignoring her instructions to hang back. Driven by rage over her sister's death to lash out at any enemy. Fire erupted from the barrels of the guns pointed at the motel room. Dream flexed her will and the bullets went astray.

Then the real fireworks began.

When it was over, the cops were all dead, their cars smoking ruins.

And Dream and her companions vanished into the night before reinforcements could arrive.

CHAPTER EIGHTEEN

The cabin in which Camp Whiskey's leaders conducted business was twice the size of the next largest cabin. Chad had jokingly referred to the large main room as an echo chamber. But now it felt too small, the air stale and the walls too close. The problem was all the extra people in the room—three Order of the Dragon representatives and several rifle-toting Camp Whiskey guards. The Order people sat at one end of the long wooden table that occupied the room's center. Jim sat alone at the opposite end of the table, his arms crossed over the front of a thick wool sweater. He and the old man who was the obvious leader of the Order delegation glared at each other across the length of the table. The tension between them made Chad jittery.

So he abandoned his front-row seat at the staredown of the ages, rising from the table to wander over to the fireplace at the rear of the cabin. A fire crackled in the stone recess, a small pile of logs shifting as the flickering orange flames consumed them. Logs Chad might well have cut himself. He examined his palms as he held his hands out to receive the fire's warmth. Calluses formed over the course of two and a half months of hard physical labor made them look like a stranger's hands. How strange now to look at these work-roughened hands and feel so good about the deceptively simple things he'd accomplished in his time at Camp Whiskey. He'd built new cabins with the other men, becoming skilled in the basics of construction and rudimentary plumbing. At some point he'd begun to genuinely enjoy the hard physical work, taking more pride in the things he'd built with his hands than he ever had in his ability to skillfully push around numbers in a cushy white-collar environment.

Which partly explained why he felt an instinctive hatred and distrust of the Order people. What they were proposing would mean an end to the new lifestyle he'd come to love. It also reeked of a suicide mission, with the people of Camp Whiskey serving as a kind of cannon fodder. Chad wasn't a coward. He had proven that during the House of Blood revolt. But the circumstances here were different. The people at Camp Whiskey didn't live each day at the mercy of brutal overlords. No one's life was being sacrificed in the name of obscure ancient deities. But now these mysterious emissaries from some arcane organization were working to convince them to give up the safety and comfort of the camp in favor of a headlong march into a lion's den. Essentially asking them to give up their lives to help avenge the death of a woman they had all despised.

The fire crackled and the silence lengthened. Chad picked up the fire poker and prodded the dwindling logs. The flames grew higher as he imagined sinking the hooked end of the poker through one of the Order leader's eyes.

The back of his neck tingled in a weird way and he turned away from the fire. The female Order representative was eyeing him closely. She was seated to the old man's left. Her eyes narrowed, projecting an intensity that made Chad gulp. She had very fine Asian features, with high cheekbones and a small, sensual mouth. Her hair was thick and dark, glossy like that of a model in a perfume ad. Unable to bear the withering stare a moment longer, Chad forced his eyes in another direction. He had the disturbing sense that she could see his thoughts and it made him want to bolt from the cabin.

Jack Paradise stalked the room like a caged beast. The big ex-marine's jaw was a tight line of tension. He circled the table with his hands clasped behind his back, as if he didn't trust what he might do with them if he didn't keep them there. Halfway through yet another circuit around the table, he came to an abrupt stop and his hands came away from the small of his back. He leveled an index finger at the old man.

"Fuck this and fuck the lot of you. Your bullshit plan is a nonstarter on every level." He pounded a fist into an open palm. The palm an obvious substitute for the old man's face. "Basically we're the Northern Alliance and you're the U.S. Army. But this ain't Afghanistan, motherfucker. It ain't our grudge and it's not gonna be our fucking war. No way I'm getting ninety-plus percent of my people killed so you fuckers can prance in afterwards and take this bitch out."

Jack's jawline quivered. The big man was fighting to maintain any semblance of control. Chad had never seen the man in the grip of such fury. Jack Paradise had always seemed the embodiment of a Marine Corps lifer—a resolute and extremely self-disciplined hardcase, a man who wouldn't rattle easily, if ever. But he was rattled now and it was clear the Order people appreciated the full range of possibilities this implied. The woman pushed her chair backward several inches and placed a small hand on the hilt of her sword. The young man seated across from her did the same. The swords were in black scabbards, but Chad had a feeling they could be drawn and put to lethal use in the blink of an eye. The Camp Whiskey guards shifted their feet and repositioned their weapons, pointing in the general direction of the Order representatives.

Chad's heart felt ready to leap into his throat. Blood was in the air. But his people were the ones with the guns. Firepower trumped old-fashioned steel. Or did it? The Order people were an unusual lot. An understatement. They seemed from another world altogether, some place wholly alien, and whatever purpose or cause they served was as inscrutable as the face of God. They were dangerous and not to be underestimated.

Chad took a deliberate step backward. He wanted to feel the fireplace poker's solid heft in his hands again. It would be no match against Order steel, but it was better than nothing. The woman looked at him again and did something that made his balls shrivel. She smiled. Her eyes remained cold, but the smile seemed to promise she would be coming for him if the tension in the room did escalate to actual conflict.

Jim's audible sigh defused some of the tension. He leaned forward and propped his elbows on the edge of the table. "There's no need for this. Jack, have your men leave the room."

Jack wheeled on him. "What? Have you gone insane? We can't trust these people. No. My men are staying put."

Jim stared into the old Asian man's eyes for another moment. Then he smiled and rose from his seat. "Pardon me. I'll be just a moment." He moved away from the table and headed for the front door, throwing a glance in Jack's direction on the way. "A word, please. Outside."

Jack glared at Jim's retreating back a moment longer. Then he sighed and spoke to a black man positioned next to the door. "Keep things under control, goddammit. Anything hinky happens . . . you know what to do."

The guard nodded. "Yes, sir."

Then Jack was gone. The door flapped shut and Chad

was alone with the guards and the Order people. He felt abandoned. The strange people in black sat silent and unmoving. To Chad they looked like incredibly precise and lifelike sculptures of human beings. The unsettling impression lasted until the woman again sensed his scrutiny and turned her head to observe him.

And she smiled in that utterly humorless way again. "You must convince your superiors of the wisdom of our plan."

Chad blinked in surprise. It was the first time any of them had spoken to him. "Um . . . okay, one, they're not my superiors. Two, I'm not personally convinced of the wisdom of your plan. In fact, I think it's pretty half-assed and want nothing to do with it."

The woman shrugged. "Your comments are fueled by emotion and not informed by rational thought. Our proposal is your only true path to salvation. In the end, you will set emotion aside and do as we say."

Chad sneered. The woman's smug words rankled. "In the end, we'll do whatever the hell *we* want, and if that turns out to be a choice you deem 'irrational,' well whoopty-fucking-do, too bad."

A corner of the woman's mouth turned slightly upward, indicating only mild amusement at Chad's speech. It was a little thing, but it was just enough to send Chad over the edge. Offense shifted to anger. His hands curled into fists. But he couldn't lose his cool in front of them. That would lend the "emotion" comment more credence than it deserved. So he turned away from them and stalked out of the cabin, banging the door open with the base of a clenched fist.

The sharp chill of the early December evening made him shiver. Jim and Jack stood near a picnic table some twenty yards away. They stood close to each other, their heads bent as they spoke in muted tones. Wisps of fog drifted from their mouths. Chad zipped up his jacket and set off in their direction. The other men glanced his way as he neared them.

Jim smiled. "Chad."

"Fuck this, I'm done with them." Chad was shaking and he realized as he spoke it wasn't solely from the cold temperature. "I say we reject their suicide mission and send those assholes packing. We've got a good thing going here and there's no reason to throw it all away. Okay, so our location isn't a secret anymore. Our supposed enemy knows where we are. Great. Let them bring the fight to us if there's to be one. We'll kick their fucking asses."

Jack nodded throughout Chad's speech. He struck a wooden match with his teeth and applied the flame to a hand-rolled cigarette. "Exactly what I've been saying." He blew a stream of smoke at the dark sky and looked Jim in the eye. "Let's say everything they've said about Giselle is the truth. So what? If there's to be a fight, it should be on our own ground and our own terms. If she's stupid enough to send a force after us, they'll be in a universe of fucking hurt."

Jim pursed his lips and slowly stroked the beard he'd been growing for the last few weeks. "I see the sense in what each of you says. I'll admit I found the notion of eradicating the remaining threat against us a tempting one. And I might have been swayed if not for the passion you've displayed. So we will reject their proposal."

A grim smile etched a tight curve across Chad's face. "Good."

But Jim's expression remained thoughtful. "But we can't be complacent. If we're to believe the Order, Giselle has a formidable paramilitary unit at her disposal as well. We'll need to beef up our own forces and rethink our defensive strategies."

Jack grinned. "I'll take care of that."

Jim managed a small smile of his own. "I'm sure

you're up to the task." He sighed and rubbed his hands together. "Let's get back inside and break the news."

Jack pinched the end of his cigarette and snuffed the flame. He dropped it in a pocket and said, "Yeah, let's do it. Can't wait to see the looks on their fucking faces."

Chad shook his head. "Go without me. I don't want to see any of them ever fucking again. If you guys don't mind, I'm gonna head home and let you take care of it."

Jack shrugged. "Cool with me."

Jim nodded. "And with me. Evening, Chad."

"Night, guys."

Chad turned away from them and started up the hill toward the cabin he shared with Allyson. But an impulse carried him past the cabin, sparing it only a quick glance as he hurried by. The lights were out, so Allyson was probably asleep anyway. He still felt agitated and was not yet ready to join her in bed. The steep ground began to level out and he soon arrived at the site that functioned as an informal communal gathering place for the denizens of Camp Whiskey. He sat on the ground near the large campfire pit and crossed his legs beneath him. There was no fire tonight, but the pit contained a few blackened logs left over from earlier in the evening. Chad pushed his hands into his jacket pockets and hunched his shoulders forward. He peered beyond the pit at the rows of cabins down the hill. A few soft lights still glowed in some of the windows.

He'd initially found it strange that the founders of Camp Whiskey had decided to establish their compound in the mountain country of east Tennessee, so near the Master's former territory. But the feeling had diminished with time. Really, it was kind of perfect. Once they had been prisoners here. And now they had returned to the country of their nightmares, transforming it into something fresh and life-affirming. The Order had no right to be here. They were intruders. Interlopers.

Their presence tainted the good things everyone here had worked so hard to accomplish.

He sat there thinking about these things for an indeterminate period of time. Perhaps a half hour. Perhaps only as long as ten or fifteen minutes. But it had been a long day. At some point physical exhaustion caused his eyes to close and he began to drowse. Then the crunch of a twig caused his eyes to snap open. He sensed movement to his left and turned his head in that direction. Then a hand seized him from behind, gripping the collar of his jacket and yanking him roughly to his feet. He let out a startled yelp as the same hand spun him around. He tottered for a moment on the edge of the pit. Then the Order woman grabbed the front of his jacket and pulled him away from the hole.

Chad let out a gasp. "Jesus fucking Christ! Where did you come from?"

"I am schooled in methods of stealth."

"No kidding." Chad's heart was pounding. "What are you doing here? You pissed that we rejected your stupid-ass proposal?"

"The plan will go forward. Your master, Mr. Jim, has been made to see the wisdom of our intentions."

Chad frowned. He didn't like the sound of that at all. He noticed the Order woman had one hand tucked behind her back and realized she was concealing something.

"What are you—"

Her right hand curled into a fist and delivered a brutal jab to a spot just beneath his sternum. Chad cried out and bent over at the waist. He tried to say something, but could only manage a wheeze. Then the woman showed him the thing she'd been hiding behind her back and bile flooded his throat. Her fingers clutched the severed head of Jack Paradise by strands of blood-slickened hair.

Anger overwhelmed his fear. Chad forced himself upright and threw a wild punch the Order woman easily avoided. She jabbed him in the stomach again, harder, blasting the breath from him and driving him to his knees. Then she kicked him in the gut and he flopped over onto his back. A white-hot center of pain expanded and rendered further resistance at least temporarily impossible. The Order woman tossed Jack's head into the pit and again seized handfuls of Chad's jacket. She began to pull him away from the campsite toward the nearby line of trees. A part of Chad's psyche marveled over the small woman's strength, impressed despite the peril he was in.

The evening darkness deepened as they entered the woods. The woman yanked him to his feet and stood him against the thick base of a tall tree. The narrow slits of her eyes seemed darker and harder now, like the eyes of a demoness. She removed the scabbard containing her sword and set it carefully on the ground. Then she moved in close and peppered Chad's midsection with a series of high-power jabs. Yet each was delivered with just enough force to maintain a steady level of pain. Chad tried to collapse several times, but the woman wouldn't allow it, forcing him to remain upright as she continued to punish him. And he knew that was precisely what was happening. She'd judged him guilty of insolence and was putting him in his place. At some point a part of his mind became disconnected from the pain and the beating. He thought of Jack Paradise, how brave the man had been, and he weeped.

Then the woman stopped punching him and said, "I have something else to tell you."

Chad sniffled. "What?"

"Your woman is an agent of your enemy. She has betrayed you and laughs at you whenever your back is turned."

Chad stood up straighter and tried to get his breathing

under control. "I . . . know. I figured . . . that out . . . a long time ago." He swallowed hard. "But she's with us now."

The Order woman smirked. "You are an idiot."

She slapped him.

Chad put a hand to his stinging cheek. "Fuck. Why don't you just kill me and be done with it?"

Her smirk gave way to a small smile. "Because I have another use for you. The Order rules this place now. And I have decided to claim you as my property."

Chad's brow furrowed. "What?"

The Order woman slapped him again. "Be quiet and do as I say."

"Fuck you."

The woman's nostrils flared. Here eyes widened with rage. She punched him in the abdomen again, a blow harder by far than any of the previous blows. Chad dropped to his knees and she kicked him in the stomach again. On his back, now, he stared up at her and watched in disbelief as she began to disrobe. In a moment she was standing naked over him, a small foot planted to either side of his head. Chad stared up at her slender, sleek body, which was rendered ghostly pale by the sliver of moonlight that peeked through the treetops.

She licked her lips. "It is time for you to begin your life of servitude."

Chad had time to draw in a breath.

Then she lowered herself to him.

CHAPTER NINETEEN

The girl bent over the edge of the bed was a white prostitute with lank blonde hair and track marks on her arms. She was a new arrival, fresh from the streets of Los Angeles, where she'd been swept up by Black Brigade scouts. In the ordinary course of things a creature already so damaged would have been banished to Razor City. But Gwendolyn's suicide had changed things. Upon learning of the loss of her plaything, Ursula had become despondent and withdrawn. Giselle attempted to appease her by allowing her to decide the fate of the new meat, a privilege she relished. Some Ursula deemed as clearly unworthy of her attention and these were sent to Razor City. Others she killed on the spot, with no apparent rhyme or reason. And every week she selected an unlucky few upon which she vented the rage and frustration consuming her.

The prostitute's mouth had been stitched shut with a needle and thread. Her wrists were bound by a length of rusty barbed wire. Ursula stood behind her, nude except for black platform heels and a strap-on dildo. A cigarette in a plastic holder dangled from a corner of her mouth as she pounded the dildo into the prostitute's bleeding anus.

Giselle lay on her side on the other side of the bed, her head propped in an upraised hand. The prostitute stared a desperate plea at her with wide, misty eyes. Giselle felt a mild arousal at the obscene thing her lover was doing to the pitiful creature. But it was a reflex. There was no real fire behind it. She still loved Ursula, but the bond between them had weakened, a steady, drip-drip erosion she feared would continue until there was nothing left. She watched the bounce of Ursula's breasts and the sway of her long blonde hair as she ass-fucked the prostitute and tried to feel more than mild arousal.

And the result was the same.

Nothing.

So she was glad for the diversion when she heard the clack of jackboot heels.

She rose from the bed to greet Schreck.

The commander's sleek black uniform was crisp and immaculate, his boots polished and gleaming. His eyes were a cold blue-gray and his hair was cut close to the scalp. His lips were thin and his features had a cruel cast, fitting for one in his position. He doffed his hat and clacked his heels. Giselle was amused. The man was an admirer of the arch militarism of Third Reich fascists, and there were times when he seemed like a particularly demented little boy playing the role of concentration camp commandant.

He bowed stiffly and said, "Mistress, there is a matter requiring your immediate attention."

Giselle smiled and moved to her wardrobe. She selected a green silk robe and pulled it on. It was short, the hem reaching the mid-thigh level. She cinched it shut with the sash and turned back to the commander, the smile still on her face.

She smoothed the fabric down over her thighs and said, "How does this look?"

A corner of the man's mouth quirked as he struggled to contain frustration. "Madam, this is a matter of the highest importance. I hardly think—"

Giselle's smile faded. "I asked you a question. Answer it."

Schreck was a coolly efficient man who didn't stay flustered long. It was what made him so perfectly suited for his role in the scheme of things. "It looks lovely on you, Mistress."

"Of course it does. Now tell me about this supposedly dire development."

She moved to the vanity next to the wardrobe and sat in the chair there, pulling at the hem of her robe as she crossed her legs. Schreck turned to face her directly and drew in a breath. A slight frown creased Giselle's forehead. Something had rattled the man. A faint alarm sounded at the back of her mind. She'd never known Schreck to be nervous, not even in the immediate aftermath of Ms. Wickman's assassination.

Her interest piqued, she sat up straighter and leaned forward. "Come on, man. Out with it. What has the likes of you in such a tizzy?"

Schreck heaved a sigh. "Madam . . . we have new arrivals. Three women. One of them is Dream Weaver, who was—"

"I know who she is." Giselle frowned and glanced toward the bed. Ursula was still pounding away at the prostitute. The backs of her long, shapely legs flexed with each thrust. The mild arousal she'd felt earlier gained a bit more heat. She had to force her gaze back to Schreck's subtly troubled expression. "She's a prize catch. You should be giddy. So why the concern?"

Schreck tugged at the stiff collar of his uniform shirt with an index finger. Giselle's frown deepened. The man was more than a little nervous. There was even a very thin sheen of sweat along his forehead. "We did not bring Ms. Weaver in. She and her companions are here of their own accord."

"But that's absurd. Why would they come here of their own free will?"

Schreck's shoulders lifted in a small shrug. "I know little of their intentions. Ms. Weaver has actually caused quite a stir in the larger world of late. She and her friends have been on a crime spree of epic proportions, with a trail of victims and robberies across several northeastern and midwestern states."

Giselle settled back in the chair and crossed her fingers at her waist. "How odd. It's not a fate I would have imagined for that woman." Her eyes narrowed. "And it still doesn't explain why they're here."

"Indeed." Schreck glanced briefly in the direction of the large double doors that stood open at the far end of the big room. He seemed anxious and his voice dropped to a whisper as he said, "But if I may venture a guess?"

Giselle frowned. "Please do."

Schreck moved closer to Giselle, kneeling slightly at the waist as he again spoke in a whisper: "I believe they've come here seeking refuge. They're weary of dodging the law and need a place to hunker down, perhaps indefinitely." A malignant smile darkened the corners of his thin lips. "Desperation brought them to our door, Mistress. They are broken. Beaten. They are at our mercy."

"*My* mercy, you mean."

Schreck blinked. "Of course."

Giselle frowned again. "If they are, as you say, 'beaten,' then why are you so afraid?"

Schreck straightened at once, indignation flaring in his eyes. "I am not afraid."

Giselle uncrossed her legs and rose from the chair. She approached Schreck, enjoying the way his jaw tightened almost imperceptibly as she neared him. "You are so very afraid," she said, still smiling as she put a hand on his shoulder. Her nose twitched. "I smell the stink of it on you."

Schreck swallowed. "Madam, I—"

"Shush." Giselle squeezed his shoulder, her fingers digging into muscle, finding a tender spot. She held his gaze a moment and allowed him to feel how easily she could tear him apart. "Your fear is a good thing, Schreck. You've always been so unflappable, even in the moments after I slaughtered your original Mistress. So this tells me something. Our guests are not to be underestimated. You believe they present a genuine threat."

Schreck drew in a sharp breath as Giselle relaxed the pressure on his shoulder. He wiped moisture from his forehead with a uniform sleeve. "Madam . . . it's true. My time in their presence left me feeling . . . unnerved. It was a subtle thing, a sense of something being . . . not right."

Giselle nodded. "Take me to them. Now."

"Are you sure, Mistress? Perhaps you should grant us time to arrange a more secure—"

Impatience flared in Giselle's eyes. *"Now."*

Shreck returned his hat to his head and snapped his heels together. "As you wish."

Giselle considered taking a moment to change out of the flimsy robe into something more formal, but she was too anxious to see her guests to waste time selecting something appropriate. She glanced toward the bed, where Ursula was still positioned behind the whimpering prostitute. The girl evinced no sign of having heard her conversation with Schreck. She was too lost in her own world. A part of her wanted to order Ursula to finish with the prostitute and accompany her downstairs, but the prospect of yet another spat with the girl made her weary.

So she looked at Schreck and said, "Lead the way."

The commander spun on his heels and strode away at a brisk rate, which Giselle hurried to match. They passed through the open double doors and moved rapidly down the long, candlelit corridor. Muffled but nonetheless distinct sounds emerged from behind the closed doors that lined either side of the hallway. Moans of ecstasy and the strangled sobs and whimpers of those in agony, laced with incongruous bursts of mad laughter. Similar sounds drifted from the hallways of each floor as they descended the spiral staircase to ground level. Schreck's boot heels struck a loud, discordant accompaniment on the marble stairs. Giselle was struck by the impression that this was how the echoing chambers of hell must sound. She was not displeased by the notion.

They reached the bottom and passed through the foyer into a large living room filled with lots of expensive oak furniture. Giselle followed Schreck through the living room as he continued toward an archway that led to the main dining hall. As they neared the dining hall, Giselle began to hear voices. Female voices. The timbre of one was instantly familiar. *Dream Weaver*. Though she'd never met the woman in person, she'd heard her voice on television numerous times. A little shiver rippled down the length of her spine. The instinctive fear made her angry. This was her domain. Her castle. She had all the power here. And yet the feeling persisted.

She detected no fear in the woman's voice. Not the slightest iota. Which was just insane. Regardless of whatever mischief she'd gotten up to in the normal world, she was now on dangerous and very hostile territory. Her every word should pulse with anxiety.

But it just wasn't there.

Giselle tensed as they passed through the archway into the dining hall. More than a dozen heavily armed Black Brigade soldiers lined each side of the room.

These were hard, brutal men. Sadists guilty of countless atrocities. The collective scent of fear was almost overpowering. Some of the men fidgeted. Others were sweating and trying not to shake in their boots. Giselle was overcome with disgust and disdain. This was her elite force. Her professional killers. The ones she entrusted with the security of her realm. But right now they looked about as fearsome as a troop of Cub Scouts wielding Wiffle Ball bats. She decided then that none of these men would survive to see another sunrise.

Schreck included.

But these pitiless thoughts were forgotten as she looked at the four women seated in relaxed poses at the far end of the table. There were two women who looked to be in their midthirties. One black and one white. The other two were younger, in their very early twenties at the most. The younger women possessed a certain similarity of features. One, slightly older and sporting choppy, jet-black hair was markedly prettier than the other. Yet they had the same thin lips, wide eyes, and slightly upturned nose. They were sisters or close cousins. There was something not quite right about the younger one. Her mouth was hanging open. Droplets of drool depended from the corners of her lips and her dark eyes possessed a flat, dead look.

A half-empty bottle sat on the table between the women—and three glasses filled with varying levels of dark liquid. The thirtysomething white woman also had choppy, jet-black hair. It looked better on her than it did on the younger girl. She was extraordinarily attractive, the kind of woman who could adopt any look and instantly make it her own. She wore a pink baby-doll T-shirt, which was emblazoned with the word SLUT in large glittering letters. On any other woman her age the shirt would look ridiculous, but . . .

Then it clicked.

Giselle forced a smile. "Hello, Dream."

Dream's smile was surprisingly feral, nothing at all like what Giselle remembered from television coverage after the fall of the House of Blood. "Hello, cunt."

Giselle blinked rapidly for several moments. "How dare you—"

"Oh, shut up." Dream eyed her up and down, a mocking glint in her eyes. "I'd tell you not to get your panties in a knot, but you're not wearing any, are you?"

The younger black-haired girl cackled. "Yeah, that's some robe, baby. Shit, it's like she's the female Hugh Hefner and this is the house of horrors version of the Playboy Mansion."

The comment enraged Giselle even as it evoked a round of laughter from the girl's companions. Even the drooling, slack-jawed girl made a chuffing sound that might have been mirth. She continued making the sound for several moments after the laughter of her friends faded. Giselle put her rage on hold as she stared in helpless fascination at the pathetic creature. She looked outwardly normal, but it was apparent her mind was functioning only at the most basic level.

Giselle scowled. "What's wrong with that one? The ugly, drooling idiot, I mean." She lifted an arm to point at the girl with the slack jaw and glassy eyes, who turned her head slowly to stare blankly in Giselle's direction. "That one, I mean."

Dream's smile remained in place, but her eyes turned cold. "Oh, that's Ellen. She's a work in progress."

Giselle frowned. "What's that supposed to mean?"

Dream drained her wine glass and filled it again. "Oh, nothing much. She died recently. Was murdered, actually. By one of your men, the late Harlan Dempsey."

Giselle shrugged. "I don't know the name. Many of our field operatives are still working under orders issued by the woman I . . . replaced."

"Yeah, okay, whatever. Doesn't matter. He's fucking dead now."

The younger dark-haired girl grinned and the fingers of her right hand assumed the shape of a gun. "Pow. Right between the eyes."

Dream chuckled. "That was right at your doorstep, as soon as we were sure ol' Harlan had guided us to the right place. Anyway, I brought our dead sister back to life. Actually, I created a whole new Ellen. We had to leave the original body behind. Physically, she's perfect. The trick is getting her mind to work again. It's slow work, but I'm getting there. Marcy is the key." She nodded at the other young girl, who was still aiming the finger-gun in Giselle's direction. "She's bound to Ellen by blood and carries a touch of her sister's essence with her. I'm drawing on that to restore her personality and memories."

Giselle nodded. "Uh-huh. Right."

She knew what was happening now. It was a little unnerving, but the mere knowing made her feel somewhat better. She had lived amongst sadists and practitioners of dark magic for so long it had taken her a while to recognize simple madness when she saw it. It was a fine distinction, the line between deliberate indulgence of dark desires and the helplessness of lunacy. Dream and her friends were dangerous, yes, but only in the manner of any other roaming pack of maniacs. And she just didn't have the time or patience to deal with babbling lunatics.

So she marched further into the room and yanked a submachine gun from the shaking hands of a startled Black Brigade soldier. She broke the trembling man's neck with a hard chop of her left hand and he fell dead to the floor. Then she got a proper grip on the gun, slipped a finger through the trigger guard, and aimed the weapon at the crazy women sitting at her table.

"I've enjoyed our visit, but I'm very busy, so I'll be killing you now."

Her finger squeezed the trigger. Fire erupted from the muzzle. The weapon chugged and spit shell casings as the barrel tilted toward the ceiling. Bullets slashed through a chandelier and a rain of glittering white shards spattered the table like crystalline rain. Giselle eased her finger off the trigger and stared at the weapon with an expression that made her look like a befuddled child. Her first instinct was to blame the weapon itself. Recoil. The gun had a strong kick and she was not used to handling firearms.

But then she saw Dream's devilish grin.

Her eyes went wide and her breath caught in her throat. She felt a moment of fear. Then she shoved the fear down and a snarl transformed her face, animal fury twisting her natural prettiness and turning it into something almost ugly. She brought the weapon to bear again, aiming it straight at Dream's face. She squeezed the trigger again and waited for the thing she ached to see more than anything else, Dream's pretty face blowing apart beneath the onslaught of a hail of high-velocity steel.

The barrel tipped toward the ceiling again and the bullets etched a jittery pattern of holes in the wood. She kept her finger down on the trigger this time and struggled to bring the barrel down, the muscles in her arms and neck bulging with the strain. But her arms seemed frozen, as if held in place by the hands of some invisible puppet master. The gun's magazine clicked empty and only then did Giselle become aware of the mad, continuous roar emerging from her open mouth. The force holding her hands in place retreated, and she threw the useless weapon across the room with a cry of helpless rage. The gun's stock struck a long, wall-mounted mirror and shattered it.

Dream's black friend—who seemed vaguely familiar—laughed. "Look at that. Seven years bad luck. You done fucked up, bitch."

The one called Marcy laughed.

The drooling lobotomy case made that unsettling chuffing sound again.

And Dream just kept on smiling, utterly unfazed by all the gunfire and drama.

Giselle's teeth were clenched and her hands were curled into tight fists at her side. From the corners of her eyes, she could see the faces of the soldiers. Here and there she was able to discern tell-tale hints of smugness. Of a grim satisfaction. *There*, they were thinking. *Now the bitch knows why the hard men are afraid.*

And they were right, damn them to hell.

She exerted a considerable effort of will and slowly composed herself. In a few moments she was able to regulate her breathing. The flush faded from her face. Her fists uncurled and her jaw relaxed.

She forced a smile. "Okay, Dream. I know that was your doing. I can feel it." She moved a few slow, deliberate steps toward the seated women. "Why don't you tell me how you did it?"

Dream chuckled. "Oh, you know. If you think about it hard enough, that is."

Giselle moved another step closer. And another. Slow. Casual. As sublimely cool and confident as a stoned surfer riding the crest of an early morning wave. Her eyes were locked on Dream's. The rest of the world faded. There was only the two of them now. There was a sweet tension in the air that was almost sexual. She was putting herself out in the open, making herself as vulnerable as she'd ever been, clearing the channels to allow only pure truth to flow between them. In those moments she learned all she needed to know about Dream, and Dream saw the extent of Giselle's own formidable powers.

Yet another step closer.

"The Master. Of course." Giselle's smile was almost

radiant now. He showed you some things, awakened a dormant power within you. A power that grew beyond your ability to control and direct." She laughed. "You're not really human. Not purely. Somewhere in the distant past one of his kind mated with one of your ancestors. This is why you have become so strong without schooling yourself in the dark arts."

Dream's smile became a smirk. "Interesting theory. Might even be the fuckin' truth. Thing is, I don't really give a fuck. Not anymore."

Giselle was within six feet of them now. Close to striking distance. Certain muscles began to subtly coil. "Is that so?" She arched an eyebrow, a faintly mocking expression. "Or are you just too much of a drunken mess to wrap your stupid head around any idea more complex than a knock-knock joke?"

Dream's face turned hard. "Stop right there."

And Giselle felt that force rise up against her again. It was impressive, the sheer ease with which Dream wielded her ability. But Giselle had been expecting it this time. And she was not without ability of her own. She threw up a psychic shield that repelled Dream's energy pulse and knocked the woman back in her own chair. Dream gaped at her. Shock radiated from her every pore.

NOW.

Giselle loosed a shriek of fury and dove across the surface of the table, her right hand extended, long, sharp nails seeking Dream's sky-blue eyes. Dream's friends tried to intercept her, but another blast of energy sent them tumbling to the floor. Giselle slid across the table at high speed, her body knocking aside the wine bottle and glasses. Then she was on Dream, her left hand closing on the woman's slender throat as the fingers of her other hand shot toward those gaping, stupid eyes. And for a flashing instant, Giselle felt her own smug satisfaction, thinking, *stupid cow.*

Then Dream's hand snapped up and seized Giselle's outstretched wrist. Giselle's momentum alone should have been enough to finish the job anyway, and the power flowing through her should have sealed the deal.

But Dream's strength blunted her momentum. The woman's hand moved backward perhaps half a centimeter. Then stopped. Giselle's wrist was frozen in place, but the rest of her body kept moving. Dream leaped to her feet and moved with the direction of that energy. She shifted her grip on Giselle's wrist and exerted some force of her own. Then Giselle was airborne and flying toward the wall with no way to stop the impending crash. The top of her head smacked the wall, and an instant later she hit the floor with a hard, undignified thud. The pain was immense. Before she could even begin to consider her next move, she was yanked to her feet and slammed against the wall.

Dream put a hand around her throat and slammed her against the wall again. "How's that feel, bitch! How's that fucking feel!" Dream's eyes were wide and bulging, pulsing with insanity and unmitigated fury. "Does it fucking hurt! Does it fucking hurt!"

Giselle's vision blurred and she realized with shame that she had tears in her eyes. She didn't bother to answer the crazy woman's question. Of course it hurt. But the pain wasn't the worst of it. The thing that really got to her was how powerless she was to stop this abuse. And she almost felt like laughing, despite everything, because now she had the gift of clarity and could see how arrogant she had been. Had she really felt like a god? As if nothing or no one could ever hurt her again?

She bit her lip. Hard. Tasted her own blood.

And called out to the void.

Azaroth! Help me!

No answer from the void.

Just the sound of her head banging repeatedly off the wall as the world turned fuzzy. She wondered if she was about to die and felt a moment's perplexion at how little she cared. As she neared unconsciousness, she thought of the essential ways in which the blood sacrifice of Eddie King had changed her. Maybe she'd really died back then, the real Giselle, and the thing she was now was just some magical construct, a joke played on her by a malicious god. Azaroth. The silent one. Her former co-conspirator against the Master. Her restored hands. A body, whole again.

Construct.

Giselle's laughter approached madness. Now who was the crazy one? Dream continued to scream at her, the words losing any meaning now.

Then, just as she thought death might take her, she glanced over her shoulder and saw a new shape enter the room. She blinked hard. Dream wasn't banging her against the wall anymore. Just screaming. Raging. Her hand squeezing. The shape came into focus as it moved closer.

Giselle's heart lurched.

Ursula.

Still nude. So beautiful. So tall in those ridiculous platform heels. The jut of her mouth so insolent. In that moment Giselle felt a rush of love and desire. It was all still there, the purity of all she'd felt for the girl over these months. It hadn't really faded at all. And seeing the fright and concern in her lover's eyes only intensified the feeling.

Ursula locked eyes with her and Giselle saw the same depth of emotion within her.

It was a beautiful, aching, glorious moment.

And it passed in a nanosecond.

Ursula screamed and came running toward her, ridiculous big heels clomping on the marble floor.

And the young girl with the black-as-night hair—
Marcy—rose up and strode purposefully forward, a real
gun, a gleaming, nickel-plated 9mm pistol, in her hands
now. She aimed the barrel point blank at Ursula's face
and fired once. The bullet hit her between the eyes. An
explosion of red bloomed behind her head even as her
body flew backward. Giselle squealed anguish and
tried to flex her power one last time, reached down
deep inside herself and tried to kickstart the core of
that power. But it was unreachable. Something was in
the way. Still she kept reaching, kept straining . . .

Dream grinned and said, "No."

Giselle's vision blurred again. "Kill me. Please. Finish
it. . . ."

Dream laughed. "No." She increased the pressure
around Giselle's neck, reducing her air passage to perhaps the width of a straw. "You're not getting off that
easy."

Of course not.

Giselle's fading gaze went to the trembling soldiers.
No smugness on their faces now. Just terror. Disbelief.
Helplessness. Trembling hands unable to wield their
weapons. Giselle wasn't sure they'd choose to use them
if they could.

And there, just inside the archway, good old Schreck.
As afraid as the rest of them, but with a hint of a smirk
playing at the edges of his mouth. She had another insight then. Another bit of truth she'd been too stupid
and arrogant to discern. He was the traitor. The Order of
the Dragon plant alluded to by Gwendolyn in her last
moments. And he must have seen the recognition in
her fading vision, because now he was baring his teeth.
Cackling, the jackal exposed at last.

Giselle sucked more blood from her torn lip into her
mouth.

Called out one last time.

Azaroth . . . why have you forsaken me?

And this time she received a response.

Disembodied, mocking laughter that boomed in her head like thunder.

Thunder that rolled on and on as the world faded away at last.

PART III:
NEW YEAR'S DAY

CHAPTER TWENTY

The caravan departed Camp Whiskey at the break of dawn, six vans and two Jeeps packed with weaponry and ammunition, carrying some two dozen passengers down a winding, snow-encrusted mountain path. They traveled all through the day and the whole of the night that followed, arriving somewhere in the approximate center of Wyoming at dawn of the next day.

Allyson blinked and emerged from the drowse she'd fallen into some fifteen minutes earlier. She sat up straight and stared through a window at the gray sky and the passing countryside. The Jeep's engine rattled and chugged, its big tires bouncing in and out of potholes as it followed the snaking stretch of rural highway. There were no houses to be seen anywhere. Just trees and more trees, their branches denuded by the season, pale and angling toward the sky like the outstretched arms of worshippers.

The Jeep was at the rear of the modest column of vehicles. Allyson shifted in her seat and peered between the front seats for a glimpse of the road ahead. The other vehicles were staying close, none of them separated by more than a car length. The van directly in front of them was old and painted olive green.

Just like a for-real army truck, Allyson thought, smirking.

But as far as she was concerned, the van's color marked the end of any similarity between this insane glorified Boy Scout mission and any real military operation. They lacked strength of numbers, for one thing. In the wake of Jack Paradise's murder and the imprisonment of Jim, the tenuous connections that had held together the always fragile Camp Whiskey community frayed and came apart. An attempt to repel the usurpers from the Order of the Dragon lacked cohesion and direction and was put down in spectacularly brutal fashion. The camp's mysteriously cowed faux-military wing stood by and let it happen. The bulk of the people saw that the Order could not be overcome and a mass exodus ensued. Allyson had felt a strong urge to run with them, but could not bring herself to do so without Chad, who was riding now in one of the forward vehicles.

Only a small, hardcore group chose not to flee. These were mostly men, and mostly members of the paramilitary unit assembled by Jack Paradise. Most of Jack's men died alongside him that night. The ones who remained took orders from the Order people, and did so without question. Chad was being held against his will by the Asian woman, but Allyson had a feeling he would have stayed regardless, at least as long as Jim remained alive.

Thinking of that stirred Allyson's anger anew. The bitch treated him like a piece of property, or a pet, dragging him along wherever she went, striking him whenever he dared to open his mouth. Allyson felt embarrassment on Chad's behalf any time she witnessed this behavior, and a part of her withered inside every time it happened, as she thought of how humiliating the ordeal must be for him. Doubly frustrating was her utter inability to do anything about it.

The Asian woman forbade any contact between them. Allyson initially wondered why Chad's new keeper

allowed her to stay at Camp Whiskey. She eventually realized the woman was deriving a sadistic enjoyment from
Allyson's predicament, taunting her by flaunting her
ownership of Chad. It was a petty, cruel thing. But it was
also a good thing. Proximity meant there would one day
be an opportunity to exploit. She kept her eyes open. The
chance to get away with Chad in tow would present itself. And she damn well intended to make the most of
that opportunity.

But now things had changed. Again.

The order to saddle up and head out to the final battle
of good versus evil (although Allyson had decided evil
versus evil was a more accurate description at this point)
had been handed down. Many hundreds of miles later,
Allyson was still looking for that perfect moment. The circumstances complicated things. She no longer had an
indefinite period of time to work with. She was separated
from her man and surrounded by well-armed hostiles.

Still, she wasn't ready to give up just yet.

She kicked the back of the seat ahead of her and
said, "How much farther?"

The man in the seat turned to look at her. He was clad
in camos and sported black shades despite the overcast
sky. "Not sure. Maybe fifty more miles." He grinned and
licked parched lips. "And hey . . . kick my seat again and
I'll come back there to teach you a lesson."

The man in the driver's seat—a black man also clad
in camos—glanced at the rearview mirror and grinned
broadly. "I'd like to tear me off a piece of that, myown-
self."

Allyson snorted. "Either of you pukebags touch me,
I'll tear your fucking eyes out. And anyway, you don't
have time for pussy. You've got a big battle to be dying in
soon, remember?"

The driver laughed. "Listen to the mouth on her."

The man in the shotgun seat leered at her. "Don't

worry, baby. I can always make time for pussy, one way or another."

Allyson slid a hand into a pocket of the heavy winter jacket she was wearing. Her fingers curled around the handle of the big switchblade she'd stashed there earlier. She eased her hand out of the pocket and clicked the little button on the side. The blade popped out and she lunged forward, slamming the blade into the man's exposed throat. The man's shades popped off his face as blood jetted from the hole in his throat. He gaped at Allyson in disbelief even as she yanked the blade out and slammed it into one of his eyes. Allyson did all of this without thinking, instinct driving her, a moment of pure awareness in which she understood on a primal level that the "perfect" moment she hoped for would never arrive. It was much like those fevered moments in the dark kitchen of Chad's house as she'd slaughtered those men in black, her mind and body operating with surprising efficiency in stripped-down reptile-brain mode.

And brutal murder was like anything—it got easier with practice.

Blood spurted over her hands and soaked the front of her jacket. The man tried to twist away from her, but she grabbed the front of his shirt and held him close, yanking the blade from his eye and whipping it around again, punching it through his temple, somehow keeping her aim true as the driver screamed and swerved on the winding back road.

Allyson turned her snarling face toward the driver and said, "Slow down and let the others get around that bend."

She pulled the bloody blade out of the dead man's head and brandished it.

"Do it or die."

The man was shaking and crying, robbed utterly of any remaining shred of bravado or machismo. "Y-y-y-yeah . . . o-kay . . . please . . ."

And he did it. The van ahead of them disappeared around the bend. The Jeep slowed and Allyson ordered the driver to park at the shoulder. Again, he did as instructed, tears streaming down his face as he mewled like a snot-nosed kid on a playground standing in the shadow of a bully. Allyson pushed the shotgun seat forward, threw the door open, and got out. She hauled the dead man's body out of the Jeep and deposited it in the ditch beyond the shoulder. The whole time the Jeep was in gear and running, its engine chugging, exhaust kicking out steam in the winter's air.

Allyson climbed back inside, assuming the position formerly occupied by the dead, would-be rapist. She pulled the pistol from the driver's holster and jammed the barrel against his side.

"Drive. Now."

The driver looked at the pistol she'd so easily taken from him. Then he looked at her, simple, numb disbelief in his eyes. "I could've killed you. Or left you. Or—"

Allyson jabbed the pistol harder against him. "But you didn't. You fucked up. Because you're not as hardcore as you thought. But I am, motherfucker. So now you're gonna drive. Catch up to the rest of those assholes before they know anything's wrong. Make me say it again, I'll shoot your ass and do it my damn self."

The Jeep lurched forward.

The engine rattled and ate up highway.

They caught up and kept rolling.

CHAPTER TWENTY-ONE

The spoon slipped from her fingers and landed with a small thump on the little card table. It landed upside down, its meager load of mashed potatoes dumped onto the scuffed and scratched black surface. Ellen groped for the spoon's handle again, managed to grasp it at an awkward angle, and raised it again to her mouth. This time the spoon actually entered her mouth. A sound of simple triumph issued from the back of her throat.

Marcy sighed. "That's something, anyway. You didn't get any actual food in your mouth, but hell, you're getting there."

She settled back in her chair and stared at the thing that was supposed to be her sister. The creature was the spitting image of Ellen. Marcy was impressed by what Dream had accomplished, this godlike act of forming life out of seeming thin air. It had been Alicia's idea, to see if Dream could deliberately do what she'd done with her, recreating a dead friend from a synthesis of memories, spiritual essence, and, for lack of a better word, magic. Dream had been wary at first, and then curious, as she became increasingly interested in testing the limits of her abilities. Marcy had been so numb, so grief-stricken, and so willing to grasp at any straw.

So one night on their way to this place they stopped at a cheap motel on the outskirts of a rural community. Dream and Marcy crawled into bed together. They wrapped their bodies around each other, limbs entwined in the most intimate ways possible. There'd been nothing sexual about this, just an instinctual understanding that they needed to be as close to each other as possible in order to effect this unique process of creation. The darkness and relative silence served to enhance their concentration. Marcy's mind filled with images and thoughts of Ellen and nothing else. She visualized her dead sister so well Ellen seemed to come alive in her mind. She fell asleep in Dream's embrace, and thoughts of Ellen followed her into dreams so vivid, so lucid, they felt as real as anything from her waking life. As she awakened in the dim light of the following morning, she heard a sound like the scared whimpering of a lost puppy. Then she'd opened her eyes and there was her reborn sister, nude and huddled in a corner of the dingy room.

She'd felt such joy in those first moments, a feeling subsequently tempered by the realization the creature they'd created was essentially an empty vessel. But the reborn Ellen did seem to recognize Marcy and the others in a dim way, and it was this little thing that provided the shred of hope necessary to keep going. Dream had pledged to work with her every day until Ellen was fully restored. Marcy had faith in her friend and believed this would eventually happen.

She looked into Ellen's stupid, vacant eyes again and sighed.

Eventually . . .

Marcy didn't doubt the sincerity of Dream's intent. They'd formed a strong bond over the course of those long, frequently surreal months on the road. The complicating factor, however, was Dream's near-constant state of inebriation. She'd stayed drunk or high much of the time during their travels, but the camaraderie of the road had obscured the extent of her problem. Now, though, the truth of Dream's dependency was plain to see. She had the perpetually dour aura of the clinically depressed. She was obviously self-medicating. In a way, it was understandable. It wasn't as if she could seek the aid of a psychiatrist or any other type of mental health professional.

But knowing this failed to alleviate Marcy's frustration. Her friend was a god. Or something very close to a god. And that was simultaneously very cool and fucked-up to the nth degree. Cool because it allowed Dream and her friends a level of freedom few people would ever experience. And fucked up because Dream inwardly remained so quintessentially human and frail despite her gift.

Ellen was eating with her fingers again, stuffing mashed potatoes and meatballs into her mouth with messy abandon. Marcy refrained from slapping her wrist this time. She watched the girl eat and tried to imagine a future in which her sister was functioning at a higher cognitive state, a time when she might exist as a reasonable approximation of the sibling she'd known. She tried to imagine having actual conversations with her, perhaps reminiscing about things from their childhoods.

Ellen's teeth chomped down on her fingers and drew blood. The girl let out a squeal of pain and stared at her mangled fingers in dumb disbelief. A thin trickle of crimson slid over the heel of her hand and down her wrist. It wasn't the first time Ellen 2 had injured herself. Marcy very much doubted it would be the last. And now she'd have to clean the idiot's hand and swab the wounds with disinfectant. Her mind did that forward projection thing again, saw years of tending to this creature, and a black despair seeped into her heart.

Then Ellen held her hand toward Marcy. Her mouth opened and emitted a single syllable: "Hurt."

Marcy's mouth dropped open. The word was the first intelligible thing Ellen 2 had uttered since the morning she was conjured into existence in that dank hotel room. Ellen seemed to misinterpret her sister's astonishment as a rebuke and uttered a second word: "*Ssssssor-rrrryyyyy . . .*"

Then tears were streaming down her face and her body began to convulse with sobs. Marcy was up in a flash, her chair toppling to the floor as she hurried to embrace her sister. The girl folded herself into Marcy's arms and clutched at her clothes with her clumsy fingers, that second word emerging from her mouth again and again. Marcy stroked Ellen's hair and made cooing sounds in her ear.

"Shush. Everything will be okay. I promise."

Tears filled her own eyes as she prayed for that to be true. She remembered with horrible clarity how she'd felt in the aftermath of Ellen's death, that gnawing, soul-shredding grief. She couldn't imagine anything more awful. It would be better to be dead than have to go on feeling that way. The train of thought made her think of the friends she'd killed after the incident in the bar, all those lives extinguished because she'd snapped or gone temporarily insane. Even now, months later, she had no reasonable explanation for what she'd done, just that sense of fate carrying her toward a dark destiny. A mad whim. She remembered every detail of that day vividly, the twitch of the gun in her hands as she squeezed the trigger again and again, the specific damage each bullet had done to the bodies of her friends, and the way those bodies had fallen. But she hadn't allowed herself to think about how these deaths must have affected the loved ones of her victims. But now she was thinking about it. Oh, yes. And now she imagined the grief she'd felt for Ellen multiplied dozens of times.

The first sob began somewhere deep in her gut and tore out of her throat with wrenching force. It was followed by many more.

The two sisters held each other and cried for a long time.

CHAPTER TWENTY-TWO

Giselle awoke in darkness, as she had every day for the last two weeks or so. At first she'd tried to keep careful track of the passage of time. It seemed important, albeit for no immediately apparent reason. It'd merely been something to do, a simple task to occupy a mind that might otherwise obsess on things more disturbing. At some point she stopped trying to gauge the length of her imprisonment, and so now her best guess was two weeks. Two weeks of numbing existence in the dark and the cold.

She'd felt a deep humiliation upon being returned to the hanging cage, the prison she'd fought so hard to escape. A life had been sacrificed to make that happen. Her own conscience had died in the process. But it had all seemed worth it for a time. She'd had her revenge and for a while had known a kind of contentment. And in time contentment bred arrogance, which led to her downfall. She should have been so much more careful. How stupid she'd been to accept Schreck's loyalty without question. That vile man. He was the reason she was in this awful place again, having suggested it when Dream and her friends had been debating about what to do with her. And he'd surprised her by knowing how to access the chamber. Just one more thing she should've guessed, one more example of how arrogance had blinded her. And now she ached for revenge again, but this time she knew she would never have it.

Her power was gone.

Well, not really gone. Not exactly. It still resided somewhere within her altered DNA, still floated in the microscopic spaces between molecules. She could feel the faint thrum of it in her every pore. That was the most maddening thing, that awareness, because the power was beyond her ability to reach. Dream had seen to that, infusing her body with a damping energy, an extraordinarily effective bit of blunt magic that blocked her every attempt to tap her own magical abilities. That Dream was able to direct energy so effortlessly boggled the mind. She was untrained. She'd never read any of the ancient texts Giselle had pored over during her years in service to the Master. She could accept the scope of Dream's abilities as an accident of nature and genetics, a dormant thing stirred to life during her ruttings with the Master. She had a harder time understanding how the woman had come to direct that raw, wild energy with such precision and effectiveness. It was either a case of practice makes perfect, or Dream was some kind of magical idiot savant. Either possibility was equally galling. It meant her years of often tedious study had ultimately been for nothing.

As bad as that was, it was as nothing compared to the desolation she felt in the wake of Azaroth's abandonment. She recalled her last communication with the death god and felt the same puzzlement she always felt. No words, just that mocking, echoing laughter. So unlike anything in her previous experience with the ancient entity.

Perhaps he'd been manipulating her all along, even all those years ago when she'd first invoked his name with a blood sacrifice after reading about him in one of the old texts. The death gods were old beyond human conception. It was presumptuous to assume to know why they did the things they did. Maybe Azaroth really had played her from the beginning, building her up with the intent of eventually betraying her. Wheels within wheels within wheels. Suffering begetting suffering down through the ages as the old ones spun out their endless, convuluted machinations. The death gods fed on suffering, this she knew. And she supposed Azaroth was feasting on her pain even now, enjoying the particular aged flavor of her despair.

An impulse caused her to call out to him. It didn't matter that he probably wouldn't answer, or that at best she would only hear that mocking laughter again. Her every fiber ached to know the truth. She realized it would not grant her peace, that it might even deepen her despair, but the need to know overwhelmed any other considerations.

She focused what she could of her will and called out to the void: *AZAROTH! HEAR ME! I BESEECH YOU! WHY HAVE YOU FORSAKEN ME!*

At first there was nothing. Just that darkness. That void. Then she felt a touch of warmth against her flesh, a subtle atmospheric shift, like the sigh of a lover against her neck. The warmth increased, displacing the cold that normally permeated the room.

Next, a pinpoint of light in the middle distance.

The light grew and pushed the darkness back. Giselle could see again, albeit dimly, the stone walls beyond the cage. The shimmering center of light in the middle of the room flared brighter still and grew to the size of a man. A mist billowed at the edges of the light and Giselle realized she was seeing a portal, a doorway between dimensions. She saw shadows within the light, forms moving, something coming closer. A shape resolved into the dark silhouette of a man.

The man stepped through the light into the dark chamber.

Giselle's screams echoed off the chamber walls.

She screamed and screamed again. Screamed herself hoarse.

The man laughed softly and approached the cage. Giselle whimpered and scooted to the far end of the cage, making it rock wildly.

"Nooooo . . ." She moaned. Her mind rebelled, fought to deny the reality of what she was seeing. But he just kept coming closer, refusing to dissipate like any good hallucination should. "Noooo . . . nononono . . ."

The Master laughed again and said, "Yes."

She groaned again. "How?"

He smiled. "I thrived in the afterlife, Giselle. You should have expected that. I destroyed the one you call Azaroth, usurped his position among the death gods. It's me you've been communicating with during your recent troubles. I'm the one who demanded the blood sacrifice of your friend. You've belonged to me from that moment. You and your dead conscience."

That mocking laughter again, filling the chamber, rattling her bones and triggering an ache behind her eyes.

Another whimper. "Kill me. Finish it."

His expression shifted again, something that was almost sadness touching his handsome features. "No. Your final judgment is in the hands of others." He stroked her cheek with the back of a strong hand. "I'm showing myself to you one final time to thank you. Your sacrifices have facilitated my return. For that, you have my eternal gratitude."

Giselle wept. She was no longer capable of articulating her despair any other way. The light dimmed as the portal between dimensions began to close. The Master remained in the chamber with her a while longer, stroking her hair and delighting in the sound of her anguish as the darkness and cold enveloped them.

CHAPTER TWENTY-THREE

In the dream, things were as they had once been. She was years younger and her long hair was a vibrant shade of blonde. Her flesh was imbued with that deep, lovely tan all the boys found so sexy. She was in a park on a glorious summer afternoon, the sun a golden ball high in the perfect blue sky. She was stretched out on a blanket, soaking up the rays in a white bikini. Her friends were there, too. Alicia sat next to her on the blanket, her long legs folded beneath her as she read a John Grisham novel. Karen and Chad tossed a Frisbee back and forth in the distance. The orange disc arced across the sky and Chad hurried into position to catch it. Music emanated from a nearby boom box, a big hit by a new band called Green Day.

It was a lovely dream, but tinged with a subtle undercurrent of melancholy. An aching sense of loss belied the purity of the images. Because this was nothing more than a snapshot of something that was gone and forever out of reach. Karen Hidecki was dead. The Alicia Jackson she'd known in those days was dead, too. The regenerated Alicia would never be anything more than an obscene approximation of the deceased woman.

And as for Chad . . .

The texture and tone of the dream began to change. The blue sky turned a shade of burnt orange bordering on red. The shape of the Frisbee was almost indistinct against that sky as a gust of wind too cold for summer carried it off course. Karen charged after the disc and for a moment it seemed she would catch up to it. But then her head tumbled off her shoulders and bounced across a patch of dead, yellow grass that moments ago had been a bright shade of green. Dream sat up and screamed, pointing at the headless body, which was still running at high speed toward a nearby line of dead trees. The sight of her pale forearm startled her. What had happened to her beautiful tan?

Then Alicia spoke in the creaking voice of a rotting corpse. "You're just an old whore now. The girl you were is just as dead as that headless bitch."

This was the regenerated Alicia now, looking as she had the moment she'd first appeared to Dream in that little shithole bar. Her flesh was bloated and covered with hundreds of weeping razor nicks.

Dream trembled and shook her head helplessly. "No . . . no . . ."

Alicia set aside the book she was reading—which had somehow morphed into *The Satanic Bible*—and began to crawl toward Dream on her hands and knees. The corners of her mouth stretched wide in a lascivious grin. The skin at the edges of her mouth cracked and a pale, dry nub of tongue emerged to lick uselessly at the new wounds. A brittle wheeze of laughter emerged from the back of her throat.

She reached for Dream with a bleeding hand and said, "Come show me some love, baby."

Dream screamed.

Then her eyes snapped open and she was awake. Above her was the heavy velvet canopy of the four-poster bed. Her head swam and her first impression was she was still asleep, had merely transitioned from one layer of dream existence to another. The old false waking dream, a wicked, but familiar, trick of her fragile psyche. Then she recognized the sensation for what it really was—borderline intoxication. She hadn't remained unconscious quite long enough to sleep off last night's binge.

Which was just as well.

She rolled out of bed and swept the nearly empty bottle of tequila off the nightstand. She held the bottle up and shook it. There was enough left for one good swig. She put the bottle to her mouth and upended it. It slid down her throat as smoothly as water. There'd been a time when so much as a single sip of straight tequila had been enough to make her retch. She returned the empty bottle to the nightstand and stretched her limbs, rolling her neck to work out the kinks.

Images from the dream came back to haunt her. Not the predictable bit at the end when it had all turned to rot. Dream had known too much real horror to care about such nightmare images. What really bothered her was the dream's beginning, which had been so vivid and true, a scene dredged from a store of long-suppressed memories. There really had been days like that. Many of them. Times when she'd been truly happy to be alive and surrounded by her friends. Happy and so young. Thinking about it triggered the old familiar ache in her heart. This was why she normally worked so hard to keep those memories locked down in her subconscious. The usual reflex to push them down failed to kick in this time. So stupid. Next would come the rush of tears . . .

Only that didn't happen. Her eyes misted a little, but that was it. And instead of burning straight through to the core of her pain the old ache just fizzled.

Dream sighed. "Nothing stays the same forever."

She looked around the huge, empty room and wondered to whom she was talking. But the answer was obvious. There was no one else around. She was alone most of the time these days. She'd granted Schreck the freedom to run the estate as he saw fit, with the stipulation that he and his men stay out of the way of Dream and her friends. So far it had worked out well enough. They were comfortable here. The law couldn't reach them here. There was one downside, but it was a big one. The sense of camaraderie they had shared had diminished by a significant degree. Marcy and Ellen had commandeered a smaller room on a lower level of the mansion, from which they rarely emerged. Alicia, however, was taking an active role in the day-to-day operations of the place. She took such delight in meting out the kinds of tortures that had once been so mercilessly inflicted upon her, which Dream found ironic as well as mildly disturbing.

And that was another thing. The interior of this house was massive, containing hundreds of rooms. And in each of those rooms resided a sadist-in-training, an Apprentice, each of them committing acts of atrocity so vile the mere contemplation of which would once have made Dream want to vomit. But the part of her that might have cared had withered and died somewhere along the way. She couldn't even feign offense at the institutionalized brutality that surrounded her. It was simply the way things were and would always be in this place—and the way they needed to be in order to sustain the dark magic that kept the place thriving.

So she supposed she liked it here well enough.

But it would be nice not to feel so alone.

Fuck.

It was insane that she could still feel such depression. She was so powerful. There was nothing she couldn't do. She could will life into existence just by thinking about it hard enough. She could change the temperature in a room with a small flex of her will. She could send a hail of fucking bullets off course by doing the same thing. She suspected she was even capable of altering her own body chemistry, of rolling back the years to erase age lines and reverse any age-related infirmities. Disease could take root inside her and it wouldn't matter because she would be able to burn it away just by thinking about it. For all practical purposes, she was now immortal.

So why was she still so unhappy? She didn't know. What she did know was she was fucking tired of thinking about it. So she strode across the room, crossing the large expanse of open floor to the area at the opposite end that functioned as both a library and den. The walls here were lined with tall bookcases. There was a fireplace and plenty of expensive-looking furniture. And there was a well-stocked bar tucked away in the corner. She stepped behind it and scanned the rows of gleaming bottles. After a few moments of debate, she selected a bottle of Stolichnaya. She opened it and knocked back several big gulps of vodka.

A slight semblance of well-being returned immediately. It felt good just to have a full bottle in her hands again. She moved away from the bar and examined the shelves of books. Many of them were classic titles she recognized. Many others were unfamiliar. Some titles weren't in English.

She saw one that called to her, the words THE SATANIC BIBLE etched in gold print along its spine. She recalled her dream and pulled the book off the shelf. Then she settled down in a plush recliner, set the bottle on the little table next to it, and flipped the book open. Her fingers moved over the pages and her lips moved slightly as she read the words. She frowned. This book was not the famous Anton LaVey tome with which she'd been fleetingly familiar in her youth. It appeared to be an actual bible for Satanists, a genuine dark equivalent to the Christian Bible, but that was . . .

"It is what you think it is, Dream."

Dream's fingers stopped moving. The intrusion of the familiar voice had surprised her, but she felt no fear and that was strange. She had helped to kill him, after all. He was standing so close, but she hadn't heard or sensed his arrival. She could hear the soft, unlabored sound of his breathing. He was alive again. Somehow. Or was he? Maybe he was like Alicia and Ellen, a manifestation manufactured by her subconscious, this time a conjuration of shameful desires she'd worked to ignore through the years. She had been thinking about him a lot of late, especially at night as she lay alone in the dark in that big bed.

Then he moved into view and she knew it wasn't true. It was really him. The Master.

She closed the book and looked up at him. "How?"

He smiled. "Does it matter?"

And now she smiled. "No. It doesn't matter at all."

She set the book on the table next to the vodka bottle and stood up. She stepped into his outstretched arms and laid her head on his shoulder. She felt his calm strength and reveled in the warmth of his bare flesh.

Her voice was a whisper: "I'm sorry."

"Shush." He stroked her hair with one hand while the other slipped to the small of her back. "Things were different then."

She lifted her head and looked into his eyes again. "Yes. And I think I've become the woman you needed me to be back then. I think I could be your Queen now."

His hand slipped beneath the thin fabric of her halter top and roamed over her trembling flesh. She felt herself grow wet and moaned as his mouth met hers. The kiss made her knees shake and she gripped his shoulders hard to remain upright. It went on for several moments, his warmth suffusing her as their bodies began to writhe in tandem. Then he broke off the kiss and smiled again.

And he said, "You are already my Queen. I knew one day you would be ready."

Dream thought, *You have no idea how ready I am.*

And perhaps he knew her thoughts, because in the next moment he swept her into his arms and carried her across the room to the big bed. And within the next few moments Dream again experienced the thing she'd secretly longed for all through her years of private torment.

Her screams filled the room.

And after the screams, tears of joy.

CHAPTER TWENTY-FOUR

The collar was too tight and chafed at his skin. Chad fought an urge to stick a finger under the strip of leather to relieve the pressure against his throat. For one thing, it wouldn't really help. But mostly he just didn't want to feel the back of Bai's hand again. She had a quick temper and would not abide even the mildest affront to her will.

The physical discomfort was only part of the problem. More aggravating was the humiliation he'd been living with every day for weeks. A masochist with a taste for bondage and discipline and a weakness for hot Asian chicks would be in heaven, but Chad didn't roll that way. He burned with the need to be free of this despicable woman, to be his own man again, able to do as he pleased whenever he wished.

He didn't know how to make that happen. Bai was too strong. Too smart and too fast by far. She was like some kind of superwoman. She anticipated his every move, seemed to know his thoughts. He looked at the long black leash hooked to his collar. It was looped around the minivan's driver's-side door handle. He imagined ripping the thing free and wrapping it around Bai's neck. The fantasy took shape in his mind, and he saw how the leash would dig into her slender throat as he drew it tight, Bai's eyes bulging out as she clawed helplessly at him and gasped for air.

Of course, the minivan would go hurtling off the road, perhaps to crash into one of the big trees beyond the ditch. The impact would send him through the windshield in a hail of safety glass. He might even die. He thought maybe it would be worth it.

He felt the heat of her gaze on him and turned timidly in her direction, tensing for the blow he imagined was imminent.

But she only smiled at him in that soft, enigmatic way. "We are almost there, Dogshit. If you wish to kill me, your best chance will come in the confusion of battle."

Chad grunted. "We both know it'll never happen."

Her dark eyes gleamed in the morning sun. "Of course. You are too weak, Dogshit. Too much the coward. Too much the sniveling little faggot. You are worthless."

This was another thing that incensed him. She hadn't addressed him by his given name since the night of the coup. To her, he was primarily known as Dogshit. A prime example of what passed for her sense of humor. One day he'd stepped in a pile of fresh shit dropped by one of the stray pooches that hung around Camp Whiskey scrounging for scraps. Bai had immediately bestowed the hated nickname. The collar and leash was her idea of a fun way to embellish the joke. It was embarrassing as hell, but there was nothing he could do about it. He'd learned not to object the hard way.

But there was a change on the horizon. The battle they'd prepared for would commence soon, perhaps within the hour. Bai wasn't saying much, but he knew they were very close to their destination. He had a feeling the end of his servitude to Bai was coming one way or another. Either he would die during the conflict, or she would finish him off once the Order had killed or apprehended Giselle Burkhardt.

Or he would find within him the courage to try to kill
her during the battle. He would be outfitted with a
combat-appropriate level of weaponry prior to the storming of the remote farmhouse. It should be an easy thing
to turn that weaponry on his true oppressor. But Bai and
the two Order men moved with a speed and deadly
grace that was eerie, almost supernatural. Should he attempt to use a gun on Bai, she would be behind him
within the space of a heartbeat, well before he could
squeeze the trigger, her sword at his throat, ready to take
his head off before he could even think to turn around.

There was just no percentage in it. Any such attempt
would be tantamount to suicide. Chad figured this was
part of the reason the surviving members of Jack Paradise's paramilitary unit had surrendered and accepted
the Order people as their new leaders. He also suspected these men had been promised a large reward
upon successful completion of this mission. Hell, you
could never underestimate greed as a motivating factor
for anything.

Bai's gaze went back to the road ahead. The minivan
was following a large vehicle that had once been a
package delivery truck. It had been repainted, the old
logos covered over. The truck disappeared around a
sweeping curve for a moment, then reappeared as Bai
guided the minivan around the same curve.

Bai glanced at Chad. "We are almost there, Dogshit.
Are you ready?"

Chad grunted. "No. Not really."

Bai's smile became a smirk. "Typical American weakness. No wonder your country isn't what it once was."

Chad chose not to reply. She was just baiting him
again. Should he open his mouth and say the wrong
thing, he could get his nose broken for his trouble. Or
lose another tooth. He looked out the window on his
side and watched the flashing, denuded trees. Several

moments passed and Bai seemed content to let the exercise in verbal humiliation lapse. Chad felt a bitter gratitude.

Then the line of trees began to thin and soon after that the minivan began to slow. Chad could now make out the twisting line of a narrow dirt side road and, beyond that, the small, dark shape of an old house sitting atop a gentle rise. The house was dilapidated and surrounded by acres of forest on all sides. Its seclusion triggered memories of another house, one high in the mountains of east Tennessee. This added to the already strong sense of déjà vu he was feeling. He'd done this before. But this time was very different. He felt no righteous sense of purpose. This time he was nothing more than a helpless puppet along for the ride.

He looked at Bai and said, "I have to ask something before we do this. I realize you probably won't tell me, but the hell with it. What's the deal with you fucking Order people?"

Her brow creased slightly. "I don't understand."

Chad just managed not to roll his eyes. "What is your purpose? What function does your organization serve? Why go to such lengths to exact revenge?"

Bai smirked. "You could never understand. These are not things for men of low nature to comprehend. All you need to know is we are an ancient Order. Our lives are sustained through centuries through the ritualized sacrifice of innocent lives. And foremost among the codes that govern us is an unswerving loyalty to the Order. When one of us is cut down, it is an attack against us all. To not exact revenge, as you put it, is not an option."

"Wait a minute . . . low nature?"

"Unpure. Unclean." Bai smiled. "And stupid. Low."

Chad thought about that a minute. He was too used to Bai's insults to be overly offended by the "low" comments, but something else she'd said triggered a faint association. He puzzled over it a moment. Then he had it and his eyes went wide. "The Master did the same thing. Was he of the Order?"

Bai shook her head as she twisted the minivan's steering wheel and followed the package truck onto the dirt road. "No. But he had a close association with us, as he practiced many of the same rituals. It is how Evelyn Wickman came to be in his employ."

"Huh." Chad settled back in his seat and felt a strange sense of completion steal over him. Learning this small piece of the puzzle after all these years meant very little in the larger scheme of things. Ms. Wickman was dead and gone. But that small sense of satisfaction was there regardless.

It didn't last long. The package truck reached the top of the driveway and rolled to a stop. Its brake lights came on, then turned off. Bai guided the minivan to a stop several feet behind it and switched the engine off.

Chad felt a lump rise into his throat as his pulse quickened.

This is it, he thought. *The end.*

But no, that wasn't quite right. The true end of his journey lay beyond the frail-looking wooden door on the other side of the house's rickety porch. Chad tensed and the fear began to steal over him. It was about to begin. The noise. The explosions and gunfire. The screaming and the death. He wasn't ready for it. Could never really be ready for it. But it was happening anyway.

He sucked in a startled breath as Bai reached behind his neck. Then the pressure around his throat was gone. She tossed the collar and leash to the floorboard and said, "This is your chance. Fight and emerge victorious. Then freedom will be yours. It is up to you."

She held his gaze for an intense moment and he felt that familiar tingling behind his eyes, as if she could see into his brain and know his every thought. Then the moment was over and she was turning away from him. She opened the door and stepped out of the minivan.

Chad allowed himself another moment to compose himself, then did the same.

The back of the package truck was open and the store of weaponry inside was being rapidly unpacked. A man clad in camos thrust an M-16 and ammunition into his hands. Chad numbly began to load the weapon as he watched other men haul out two cylinders that vaguely resembled the bazookas he'd seen in old war movies. But he recognized them as AT7's, shoulder-launched antitank weapons. Jack Paradise had schooled him on the subject.

The men with the AT7's were setting up to begin the first thrust of the assault even as the remaining caravan vehicles rolled up behind the minivan. A Jeep at the end of the column swerved around the van ahead of it and skirted the edge of the dirt driveway as it rattled toward them. Chad felt a knot form in his stomach as he glimpsed Allyson at the wheel. He frowned. He was sure there'd been two paramilitary men with her in the Jeep, but they were nowhere to be seen.

Allyson stomped on the brake and emerged from the Jeep a moment later. There was a handgun tucked in the waistband of her jeans. She wasn't wearing the heavy jacket she'd had on earlier. She looked Chad in the eye and strode purposefully toward him.

Bai's lips pursed as she observed Allyson's approach. "Where are the men who were with you?"

Allyson pulled the handgun from her waistband and thumbed the safety off. "One of them bailed. Kept talking about how he didn't want to die for something he didn't give a shit about. He ordered the other guy to pull over at gunpoint. Far as I know he's making his way back to that podunk little town on foot. The other guy, he lost his nerve a little later. Maybe his buddy taking off got to him, I don't know. He blew his brains out with this thing." She waved the gun around and Chad flinched, expecting to see the flash of Bai's sword at any moment. "I could've run after that, but you already know I'm not going anywhere without Chad."

She said all this fast, as if she'd been frantically rehearsing it in her head for the last leg of the journey. He was sure there was only a small thread of truth in it. She had the determined air of one on the cusp of a brave and dangerous act. He couldn't fathom why she would've killed the men rather than allowing them to bring her here as planned.

Bai's expression was openly skeptical. But then she smiled and said, "No matter. The time has come. You will fight with us."

Allyson didn't bat an eye. "You bet your ass I will."

Bai spun about on her heels. She unsheathed her sword and waved it at the sky. "Begin."

Suddenly free of Bai, Chad hurried to Allyson and leaned close, whispering frantically, "What the hell's going on?"

Allyson touched his face. "I love you. I'll do anything for you."

Chad frowned. "But—"

Allyson leaned closer, her lips grazing his ear. "It's simple. We'll follow them in. We'll fight and stay alive, hanging back at the rear, staying close to each other. Then as the others press on we'll get the hell out." She inclined her head very slightly toward the Jeep. "Then we'll take that thing and run for our lives."

Chad didn't know how to reply to that. Her plan was dangerous, but maybe it could work. Hell, they didn't have a lot of other options. Then Bai was shouting again and he looked her way, half-expecting her to have somehow heard their muted conversation with her super ninja hearing. But she was facing the house and waving her sword around.

The rear lights of the package truck came on again and an instant later a blast of hugely amplified music boomed like an explosion. Chad recognized it as something early by Metallica, but he didn't know their stuff well enough to identify the particular song. He gulped as the front door of the house began to creak open. He saw dark shapes come into view, hands clasping weapons.

Then there was a loud WHOOSH of sound, followed immediately by another identical sound. The AT7's. Heavy shells passed through the front door and the bone-bruising sounds of explosions followed.

The AT7's weren't reloadable. The men dropped the spent weaponry and cleared the zone for two more men wielding AT7's. There was that WHOOSH again. And again. Followed by still more explosions. They were softening up the enemy, paving the way for the initial push into the house, which would begin within seconds. Chad kept expecting the fragile old house to collapse beneath the brunt of the heavy ordnance, but somehow, almost miraculously, that didn't happen.

Then Allyson was in front of him, moving to the rear of the package truck. An M-16 was thrust into her hands by a man in camos. Like all of them, she'd been trained on the weapon in preparation for this moment. She took it and hurried back to Chad's side. Then Jim emerged from the back of the truck, hair ruffled as if he hadn't slept in days, eyes bleary and haunted. Chad had barely seen the deposed Camp Whiskey leader since the night of the coup. But like the rest of them, he was armed to the teeth. He looked Chad's way and acknowledged him with a nod. Then he turned and hurried to a forward position.

Chad wanted to call after him, but it was too late.

He dimly heard Bai's screamed exhortations over the buzzing in his ears.

And then they were moving forward, all of them.

Gunfire erupted from both sides.

Chad lifted his weapon, aimed quickly, and squeezed the trigger. The weapon chugged and the scent of blood was heavy in the air as Chad and the woman he loved rushed into the thick of battle.

CHAPTER TWENTY-FIVE

They were out on the long balcony overlooking Razor City as they heard the muffled thumps of the first explosions.

Dream frowned. "Something's happening."

The Master stood with his forearms balanced against the balcony railing. He looked just as he had the last time Dream had seen him, and she understood that what she was seeing was part illusion. He had a chameleonic ability to shift his appearance at will—it was one of the traits of his race—and he'd chosen to present himself the way she remembered him. He was handsome, with fine, chiseled features, and a muscular body with a deep tan. The same thick, broad shoulders that had so turned her on the first time. The same intense, passionate eyes. The strength, confidence, and poise he'd possessed in such abundance was still there too, perhaps even to a greater degree than before.

Because something serious was definitely happening somewhere in the house and he didn't seem the least perturbed by it. Dream heard more explosions and a rapid, snapping sound she assumed was automatic gunfire.

Still looking at the red sky of the alien world beyond

the balcony, he said, "Do you know what this place is, Dream? That world out there?"

She frowned again. "No, but—"

He stood erect and turned toward her, took her gently into his arms. She shuddered and slid with a sigh into the embrace. He stroked her hair and kissed the top of her head. "That red-sky world is where my kind originated. Our race thrived there for many thousands of years. Then some ravaging disease blighted it and the survivors took to the stars in silver ships." He glanced over her shoulder at the barren landscape beyond Razor City. "It is still a dead world, all of my kind are long perished, but for some reason it calls to me. See that pyramid in the distance?"

Dream looked at it. "That's new, isn't it? Or relatively new. The slaves were working on it for a long time before I got here."

The Master nodded. "New, yes. However, it is being built according to ancient specifications. When finished, it will be a precise replica of the pyramids my ancestors used as holy temples. I believe Evelyn intended to eventually use it in an attempt to resurrect my mortal form."

Confusion creased Dream's brow. "Evelyn?"

"You knew her as Ms. Wickman."

Dream stiffened slightly. "Oh."

"Of course, she had no way of knowing how close I was to achieving that goal on my own." His smile this time had a rueful quality. "It isn't easy to send information through the veil separating the mortal world and the various afterlife dimensions. Even those skilled in such things frequently get it wrong. Poor Giselle, for instance."

Dream shivered and turned her head against his chest again. "What will happen to her?"

"Those sounds you're hearing? The approach of

invaders. They have come for her." He lifted her head from his chest and stared into her eyes. "And they will have her."

Dream felt a fresh sense of alarm. It had been so easy to allow herself to be hypnotized by the sound of his voice, to slip into a cocoon of comfort while wrapped in his arms. She pushed away from him a little and said, "Shouldn't we be doing something? They're coming here." She nodded at the open French doors. "She's in there, in that nasty chamber on the other side of that wall."

He smiled and stroked her hair again. "We will do nothing."

Her eyes gleamed with sudden fright. "Why?"

His smile remained unwavering. "We are in no danger. We could repel the invaders, if we so chose. You are strong enough to do it on your own, in fact. But we will not do this. They will take Giselle and depart this place, never to trouble us again. Then we will rebuild this kingdom, perhaps even expand our presence in the land of my ancestors. And we will reign as king and queen for a thousand years."

Dream laughed. "A *thousand* years?"

"Yes. It is part of the bargain I made with the death gods."

Dream stopped laughing. "You're not kidding, are you?"

The Master shook his head. "I am not."

Dream shivered. It was a strange thing to contemplate. Suicidal impulses had plagued so much of her younger years, and now she was looking at a potential lifetime stretching across centuries. The concept was initially jarring, but the more she thought about it—and the more she stared into her lover's intense eyes—the more right it felt.

She smiled and touched his face. "Okay."

He took one of her hands in his, kissed the back of it. "I love you, Dream."

She tugged at the sash around her bathrobe and pulled open the flaps, exposing the front of her body. Her breasts were pale in the alien sunlight. The sound of the gunfire was growing louder as she said, "Come fuck me."

The Master smiled again.

And did as his Queen bade.

CHAPTER TWENTY-SIX

Marcy was in the bathroom with her sister. Ellen was perched on the toilet, with her jeans down around her ankles. Marcy knelt in front of her and coaxed her sister with words she almost certainly didn't understand. Hygiene was a big problem for Ellen. It had been hard to get her to understand that she couldn't just squat and shit on the floor any time she felt the urge to go. Nor had it been easy to instruct her on proper use of the toilet. You had to watch for signs indicating she was on the verge of needing to take a dump. She would get restless and start pacing about their room, panting and whimpering like a dog in need of going outside. In fact, the process had been very similar to potty-training an animal.

Ellen whimpered again. "Muhmuh . . . muh—"

Marcy sighed. "Come on Ellen. Squeeze. You can do it."

"Muh . . . muh—" Tears of frustration welled in Ellen's eyes. "Muh—"

"Oh, the hell with it."

Marcy stood and extended a hand to her sister, who accepted it with dumb gratitude, a drool-flecked smile tugging at the corners of her mouth. Ellen stood, and Marcy helped her get her jeans tugged back up and snapped shut. They had just reentered the bedroom when Marcy heard the faint sound of something she needed a moment to recognize as heavy metal music.

She frowned.

It was the first time she'd heard recorded music of any sort since arriving at this place. Though the music was muffled, she had a sense that it was coming from somewhere outside the house. She was moving toward the bedroom door to investigate when the boom of the first explosion sent a hot spike of fear through her heart, freezing her hand on the doorknob. The sound was massive and the concussion seemed to rattle the whole house. It was followed immediately by more explosions, just as big and loud, which was followed by the stuttering sound of gunfire. Ellen screamed and threw herself against Marcy, jarring her hand away from the doorknob. Her hands clawed and scrabbled against Marcy's clothes as she mewled inarticulately. Marcy shoved her away, sent her tumbling to the floor. Ellen landed on her ass and let out a pained squeal. The sound ripped at Marcy's heart, but the panic engulfing her was too immense to allow any room for coddling her simpleton sister. She had to figure out something to do, and fast, before whatever was happening downstairs got any closer.

Then she had it. The only answer possible.

Dream. We've got to get to Dream.

"Upstairs." She looked at Ellen. "Get your ass up. We're going upstairs. *NOW.*"

She hurried over to the nightstand beside the bed, yanked the drawer open, and pulled out her Glock. She checked the magazine. Full. She popped it back in and turned around in time to see her sister moving toward the door. Ellen's hands fumbled with the doorknob for a moment before seizing it. A burst of adrenaline sent Marcy dashing back across the room.

The door came open and the sound of gunfire grew abruptly louder. Screams and confused shouts echoed down the hallway.

Ellen stepped into the chaos and Marcy followed.

CHAPTER TWENTY-SEVEN

The straight razor felt good in her hands, like it belonged there. Alicia flicked it open and moved to the head of the bed, where she stared down into the wide eyes of the girl tied to the headboard. She was a young thing, slim and blonde, with a cute face and a nice figure. The ball gag affixed to her mouth and face enhanced her prettiness in a perverse way, emphasizing her youth and vulnerability.

Alicia sat next to her and pushed sweat-soaked strands of blonde hair away from the girl's forehead. The girl shivered at Alicia's touch.

Alicia smiled. "Once upon a time, girl, I was in your place. Tied up for no good reason other than the pure hell of it. A damn shame, ain't it? That there are people in this rotten world who get their kicks this way?"

Tears welled in the girl's eyes and spilled down her flushed cheeks.

Alicia wiped the tears away and licked them off her fingers. "Mmm. Anyway . . . as I was saying, it's a shame there are people like me in the world." She laughed and placed the blade flat against the girl's white belly. "A shame for you, anyway."

She pressed the blade into the girl's flesh, penetrating

just slightly, perhaps an eighth of an inch, and drew a red line all the way down to her hip. It wasn't a mortal wound by any means, but the girl squealed and rocked against her restraints. Then she was panting in agony behind the ball gag. Her whole face was red and Alicia wondered whether it was possible to scare a person this young enough to induce a heart attack. It didn't seem likely, but she supposed it was possible. It would be regrettable.

She was just getting started on her.

It was funny. This thing she was doing to this girl, some anonymous runaway she didn't even know, was exactly what she'd planned for Dream back when she'd first recorporealized. But things had changed somewhere along the way. Being with Dream made her stronger and made all sorts of interesting things possible. The time she'd spent on the road with Dream and those kids had even been kind of fun. So she'd stuck with them, resisting the sometimes powerful urge to kill them all, and things had worked out just fine. She was in a perfect situation now, in just the right place for indulging the dark compulsions that were always lurking in the back of her mind.

Strange.

She'd never had impulses like these in her first life. The original Alicia Jackson had been just as tough and no-nonsense, but she'd also been a highly moralistic person. That conscience had not made the journey back from the other side of death with her. It bothered her a little, that some piece of her essence was missing, but not enough to matter.

There were three black-clad Apprentices in the room with her. Two young men and a slender girl about the same age as the runaway tied to the bed. The men were lounging in chairs. They looked bored. This wasn't anything they hadn't seen a thousand times by now. The girl, though, was sitting in a chair close to the bed, an avid expression on her face, her eyes glittering with a dark, eager hunger.

Alicia smiled again. "Sophie? Could you do me a favor?"

Sophie looked at her. "Yes, Mistress?"

"There's a bottle of perfume over there." She nodded at the vanity sitting against the wall behind Sophie. "Fetch it for me, would you?"

Sophie grinned. "Of course."

She hopped up and bounced over to the vanity, displaying an adolescent enthusiasm Alicia found charming. She found the bottle and brought it over to Alicia. "Here ya go."

"Thanks, Sophie. Now sit down again and watch. This will be fun."

Sophie did as ordered and Alicia looked into the bound girl's eyes again as she removed the stopper from the bottle. She moved the bottle into position over the long incision. "This is another thing that was done to me years ago. Let me tell you something, girl. You may think you're hurting now, but—"

The blast of bludgeoning heavy metal riffery startled Alicia and the bottle slipped from her fingers. The music was very loud. Very close. She thought about it a moment and realized she'd been hearing another, lower sound prior to the intrusion of the music, a sound she now recognized as the rumble of engines.

Alicia stood and moved toward the bedroom door. "Just what the fuck is going on out there?"

She opened the door and stepped out onto the second-floor landing. She peeked down the stairs and saw a number of Black Brigade soldiers heading into the foyer. Curiosity got the better of her and she started down the stairs. The gunfire was already starting by the time she was halfway down. Then the first AT7 shell slammed through the door, passed through the foyer, and detonated when it struck the wall arch outside the living room. The explosion ripped apart bodies and rocked Alicia off her feet, sent her tumbling down the stairs.

She was just getting to her feet when the next shell came streaking in. The next explosion knocked her off her feet again and for a moment all she felt was a stunned confusion. She heard loud voices and bullets buzzing by everywhere. Then she felt an immense pain and lifted her head to look at her stomach. A piece of shrapnel had ripped through her abdomen, eviscerating her.

Then the black boot of a fleeing Black Brigade soldier came down on her face as she died a second time. In the last moment before she expired, she experienced a surprising—and intense—feeling of relief.

CHAPTER TWENTY-EIGHT

The invading force stormed through the demolished entrance to the house and spread out through the ground floor. The sound of gunfire was ceaseless, the stuttering eruptions blending into a cacophonous din.

Chad and Allyson were among the last through the entrance. They came in charging, then fought not to stumble over the strewn body parts and debris. The large foyer had been transformed. It was now a hellish slaughterhouse. Blood and pieces of bodies everywhere. Chad had seen the aftermath of brutal, violent death before, but never in such abundance, not even during that seemingly endless firefight through the tunnel to the Master's house years ago.

He saw the body of a brown-skinned woman lying still in the middle of all the carnage. He frowned and moved closer. "It can't be."

The dead woman looked just like Alicia Jackson, Dream's long-dead best friend. And it wasn't just a strong resemblance. That wouldn't have troubled him. No, this woman was a precise replica of the woman Chad remembered. He knew Alicia had no siblings—identical twin or otherwise—so he was unable to make sense of what he was seeing on any level. He stared at

Alicia's slack features and forgot his surroundings. The moment nearly cost him his life.

He detected a blur of movement in his peripheral vision and looked to his right in time to see Allyson raise her weapon and send a burst of automatic fire at the second-floor landing. Red dots blossomed across the black shirts of two armed men. The men fell backward against more black-clad men behind them. Allyson hurried to the foot of the staircase and kept firing the whole time. More men in black fell dead before they could get a bead on Allyson with their own weapons, and in a moment the landing was clear, the surviving enemy combatants retreating to a safer position.

The sound of gunfire became more sporadic and eventually died down to the occasional pop. Allyson seized Chad's arm and tried to tug him back toward the front entrance, leaning close to whisper into his ear. *"Come on, goddammit, this is our chance, let's get out of here."*

Chad was numb. Part of it was the mystery of Alicia. The wall-to-wall gore was another part of it. But a bigger factor was this firsthand experience of Allyson's total willingness to kill anyone in the way of what she wanted. She'd done it before, of course, starting with the men who'd broken into his house. Then again on the way up here, dispatching the men who'd been her traveling companions. But now he'd watched her mow down at least four more men, acting with deadly precision and concentration, not stopping until she was certain the threat was gone. In a flash, Chad realized no one had ever cared for him as intensely as Allyson did. No one had ever been so willing to step into harm's way and sacrifice for him.

So he let himself be dragged toward the door. He would follow her anywhere now. They reached the door and would have stepped through it if not for the presence of the older Asian man and his younger male sidekick on the porch. The men regarded them with even, unreadable expressions. Each held an identical silver sword. Chad immediately understood that they had assumed this position to prevent the very thing he and Allyson were attempting.

"Fuck. We're not going anywhere yet."

Allyson started to raise her weapon. "Goddammit."

Chad pushed the barrel down. "Don't. You'd be dead before you could squeeze the trigger."

Allyson made a sound of frustration and twisted away from him. "Fine. Fuck them. Let's finish this thing."

A number of the Camp Whiskey soldiers had filtered back into the foyer. Jim was among them. There was a bright splash of blood across the front of his shirt, but he did not appear to be wounded. Chad assumed he'd killed someone in close combat. Bai reappeared, too, her sword dripping blood. She pushed her way to the middle of the throng and rattled off a quick set of instructions. "The ground floor is clear. Now we advance. You. And you." She pointed at two of the camo-attired men. "Up the stairs. Get close, but not close enough to draw fire. You know what to do."

The two men nodded and wasted no time following her orders. They unclipped gas masks from their belts and slipped them on. Then they crept up the stairs one careful step at a time. They stopped at a point about halfway up and hunkered down. One man kept his weapon trained on the second-floor landing while another man unsnapped two stun grenades from his belt. He tossed one up to the landing. It landed with a loud thump on the hardwood floor and rolled down the hallway. The second one bounced off the wall beyond the landing and for one tense millisecond Chad was sure it would come tumbling back down the stairs. But the grenade caught a funny bounce as it hit the floor and went backward down the hallway. This all happened in the space of maybe five seconds. Terrified screams resounded in the second-floor hallway as several people saw the bouncing black objects and recognized them for what they were.

Then there came a loud, teeth-jarring BANG!

And another.

Then smoke was billowing from the hallway and a number of Camp Whiskey soldiers went racing up the staircase as Bai screamed at them: "UP! UP! UP! FIGHT! FIGHT! FIGHT!"

To Chad she seemed like a madwoman herding human cattle. Then she was at his back, the heel of her hand slamming between his shoulder blades, driving him forward. "GO! FIGHT!"

Chad's feet found the staircase and he began to move up even as he heard gunfire erupt anew above him. He fumbled with his own gas mask and somehow managed to get it on. Then Allyson was racing up the staircase, hurrying past him to put herself between him and the bad guys yet again.

Chad ran after her.

CHAPTER TWENTY-NINE

Marcy burst through the bedroom door into a hallway choked with black-clad Apprentices and a handful of Black Brigade soldiers who were attempting to herd the frightened sadists back into their rooms. She looked to her left and right and saw no immediate sign of Ellen. Shit. She went up on her toes and lifted her chin in an attempt to see above the heads of the babbling morons in her way. Sometimes it was a real pain in the ass being a short girl. Then she finally caught a glimpse of the bobbing head of a person weaving between the gathered Apprentices.

Ellen.

She was heading toward the staircase to the second floor. Toward the source of all that gunfire. Marcy shoved people aside with one hand and waved the Glock around with the other as she set off in desperate pursuit. She ignored the frequent shouts of protest and pushed her way forward with reckless abandon. One big male Apprentice glared at her and moved back into her path. He was opening his mouth to say something when she shot him between the eyes. She hopped over his falling corpse and continued forward with greater ease, the Apprentices and Black Brigades shrinking away from her, creating a wide path straight down the middle of the hallway.

Marcy caught sight of Ellen's back. She had reached the staircase landing and showed no signs of slowing down. Marcy put on a burst of speed as her sister started down the stairs. Some part of her was aware of how crazy this was. The thing she was risking her life for wasn't really her sister. Dream could conjure another one into existence if it died. But some deep, familial instinct drove her forward anyway.

She reached the staircase and went full-throttle down the stairs. The second-floor hallway was choked with smoke. Ellen reached the bottom of the stairs and stepped into that billowing white cloud. God alone knew what was driving her. She was heading into the worst of the danger rather than away from it. The only thing Marcy could figure was she was trying to get out of the house. Too bad she lacked the intelligence to recognize the impossibility of escape by that route.

Marcy leaped over the last four steps and landed hard on the floor. Pain exploded in her ankles, but she ignored it and moved into the hallway. A lot of Black Brigade men were in front of her now. And Ellen. Bullets whined in the air, punching holes in the walls, blowing out lights, and occasionally shredding the flesh of the soldiers. The smoke wasn't as thick at this end of the hallway, and Marcy was grateful for that. She figured they had a few moments of relative safety, a narrow window of opportunity of which she meant to take full advantage.

She grabbed Ellen by the wrist and spun her around. The girl yelped and looked at her with eyes wide with fear. She didn't seem to recognize Marcy at first. Then she cried out and threw her arms around Marcy in a rough embrace. Tears welled in Marcy's eyes. She broke the embrace and grabbed Ellen by the wrist again.

"Come on, girl, back upstairs. We're gonna go see Dream."

Ellen opened her mouth and said, "Muhmuh . . . muh—"

Marcy began to drag her back toward the staircase. "Yeah, yeah. Tell me later, okay?"

Then Ellen let out a startled wheeze and Marcy turned to look at her. The front of Ellen's shirt was red, and there was a big, ragged hole between her breasts. A stray shot had caught her when Marcy had her back turned.

Ellen dropped to her knees and Marcy dropped with her. She put her hands on her dying sister's shoulders and tears filled her eyes again as she said, "Ohno. Ohnononono. Not again. Not again."

Then Ellen sagged forward into her arms and Marcy guided her gently to the floor. The battle continued to rage ahead of them, but for the moment Marcy was oblivious to it. She stroked Ellen's hair and continued to utter her desperate denials. Ellen's breathing was shallow and uneven. Blood spilled from the corners of her lips. Her eyes were glassy and Marcy could see the life seeping rapidly out of her. She would be gone within moments and there was nothing she could do about it. Not a single goddamned thing. It was that night in that fucking hotel room all over again.

Ellen's eyes cleared for a moment and focused on the distraught face of her sister. Her lips moved and a soft sound emerged: "Muh . . . muh—"

"Shush. It's okay. Don't try to talk." Marcy sniffled and hot tears spilled down her cheeks. "I'm gonna take care of you, okay? Just like I've always done, you'll see."

But Ellen wasn't listening. She grabbed the front of Marcy's shirt, seized it with surprising strength, and struggled to lift her head off the floor. She opened her mouth one last time and this is what she said: "Muh . . . muh . . . Marcy."

Then she was dead. Again.

Marcy felt a moment of total despair. Her mind replayed Ellen's last moments, that heroic struggle to speak her sister's name for the first and only time.

The despair evaporated.

Marcy stood and did a quick appraisal of the situation in the hallway. Many of the Black Brigade men had fallen, were either dead or dying on the hallway floor. Some went racing past her, heading for the staircase and the third floor beyond. A handful remained behind, valiantly defending their position against all hope of success. The smoke at the far end of the hallway was beginning to dissipate. She could make out the forms of the invaders as they drew steadily closer. She saw red bursts from the muzzles of their weapons. A stray round from one of those guns had ended the life of her reborn sister.

Marcy acted then on instinct, without even considering the implications of what she was doing. She raised the Glock and dashed into the fray, rushing past the Black Brigade men hunkered down in doorways. She squeezed the Glock's trigger over and over and some of the bullets found soft flesh. She saw one round penetrate the throat of one of the camo-clad men. The man dropped his weapon and clamped his hands over the wound. Blood pulsed over his fingers as he sank to his knees. Another bullet punched through the faceplate of another man's gas mask, sending him lurching into the arms of a startled comrade. She kept firing and two more men fell. The enemy returned fire, of course, but they kept missing, seemed somehow unnerved by the sight of the young girl coming straight at them. Marcy felt invincible. It was just like those months on the road with Dream. She was killing at will and nothing could stop her.

Then a bullet caught her in the thigh and spun her to the floor. The pain was immense and startling. Not invincible after all, then. The hell with it. This was the end for her. But she would not go down easy. She rolled to her side, lifted the Glock, and fired again.

Another man fell.

And another.

Then the Glock clicked empty and a moment later a burst of automatic fire tore apart her chest. The Glock slid from her suddenly numb hand and she rolled onto her back. She was still alive, but just barely, could feel the strength leaving her body. A fleeting thought crossed her mind in those last moments, the possibility that Dream might try to conjure her back.

She hoped not.

Then a man in camos was standing above her. He peeled off his gas mask and shook his head. The hallway was almost quiet now. The remaining Black Brigade fighters on this floor had been vanquished. The camo-clad man's tone was incredulous as he said, "Any of y'all see that shit? That bitch was crazy."

A small woman in black appeared next to him. She unsheathed a long, gleaming sword and said, "She is a warrior and deserves a warrior's death."

Marcy anticipated the arc of the sword and closed her eyes as it flashed through the air. It hurt for only a fraction of a second as the blade chopped through her neck.

CHAPTER THIRTY

The fiercest fighting was happening well ahead of their position. Chad was glad of that. But they were by no means out of harm's way. Stray rounds whizzed by intermittently. Most of them thunked harmlessly into the walls, but one found the head of a man just behind and to the left of where Chad was standing. Chad felt a tightness in his chest and dropped to the floor, unable to breathe for a moment.

Then Allyson was kneeling over him, gas mask pushed atop her head, panic etched into her strained features. "Chad! Can you hear me? Are you okay? Are you hit?"

Chad sucked in a deep breath and sat up. "I'm fine. I—"

The smoke was thickest at floor level. But now some of it rolled away and he saw a black-clad man prone on the floor. The man had been shot multiple times, including one round that had passed through his cheek. At a glance, anyone would assume the wound to the face had been a mortal one. It was ugly and spectacularly gory. But a closer look revealed the truth. The round had passed through one cheek and out the other, leaving behind a mangled face and a mouthful of shattered teeth. But he was alive. And clutched in his right hand was a 9mm pistol. He raised it and aimed it at the back of Allyson's head.

Chad snapped out of his stupor and shoved Allyson aside a moment before the 9mm discharged. The bullet smashed into the wall. Chad leaped to his feet and kicked the gun out of the man's hand. It went skittering down the hallway, disappearing beneath the curling tendrils of smoke. Chad switched the M-16 to semiauto, jammed the barrel against the man's forehead, and squeezed the trigger. The bullet punched a hole through his forehead and blood fanned out around the base of his skull.

Allyson was on her feet again. She looked at the dead man. Then she looked at Chad and smiled. "You saved my life."

"I owed you."

A figure emerged from a doorway to his right and Chad lifted his weapon again. Then he saw who it was and heaved a sigh. "Fuck, man, you scared the shit out of me."

Jim's weapon was slung over his shoulder. He wasn't wearing a gas mask and his eyes were bloodshot and watering from the smoke. Eyes that projected a deep sadness. "All this madness, there's got to be an end to it." The continuing sounds of battle failed to mask the haunted tone. He sounded like a man contemplating the end of the world, like a president on the brink of launching nuclear warheads. He looked Chad in the eye and said, "It ends here. I'll see to it."

And with that he turned from them and continued down the hallway.

Chad glanced at Allyson. "The hell's that supposed to mean?"

She pushed her gas mask down and shrugged. "No idea. Let's keep moving."

And move they did, following the advance guard to

the end of the hallway, then up the stairs to the third floor. They continued to encounter resistance as they progressed through the house, but it thinned out as they gained each floor and they stopped using the stun grenades to pave the way. It just wasn't necessary and only served to slow them down. Chad followed Allyson's lead and removed his gas mask. He remained vigilant, but he had a feeling his time as an active participant in the battle was at an end.

Chad didn't fire a single shot as they moved more quickly through the fourth and fifth floors. The gunfire ahead of them was sporadic, limited to occasional pops. Chad felt almost giddy for a time, buoyed by the apparent quick success of the invasion. Then something troubling occurred to him, the notion that success had come too fast and too easily. Yes, the enemy was fighting back, had even killed a number of the Camp Whiskey men, but the defending force was less formidable by far than Chad had anticipated. There didn't seem to be that many of them. Thinking about it, he began to feel a touch of paranoia. It was almost as if the enemy was holding something back, only offering a token resistance. Chad looked at Allyson and saw the intent look on her face. He wondered if any of this had occurred to her. Probably not. She was too focused on the task at hand.

He cleared his throat and said, "Hey, there's something—"

The thought went unfinished as something peculiar caught his eye. There was a bullet hole just below one of the wall sconces. It appeared to be . . . healing itself. The hole was filling in, the fabric of reality—or appearance of reality—reassembling itself. There was some sort of sorcery at work. If he survived to make a return journey back through this house, he thought it likely he would eventually arrive at the foyer to find it perfectly restored. Upon reflection, this shouldn't have surprised him. This place was just like the Master's house in many ways. Bigger by far on the inside than out, for one thing. Populated by a coterie of wayward psycho children turned professional sadists, for another. And sustained by a brand of magic so powerful the mere contemplation of it was staggering. Surely anyone capable of wielding that kind of power was also capable of swatting aside the Camp Whiskey invaders like so many gnats.

Allyson shot him a puzzled, impatient look. "What?" Her gaze remained on the hallway ahead, occasionally drifting to the left or right as they passed open doorways. "Keep your head out of the clouds, Chad. Stay focused."

The formerly ragged bullet hole had dwindled to a small black speck on the wall. In another moment even that was gone. "Yeah. Right." Chad shook his head and poked the barrel of his weapon into the open doorway on his right. He peeked around the doorjamb and saw a shivering, terrified Apprentice huddled beneath a desk on the far wall. He moved past the doorway and said, "It's not important."

She shot him another puzzled look. Her hair was pulled back in a ponytail, with little blonde tufts hanging loose at her temples. Her face was grimy with sweat and soot. But it was funny. He felt a sudden and powerful urge to kiss her. She was so amazingly beautiful. He didn't think he'd ever fully appreciated just how beautiful until this very moment. Somehow she even managed to make combat look sexy.

She arched an eyebrow. "Are you okay? Would you get that goofy grin off your face. We're fighting for our lives here."

Chad forced the smile away and nodded. "Right. Sorry."

They ascended another set of stairs to yet another floor. Chad had lost track of how many floors they'd climbed, but he knew it was a ridiculously high number for a house that looked like a one-story wreck from the outside. But there was something different about this floor. It was wider and better-lit. The light fixtures and wainscoting were more ornate. And at the end of the long hallway stood a massive set of double doors that seemed to reach for the sky. Chad noticed now that the ceiling curved upward, rising dramatically toward the end of the hallway.

One of the men ahead of them said, "Goddamn. I hope we ain't goin' in there."

The man to his immediate left snickered. "No shit. Look at them fuckin' monster doors. Giants must live in there."

The other man shuddered visibly and said, "Fuck. Don't say that. This shit's been weird enough already."

Bai was at the head of the decimated column of fighters. She arrived at the double doors and turned her back to them, waited with arms crossed beneath her breasts for what remained of the Camp Whiskey force to assemble before her. Only now, clear of the smoke and exposed in this wide hallway, did Chad realize just how little was left of this force. Their numbers had been reduced by more than half.

Bai spoke. "Victory is ours."

Then she unsheathed her sword and waded into the loose circle of surviving Camp Whiskey fighters. She was a black, untrackable blur moving side to side across the hallway, the long blade a flashing silver streak of light. The soldiers fell in rapid succession beneath her blade. Most were too startled to put up a fight. One or two tried clumsily to resist, but died in the attempt. It was over almost as soon as it had begun.

When Bai returned her sword to its sheath, the only people she'd left alive were Chad, Allyson, and Jim.

Chad gaped at her. "Why the hell did you do that?"

Bai's expression was serene. The anger and terror in his tone failed to move her. A little smile darkened the corners of her mouth. "They were no longer necessary."

Chad's heart was slamming in his chest. "Yeah? And what about us? Why are we alive?"

Her smile deepened a little. "Because I am of the Order. I am merciless and I do not care about you. But I am true to my word. Survive this and you and your woman will be free."

Chad's chin jerked in Jim's direction. "And what about my friend?"

"He has also cut a deal with the Order."

Chad's expression turned quizzical as he moved closer to Jim. "What's she talking about?"

Jim sighed. "You wouldn't understand. You don't need to understand." He turned away from Chad and looked at Bai. "Let's end this."

Bai nodded and moved to one of the huge doors.

She took the knob in one of her small hands, turned it, and pulled the door open. A brilliant white light made their eyes water.

Then Chad glimpsed what was waiting for them inside and gasped.

CHAPTER THIRTY-ONE

Down in the depths of a fevered sleep, Giselle's body shook as she dreamed of blood. Blood everywhere. Spouting from freshly opened wounds. Jetting from the stumps of severed limbs like semen ejaculated from a throbbing cock. A great, crimson ocean drained from the bodies of hundreds of victims, a deep red tide filling the hallways of a very old mansion that only vaguely resembled the one she'd ruled over so mercilessly for a handful of months. Then a flashback, a jump backward in time, and the blood she sees is weeping from the wounds in her little brother's body. Wounds she inflicted at the Master's behest in order to save herself. He'd rewarded her for that blood betrayal, using his magic to arrest the aging process in her body, freezing her in an image of perfect late adolescent beauty. She had lived for more than fifty years, but she would never look any older than seventeen or eighteen. But the psychic price for this dubious gift was high indeed. The look of agony on her dying brother's face was always lurking at the back of her mind, perpetually threatening to rise to the surface with its screaming accusations.

And so of course he returned to haunt and taunt her now.

Giselle awoke gasping, her psyche still reeling from the long-supresed images of her decades-dead brother. Wakefulness failed to banish the memories. Her body shook and her heart raced like an athlete's at the end of a series of sprints, a manic *thump-thump-thump* that made the blood sing in her ears. Or was that just the memory of her brother's wailing pleas for mercy? Hot tears filled her eyes and spilled down her cold cheeks. She remembered it all now. How he'd called out for his mommy and daddy over and over, even though they were already dead. Even though he'd watched them die. As if some part of him really believed their mutilated bodies could reanimate and come to his rescue. Because that's what mommies and daddies did. They came to your rescue. They kept the boogeyman away and held you and rocked you when you were feeling bad. He was just a little kid and he'd been unable to accept that there was no one to play that role for him anymore. Not even his beloved older sister, who had turned against him so cravenly, just to save her own hide.

Giselle's scream echoed in the dark chamber.

She shook her head hard, her sweat-soaked, stringy hair flailing in the darkness. She cried and jibbered like a madwoman locked in the padded room of some asylum.

NO!NO!NO!

NO!NO!NO!NOOOOOooooooo . . .

But the images refused to recede. It was as if, having thought of them, having allowed them room to breathe in the haunted cavern of her mind, she couldn't *not* dwell on the awful memories.

She let out another keening cry of grief, raised her hands to her face—and felt the stumps prod her cheeks.

A moment of perfect stillness elapsed. In this moment, she held her breath, not daring to breathe. Not daring to acknowledge existence itself. Her mind was blank. Then she released that breath and gently touched the stumps to her cheeks again.. There was a faint phantom limb sensation, but it diminished as her mind accepted the simple physical evidence of her mutilated flesh.

Her hands were gone again. She experienced a moment of desperate, yawning disorientation, as if she were standing at the edge of a great abyss. One more step and she would plummet into forever darkness. She struggled to comprehend what had happened. There was no pain. No throbbing ache of infection. These were not fresh wounds. Rather, these were wounds that had healed over time. Months, maybe. Her "restoration" had been a kind of illusion all along, an elaborate trick played on her by the Master while he masqueraded as Azaroth and awaited her inevitable downfall. She'd even half-suspected it near the end of her reign here.

She was as she'd once been.

Completely.

Her body was real again. Not whole, but real. Unenhanced by magic. In fact, she felt not the faintest trace of magical energy lurking anywhere within her. Whatever abilities she'd possessed were gone, beyond any hope of recapture. The damping energy Dream had wrapped her in was gone, too, no longer needed.

She was as she'd once been.

Completely.

With a broken body.

And a fully functioning conscience.

This realization at last banished the memories of her brother, but there was no relief in this. Because now her mind was flooded with a ceaseless series of images of the horrible things she'd done over the last few months. A nonstop film loop of atrocity with her in the starring role. And Ursula in a second-billed role, always by her side, inflicting pain and death because they enjoyed it, because they reveled in the screams and cries of their victims. Had she really thought she loved Ursula? Because she felt no connection to that emotion now. It, too, had been an illusion.

Giselle pressed the backs of her forearms to her face and cried some more, her chest heaving with the force of emotions artifically held in check for too long.

She thought of Eddie, her blood sacrifice to "Azaroth."

Sweet, trusting Eddie.

And that look of confused betrayal on his face in his last moments.

The crying only began to dry up as she felt the subtle vibrations in her bones. She sat very still for a moment and waited. And felt the vibrations again. Then she drew in a series of deep breaths and felt herself grow calm.

She then situated herself in a corner of the swinging cage and awaited the arrival of the ones who had come for her. She thought about them and wondered what they would do with her. She supposed they would torture her. And then kill her, of course. There would be much pain. But contemplating this failed to disturb the new, sudden sense of peace that had settled over her. She supposed she deserved whatever they had planned for her. She thought about the dragon tattoo. If she could see herself in a mirror, would she still see the dragon? She thought not.

She was as she'd once been.

Completely.

She closed her eyes in the darkness and thought of a time when she'd done heroic things. Memories that were bittersweet now, but no less true than the memories of horror. When the tears came again, they were the soft, noiseless tears of a black-clad mourner at the grave site of a long-estranged former lover or friend.

CHAPTER THIRTY-TWO

The room was enormous, a large, open space big enough to encompass some of the smaller rural homes Allyson had seen on the way to this place. A portion of it functioned as a library and den. At the far end was a living space, with a canopied four-poster bed, wardrobe, and vanity.

A man in a black uniform stood in the center of the room, hands upraised, lean body in a stiff pose of surrender. Allyson tightened her grip on the M-16 as they moved deeper into the room. Something about the atmosphere here didn't seem right. It was warm. And yet she felt a bone-deep chill. She shivered slightly as they advanced on the man who looked to be all that was left of the pathetic security force they had just vanquished.

The man was smiling as they neared. There was something unsettling in the man's steady gaze. His dark eyes were the cold, unblinking eyes of a lizard. Allyson, seized by the absurd notion that he would have a forked tongue, suddenly didn't want him to open his mouth. She imagined that tongue flicking out between teeth too sharp and too white, the only sound emerging from his mouth a low, sibilant hiss.

The image was so vivid she drew in a startled intake

of breath when he opened his mouth to say, "Welcome, honored representatives of the Order of the Dragon."

He bowed slightly at the waist as he said this.

Bai bowed in return and said, "I am Bai, designated by the Order to retrieve Giselle Burkhardt from your custody. And are you Schreck?"

The man in black straightened and nodded. "I am."

Bai sheathed her sword. "At ease, then."

The man called Schreck lowered his hands with deliberate slowness, as if he did not yet trust that he was safe in their presence. He looked at Allyson, then, a glance so quick she almost missed it, and her sense of unease deepened. It wasn't just that oily, insincere smile that bothered her. She thought she'd detected something in that glance, something inscrutable directed at her. But that was crazy. And paranoid. She'd never met this man before, had no knowledge of him prior to walking into this room.

Then he spoke again, a comment directed at Bai.

"Shall we finish our business now?"

Allyson frowned.

There was something familiar in the timbre of his voice, a faintly insinuating and mocking quality. She had heard this voice before, she was sure of it, but the connection eluded her as, for some unfathomable reason, Schreck and Bai approached a drab and blank expanse of wall opposite the big bed. Schreck leaned close to Bai and said something she couldn't make out, a mumbled whisper. Then Bai nodded and extended a hand to the wall. Her forefinger described a vague shape on the wall. It might have been a door. She spoke in a whisper and Allyson moved a step closer, straining to hear. The words became slightly more distinct, but Bai was speaking an Asiatic language, so the meaning remained elusive.

She turned and looked at Chad, who was staring past

her at the far end of the room. She followed his gaze to an open set of French doors. Beyond the doors was a balcony. And on the balcony, their backs turned to the people in the room as they leaned against the railing, were two people, a man and a woman. The man wore only black slacks. He had long, sandy brown hair and a sculpted physique. The woman wore a small robe that barely reached the middle of her shapely thighs. She had long, slender legs and a tapered waist. She had short, jet-black hair.

No . . . wait.

She blinked hard and rubbed at her eyes. Then she looked at the couple on the balcony again. The woman's jet-black hair was gone. She now had long, flowing blonde locks. Allyson decided her eyes were playing tricks on her. It had been a long day. A combination of fatigue and a trick of the light had conspired to make her initially think the woman's hair was shorter and black.

A nice theory. Except it was pure bullshit and she knew it. The woman's hair had grown and changed color in the blink of an eye. She was seized by a sudden conviction—she didn't want the people on the balcony to turn around. Didn't want to see their faces. That nagging sense of familiarity she'd felt while listening to Schreck had returned. She thought she knew who that woman was. It made no sense that she was here. Or maybe it made as much sense as anything.

She looked at Chad again and the look on his face pierced his heart. It was a combination of disbelief and longing.

He took an unconscious step toward the balcony.

Allyson hated herself for the tears that came then. She had no right to feel this sense of betrayal, not after the things she'd done. Maybe this was what she deserved in return for all those months she'd deceived Chad. Maybe this was karma.

Then Jim clamped a hand on Chad's shoulder, stopped him in his tracks. He turned Chad toward him and locked eyes with him, spoke a single word: "No."

Chad blinked rapidly. "But . . . I think that's—"

Jim shook his head, his expression stern. "Doesn't matter. You have to leave the past behind." He looked at Allyson now. "You both do."

Allyson shuddered, feeling again that bone-deep chill that belied the room's temperature. She opened her mouth to reply, but whatever it was she'd been about to say went unspoken as her attention was drawn to the wall where Schreck and Bai had been standing moments ago.

She frowned again. "What the fuck?"

The men followed her gaze and saw the vertical, black rectangle in the wall, a door to some dark place. It hadn't been there before. And Bai and Schreck had vanished, presumbably into that darkness. Looking at the darkness beyond the opening triggered a sensation of creeping dread. Allyson felt it crawling through her intestines like a tapeworm. She didn't know what that dark place was, but she did know she would sooner die than set even one foot inside it.

Then there was movement within the darkness and a moment later Bai and Schreck reemerged into the room. Between them was a young woman, maybe seventeen or eighteen. Allyson's heart leaped at the sight of her charred wrist stumps. Some monster had mutilated her. She was nude, except for a very small pair of black panties. She was pale and her long black hair was tangled. The girl was pretty, but there was obvious madness in her jittering eyes. She shivered and leaned close to Bai.

"What the hell? *This* is the person you came for?" Spittle flew from Allyson's lips, each word a jab, imbued with an implied sneer. "Look what's been done to her.

She's pathetic. I don't care what she's done. Now you're going to torture her? You fucking animals."

Bai's smile was thin and strained. "It is no concern of yours." She placed a hand on the hilt of her sword. "Unless you would like me to rescind the Order's deal with your lover. Then I suppose we could—" Her smile broadened. "—discuss it."

Allyson watched the woman's hands curl around the sword's hilt. There was something almost sensual about the gesture. A vaguely sexual eagerness. Allyson recognized the futility of her indignation on the girl's behalf and bit back any further expressions of rage. She sighed. "That won't be necessary. Could we please just get out of here now? No offense, but I'd like to never see any of you fuckers ever again."

Schreck laughed softly.

Allyson glared at him. "Something to say, asshole?"

Chad reached for her, brushed a hand across her arm. "Allyson, stop this. There's no need—"

Allyson shrugged his hand away and approached Schreck, halving the distance between them. "Do I know you?"

Schreck's dark eyes glittered. "Certainly, Ms. Vanover."

Then she had it. The wheels in her mind stopped spinning as the connection clicked. Hearing him say her name did the trick. It was *him*. The voice on the phone. Her contact during the months she'd spent spying on Chad. How that voice had haunted her during her months at Camp Whiskey. She heard it in her dreams and like a whispered promise of pain in idle waking moments.

She managed one word, pushed through gritted teeth: *"You."*

Schreck grinned, baring rows of horrible, too-white teeth. He looked like a shark. "Have you told your boyfriend about—"

Allyson looked at Bai as she jabbed a finger in Schreck's direction. "What about this son of a bitch? Has the Order made any deals with him?"

Bai kept her expression neutral as she said, "None that have not already been fulfilled."

And now it was Allyson's turn to grin like a crazy person. The sight of it must have unnerved Schreck. He frowned and glanced at Bai. "What's the—"

Allyson moved with explosive speed, reversing her grip on the M-16 and raising it above her shoulders. Schreck cringed and shuffled backward. But the black door was gone, the blank wall restored. His back met the wall and he could move no further. He raised his hands to cover his face, but he was too late—the stock of the M-16 crashed into his mouth, pulping his lips and shattering teeth.

Allyson moved out of his way as he tumbled to the floor and rolled onto his back. She tossed the M-16 aside and pulled the 9mm from her waistband. She set the safety and moved to where Schreck was sprawled. She avoided Chad's gaze, not wanting to look too long at his expression of horrified astonishment. Jim remained stoic, his hand on Chad's shoulder again.

Schreck opened his bleary eyes and saw her standing over him. He let out a wail and tried to scoot away. Allyson seized a handful of his black shirt and lifted him a few inches off the floor. Then she adjusted her grip on the pistol, raised her hand, and brought it around, smashing the nickel-plated butt against the side of his head. Shreck shrieked and bucked on the floor, but Allyson held on to him with ease, galvanized now by the most righteous sense of rage that had ever possessed her. She raised her hand again and whipped the pistol across Schreck's face another time. Then another and another. Again and again. Mashing flesh and pulverizing bone. The man barely looked human by the time she stopped swinging the pistol back and forth. He sagged in her grip, unable to resist, barely alive.

She let him go and stood up straight. Schreck's blood-filled eyes looked up at her. Whether he could see her or not she didn't know. She hoped so. She hoped he saw an avenging angel about to hand down judgment.

She hoped he was afraid. Of her and his impending rendezvous with the denizens of hell. She switched the 9mm's safety off and aimed the barrel at the center of Schreck's ruined face. His lips twitched, seemed to curl upward. A last, mocking smile of the damned.

Allyson pulled the trigger and Schreck died.

CHAPTER THIRTY-THREE

Back outside, now.

It wasn't yet noon, which didn't seem possible. Allyson felt as if a lifetime had passed since they'd gone charging into the strange house. So much had happened. So many people had died. It didn't seem right that a space of little more than an hour could encompass the extinguishing of all those lives. But it had. The sun was obscured by clouds and the air was tinged with winter's chill. But Allyson didn't mind that. It was a clean chill. Natural. She remembered her glimpse of that black room and shuddered.

The girl called Giselle had been loaded into the minivan parked behind the package truck. She was in the rear, her wrist stumps bound with a thick layering of silver duct tape. The girl looked numb, her eyes staring at something beyond this place. The young Asian man was sitting beside her. He sensed Allyson's scrutiny and his head swiveled slowly in her direction. A very small smile darkened the edges of his cruel mouth. Allyson turned away and moved to the Jeep.

Chad and Jim were there, arguing in low voices. Chad was doing most of the arguing, though. Jim kept his head down and stared at the ground as he listened to his friend rant.

"Jim, you just can't do this. You can't go with them. It's insane."

Jim sighed—an immensely tired sound—and at last lifted his head to look Chad in the eye. "Perhaps. Regardless, I am going." He looked at Allyson and managed a tired smile. "Hello, Allyson. I want you to know how proud I am of you."

Allyson flushed with embarrassment. She smiled and abruptly threw her arms around the old singer. He laughed and after a moment returned the embrace. Then she broke the embrace and stepped back, saw that he was smiling, too. It transformed his haggard features, making him look decades younger. For a flickering moment, she glimpsed the rock god of old, the impossibly good-looking and intelligent young lion who had taken the world by storm.

She swiped tears from her eyes with the base of a palm. "Chad's right, you know. You should go with us. There's nothing you can do for that girl."

Jim's smile slipped some, but didn't fade entirely. "I wouldn't be too sure of that." He glanced at the minivan and the last of his smile evaporated as he looked at the frail form of the girl huddled against the door. "Giselle has made mistakes. She's done bad things. Unforgivable things. But there was a time when she did amazing things. A time when we worked toward a common goal. She was incredibly brave then, and her actions ultimately saved the lives of thousands. Including—" He indicated Chad with a tilt of his chin. "—your man here. For that alone, I owe her my company for what's left of her journey. I owe her whatever comfort I can give her, meager though that may be."

Chad made an exasperated sound and shook his

head. "Look, I get what you're saying, okay? I understand it. But you're putting your life on the line here."

Jim's smile this time was smaller, sadder. "It won't be the first time."

Chad opened his mouth to respond to this, but hesitated at the sound of the minivan's front passenger door slamming shut. The old Asian man was ensconced in the shotgun seat now. Bai was standing outside the open side door, watching them expectantly.

"Leaving now!" she called to them.

Jim shuffled a few steps in that direction. Then he turned toward Chad and Allyson, addressing them one last time as he walked backward. "I wish you both the best of luck with whatever the future holds. You can be happy, but you should stay underground."

He reached the minivan and turned away from them. He slipped into the rear compartment and settled into the space between the younger Asian man and Giselle. Bai threw the door shut and moved to the other side of the van. She slipped behind the wheel and pulled the driver's-side door shut. She didn't so much as glance Chad's way. There was something dismissive about this. He was already a part of the past for her. A toy she'd amused herself with for a time and was now discarding. The lack of even token acknowledgment made Allyson hate the bitch more than ever.

The minivan's brake lights came on and the engine purred to life. It was a well-maintained car, easily the best-running vehicle in their meager fleet, so of course Bai had commandeered it for the drive up here. But Allyson's resentment on that count faded as she watched Bai quickly execute a three-point turn and start down the hill. The sooner the Order people were gone from her sight the better.

Chad sighed and slumped against the side of the

Jeep, watching with numb resignation as the minivan quickly made its way down the winding dirt path. "I can't believe he's going with them. How could—"

The explosion made Allyson stagger backward. Chad dropped to his knees and screamed. The minivan's interior was on fire. The roof had been blown out, its mangled remains a soot-gray mess. A column of black smoke rose into the air. Allyson's mind reeled. She couldn't begin to process what had happened. And then the fire ignited the gas tank and a second explosion demolished much of what was left of the minivan. Allyson's knees went weak and she clutched the Jeep's side mirror to remain upright.

Chad got to his feet and rushed down the hill. He was screaming something. Useless words of denial. Allyson watched him stumble and fall, banging his knees on the hard ground. And then he was on his feet again, charging full-out toward the smoldering wreck of the minivan. Allyson regained her composure and shoved herself away from the Jeep, hurrying down the hill after him.

Chad stopped a dozen yards from the burning van. The heat was too intense to get any closer. He was on his knees again and sobbing by the time Allyson reached him. She dropped to her knees and wrapped her arms around him, forcing his head away from the awful sight. He buried his face against her breasts and wailed. Allyson stroked his back and cooed to him. Nonsensical things. The things a mother might whisper in a baby's ear. She felt useless and stupid. She looked over his shoulder and was able to make out smoking remains in the minivan's seats. A scent of burning meat permeated the air. Allyson's stomach did a slow roll.

She gripped Chad by the hand and stood up, pulling him upright against his will. He looked at the minivan again, a stricken look contorting his features. Allyson turned him away from it and they began a grim march back up the hill. They reached the Jeep and Allyson helped Chad into the passenger seat. He was pliant, now, acquiescing to her every instruction without resisting.

Allyson climbed behind the wheel, dug the Jeep's keys out of her pocket, and twisted them in the ignition. The engine sputtered a few times, then came to reluctant life. She goosed the gas pedal a few times, and when the Jeep was running more smoothly, she put it in gear and started down the hill.

They gave the ruin of the minivan a wide berth.

They drove in silence for miles, leaving the house on the hill far behind.

Chad spoke up when they at last left the rural road behind and started down a much busier state route. "Jim planned that, didn't he?"

Allyson hesitated a moment before replying. She'd been working toward the same conclusion, but it was nonetheless a hard thing to admit. "Yeah," she said at last, "I think he did."

Chad slumped in his seat and stared blankly at the road ahead. "Hell. It makes sense, in a really fucked up way. He couldn't take out the Order people in a direct confrontation. So he waited until he had them where he wanted. He sacrificed himself to avenge the deaths of his friends and to save Giselle from whatever sick thing they had planned for her." He laughed, a short, sharp, bitter sound. "I've got to hand it to him, I guess. I'll bet those arrogant assholes never saw it coming."

Allyson frowned. "Okay. But *how* did he do it?"

Chad looked at her. "You saw that big jacket he had on, right? There was a lot of ordnance in that truck. I bet he helped himself to some grenades before we went into the house. Hid them deep in that jacket. It must have been so easy to just reach in his jacket and slip the pin out of one of those grenades. All he had to do then was wait a few seconds."

Allyson's eyes misted. "That . . . shit, that really took some guts."

Chad nodded and said, "Yeah."

They drove in silence for several more miles. Traffic thickened as they neared the exit that would carry them back to the interstate. Allyson thought of something as she hit the turn signal. "He said we should stay underground. "Why do you think he said that?"

Chad shook his head. "Jim spent most of his life underground. Probably he just thinks . . . thought it would be the smart thing to do."

"Or maybe he thought we might still be in danger somehow. Either from the Order or . . . whoever's in charge now at that house we just shot up."

Chad shrugged. "Could be."

Allyson steered the Jeep along the curving interstate ramp. "So what do you think we should do?"

"Right now?" Chad grunted. "Let's just keep driving and figure it out later. All I want at the moment is to get to a hotel somewhere, preferably one at least a hundred miles from here, then shower, have sex with you, and sleep for a day."

Allyson smiled. "Sounds good."

The Jeep hit the interstate and Allyson put the pedal down.

EPILOGUE

Six months later

Dream sat on a high throne made of gold in the pyramid's main pavilion. Seated to her left in an identical throne was the Master. He looked resplendent in his long, tousled hair and fine clothes. He sensed her looking at him and smiled.

Dream shifted her attention to the mass of people gathered below. They sat in rows with their heads bowed. Perfectly still. Afraid to move until instructed to do so. They were right to be afraid. These were the denizens of Razor City, the now-thriving slave community founded by the late Giselle Burkhardt. Theirs was a brutal existence. They lived day-to-day, never knowing when they might be summoned to sacrifice or be killed by some other cutthroat member of their own community.

They were gathered to pay official tribute to their new Queen and Master. A few of them would soon be called to the altar situated between the crowd and the high thrones. They would give their blood to honor the death gods and exalt the reign of their new rulers. The perimeter of the pavilion was ringed with armed men clad in black. Formerly called the Black Brigade, Dream had redubbed them the Palace Guard. She liked the sound of that better. It was like something out of a fairy tale. And therefore more fitting for a Queen.

It was far from the only change made in the months since she was reunited with the Master. She had more control over her powers than ever, could conjure things and mold the fabric of reality with astonishing precision. She had reshaped herself into a replica of her younger self. Her hair was golden blonde again, long and flowing. Her skin was a sun-kissed tan again, and the age lines at the edges of her eyes and mouth were gone. Some of her improved control was a result of the Master's guidance. More of it was her exponentially increasing natural skill level. A shining example of what she could do was standing in front of the altar.

Marcy stood with her hands clasped before her, facing the crowd. A ceremonial dagger was in a sheath attached to her belt. The girl was perfectly restored. Dream had recreated her down to the finest detail, including memories and personality. It had become so easy to retrieve such things. The recreated Marcy didn't know she had died. It was the one bit of memory Dream had seen fit to erase.

A marshal drum beat resonated in the pavilion. The man beating the drum stood next to the altar. The drumming abruptly swelled and ended with a flourish.

There was a moment of perfect silence.

No one inhaled or exhaled.

Then Marcy unclasped her hands, unsheathed the ceremonial dagger, and turned toward the thrones. She bowed slightly at the waist and said, "Your Highness, we are ready and await your command."

The Queen nodded. "Begin."

Marcy bowed again and turned away from her. She issued a silent command with a head gesture and the Palace Guard moved into the crowd. They jerked a number of men and women to their feet and prodded them toward the altar. The doomed ones went to their fates with their heads bowed. Each of them knew there was only one means of deliverance from this place. They accepted this because they had no choice. Many of them even embraced it.

Dream settled into her throne again and watched happily as the evening's first blood was spilled. By the end of the ceremony, the blood ran in thick, red rivers from the altar, staining the floor around it a stark shade of dark crimson.

Blood was everywhere.

Dream saw this.

And she decided it was good.

There was no greater glory than that derived from the sacrifice of innocents. It ignited her senses and fueled the darkness that had always lurked in her heart and had now been unleashed, given freedom to reign. It was a thing she hoped to enjoy for centuries to come. With her perfect lover at her side, she would happily wade through an ocean of blood. And with any luck, the wider world would one day bow before them.

She looked at the Master and he met her gaze.

He smiled again.

And she saw the promise of eternity in his dark eyes.

She reached toward him, clasped hands with him.

The Queen shivered at her King's touch.

NATE KENYON

"A voice reminiscent of Stephen King in the days of *'Salem's Lot*. One of the strongest debut novels to come along in years."

—*Cemetery Dance*

A man on the run from his past. A woman taken against her will. A young man consumed by rage…and a small town tainted by darkness. In White Falls, a horrifying secret is about to be uncovered. The town seems pleasant enough on the surface. But something evil has taken root in White Falls—something that has waited centuries for the right time to awaken. Soon no one is safe from the madness that spreads from neighbor to neighbor. The darkness is growing. Blood is calling to blood. And through it all…the dead are watching.

BLOODSTONE

ISBN 13: 978-0-8439-6020-4

GRAHAM MASTERTON

A new and powerful crime alliance holds Los Angeles in a grip of terror. Anyone who opposes them suffers a horrible fate…but not by human hands. Bizarre accidents, sudden illnesses, inexplicable and gruesome deaths, all eliminate the alliance's enemies and render the crime bosses unstoppable. Every deadly step of the way, their constant companions are four mysterious women, four shadowy figures who wield more power than the crime bosses could ever dream of. But at the heart of the nightmare lies the final puzzle, the secret of…

THE 5TH WITCH

ISBN 13: 978-0-8439-5790-7

From Horror's greatest talents comes

THE NEW FACE OF FEAR.

Terrifying, sexy, dangerous and deadly.

And they are hunting for YOU...

WEREWOLVES

SHAPESHIFTER by J. F. Gonzalez
JANUARY 2008

THE NIGHTWALKER by Thomas Tessier
FEBRUARY 2008

RAVENOUS by Ray Garton
APRIL 2008

"If you've missed Laymon, you've missed a treat!"
—Stephen King

RICHARD LAYMON

Many people have a hobby that verges on obsession. Albert Prince's obsession happens to be cutting people, especially pretty girls. There's nothing he loves more than breaking into a stranger's house and letting his imagination—and his knife—run wild. Albert's on the run now, heading cross-country, but he's not about to stop having fun....

A pregnant young woman, a teacher, a librarian, an aging Southern belle, a famous writer and a budding actress. All of them have troubles and all of them are looking for something in their lives. Unfortunately, what they'll find isn't necessarily what they wanted. What many of them will find instead is Albert and his very sharp knives.

ISBN 13: 978-0-8439-5752-5

To order a book or to request a catalog call:
1-800-481-9191
This book is also available at your local bookstore, or you can check out our Web site **www.dorchesterpub.com** where you can look up your favorite authors, read excerpts, or glance at our discussion forum to see what people have to say about your favorite books.